THE
SENTINEL'S
DAUGHTER

THE
SENTINEL'S
DAUGHTER

DAUGHTERS *of the*
NEW AMERICAN REVOLUTION

★ ★ ★ BOOK THREE ★ ★ ★

MARIA ERENI DAMPMAN

The Sentinel's Daughter
Daughters of the New American Revolution
—Book Three—

Copyright © 2024 by Maria Ereni Dampman

A Lickenpoodle Press Publication

Lickenpoodle Press
Attn: Permissions Coordinator
P.O. Box 255
Round Hill, VA 20142

ISBN: 978-1-7371770-4-3 (paperback)
ISBN: 978-1-7371770-5-0 (ebook)

Editorial development and creative design support by Ascent:
www.spreadyourfire.net

*"Women, if the soul of the nation is to be saved,
I believe you must become its soul."*

—*Coretta Scott King*

1

July 2, 2046

Emma

I've never felt this uncomfortable in my entire freaking life.

It's not even 10 a.m. and the temperature is already in triple digits. The rocky cliffside we wait on is dry and dusty, with any speck of life having been broiled out of it years ago. With no trees for shade, I feel equally desiccated as I sweat out the very last drops of water inside me. Even my brain feels parboiled under the helmet Adam told me to not even *think* about removing. I tried to explain that the headgear is far more likely to cause a heat stroke than to save me from a wayward bullet, but my words did nothing to change his explicit order. I'm not sure if the command comes more from concern for his little sister's safety or fear of what my husband will do to him should I get killed. I imagine it's both, especially because I'm not supposed to be here, at all.

We're already in position, lying on our bellies with our weapons propped up before us, so it's too late for Adam to change his mind. I'm here until the mission's over, and although I'm glad to be a part of it, I wish there's some way to hurry it along. Everything about today has been hurry-up-and-wait, with the waiting proving to be far harder than the hurrying. When I look around to see how others are dealing with their boredom, I find some of the men chatting quietly while others somehow manage to snooze. I envy their effortless comfort.

The soldier to my left opens a pack of peanut butter crackers and offers me one. At this stage of my pregnancy I'm almost always hungry, so I accept it with a smile of thanks. As I reach over to take it from his outstretched hand I wince as the buttons of my jacket dig deeper into my belly. And just when I think my current situation can't become more unbearable, the baby gives one of my internal organs a hard, swift kick.

Well, *that'll* teach me to think things can't get worse.

I close my eyes and take a deep breath and let it out slowly, fighting off the little fairy lights in my peripheral vision caused by the pain. After it passes, I try to stealthily dig a larger divot in the sand for my belly, but my tactics fail when a small cloud of dust poofs into the air. Then, the teasing begins.

Assholes. I'd like to see how they'd fare in my situation.

My brother glares at the jokesters, cutting off their remarks but not their sniggering. He turns his steely gray gaze to me and I roll my eyes, snottily mouthing the words "I'm fine" for what feels like the eighty-fifth time. I know I don't look it, with my sunburned face and eyes bloodshot from the dust. I reach for my canteen before remembering I'm almost out of water, then surreptitiously slide my arm back against my body, hoping no one noticed.

I honestly thought this would be a quick mission, and that we'd be well on our way home by now. I packed light on purpose, refusing the extra canteen Adam offered each of us before we left. Just as I'm wishing Adam had tried harder to make me take one, a canteen slides across the dirt and stops directly in front of me. I glance to my side, meeting Adam's smug face.

Feeling particularly churlish, I almost slide it back. But if this mission goes south and we have to run, I'll put everyone in danger if I pass out from dehydration. The cool water refreshes my throat, but I don't drink as much as I want. I don't want Adam to suffer for my stupidity. When I hand it back he tells me to keep it, telling me he brought an extra for me "just in case."

I want to hug him and kill him at the same time. "Stop staring. I'm fucking *fine*," I mutter as I turn away, watching the heat rise off the asphalt below. I hear a couple of men chuckle, but a few others bolster my show of independence with their *oorahs*. Adam lifts his head just enough for them to see his glare, silencing them instantly until someone snorts out a laugh a few seconds later.

"Seriously, Adam. I'm good," I whisper more kindly, but he still looks worried. It's been hard to get Adam and Declan to understand that pregnancy isn't a reason for me to stay home, at least not yet. It hasn't diminished my ability to use my wits in a crisis, and it certainly hasn't affected my aim. There's absolutely no reason for me to stay home when my skills are needed here.

It's hard to believe it was exactly one year ago today that I was reluctantly preparing for my Presentation. It feels like just days ago when I was stuffed into that ridiculous white gown and forced to smile as I met the monster my father contracted me to marry. So much has happened since then that everything's still pretty much a blur. I'm out from under my father's control and married to the man I chose. It's my beloved's son I carry, and my feelings for him are already so strong they often bring me to tears.

I cannot wait to meet my child, but I'm also terrified to bring him into a world as terrifying as ours. As the first Heir to be born and not named, people have become fanatically fixated on "The Big Day." He's not even born yet and people are acting like I'm about to deliver a Messiah, and instead of calming the nation, the New State Church has encouraged the rhetoric. The Supreme Pontiff claimed just last month that people who have been blessed with the opportunity to touch my belly have been cured from everything from colds to end-stage cancer. This inane idea has been repeated often enough that most of the nation now believes it. Every day, desperate people crowd the barricades surrounding the Executive Mansion where they think I live, screaming themselves hoarse for me to come out. I can't imagine how disappointed they'll be when they find out my son is not a savior with mystical powers. Hell, if I have my way, the nation will never get to know my son at all.

But the second after Supreme Archon Ryan Gregory died, my father declared himself the Supreme Regent, claiming he will rule for my son until he turns twenty-one. Why he didn't just declare himself the next Supreme Archon is beyond me, as he's murdered everyone powerful enough to usurp him. Yet even a self-proclaimed regent cannot rule without a ward, so since I escaped the Premier City, finding me has been his top priority. Needing to keep my MIA status quiet has hindered his efforts, but he must be deeply concerned by now. He's running out of time as my due date nears. Although he's done an excellent job hiding my absence so far, there's only so long the nation will accept his excuse that I've sequestered myself in the Mansion, bereft with grief over Ryan's death.

How the people of this nation believe whatever they are told without question baffles me. I know that any form of dissension is considered treason and punishable by death, but is nobody capable of thinking for themselves? Declan and I exposed our government's lies, the Universal Church's greed, and detailed the human rights horror show that is the Purity Police, and yet few are willing to join us and fight for change. Everyone is so afraid that things will get worse that even those with nothing left to lose are reluctant to stand up against my tyrant father. Especially after the examples he made of George-town, Baltimore, and the underground community of Philadelphia, the population has been exceptionally compliant. In some ways I can understand that. If my father has taught us nothing, it's that things can always get worse.

I fear what this means for those of us determined to resist. I'd been so certain that if we exposed the truth we'd enrage the nation to the point they'd want to rise up. Our tech guru, Amy, even managed to get several of our international broadcasts shown in full on a hijacked mandatory evening news program, but before our message could gain traction, my father denounced everything we said as "fake news." He claimed each video was made by either malevolent foreign powers, enemies of the Universal Church, or some minority group who then became the latest brutal example of what happens when someone speaks against him.

While Declan's been traveling the country trying to unite a number of smaller resistance groups into one cohesive army, I've been speaking with leaders from all over the world. At first I'd been nervous that they wouldn't take me seriously, but it turns out my name means far more to world leaders than my sex, youth, or lack of political experience. The fact that the Supreme Regent's own daughter, a *Bellamy*, is willing to speak against him, makes my message one they cannot ignore.

I especially enjoy speaking with female Presidents, Prime Ministers and Ambassadors who indulge my more personal questions about how they rose to power and managed to keep it. Until Declan told me, I never knew that women leaders once were the norm not just overseas, but here, too. I had been thoroughly surprised to learn that before the war, women had been Supreme Court Justices, Governors, and members of Congress. Hell, one even became Vice President!

I am desperate to understand how our nation, with a population that at one point was fifty-one percent female, and many of them quite wealthy and powerful, was unable to stop what came to pass. One of the banned books Amy lent me said that when abortion rights for women were overturned, there had been an uproar. There had been marches, protests in front of the Supreme Court, and letter writing campaigns, and although their collective fury could be felt in the moment, the passion faded as time passed.

Causes become less important when money is tight, food is scarce, and the threat of retaliatory violence is high. When one is forced into survival mode, instinct takes over. Who has the time to protest when they are working around the clock to scrape together enough money to feed their children and to keep a roof over their heads?

In my studies, it was easy to see how the death of democracy had been insidious; in hindsight, the framework put in place to topple it laid over a course of decades. It had been done so cunningly it was damn near Machiavellian, and by the time the nation realized what happened, it was too late. We had a Dictator more unhinged and punishing than any the world had ever seen.

If only he'd never come to power. If only my mother's generation, both men and women, had fought harder, protested louder, and gotten off their asses to vote, maybe we wouldn't be in the situation we're in now.

A year ago I never thought about things like this. I believed what I'd been told, and behaved like the pawn I'd been trained to be. I honestly didn't know there was any other way to live aside from being the property of a father or husband. Now it's my mission to not only teach every young American what they lost, but to inspire them to fight to regain the rights every man and woman are due.

But in order to take back our nation, the people need to first relearn how to think for themselves. In the months I've lived in Lancaster, Pennsylvania, I've learned I'm far more capable than I ever imagined. Aside from my diplomatic duties, I've also become an incredible shot with a rifle and proficient in hand to hand combat. Living with the Zooks means helping out on their farm, with days beginning and ending the same way—when it's dark. I've learned how to sow and reap crops, feed animals, milk cows, and mend clothes. When we have time, Keira and I also hunt and trap wild animals that are plentiful in this area and provide an extra source of food for us all.

As if that's not enough to keep us busy, Declan and I are also the proud parents of a perpetually screaming infant. We kept the baby girl orphaned after the cyanide attack in Philadelphia, the child developing an affinity to us both as well as to Keira. I smile as I think of little Anya, who is every bit as hot-headed and volatile as her namesake. When Declan mused that we should name her after our recently deceased friend and former Commander, I knew there was no better person to honor. I can only hope our Anya will grow to have even a tenth of her spirit.

I'm broken out of my mental rambling by the sound of approaching vehicles. Adam raises his hand, signaling us to get ready. We are expecting two tractor trailers to roll through here any minute, their cargo the population of a small Ohio town deemed guilty of "treasonous acts." As pretty much any action the Purity Police dislikes is now considered treason, God only knows what they did to be punished so harshly. Last month, while administering the Oath of Fealty to the Supreme Regent to a large group, they arrested a man for *sneezing*. Scott had rolled his eyes and huffed that if that wasn't a commercial for allergy medicine, it should be. He stopped joking about it when, a few days later, the poor man's tortured body was reportedly found face down in the Reflecting Pool.

Adam tells us to get ready before radioing down to the team below. Our job is to cover the ground forces who will intercept the vehicles. One of the men behind me radios our medical team, alerting my husband, Scott, Keira, and a few other members of the Broad Street Bullies who guard them, that the trucks are now in sight. We have no idea what shape those poor prisoners are going to be in, and considering the heat, I feel terrible for having little hope they are still alive.

The broken-down farm truck blocking the road is how we plan to stop the tractor trailers in an optimal location for our attack. The primary extraction team is led by a retired Marine, and hidden within the underbrush at the side of the road are forty or so men and women tasked with liberating the prisoners.

The trucks advance around the sharp turn and brake hard, narrowly avoiding the vehicle blocking the road. Nothing happens for a few minutes as the drivers and the Purity Patrolmen accompanying them confer before exiting their vehicles. The drivers' uniform jackets are off, their undershirts stuck to their lumpy bodies with sweat. The scope is powerful and lets me see things in freakishly good detail down to the officers' beet-red faces dripping with sweat. They hastily do up the gold buttons on their uncharacteristically dingy-looking white jackets.

The patrolmen demand the drivers help the farmer move the broken vehicle, and judging by their pissy-looking faces, they don't want to. After a few sharp words, the drivers head over to help the farmer as the patrolmen step away to light up cigarettes and wait.

I hold my breath. When the patrolmen have their backs turned, our undercover "farmer" whips out the Glock tucked in the back of his pants and blows a tidy hole through the back of their heads. The drivers get on the ground with their hands in the air, and although I can't hear what they're saying, it looks like they're begging for mercy right before he kills them, too.

The ground team springs into action as Adam's radio bursts into a cacophony of overlapping voices. This is the moment for which we've been called into action. If this is a setup and a bunch of patrolmen jump out, we have to be ready to fire in an instant. I place my finger aside the trigger.

Two men use bolt cutters to snip the locks on the back of the trucks, release the doors, then flatten themselves against the side of the container to give us a clear shot. We're the first to see that despite evidence they had once been crammed tight with people, they are now empty.

"Something's wrong," Adam grumbles. His trepidation is palpable as we watch more of our ground force hurry forward, their weapons raised against a nonexistent threat. As much as I want to chide Adam for being overly cautious, I feel it too. Just as the head guy on the ground radios Adam to ask what he sees, Adam's face drains of all color. He screams for them to retreat with panic thick in his voice.

BOOM.

The explosion rocks the ground, the noise deafening as the trucks go up in flames. The brush where our troops are hidden is engulfed, with no time for them to even scream before their bodies are consumed. The inferno races towards us, but up here on the side of this cliff, we are safe, only victims of a blast of breath-stealing heat and painful ringing in our ears. Adam commands us to get back to the trucks as fast as we can. Air reinforcements undoubtedly are next.

We run as a unit, all of us wary of ambush as we race back to our trucks parked a mile away under a coppice of half-dead trees. I'm running as fast as I can, but within a few minutes, I can't keep up.

Declan was right. I should have stayed home.

We'd been smart enough to intercept the trucks as far away from where we live as we could, not wanting to give ourselves away by conducting missions too close to home. Yet what we did was not without risk. Now we face a long ride home with the growing concern we might be intercepted along the way.

Adam slows the unit when I begin to lag behind, his eyes silently begging me to run faster. As if I'm not having enough trouble keeping up, my son kicks some squishy inner organ that hurts badly enough to make me stumble. Adam grabs my arm in alarm as I double over and pant for a few long moments. He demands to know what's wrong, our entire unit returning to surround us. Every one of them looks deeply concerned.

"I'm okay," I blurt. "Your nephew's just trying out for professional soccer with my uterus." Adam smiles but still looks worried, probably thinking Declan's going to be even more pissed that he brought me considering how badly things turned out.

"Go on ahead, just leave a vehicle for us to get home in," Adam commands his lieutenant, Nathan, and the rest of our unit. Nate gives him a blistering glare.

"I don't know how you Navy men do things," he snarls. "But Marines never leave a soldier behind. We stay together. Sir." The rest of the unit nods, a few *oorahs* thrown in for good measure. Adam takes my pack and slings it over his like it weighs nothing just as Nate lifts my weapon off me. I feel naked without them.

Even though it's a lie, I tell them I'm ready to jog out. I can't remember the last time I felt this sick. It feels like forever before we get back to the trucks, and I practically fall into the vehicle the second I reach it. Adam's on the phone with Declan, shaking his head and giving one word answers. The second he gets me situated, he demands I ride back to the farm with the others while he heads over to help the medical crew pack up. I can tell he's lying, that he and Declan are up to something, but I don't have the energy to fight with him. His worry for me is written all over his face, and it only worsens when I lean over and throw up on his boots.

Adam curses out loud, telling Nate to get me out of here as he looks disgustedly at his vomit covered legs. I don't try to change his mind, nor do I tell him to not do anything stupid, as I'm in for a whole raft of shit for my own idiocy. I instead settle for "Please, be careful," as Nate hops in the driver's seat and floors the vehicle. Before we even reach the gravel road, I pass out from exhaustion.

2

Keira

I don't know what happened out there, but judging by the way Declan's slamming bags of IV fluid back into their cardboard box, the mission failed spectacularly. His brows are knit so tightly they nearly meet, the crease between his eyes, the one that's gotten much deeper since he took over as Commander, almost deep enough to qualify as a tunnel.

Scott catches my eye and shakes his head, damn near begging me to keep my trap shut. So of course, I don't. "Declan? What happened?"

He stops for a moment, turning his terrifying black gaze to me before he slams another bag into the box. I fight the urge to cringe, now understanding Scott's unspoken wisdom. But instead of him yelling at me, Declan releases a shuddering sigh.

He drags one neoprene-gloved hand through his curly black hair, grips it fiercely, and then yanks on it in frustration. When he finally speaks, his voice is thick with misery. "The trucks were empty. Well, except for the bomb, that is. We lost our entire ground force."

I don't even know what to say, and except for an exasperated-sounding "fuck" coming out of Scott, nobody else does either.

"I don't understand," Scott finally pipes up. "This doesn't make any sense."

"Tell me about it," Declan mutters, picking up the heavy box and carrying it outside. We hear the tell-tale sound of the overfilled cardboard being thrown into the back of a vehicle, followed by the unmistakable sound of a fist hitting metal.

I'm just about to go out there, to see if I can say or do something to make him feel better, but Scott stops me. "Hey, kiddo, just give him a few minutes, alright?"

I scowl at him. "Don't call me that."

"Whatever you say, short stack."

I huff in frustration. "Quit it, asshole."

He smiles, but it's not heartfelt. We hear another loud slam outside followed by another long string of creative cursing. We both cringe.

"Well, it's nice to see some things never change," Scott drawls. "It doesn't look like either of you have reformed your mouths since living with the Mennonites. If anything, you're worse."

I flip him off while continuing to pack, and I'm just about done when a vehicle pulls up. I come out with one of the last boxes just as Adam jumps out, Declan already in his face demanding answers it's clear his brother-in-law doesn't have. The frustration is thick in our Commander's voice, as is the guilt. He's probably thinking if he'd only been there, things might have turned out differently. That's the kind of guy he is, always thinking of everyone else first.

I'm sure Declan knows that if he'd been down there, the only thing different would be we'd be once again looking for a new Commander. But when Adam stupidly says to Declan pretty much exactly what I'm thinking, I really think he's going to get punched—not that Adam looks at all worried. Although Declan's finally fully healed from being shot earlier this year, his punching arm suffered some pretty severe nerve damage, making him a shitty fighter. Just don't ever say that to him, because he gets really pissed when you do.

I pretend to be rearranging boxes so I can listen to their conversation, getting a dirty look from Scott when he comes out with the final load. After securing the last box, he tells me to stay put as he walks over to talk to the guys. I follow him anyway.

"Something is off," he adds after Adam tells us what happened. "This just doesn't feel like something Bellamy and his goon squad would do. Or maybe this is just a part of some bigger plan? Is there something else we should be looking out for?"

I peek through the open doors just in time to see Declan grab his radio and tell Amy to continue monitoring the skies over all the planned routes for our returning troops. She snarkily spits out something that sounds like "this isn't my first fuckin' rodeo," and then less caustically tells him there's not so much as a bird overhead.

Based on radio chatter, she does say that trucks are coming to investigate the noise and to get out of there ASAP, but they are still about forty-five minutes out. With that intel, Declan tells Adam he wants to see the scene while Scott and I head home. I want to go with them, but Declan doesn't even let me finish asking before he says no, that it's no place for a *girl*.

I bristle at his dismissal. I'm not a *girl*, or a *kid*, or whatever demeaning word he wants to use to brush me off. Shit, I've *never* been a kid. After watching my parents get murdered, I hid in the sewers of Philadelphia like a rat for almost a year until Brother Love found me. I was six at the time. I grew up as the only person under the age of twenty living in an ancient air-raid bunker under the streets of a destroyed city. I learned how to read off of old copies of sticky *Playboy* magazines when Brother Love wasn't around to force me to read outta the Bible. Seriously, I learned what teabagging was before I grew a set of boobs, so don't *ever* fucking call me a kid and expect me to not get pissed.

Not to mention, I turned sixteen just last week. I'm a *woman* now. According to the new laws, I could have been married for two years by now. Whenever I remind Declan of that he gets mad, snapping that there's no way in Hell I'm getting married until I'm at least thirty.

I'm not gonna lie. I kinda like it when he gets all protective of me. It means he cares. I've dropped enough hints that I really, *really* like him, but he's either ignoring them or hasn't picked up on it. Whenever Scott catches me staring at Declan, he teases me by calling me "jailbait," another nickname that pisses me off to no end. If any of us get nabbed by the Purity Police, it's not gonna be an age-gap romance that lands our sorry asses in the Reflecting Pool. It's gonna be all the other shit we've done that'll get us killed.

When we fled Philly a few months ago, the BSB had no choice but to split up. I begged to go to New York with Brother Love, Scott and Amy. But everyone said the area was too dangerous for a *kid*. So I asked to go help with the rebuilding down in Baltimore, and that request was also denied. Brother Love said the ruined city "was no place for a young lady." I snorted out a laugh at that one. *Young lady*? Christ Almighty, it's like he's never fucking met me.

I got pretty scared at that point, because if I wasn't going to New York or Baltimore, where would I go? Was this when they finally told me to fuck off and get lost? I've been afraid of that day for years, knowing eventually it's gonna happen. I must have looked ready to crap my pants because Brother Love looked at me with sympathy, Declan with confusion, and Emma with barely-constrained pity.

I'm not proud to say that when Declan told me they decided I would stay on the farm, where I "could have a chance to be a child," I completely lost my shit. I screamed that I'd never been a child, and I had no interest in becoming one now. I know as much about being a child as I do about being a young lady.

Motherfuckers.

I'd been so frustrated that I gave Declan a shove that barely moved his stout frame. He had quirked an eyebrow, saying something snotty about me having "maturity issues," and I spat back that I spent over half my life living in an underground bunker with a secret rebel unit, and that I was *way* more mature than most people my age. He stomped off in a snit because he knew I was right, and I had stuck my tongue out at his retreating back as he called over his shoulder that he wasn't changing his mind. Then he *ordered* me to stay at the farm. *Ordered*. Now that he's Commander he's become a real asshole about ordering people around.

I roll down the window on the ancient Jeep, the AC not working and the truck hotter than fuck from baking in the sun. The cracked pleather seat sears the back of my thighs, but it's not enough to make me want to change into my stupid "plain" clothes yet. I despise the pale lavender dress and apron, and really hate the black stockings and clunky boots. Unlike Sarah and Emma, who both somehow always look like Mennonite runway models with their pristine aprons, unwrinkled dresses, and shoes that are never dirty, everything about me is always rumpled, torn, and filthy. Every night there's a new rip or hole in my clothes that needs to be patched, and since the only thing that happens when I sew is I stab myself a thousand times, Sarah has taken over repair duty. She clucks at me the entire time she's working that I need to be more careful, and by the time she's done, I'm so irritated I'm ready to scream.

I tried to explain to her that I've never worn a dress in my life and that I'm not a dress-wearing kinda gal. But she doesn't understand me. Fuckin' none of them do. They're trying to cram a square peg into a round hole and in the process the only thing that's happening is we're all getting more rough around the edges.

I wish they would listen more to what I want. I wish they would let me fight more. Hunt more. I want to do more than the boring shit expected of a teenage woman in a world that stopped existing long before I was born. They want me to have the childhood they didn't get, and yeah, I appreciate that, but that's not what I want.

I keep hoping that one day they'll finally wake up and see that I'm a smart, capable woman worthy of more. They already trust me in surgery, so why not trust me with other stuff I'm good at? I've taken down a number of deer cleanly with both my crossbow and rifle, proving I've got great aim. So why do they think I'm not capable of fighting just because I'm younger than the average rebel?

At some point, I'm going to have an opportunity to prove that I'm not just a dumb kid, but a badass to be reckoned with. I'll do something so incredible that they'll be forced to see that I can be trusted. Then they'll be sorry they ever doubted me.

Yeah, I can't wait for that day to come.

3

Declan

I'm so fucking pissed off I can barely speak.

I sit in silence as we bounce over the rutted ground, Adam driving us back to the overlook so I can get a glimpse at the explosion site. He's twitchy and anxious, the pulse point in his neck galloping as we reach the place where we ditch the cars and walk.

I trudge through the scratchy underbrush, the protective gear he demanded I put on making me even crankier as I sweat myself into a deeper state of irritation. My brain is juggling somewhere between medical and recon modes, registering heat index temperatures and blast radius intel and multiplying them by the number of beers it will take to make me forget this day ever happened.

There are so many questions clamoring for precedence in my head that I can't answer a single fucking one. I can't help but think there's another shoe yet to drop. I keep thinking something's wrong, well, something more wrong than hundreds of missing people and forty of my best fighters dead, and I have no idea what that thing is.

Amy lets us know that the incoming patrol trucks are making better time than expected and to hurry up, but I need to see what happened. Adam and I crouch down as we near the ridge, Army crawling on our forearms until we reach the overhang overlooking the road.

Judging by what I see, it's clear that this isn't a case of an overheated truck. There's too much damage. Adam said he'd seen a red blinking light come on just seconds after the truck doors opened, but by then it was already too late. We agree that explosives had been involved.

We walk back to the truck in silence. I'm sweaty and thirsty and completely miserable, only feeling marginally better when Adam gets another call saying everyone made it out of the immediate area safely. Amy calls a few more times to detour us around caravans of patrolmen heading towards the scene, the sound of her fingers flying over a keyboard in the background music to my ears. She's still trying to reach Trinity to see if she knows what happened, but it's almost impossible to reach her during the day. I have no doubt Amy's gonna grill the shit outta her to find out why I'm now going to be attending memorial services for the next week.

Adam and I ponder the possibilities of what happened, and although it's a longshot, the best we come up with is Trinity somehow thought we were taking too long. Maybe she sent in another group to save the people before we could get there. We know she's got her own personal force that's mainly active military leaders who are too afraid to quit Bellamy's service, but hate him enough to aid us when they can. But even if she somehow pulled that off, that doesn't explain her not getting word to us to abort our mission, and it sure as shit doesn't explain the bomb.

The last vehicle we switch into has a box full of "regular" clothes in it, and I strip out of my sweaty scrubs and Adam out of his tactical gear. We dress in the clothes of our new community, our plain attire and straw hats still foreign enough to usually make us laugh, but not today.

I always keep my sleeves down and wear gloves to keep from giving myself away with my tattoos and scars, but it's so fucking hot I decide to wait until we're closer. I see Adam's in a similar state of mind, his shirt collar unbuttoned, exposing the huge, dark love bite on his neck. If I was in a better mood, I'd probably bring up the hilarious story he told us about Amos pulling him and Dex aside about a month ago, chastising them for the couple's propensity for giving each other "visible tokens of affection." When Adam first told me the story I laughed so hard I snorted, while Dex deflated in horror almost as badly as when I walked in on him and Adam doing the deed in the surgical suite in Philly just a few months before. Fuck, that'd been funny. Yet today, neither memory even makes me crack a smile.

I scratch at my beard, a new part of my disguise that irritates me to no end, especially when it's this goddamn hot. It itches to high hell, the ingrown hairs creating an ever-present smattering of zits I've never had before, not even as a teen. But as a married man in Mennonite territory, it's expected for me to have facial hair, and the last thing I want is to make myself stand out more than I already do. The beard also helps me not look as much as the face on the wanted posters that I swear to God are plastered *everywhere*, even out here in God's country. The only upside is that Emma thinks my beard's sexy, and I pray that it's just her pregnancy hormones reacting to something new. I haven't told her yet, but the first thing I plan to do after we finish setting up our new community is to shave it off. I want my face back.

We drive to the vacant barn where we dump our vehicle and carefully scrub it of any traces of us before we go. The vehicle Scott, Dex, and Keira were in is already back and unloaded, our medical supplies too precious to leave out in the elements. We shake hands before heading in opposite directions, the men living in a cabin in the woods about a mile from the Zook's.

Judging by the lazy dip of the sun in the sky, I'm getting home just in time for dinner. When I get within a hundred yards of the old farmhouse, the smell of roasted chicken and fresh-baked bread makes my mouth water and my stomach grumble.

Gritty comes bounding out of the house barking his fool head off until he spots a chewed shoe that once belonged to Amos in his mouth.

He runs up to me and drops the slobbery hunk of leather at my feet, bouncing on all fours in anticipation of me throwing it. For a dog that once hated me with a passion, I've become his new best friend when it comes to playing fetch. I give the slimy shoe a hearty toss and he races after it, barking with delight. I can't remember when I last felt as carefree and jubilant as that mangy beast.

When I realize I'm actually jealous of my goddamn dog I start to wonder what the fuck is wrong with me. Then again, why shouldn't I be envious? Gritty doesn't have to worry about missions that fail and people who die. He doesn't feel guilt, or shame, or even worry about the consequences of his actions more than three minutes after he's done something wrong. He has the luxury of only thinking about one thing at a time, and right now, that's to retrieve his toy and bring it back to me so I can throw it again.

I'm suddenly so weary I can hardly stand. Gritty slams to a stop next to me, drops the shoe, and barks at me to throw it again. I pick it up and toss it as hard as I can, watching him as he races after it, yipping with excitement. It's only then that I realize how much Gritty and I have in common; we're both constantly chasing the thing we want most just to have it thrown further away the second we grasp it. The only difference is he enjoys the chase.

If I was a good Commander, I'd already have a plan. I'd already have the next ten steps in process, my tasks delegated out to people who are already at least halfway finished them. But I'm not a good Commander. I'm an imposter. I warned Anna I was the wrong person for the job, but she didn't listen. Nobody listened. And now I have to inform forty next of kin that their loved ones are never coming home because I fucked up, and the worst part about it is I still don't know what I did wrong.

How am I supposed to stand there, unscathed, and comfort the families of the dead? How do I express my sorrow for their pain when the people closest to me, who had also been there, all came home without a scratch? How do I reconcile the pain of all those lost lives with the relief of knowing my beloved wife, daughter, and yes, even my goddamn dog, had been safe and sound a couple hundred miles away?

What does that say about me, as a leader, that I flat out *ordered* Emma to stay at home "where she belonged?" Goddamn, I hate it when shit like that comes out of my mouth, but if I had to do this all over again, I would do the exact same thing. What kept me sane out there was knowing Emma was safe. If anything happens to her or my children it will kill me. I can't live without them, and yet I expect the families of those fighting with me to do just that.

Wow. You couldn't be a bigger hypocrite, could you?

I squeeze my eyes shut and sigh heavily as the fucking voice in my head laughs.

That's right, motherfucker! I'm back.

No, no, no, no. . . This can't be happening. Not again. Not now.

Tears of frustration prick my eyes. I try to think of why he's returned and come up with all sorts of excuses. I'm stressed. Exhausted. Grieving. Furious. Exhausted.

You already said that one.

The screen door slams, forcing my eyes open. Emma exits the house and looks off both ends of the porch, calling Gritty to come in for dinner. She hasn't seen me yet, giving me a moment to take in the sight of her. Her face is pale despite the always slightly-burned tan she's developed, her eyes tired. She rubs her palm over where my son grows inside her, and I wonder if he's been kicking the shit out of her again. I keep telling her she's doing too much. She needs to eat more. Rest more. But she doesn't listen. Fucking nobody listens to me.

When she finally spots me she startles, but then her face breaks into that wide, beaming smile of hers that I love. No doubt she's as happy to have me home as much as I'm glad to be back.

As she hurries towards me, tears form in my eyes from just the thought that something could have happened to her today. I swipe at them in irritation, looking up at the cloudless sky for a second and inhale a deep, grounding breath. When I look back my eyes are clearer, allowing me to drink in her every detail. I love how her pale blue dress and starched white apron no longer hide her pregnancy, her body now possessing the curves of a woman just a handful of months shy from giving birth. Her blonde hair is back in one of the little mesh bonnets the married Mennonite women wear, with just a few loose tendrils waving in the breeze as if they, too, are excited to see me.

I add this mental snapshot to the vast collection I hoard in my mind. With the farmhouse in the background and the windmill spinning in the distance, Emma could be any woman in any number of pieces of art. But she's not. She's mine, just like I'm hers.

When we come together, I fold her into my arms without a word, hugging her tight. She asks no questions, content in our embrace, and I am so thankful for this precious moment, for my sweet, understanding wife—

That's when I smell it—the lingering scent of motor oil and smoke in her hair that matches the stronger one trapped in mine. She probably thought Sarah's homemade lavender soap would be strong enough to erase the proof of her disobedience, but all it does is create a disconcerting dichotomy of windswept fields and fiery death.

I sigh heavily. I keep telling her that I can't do my job effectively if I'm constantly worrying about what she's up to when I'm not around. I thought she finally understood that during the last few months of pregnancy she really needs to do less, not tackle more. I need to say something, but right now, she feels too good in my arms, and I'm too exhausted to argue. Every fucking time I bring this topic up we fight, and right now, I only want to bask in my wife's love for a few more moments. I don't think that's too much for me to ask for right now.

Gritty returns with the slimy shoe, slapping me in the thigh with it while whiningly demanding I throw it. I know he won't leave me alone until I do, so I disentangle myself from my wife and reach for the shoe, but Emma grabs it first and gives it an impressive toss. Together we watch the dog gleefully run off, my arm slung over Emma's shoulder, her head resting against my chest. I sniff audibly and she stiffens, an entire unspoken conversation occurring within a single second.

I rake my hands over my eyes, my fatigue giving way to reluctant pride. Emma always manages to handle things as they come, taking things in stride way better than I do. There are plenty of days when I think she should take over as Commander, as she's better suited for the job. She lives this dual life so much better than I do, even if she sometimes does stupid shit that will eventually get her killed. Yeah, I'm a lucky son of a bitch that my wife's bravery is the biggest complaint I have about her, but fuck, does it add to my worries.

I look down at her in feigned disapproval. "One of these times I'm going to make good on my threat to take you over my knee."

She looks up unapologetically with a saucy twinkle in her eye. "You keep promising, but you never do," she responds sweetly as she turns her back to me and smacks her ass in playful invitation. My dick twitches in my pants as she saunters away, her skirt swinging with the sway of her hips, her laughter tinkling behind her like the most beautiful windchimes.

Jesus J.R.R. Tolkien Christ, this woman's going to be the death of me yet.

4

Trinity

There are many people I've met over the years that I've despised for one reason or another, but never have I hated someone more than I do our *beloved* Supreme Regent, Edward James Bellamy.

That I despise him more than our second Supreme Archon, who was a drunken, misogynistic bigot who did unspeakable things while hiding behind recitations of religious scriptures cherry picked for his specific needs, isn't even a close contest. That I hate him more than the first Supreme Archon, the miserable bastard who destroyed our nation with his demented mind and lying tongue, says even more.

I do get some comfort out of knowing they are both dead, and yes, I do get a perverse sense of satisfaction from rewatching the hospital security footage of Ryan Gregory's excruciating death. It makes a fabulous "pick me up" for times like these when everything's going wrong. It's a crying shame I can't share it with the world, as I think a lot of people would feel the same way, but sadly, the video incriminates the wrong man. Although Alex Smith delivered the lethal injection, Bellamy was the impetus behind his hand. I have proof of that too; I'm just not sure how to use it to my best advantage. At least not yet.

Most of the nation mourned Gregory's death, if not out of feelings of true loss, out of fear of someone turning them in for not feeling enough. The nation walked a fine line during those thirty days of mandated mourning, careful to be sufficiently somber to escape the watchers' eyes, but not appearing too bereaved to be considered a threat to our ascending lord and master.

I'm old enough to remember the good old days, when you could verbally bash leadership and not have to worry about repercussions. Say what you want about the law that forbids us discussing the time before the war, but telling us we can't talk about something doesn't mean we forgot. There's nothing the watchers can do to keep us from remembering how much better things had once been, and there's even less the Purity Police can do to keep us from secretly hypersalivating over thoughts of regained freedom. I've made it my sole mission in life to do whatever I can to overthrow this regime, and if it kills me in the process, so be it. At least I'll die knowing I've made life more difficult for the man I pray nightly that God will allow me the honor of killing.

I had hoped our former allies would have saved us by now, but they've proven to be too afraid of our nuclear arsenal to step in. Our enemies have done likewise, confirming that the tenets of self-preservation are alive and well in their nations, too.

So with no one coming to save us, our salvation must come from within. I have more hope with our current resistance leaders than with any we've had in the past. Don't get me wrong, Anna Vasiliev was a ballsy Commander. I knew from the very beginning that any Russian woman who defied custom by not adding the "a" at the end of her name would be a force to be reckoned with. But she loved her people too much, and was too afraid of them dying to risk actions of true significance. As bad as her bark was, she didn't have the bite.

This new leader, Declan Byrne, is just the opposite. I wouldn't go so far as to call him reckless, but sometimes he needs to rein in his enthusiasm. I'd been clear in my message to Amy that he needed to take extreme caution with the information I'd received. It had come from a new source I had yet to fully vet, and although the intel seemed credible, something about it had just felt off.

As I search for answers to today's disaster, I see that I was not the only person who found the Purity Police order to "liquidate" those towns. It takes little effort for me to find the location of the other viewer; their juvenile attempts at remaining anonymous are no match for my skills.

There's a new group of rebels in western Pennsylvania who have been making enough waves that I've found it necessary to keep tabs on them. I'm not surprised to see their interest in the post, as they would have been logistically closer than Declan and his crew and thus able to intercept the trucks quicker. But even if I had known of their interest to help, I still would have told them to stand down. The mission was too close to where they've set up their community, and it would take very little searching for the Purity Police to find them. Even now I doubt they know how much danger they're in.

I can tell someone from their camp is currently online so I reach out to them. I ask them if they know what caused the explosion today, and await their response. Whoever is there tries to decrypt my many layers of heavily coded protection, and fails. Then they log off.

It's smart of them to not answer. They have no idea if I'm friend or foe, and judging by their flimsy attempts to hack me, they're in way over their head. But vanishing without a word also infers guilt, making me that much more determined to find them and force them to toe my line.

I sigh. As if I don't have enough issues, I now have to locate a rogue group of revolutionaries causing more harm than good. I don't doubt their hearts are in the right place, but until I can get them to play nicely with Declan's army, they are just making my job harder. I'm not sure how, but I'd bet my left breast that they are the reason forty of our best soldiers are now dead.

A few years ago, I stumbled across encrypted messages from several high-ranking military officers determined to find a way to get the first Supreme Archon and the entire Committee out of office. In the pits of the dark web, I found a great deal of support for returning to the Democratic Republic we'd once been, and that had been enough for me to put the wheels in motion.

But finding capable leaders willing to actually risk their lives and those of their families was no easy task. Suddenly everyone wanted to be a bridesmaid and not the bride. I had no choice but to blackmail a few people into leadership positions by digging up their darkest secrets and using them as incentives. After they were involved, more joined us with considerably less persuasion needed.

I flip through files and interpret some more code, the running scripts of letters and numbers soothing my anxiety better than any pharmaceutical. I find that the Purity Police upped the reward for finding me to twenty-five million, a number so outrageous it worries me. Most people would willingly cut off a limb or two with a rusty butter knife for that sort of money. I've always known that what I'm doing is akin to suicide, and at some point, things will end badly for me. That is why my true identity is known to only two people, and sadly, one of them is already dead.

Someone else needs to know the truth, for if anything happens to Cassiel, my link to both the military and the rebels is gone. If we want to succeed, both groups must work together. If we can turn enough people against Bellamy, if we can prove we are capable of not only a successful overthrow of the government but can create a new, better one that will benefit everyone and not just the very rich; if we can get more help from other nations, then maybe, *maybe*, we can pull off a coup, and return to normalcy from there.

Girl, that's an awful lot of ifs. . .

Oh, and that's forgetting the most important if—*if* I manage to stay alive long enough to keep all the moving pieces together. Because unlike Cassiel, Declan, or even Emma, there is no replacement for me. I don't wish to sound conceited, but there is simply no one who can do what I can.

So far, the Purity Police don't have a clue of who or where I am, and I intend to keep it that way. Even though I'm currently number one on the nation's Most Wanted list, I am little more than a ghost. The Wanted posters for me are downright comical, with no poorly-wrought sketch of my face, just a giant black question mark taking up half of the page. A patrolman sharing a vehicle with me last week spoke in hushed tones to his compatriot about how odd it is that no one even knows if Trinity has "a cock or tits." It took all my composure to keep a straight face, not wanting to be reprimanded for eavesdropping, or worse, to raise even a hint of suspicion.

I highly doubt that they would think me capable of Trinity's illustrious crimes. After all, I'm *only* a woman. And what could a woman in this day and age possibly know about subterfuge?

Absolutely everything.

I still can't get over how, within a single generation, the men in this ass-backward nation can honestly believe women have somehow become stupid. Just because the new government insists we need to be protected from ourselves doesn't make it true. In fact, those of us who dare to defy the laws are becoming ever stealthier, more cunning, and far more dangerous for the simple reason we've been forced to learn how to subvert their laws.

It infuriates me how our leaders continually underestimate the female sex, even as their ever-worsening misogyny adds an ever-thickening layer of safety around the bubble in which I exist. Because of their myopic ways, many American theorists believe I'm not an individual, but a malicious foreign organization; others think I'm a disgruntled group of American men who somehow evaded the GTPC—the Great Traitorous Persons Cull. I was surprised they didn't call it what it really was, the Great *Educated* Persons Cull, even though many believe an M should have been added for Minority. I imagine by that point in our history it was already believed redundant..

A noise in the driveway startles me from my thoughts. The bright security lights flash on with blinding force, lighting up the outside brighter than the surface of the sun. I don't know what's going on, but things happening around here in the wee hours are never a good thing. Tires roll smoothly to the front door, my cue to quickly shut down my computer and stash it where it can't be found. I'm annoyed that I cannot complete the message I'm composing, as it's information that needs to get out tonight. I berate myself for my inability to stay focused, a problem I've always had but seems to be worsening of late.

I crawl into bed and pretend to be asleep, listening for clues as to what's got the house astir at four a.m.. There are loud voices and feet scuffling, and then yelling. *Lots* of yelling. I want to look out my window and see what's happening, but then I hear someone approaching my bedroom. They open the door, letting in just enough light to verify that I'm in my bed before closing and locking my door from the outside. Whatever's happening they don't want me to see.

I just hope no one needs me before they unlock the door, because if it's an emergency or not, I'm going nowhere. This isn't the first time we've all been locked down for "security reasons," and I can only hope for everyone's sake this is a short one, as my patient gets severely agitated when she finds herself confined. She's got a mind full of scorpions, and I'm tired of wrestling them back in their cages after the House Guard or the Purity Police rile them up. Some days I wonder, if one were to slip out, how bad would it really be? What damage could it really do?

Then I remind myself I may be old and tired, but I'm far from suicidal. Until the Lady Consort dies, or until I'm ready to give up, I need to keep track of those foul buggers like my life depends on it, because in all honesty, it does.

The sound of scrabbling feet on marble floors, and then of something most likely precious and irreplaceable shattering downstairs, proves that the battle has made its way inside the house. I hear muttered curses coming from the men, and then shockingly, a woman's voice. She sounds screechy and furious in all her accented indignity, but under her rage is a tone far too familiar among all of us in this house. Fear.

"Get your fuckin' grabby ass hands off me. You hear me? There's gonna be hell to pay when I tell Edward how you treated me tonight. He'll have your asses floatin' in the Pool before lunch. Now get me a phone so I can call him. Now!"

A few of the men laugh at her demands until one of them shouts out in pain, "Watch out for her fucking nails!"

She screams out something about breaking one, which I hate to tell her, is the least of her problems right now. Just as I'm thinking the Purity Police aren't going to take much more of her malarkey, her threats are silenced with the unmistakable sound of a harsh slap. She whimpers mournfully for a few moments before breaking into a howling sob.

"I told you to shut the fuck up, and you didn't listen," one of them says. "So I don't know what you're crying about." He orders the men to take her to the East wing, a section of the house rarely used and recently closed off for renovation.

I thought I knew everything going on inside these walls, but I apparently don't. Although it's common knowledge that Bellamy's unfaithful to his wife, he knows better than to bring women here. Not after what happened the last time.

I wonder why this woman's voice sounds so familiar, and when it comes to me, I laugh so hard I have to bite my knuckle to the point it bleeds to keep from being overheard. The old saying that Karma's a bitch is absolutely true. Through the years, I've witnessed Her topple the unassailable and humble the shameless, but this is the first time I can honestly say that if She were corporeal, I'd give her a big ol' sloppy kiss right on the lips.

The banshee downstairs is none other than Bellamy's whore, Caitlin Brown.

Tucked away in the Executive Mansion, it's been impossible for me to speed up her inevitable fall from Bellamy's grace, not that I needed to. It turned out she was more than capable of slitting her own throat without even a speck of help from me. She thought she was so smart, believing she could trap Edward into divorcing his wife and marrying her when she "accidentally" got pregnant.

Accident my ass.

We all assumed he would kick her to the curb the moment the pregnancy started to show, but instead, Edward kept Caitlin hidden away in the Executive Mansion's residence. Her baby became an "insurance policy" should anything happen to Emma or her son, as Caitlin conveniently was only a month or so ahead of Emma's due date. After Emma escaped, Edward had no choice but to keep Caitlin around. And if he doesn't find his daughter soon, Caitlin's brat will then be passed off as the Heir.

I shudder to think what sort of mind the child of a scheming, selfish bitch and a ruthless, power-hungry psychopath might have. If he ends up on the Throne, there's no telling how much worse this nation will become. As long as there's breath in my chest and blood in my veins, I have to keep Caitlin's bastard out of power because he'll undoubtedly be the worst Supreme Archon yet.

The house returns to its sleepy, early-morning routine. The patrolmen have delivered their charge and now clomp en masse towards the kitchens, talking eagerly about raiding the refrigerators. One guy's still bitching about the gash on his face needing stitches, another tells him to pour some vodka on it and to shut up about it. He replies cockily that he has every intent of hitting the bar to make himself a drink. He claims he *earned* it.

When Bellamy hears about their feelings of entitlement he will not be pleased. His need to feel respected at all times has caused him to ruin better men for much less. I doubt these patrolmen have any clue how dangerous their seemingly innocuous actions are, naively thinking he'll never find out. They have no idea their every move is being watched and their every statement recorded, and not just by me.

The sky begins to brighten, my bedside clock reminding me that I'm only going to get a few hours of sleep. My day's work unfurls before my closed eyes, my various duties of nurse, protector, informant and spy yet to determine if the day's labors will land me closer to either heaven or hell, or as on most days, a little closer to both.

As I drift off to dream of better worlds, I smile sleepily when I remember my earlier thoughts, and how incredibly wrong I'd been.

Sometimes good things do happen in the middle of the night.

5

Emma

My husband is pissed.

Before we sat down for dinner, he pulled me aside and let me know gently, but in no uncertain terms, that when he gives me an order, I'm expected to follow it.

Needless to say, that statement went over like a lead balloon.

The next thing I knew, I was yelling, he was yelling, and then my hormones kicked in and I started crying while he quietly cursed himself for upsetting me. Again. He looked miserable as he took me in his arms, apology written all over his face but the words not passing his lips.

As the minutes passed with him rubbing my back and kissing the top of my head, I realized not only was I not going to get an apology, I didn't deserve one. I should have either told him I was going on the mission or stayed home. I shouldn't have snuck off like an insubordinate teenager. If anyone should apologize, it's me, yet I can't bring myself to do it. I'm still too furious at being *ordered*.

Now, we sit in uncomfortable silence punctuated only by an occasional sniffle from me or an agitated sigh from Declan until Sarah calls us down for dinner. I barely stay awake through our meal, a miserable affair filled with sidelong glances and palpable resentment. Even Sarah and Amos are tense, the anxiety radiating off of them adding to the air of suffocation in this beastly hot house. I never realized how spoiled I was growing up in an air-conditioned home that was often so cold during the summer I needed a sweater.

When I say that I need to lie down halfway through the meal, Declan takes one look at me, wipes his mouth with his napkin, tosses it aside his plate, and silently rises. He scoops down to pick me up off the bench, and I squeal for him to put me down but he refuses. He carries me upstairs and lays me down on the narrow bed we share.

Firmly in "doctor mode," he wants to know what hurts, or if I'm dizzy, cramping, or nauseated. He's obviously worried, but also still angry with me. It changes the tone of his relentless questions into an interrogation.

We could easily get past our anger and frustrations if one of us would just open up about why we're really upset, but we're both too busy being stubborn. I can't help but think if it wasn't so damned hot in here, maybe we wouldn't be so irrational.

After completing his exam, Declan sits on the edge of the bed with his back to me. His elbows rest on his knees, his unfocused eyes staring at some point between his feet on the floor. He sighs heavily. He doesn't look at me, instead staring blankly at the floor.

"You could have lost our baby today." His voice is as flat and unemotional as his face. "You're dehydrated, slightly dilated, and your blood pressure is higher than I'm comfortable with. I think that with hydration and a few day's bedrest, you'll be fine, but if you do something like this again, you might not be so lucky."

He turns to me, his eyes filled with simmering anger. This is the first time he's ever looked this furious with me, and he's absolutely at his most terrifying when he's like this. I've heard stories of some of his rage-fueled moments, and even seen him lose it on a few occasions. But the fear I feel right now eclipses those other times by a million. Even though I know he would never hurt me, my past trauma experiences lead me to freeze up like a terrified rabbit.

When he notices my reaction he looks ashamed, his entire body softening and his voice gentling in an attempt to relax me. "Look, I was going to leave tonight to get up to New York, but I'm going to stay here until you're feeling better," he says quietly. "I'm serious Emma. You are in no condition to go galavanting around no matter how much you think you can. I've been trying to shield you from the truth, but there are things about your pregnancy that worry me, and no, it's not because I worry about everything concerning you. It's because there's medical reason. I want you to be as healthy as possible before you deliver. You aren't going to be able to deliver in a hospital with fully trained obstetricians and every possible piece of equipment necessary in case. . .in case. . ."

He doesn't have to finish the statement, his watery eyes saying it all. His voice is choked when he reaches for my hand, kisses my knuckles, and whispers, "I can't live without you, Emma."

When a single tear drips from his eye, I clumsily brush it away. "I'm sorry. I really am. I just thought. . ."

He places a single finger to my lips, silencing me. "You do know what Benjamin Franklin would say right now—"

"Don't ruin an apology with an excuse," we recite together, and we both smile as we think of Brother Love and his ability to have just the right quotation for every occasion. If he were here, I wonder what he would say.

Declan changes the subject. "Well, now that there's nothing to hide, tell me everything you saw from the minute the trucks pulled up. Especially if it's something you thought was weird, or out of place. It doesn't matter how small or insignificant. There could be things you noticed that Adam didn't that might help."

I close my eyes, settling into my pillow and take a deep breath before beginning a running monologue. When I'm done, Declan says Adam and I are really close in our retellings of what happened, but mine is in greater detail. He also thought the begging drivers and dirty patrolmen were interesting enough to look into. In all my life, I've never seen so much as a spot on a white-uniformed patrolman unless they were actively beating the hell out of someone. I often wondered if they wore white because it's the easiest color from which to bleach out blood.

We talk for a long while, Declan finally relaxing when my blood pressure falls to safer numbers. He sighs tiredly, stopping for a second to scrub his palm over his eyes. "Emma, tell me—how am I supposed to do this if I lose you? How am I supposed to go on if you die?"

When he looks at me again I realize that this wasn't a fight—at least not for him. He's *terrified*. He's lost so many people in his life that the mere thought of something happening to me or our children makes him panic. I can understand his fear because I feel the same way every time he walks out the door. When he's gone, I live for his texts, and I'm never happier than when I see him walking across the fields coming home to me.

We talk a while longer. Declan lies beside me on our narrow bed, his fingers drawing gentle figures on my baby bump, and his face lights up like the sun when he receives an answering thump from within. By the time we're back to being good with each other, he's becoming antsy, the long list of things he needs to do running through his head despite him trying so, so hard to stay here with me in the present.

I know I'm being selfish, wanting him to stay when we both know he needs to go. I promise that I will behave myself while he's gone, telling him that I have Sarah, an experienced midwife, to help me. I swear that at the slightest hint of something being wrong, we will call him. Immediately. I even manage a brave smile that is convincing enough to make him look at the door and then back at me. I nod encouragingly when he finally stands, and when he reaches for the packed bag of civilian clothes he keeps in the corner for emergencies, I know he believed my lies.

"If you're sure you're okay, I am going to go. You need your rest, and it's safer for me to drive at night. I'm too wound up to sleep, so I might as well head out now. Today just sucked and I've got a lot of shit to do that I can't do here. I just wish I could stay here with you, even if it's just to hold you."

With those words, I swear to God, my heart begins to bleed. He doesn't need to raise his voice, or point fingers, or use that sneering tone I hate so much to break me apart. It's the desultory voice that matches the yearning in his eyes that restarts my tears.

"Baby, please, don't cry," he breathes as he drops the bag and comes back to hug me again. "I'll be gone for about a week, and then I'll be back for a while. Amos needs my help with the harvest, and I promised I'll be here for as long as he needs me. But I want you to stay in bed until I get back. You can get up to pee, and that's about it. No stairs, no work, and no lifting—not even Anya. I'm going to tell Keira to watch you, and you know she will *absolutely* rat you out if you even blink too hard."

I crack a small grin, but I'm still about two seconds from sobbing. He places my chin in the palm of his hand and tilts my face up so our eyes meet.

"I love you so much, Emma Byrne. Don't you ever forget that," he whispers before giving me the sweetest, most loving kiss. Then in a blink of an eye, he's gone, softly closing the door behind him.

6

Declan

After making it crystal clear to Keira and Sarah that Emma is to do abso-fucking-lutely *nothing* until I return, I head out into the dark. Sarah looks nervous and worried, and Keira is a mix of annoyed at the added responsibility of watching the "devil child," and thrilled to be able to boss Emma around. I remind her to watch her mouth, to which she tells me to "fuck off." I don't know if I want to strangle her or laugh, so I jokingly do both, eliciting a rare giggle from the kid and a shocked look from Sarah.

The sun's setting and evening chores are over. I'm sad to leave right before my favorite time of night, that sliver of day when the heat finally becomes almost bearable and mere minutes before the mosquitos come out to play vampire on anything that will bleed. Sarah and Keira are putting away the dishes in the kitchen, and Amos sits out on the front porch swing with his pipe sticking out of his mouth and a farm journal in his lap.

"You headed out of town again?" He frowns. "I was hoping to get a few minutes of your time."

"Something wrong?" I could kick myself for how stupid I sound. Of course something's wrong. I can count on both hands the number of times we've spoken, not because we don't like and respect each other, but because Amos is a man of few words.

"Not really. It can wait if you're in a rush."

"I promise we'll talk when I return," I respond quickly, not wanting to stick around any longer than necessary. I've got a long drive ahead of me and a lot to do once I get to New York. He kindly wishes me safe travels before turning back to watch the stars emerge over his pasture.

As I head into the fields, the screen door slams as three sets of little boots stomp along the faded wood porch. Amos and Sarah's children line up to wish their father goodnight, and with Anya already in bed and snoring away, I almost turn back to warn them about slamming the door on their way back in and waking her. We adults have learned the hard way to never do *anything* that might wake her out of a sound sleep. She'll make you pay for it by shattering your eardrums with her screams, and once awake, she usually doesn't fall back asleep until minutes before it's time for morning chores. I guess because the kids don't have to personally deal with her vindictive vocal gymnastics they have yet to learn that silence is golden when there's a sleeping baby in the house.

I amble past the few neighboring farms, drinking in the peaceful sounds of chirping crickets and the occasional moo of a cow. Everything about this rural community is beautiful, and it would be a wonderful place to raise a family. The land is gorgeous, the community gracious, and the lack of patrol presence a welcome blessing. I often wish Emma and I could stay here forever, but we can't. When you're black carded and on the run, you can't get comfortable anywhere because that's when you get caught. I cringe to think what would happen to these people if Emma and I are found hiding among them.

Although I'd initially been against it, Anna's plan to have some of us hide among the Mennonite community of Lancaster should Philadelphia fall had been a genius idea. Nobody's going to even *think* about looking for us here. Lancaster, Pennsylvania is known for following the Committee's rules and taking their abuse to the point of subservience. I always thought that meant they were okay with how the nation was run because they never put up a fight. I had assumed they adopted the new ways because they believed in them.

You know what they say about people who assume. . .

Yeah, and I have no problem admitting now that I was wrong. I knew almost nothing of their culture before I got here aside from their refusal to fight in wars and the fact they're mostly farmers by trade. But since I've lived among them, I've learned about their history, their faith, and their beliefs. I've listened to their stories, and despite their adherence to the rules, almost none of them have happy endings.

From the day the Committee took over, the lives of the Amish and Mennonites changed dramatically. The community, despite their profession, were forced to work hand-in-hand with the new Agriculture Department. In the beginning, their areas of expertise and years of experience were taken into consideration, allowing them to continue their old-school methods for everything ranging from animal husbandry to canning. They may not have yielded as much final product as with newer techniques, but what they produced was always of considerably higher quality. Most of their produce went overseas to fulfill our export requirements to China, with some carefully held back to be consumed only by the wealthiest Americans who could afford it.

As the years went on, and we failed to do anything about our ever-worsening global climate, our weather patterns once again shifted. The midwest became a dust bowl where rain rarely fell. The proliferation of tornadoes in Oklahoma and Kansas now spread east through most of Tennessee and Kentucky, destroying crops and facilities faster than they could be replanted or rebuilt.

Eventually, life became unlivable in areas where, only a hundred years ago, vast fields had rippled with wheat and been filled with sturdy stalks of corn as far as the eye could see. With no grass to graze, entire herds of cattle grew thin and died off in alarming numbers. Chickens died out from increasingly virulent bird flus, and more and more pigs were mysteriously growing sterile.

As food became more scarce and the prices rose to the point of the ridiculous, people began to panic. Few things make people riot faster than a lack of food, and combined with growing political unrest, the fledgling Committee was eager to fix the problem before the people could revolt.

It shouldn't have come as a surprise, but putting bureaucrats in charge of shit they knew nothing about only made matters worse. When presented with untried ideas for "new cost-cutting advances" and "improved profitability," they adopted practices that anyone who knew anything about growing food could have told them would never work.

Despite a massive outcry from the remaining small farmers in America, the government put every last penny of their Agricultural budget into expanding the size and number of Confined Animal Feeding Operations, known less formally as CAFOs. With no subsidies to aid other forms of farming, most small farmers had no choice but to abandon their lands and try to find other work in the cities.

Unsurprisingly, it didn't take long for these enormous commercial entities to begin having problems with the animals contracting and spreading chronic disease. No creature can remain healthy for very long when trapped, by the hundreds, in tiny stalls in hot, airless buildings. Infections and disease ran rampant, and the animals had to be pumped with increasingly higher doses of ever-stronger antibiotics and antivirals. Steroids and hormones were liberally used to fatten animals and quicken their growth to maturity.

Virulent forms of bacteria and fungi began infecting and killing the people who worked inside the CAFOs, and once word got out, no one, no matter how poor, or hungry, wanted to work in them. After a few of these new diseases were determined to be zoonotic with a death as equally horrible as that of Rabies, death-row inmates from prisons were forced to work in them until they died.

It rapidly became clear that the only sources of safe meat came from old-school farmers and their proven, time-tested methods. With the middle of the nation too arid and climatically volatile for farming anything, and the SouthEast rampant with animal-killing disease, that left only the NorthEast and the West coast. But after a few uprisings in California, Washington State, and Oregon were stupidly dispelled by nuclear weapons, that left only the NorthEast capable of growing anything edible.

The minute the Committee determined the nation's survival depended on the farming efforts of a handful of states, they seized most of the farmland and put it under Ag Department control. People whose farms had been handed down from generation to generation now found themselves paying rent to live on and farm land they once owned. They were told what to grow, and how much to grow. If they couldn't meet their quotas, they were evicted from homes their ancestors had owned for generations and new tenants were brought in.

When Amos first told me the history of Lancaster and the surrounding areas, it had blown my mind. New resentments against the Committee built within me in honor of my new friends. It amazed me that the farmers didn't rebel against the injustice, instead taking the abuse in stride.

When I asked him why they didn't fight back, he made a sour face, and shrugged. "There was no way for us to win then, just as there is no way to win now. All that we would accomplish is killing our young men and leaving our mothers, wives, sisters and daughters unprotected and destitute. We worried what would happen to them."

They carried on, working, working, working, only to have their rent and quotas rise each year, in an endless, thankless circle of back-breaking toil. Every inch of farmable land is now in use, and when it's time to harvest, there are never enough hands to bring it in. The few pieces of machinery given by the Committee to help the farmers years ago now lie in rusted heaps; the exorbitant prices for imported parts and skilled maintenance far beyond what the farmers can afford and the government is willing to provide.

They also can't afford to hire the number of manual laborers needed to pick the crops, often leaving large quantities of crops rotting in the fields. When crops grow ripe, everyone, from the very young to those barely able to walk with a cane, toil until they're ready to drop.

No wonder they're willing to risk taking in the people from Philadelphia. They're fucking *desperate*, and desperate people forced to make dangerous decisions often regret them. I can only pray this one doesn't bite them in the ass.

The community's historically strict obedience of the law does allow them one enormous perk: there's almost zero Purity Police presence within the Mennonite area year 'round, and only quarterly visits from the Ag Police. This allows them to secretly practice their faith instead of that of the New State Church, only switching over to the nationally-sanctioned services the few times a year government workers are present.

It also allows them to aid those suffering persecution for their beliefs, both religious and otherwise. They've sold, as well as donated, some of their limited food surplus to communities forced into hiding, not to mention aided a few black-cards, like myself, the few times one made it to their neck of the woods. Considering the sentence is death to anyone who aids a black-carded individual, I find their willingness to aid us truly commendable.

After the city of Philadelphia fell for good, and we showed up unexpectedly at their door one night, Sarah and Amos helped a number of us find homes within the community. Unmarried people found themselves to be "long-lost nephews" or "nieces" of families willing to board a stranger in exchange for labor. Couples and families moved into the few vacant, but fully-furnished homes, still standing smattered between the fields or in areas unsuitable for farming.

Although curious, none of us really want to know what made the properties available.

Amy was busy for a few weeks forging papers and identities for those of us relocating. Emma and I are now "cousins" visiting the Zooks from a nonexistent community in Oklahoma. My wife told the few neighbors she's met that we came to Lancaster because where we lived we did not have a midwife, and luckily, Sarah is quite experienced. Adam and Dex adopted personas of "bachelor brothers" after moving in together. After word got out that two good-looking single men moved into town, no shortage of hilarity ensued as, I swear to God, every unmarried female within a fifty-mile radius took notice.

Although it's really fucking obvious we aren't Mennonites, with our tattoos and dirty mouths, these people are desperate enough to welcome us into their community. In return for their hospitality, we're doing our best to blend in, be helpful, and stay out of trouble. Once I understood what they've been going through, I feel more of a kinship with the community, and considerably safer whenever I must leave Emma and the kids behind.

I pass the small cottage where Adam and Dex live, deciding at the last minute to poke my head in and ask them to check on Emma while I'm gone. With their front door open and only their screen door closed against the bugs, I can hear Adam singing in the shower while Dex is cooking something that, for the life of me, I can't tell whether is fish, fowl, or beef. It smells like shit. He's concentrating so hard he doesn't hear me knock, so I quietly let myself in. I peek over his shoulder and whisper, "What's it supposed to be?"

He nearly craps himself, jumping about a foot off the ground as he lets out a distinctly unmanly shriek while pointing a spatula at me like it's a weapon. "Jesus Christ, Declan. Are you trying to give me a heart attack?"

I smile. It wasn't long ago I would have been thrilled to see him dead, but after he helped rescue my wife, I felt it was only right to give him a shot at redemption. When he tells me the charcoal briquettes in the pan are supposed to be fish, I recommend he toss them before he poisons himself and his boyfriend.

Oh, excuse me, *fiancé*.

Somehow I keep forgetting that Adam popped the question to Dex just minutes before he went on a dangerous mission in Philly that ended with me fishing a bullet out of his arm and sewing it back together on the Zook's dinner table. They've yet to set a date for the big day, I think enjoying their reunion after nearly five years apart far too much to worry about wedding details just yet.

Adam wanders out of the bathroom minutes later with a towel slung low on his hips and using another one to dry his hair, and when he sees me standing in the kitchen he blushes. I ask him with a straight face if he still thinks Dex is trustworthy, and he glares at me until I point to the nasty shit in the pan. I crack a grin and quickly add that I think his boy toy is either the worst cook on the planet or trying to poison him. The tension in his shoulders eases when he realizes I'm joking.

After he slings on a pair of jeans, I give Adam my itinerary as well as my latest burner phone number in case he needs me for anything. I give him strict instructions to check on Emma, and if she's out of bed, I'm to be called immediately. He pales when I tell him that because he disobeyed my order, Emma could have miscarried, which isn't much of an exaggeration.

I realize now that by trying to protect my wife from the concerns I had about her pregnancy that I'd helped create today's situation. She had honestly thought I was just being overprotective because I never told her anything was wrong. But my complicity in the wrongness isn't enough to let Adam's disobedient ass off the hook. By the time I'm done giving him hell he looks miserable enough that I tell him that things are okay, but from here on, he needs to fucking listen to me. He swears that he will.

As a peace offering, I tell him if they don't get called out on business over the next few days that they should help Amos around the farm while I'm gone. It'll be a good excuse for them to keep an eye on Emma, not to mention that Sarah will feed them while they're there. Both men perk up at my suggestion because they know Sarah is a helluva good cook.

By the time I reach the barn where our truck is hidden, only the stars and a sliver of crescent moon light my way. I'm deep in my thoughts, counting all the things I need to accomplish on this trip. Topping the list is finding a place where I can bring my people together; a place that's safe enough where we don't have to hide underground or in equally miserable conditions. I think not just about all the things my people will need in a new community, but the things they might want, too.

I think about what I want in the place I call home, and realize I've never once envisioned the actual house. What I see in my mind are almost like snapshots of the moments spent within. I smile, picturing eating dinner at our large kitchen table surrounded by my wife and our brood of children. I see myself laughing as the kids taunt each other while shoveling food into their mouths, Emma mockingly scolding our shenanigans as she daintily lifts a forkful of food to her lips. She then puts down her fork and bursts out laughing, finding our silliness as funny as the rest of us.

I envision checking on my children in their beds before heading to sleep on Christmas Eve, rearranging loose blankets and kissing their warm, baby-fat cheeks goodnight. I daydream about curling my body around my wife in our bed, and the two of us making love under thick quilts while snow falls steadily outside our window.

I imagine growing older, my hair graying, my children now adults and bringing home boyfriends and girlfriends, and then future wives and husbands, who I sternly interrogate to make sure will meet my very high standards to marry. The young men think I'm teasing when

I say that if they hurt my girls, I have a gun and a shovel and am skilled with both. My smirking daughters know me well enough to inform them that I'm not joking.

As I age into my twilight years, I welcome swaddled, newborn grandchildren into my arms with tears of joy and giant smiles. Years later, I'll teach those same boys and girls how to ride bicycles and swim in the ocean. And if I make it that long, I'll cry at their weddings as I remember my own wedding day, so many years ago. At the reception, I'll dance with my still gorgeous wife, gazing lovingly into her sapphire eyes and realize that despite everything I've been through, despite everything we've endured, my life was perfect because it all led to this moment.

I'm a bit teary eyed as I close my eyes for a moment and pray. *Dear God, if you're listening, I will give you anything and everything you ask if you allow these dreams to come true.*

By the time I reach the barn I'm smiling like an idiot as I think of potential names for my future children. The barn door squeals when I push it, loudly reminding me that it desperately needs oil. I fumble with my phone, needing the flashlight to see what I'm doing inside the pitch-black structure. I don't even realize I'm not alone until the muzzle of a gun is pressed sharply against the back of my skull, and I feel the unmistakable pinch of a needle being jabbed into my neck.

Fuck. Me.

7

Trinity

It's been five days since that contemptible homewrecker was dropped off on our doorstep, and I haven't had a moment's peace since. After the guards smacked her around enough to remove any thoughts that her tantrums would get her an audience with Edward, I thought the commotion would die down. Instead, she continued to shriek demands and pound on the door as if she'd been locked inside with a chainsaw murderer and a rabid raccoon.

This morning she resorted to more civilized, and blessedly, far less noisy requests. Then she gave up on being polite shortly after lunch, instead turning to despondency as she wailed and bemoaned the tragedy that is her life.

Now she's taken to begging *"Please, someone help me!"* over and over through the thick wood doors, a tactic that worked the first time when a member of the House Guard worried that maybe she'd taken ill. The second he opened the door, she made an easily-foiled break for the stairs that then necessitated a visit by a visibly irritated Purity Officer. I don't know what he did, but she's been quiet since he left.

Although some of the maids feel sorry for her, I have zero sympathy for the gold-digging bitch. She made her bed, and now she can lie in it. I might feel less animosity towards her if she was more considerate of my staff, but alas, her entitlement knows no boundary. She's exhausting to deal with, and nothing is ever good enough, not to mention, she has yet to utter a single word of gratitude to anyone.

We're doing our best to keep things unchanged for the Lady Consort, and so far, I don't think she's realized we have a new "guest." The ladies and I are doing our best to steer her away from areas of the house where she might overhear one of Caitlin's tirades and begin to ask questions. I thought it best to not tell Louise just yet that her husband's pregnant mistress is currently housed in the opposite wing. In all honesty, I'm hoping the conniving whore will only be here a few days so I don't have to tell my mistress, at all.

But it's impossible to hide the increased number of patrolmen on guard, and we give our Lady vague answers when she asks why her home has been besieged. The clomping of boots and the blaring of staticky radios ruins the tranquil atmosphere the staff and I work so hard to achieve. My mistress' health requires a stable, stress-free environment, and that's impossible to maintain when the house feels thick with hostility.

The House Guard is made up of members of the military, and those men have mostly been handpicked by Sir James, so we have no problems there. They are our usual security team, and they are always kind and respectful. My ladies and I do not fear them. It's the patrolmen who frighten us, as their behavior is unpredictable, and their attention always unwanted.

I've trained the women how to tell who's headed in their direction before they might be unhappily surprised. If you listen carefully, the different units' shoes make distinctly different sounds. The House Guard wears a boot with a rubber tread, something I specifically demanded to keep the noise down inside the house. Even if you don't hear them coming until they are near it's not worrisome, as they are merely coming to ask a question or to ask if we need help with whatever we are doing. The crisp click of leather soles means a Purity Officer is headed your way, which is never a good thing. I'm glad their shoes are noisy, as it's audible from quite a distance, and usually gives us enough time to escape their notice.

Yet knowing who's headed your way isn't the only thing you need to be aware of, as it's the cadence of their step that usually betrays their intended level of threat. A brisk, yet steady footfall usually means someone's en route for a purpose. There's usually little chance they will take the time to bother even the prettiest of employees if they are imminently expected somewhere. An erratic, slapping pace almost always signifies someone's either in a foul mood, or about to rain down Holy Hell on someone. Again, this one rarely pertains to us.

It's the leisurely amble that my ladies fear the most. A Purity Officer with nothing to do is a dangerous individual. And if there's a group of them coming towards you? Or if it sounds like they're trying to sneak up on you?

Then, it's time to run like hell.

One would think the Purity Police would behave better inside the personal residence of the Lady Consort, but alas, there seems to be very little thinking done by these men unless it's done with their dicks. The poor maids have resorted to racing from room to room and locking themselves inside when they work. They now work in pairs, or even groups of threes, in an often futile attempt to do their jobs without being molested. The kitchen staff is overwhelmed at all hours of the day and night by men sauntering in with their impertinent demands. They leer at the women as they eat, often complaining about what they are given and leaving a mess in their wake. I've often thought if I worked in the kitchens, I'd be hard pressed to not slip rat poison in their food.

Then this morning, all my hard work went straight to Hell when the Lady Consort managed to slip away from me. She followed the screams and curses to the door of her uninvited guest, and by the time I found her, Louise had already put the pieces together and grown terribly agitated, much to Caitlin's amusement.

As I led my heavy-hearted charge away from Caitlin's cackling laughter, I tried, and failed, to understand how Caitlin could be so cruel. I badly want to barge into her room and give her a verbal lashing she'll not soon forget, but it would inevitably be a waste of time. People who only know how to tear others down are the ones who hate themselves the most, and Caitlin's self-loathing is evident from quite a distance. I decide the harshest punishment I can inflict is to simply leave her to the torments of her own thoughts.

Now that Edward has sentenced her to spend the remainder of her days here, with the rest of his broken, misfit toys, she must know her days are numbered. As soon as the baby is born, she will become redundant, and I have no doubt that shortly after the birth, Caitlin will either "disappear" or suffer some form of "accident." And I think a large part of her increasing hysteria is because she knows that, too.

* * *

It's warm and humid in the conservatory where we sit, the sun beating down on us as my patient tends to her flowers. The calm, vacant look in her eyes is not from doing something she loves, but from the extra pills crushed up and slipped into her breakfast. I feel bad for letting her believe she's doing better by not needing extra medication to deal with yesterday's trauma and today's upcoming activities, but not badly enough to have risked going without. So far, she's outwardly calm, but her furtive glances at the clock and the way her shoulders inch closer to her ears with each ensuing chime, reveal that she's anything but.

Louise usually prefers silence when she spends time with her plants, but today she's requested Rachmaninoff. To further distract herself, she sings along to the orchestration, her vocal range and abilities every bit as stunning as when she was young. She's changed little over the decades; only the fine lines around her eyes and mouth give away that she's no longer a young woman. Even her hair has not darkened with time, as proven when a strand of pale gold hair falls out of the elegant, upswept style she prefers. She swipes at it absently, leaving a smudge of dirt across her cheek that does nothing to mar her beauty.

I often wonder if she hadn't been so stunning if she would have had a better life. Everyone expects pretty people to be happy, and extraordinary beauties, like Louise, to live exceptional lives. People often shallowly think life is easier for beautiful people, that their looks somehow smooth life's rough edges, but they don't. Louisa May Bellamy is proof of that.

I look at my watch, grimacing when I see it's about time for the dreaded annual luncheon with her mother. I hate to tell her it's time to remove her apron and wash her hands and face, that she needs to refresh her makeup and apply a new coat of lip gloss before Mother Barbara descends upon us. I've made sure the menu is set and the serving staff knows the precise timing of the courses, shaving off a minute here and there to get this sixty minute production over in less than fifty without the old bitch realizing until she's back in her car.

I stand slowly, not wishing to spook Louise as I look out the window and watch the photographers prepare for their chance to snap a photo of the Lady Consort with her mother. Every year, they are prepped en masse by one of Bellamy's goons to not ask Louise questions, but every year, they do. The cacophony they'll create will only further disturb her, making her tremble and quake as she fumbles for answers.

"I know. It's time," Louise whispers, untying the apron from her waist and placing it in the basket next to the gloves she refuses to wear. She frowns once more at the flowerless, droopy orchid that refuses to perk up, as unsure of what it needs just as I often find myself with her.

I take my Lady to tidy herself, her hands trembling to the point I have to help her freshen up her makeup. Unfortunately, there's not enough time to repair the chip in her nail polish that her vulture of a mother will absolutely comment upon.

We head downstairs slowly, Louise never wavering in her death-grip on the banister. She never recovered from falling down the stairs shortly after Emma's birth, and being forced to use the dreaded stairwell every day hasn't helped. Why they didn't sell this house and move elsewhere is beyond me, and when I finally mustered the nerve to ask her, all she gave me was a sad smile. I needed no words to know she lives in this house because *he* wants her here. Reliving that fall each and every day is part of her punishment.

The mansion's grand entrance is silent, cold, and uninviting. Louise shivers despite the fact it's nearly seventy-two degrees in here and she's wearing a long-sleeve dress. When her mother's motorcade pulls in, I squeeze her hand one last time before backing away, and she looks back at me in terror. I feel horrible for leaving her, but I can't stay. I simply don't have the inner strength to not strangle the old cow.

I head off to my room where I watch Lou on the camera feed, preparing myself for the inevitable disaster. I flip to an outdoor shot that shows Mother Barbara exiting her vehicle. She waves like she's the Queen of England to a nonexistent throng of people who will later be photoshopped into existence.

She greets Louise loudly enough to make everyone near her startle. "May the Lord rain blessings down upon you on this, your special day, my beloved daughter! It's been far too long since I've last seen you, Louisa May. I am assured you are well, as you look beautiful, as always. May this year bring you the greatest happiness yet!"

I catch the subtle darkening of my patient's eyes, knowing how much she hates her given name that only her mother still calls her by. She's always preferred to be called Louise, and those closest to her, like me, call her Lou in private.

She stands stiffly as her mother air kisses her on both cheeks, the bright pink dress and matching jacket, shoes, and hat Mother Barbara wears making her look like a giant bottle of Pepto Bismol. Everything about her screams over the top, from her theatrical entrance to her clothes; the ostentation compounded by her daughter's demure, ice-blue dress and even colder demeanor. I'm almost proud when Louise smiles at the reporters and then turns on her heel, cutting short her mother's time in front of the press as she's forced to follow the birthday girl inside.

They stand in the vestibule as Mother Barbara removes her hat and gloves and hands her purse to the maid, who nods and curtsies, her hands shaking badly enough that the feathers on the hat rattle. She smiles at the young woman, thinking she's overwhelmed by her glorious presence, when in reality it's the force of her hatred for the aged woman that makes her tremble. There's not a single soul in this house who can tolerate our *beloved* Mother Barbara, a fact I well know. As I am in charge of hiring the mansion's staff, I've made sure of it.

"I see you're in a hurry to get this over with, so let's just go straight to the dining hall, shall we?" Now that there's no one around, her voice is clipped and harsh, her eyes roving over her daughter and picking apart her appearance. She has yet to see the chip in her nail polish, a stroke of luck for my sweet Lou. They head into the formal room, the giant table looking particularly silly being set for only two.

"Is Emma not dining with us?"

Oh, shit.

Louise looks at her quizzically. "Why would Emma be joining us?"

Now, it's Mother Barbara who looks bemused. "She moved in here earlier this week. It's been all over the news. You must be doing quite poorly indeed if you cannot remember you share your home with your daughter."

I hold my breath, waiting for Louise to respond, but she only lifts her water glass to her lips and takes a long swallow. Her mother's eyes alight upon the chip in her daughter's nail polish, a flaw that sets off a ten minute diatribe about how Louise will never lure her husband back if she doesn't look after herself. She's so wrapped up in her speech she doesn't notice her daughter's hand wrap slowly around the steak knife next to her plate, her knuckles blanching from the deathgrip as she slowly lowers it into her lap.

"I've decided we need to get you out into society more, and it's high time you attend more events with Edward. After all, you are the *Holy Lady Consort*, and soon you will be grandmother to the *Blessed Heir*. Both you and your daughter need to set an example for American women, and you are shirking your duties. Honestly, Louisa May, I raised you better than this."

The look on Louise's face could boil a glacier to steam in under a minute. The hate she feels for her mother exudes from her eyes in twin beams of rage that her mother is either wholly oblivious of or just used to ignoring.

I've never seen Lou like this before, and I don't know what to make of it. Her mother's insults usually reduce her to tears of self-loathing as she gobbles down every cruel word she's fed and digests it into truth. But today she's turning her mother's torments into something else, something I've wanted to see happen for so long I'd almost given up hope. Now that it has, I'm actually afraid of what Louise might do, especially with that knife in her lap. I know I should get help, but I'm strangely rooted to my seat. Even if my actions might prevent a murder, I find myself unable to do anything but watch the scene before me unfold.

"Your husband has a big birthday coming up. Wouldn't it be a lovely idea to throw a party in his honor?"

Wow. Just when I think I can't hate that old crone more, she has to ruin Louise's birthday by bringing up her odious son-in-law's upcoming sixtieth. But her daughter doesn't get angry or upset; in fact, the only change in her demeanor is the frightening-looking smile forming on her perfectly painted lips.

"I agree, mother dearest," Louise responds with blatant scorn that her mother once again either misses or ignores. She takes her fork in her hand and spears a piece of her salad. "There are so many people I haven't seen in quite some time. A party just might be fun."

Mother Barbara looks about as surprised as a person can for having a face so incredibly full of Botox and fillers. "I'm glad you agree," she says slowly, taking a bite of her salad and chewing thoughtfully. "I'll start planning it this afternoon."

"No," Louise responds quickly, the word sounding harsh coming out of lips that haven't uttered a word of dissent since the day she went headfirst down the stairs. "I would like to put it together. It will be nice to feel useful again. And if I get stuck, or need advice, I can always call you for help."

What?

Okay, now I know Lou's up to something. She wouldn't call her mother if she was bitten by a venomous snake and her mother had the last vial of anti-venom. Even her mother looks at her with disbelief, but says nothing.

As the luncheon continues, Louise's focus fades in and out. Even when Mother Barbara demands the chef be brought in so she can complain about the seasoning of her entree, my mistress barely looks up from toying disinterestedly with the food on her plate. Only after the chef takes the old lady's rebuke and stomps back to the kitchen with barely concealed rage does Louise look up from her meal. She casually mentions how unwise it is to chastise a chef who has yet to produce the cloying fruit tart Mother Barbara always requests; especially one sweet enough to mask even the bitterest of poisons.

"Really, Louise," her mother gasps in horror. "The things you say to me, sometimes. Especially after everything I've done for you. . ."

As her mother prattles on, Louise mentally retreats from the onslaught of insults by zoning out. When this happens I worry about where she goes, as there's so much unchartered darkness in her mind that almost anything can happen should she venture down the wrong path.

But when dessert is served, she comes out of her trance. She looks up into the camera I'd hidden in the lavish floral centerpiece and flashes me a wicked smile. Although I have no idea what she's thinking, I'm happy to see that the glittering, mischievous look in her eyes, the one I love but haven't seen in far, far too long, is back.

When their conversation again turns back to Edward's party, Lou winks at the camera before settling back into her chair with a sly grin. It's then that I know without a doubt that this party is destined to be one to go down in history.

8

Declan

I wake up to find myself in a car with a bag over my head and my hands cuffed behind my back.

Howya gonna get yourself out of this one, hot stuff?

I would tell the voice in my head to fuck off, except there's a gag in my mouth, and my tongue feels like it's made of lead. My head hurts, my brain not nearly up to the speed it needs to get my groggy ass out of my current predicament. I pretend to still be asleep, allowing the drugs I vaguely remember being shot up with more time to wear off.

My ass has fallen asleep despite sitting on some of the cushiest leather imaginable, so I've apparently been immobile for a while. I listen carefully, taking slightly stronger inhales to see if I catch a whiff of something that can give me a hint as to who I'm with or where we're going. I come up with nothing.

I can only imagine I'm being turned in to the Purity Police for the reward. Although I've only met a handful or so of Amos and Sarah's most trusted friends, you never really know who's watching you at any given time. Hell, was this what Amos wanted to talk to me about? Did he have suspicions that someone was going to turn me in? Last I heard, the reward for bringing me in alive is up to five million dollars. That's a lot of incentive.

Though those that are betray'd do feel the treason sharply, yet the traitor stands in worse case of woe.

With all due respect, just shut the fuck up, voice. I can guarantee that whoever turned me in is going to be *significantly* happier. They're getting five million dollars. I'm going to get tortured.

I squirm a bit in my seat, trying to get comfortable for however much longer I'm stuck in this car. The person next to me stiffens before speaking a muffled word or two to the driver. They are speaking a foreign language. Something Slavic-sounding.

I wonder if whoever has me took Emma, too. Fuck, if they get rough with her, she could lose the baby. Even worse, they could both die, as the stress of being taken into custody could easily be more than enough to start premature labor in her weakened state.

The car turns onto a gravel road that, judging by the way we're bouncing, hasn't been maintained in the past ten years or so. We slide to a stop sharp enough to launch me forward into the seat in front of me, my nose taking the brunt of the impact and making my eyes water as I grunt in pain. The person sitting next to me jerks me back into my seat by my arms, but not before I catch the floral scent of the driver's shampoo.

The driver is a woman.

Car doors open, and then there are more sounds of them speaking right before my door opens. I'm hauled out of the vehicle and the muzzle of a gun is pressed against my temple. A harsh, accented voice warns me to behave as a small hand digs its fingers bruisingly into my biceps. Based on where the voice comes from and where the other hand is, I've been apprehended by two women.

If I wasn't trussed up like a holiday turkey, I'm pretty sure I could overpower them, but I'm at a serious disadvantage right now. I'm waiting for the voice in my head to rip me apart, no doubt overjoyed that big, bad Declan Byrne's going to meet his end at the hands of two women barely bigger than my wife, but the voice remains quiet.

The building we enter requires a code. The telltale beeping of digits entered and an answering buzz of assent occurs three times before we march through a maze of long halls. The gun is still digging into my head, the women taking no chances. I don't bother to fight, instead doing my best to remember the series of turns. If I can get loose, it's paramount to know the quickest route out of here. Wherever the hell *here* is.

We finally stop, one door clicking shut before another one opens. A pair of high heels clicks towards me on the tile floor. Another woman.

I had pretty much assumed the women who apprehended me were civilians turning me in to the Purity Police, but there's no way they'd be allowed inside the Interrogation Center. Not to mention, nobody's screaming bloody murder, which is sorta the soundtrack of an IC. They also aren't members of the Purity Police taking me to a higher-up, as the Purity Police don't allow women in their ranks.

That's all great sleuthing, Sherlock, but who the fuck's got you?

As much as I hate to admit it, I don't have a clue.

I'm dragged forward a few steps and then shoved in the center of my chest hard enough to make me fall back, my body landing awkwardly in a large leather chair. The woman with the clicky heels sits across from me with only a few feet between us.

The bag is untied from my throat and dragged over my head, the brightness of the room making my head hurt as if someone's shoved an ice pick in my brain. My eyes tear as they attempt to focus on the woman seated like a queen in the chair before me. She has dark blonde hair that's pulled back and twisted tightly behind her head. Her brows and lashes are dark, contrasting prettily against milky skin. Her fitted dress looks expensive, the dark blue silk draping flatteringly around a toned body used to regular workouts.

She crosses her legs at the knees as she makes herself more comfortable while staring at me in the most unnerving way. Next to her chair is a small table with a crystal glass containing a single mouthful of clear liquid, and she delicately picks it up with one manicured hand with her eyes never once leaving mine. She finishes off the liquid just as the first beads of sweat appear on my forehead. As she places the glass back on the table, her lips curve into a satisfied smirk—lips that are painted the color of deep, red wine.

It will have blood, they say; blood will have blood, the voice in my head whispers in awe.

There's something dangerous about this woman. As the voice so eloquently said, this woman's not just seen, but shed her fair share of blood, and I'm pretty sure the next blood shed is going to be mine. She regards me with critical eyes the color of the most valuable rare, green gemstones, and when she finally finds me unworthy, she makes a small scoffing sound in her throat.

I'm still in my plain clothes and in desperate need of a haircut, and I reek of motor oil, smoke, and sweat. She seems the type to sense more than the average person, so she probably can also pick up the stink of fear I'm trying my damndest to suppress.

I don't know why she has me so unnerved. I was beaten nearly to death in an IC less than a year ago, and even while chained and on my knees, I was mouthing off to my captors. Yet this woman hasn't said a single word or even remotely hurt me, and my internal oh-fuck-o-meter is already off the charts. I shift in my seat, trying to find a more comfortable position, and only manage to look like I'm squirming under her intimidating glare.

Great.

Why I give a shit what I look or smell like right now is absolutely beyond me. I should be trying to get out of these cuffs, or figuring out how to overpower the chick with the gun without using my hands. So why am I currently more concerned with the fact she's looking at me like a piece of shit stuck to the bottom of her shoe?

Get your priorities straight, asshole, before you're too dead to have priorities.

When the other two women move from behind me to stand to either side of the seated one, it's clear they're younger versions of the same woman. That's not to say they don't look nearly identical. Aside from a few very small wrinkles at the corners of her eyes, and an air of maternal affection towards them, they could totally be sisters.

The three of them don't say a word and yet somehow appear to be having a lengthy discussion. Whatever their deal is, it's apparently beyond my scope of understanding. Are they demons? Succubi? Witches? Some other form of terrifying occult beings I've never heard of?

The youngest one chuckles lightly while the other two smirk. It's as if they've read my mind, found my thoughts humorous, and are now sharing silent jokes at my expense right in front of me.

How fucking rude.

Then I give myself a good, old-fashioned, metaphorical kick in the pants, reminding myself that witches and soul-sucking seductresses aren't real. I inspect them closer for some clue as to why the three of them are looking at me like I should know who they are, the three of them staring holes into me with emerald eyes sharper than the edge of a knife.

Holy motherfucking shitballs.

When the women realize I've figured out who they are, I swear on all things Holy, I see a momentary flicker of flames in their eyes. I gasp, the three smiling devilishly as I gulp down the giant lump of shock in my throat.

"Don't be afraid," the more terrifying of the daughters says in a voice that tells me I'm absolutely right to be pissing-myself-terrified right now. "If we wanted you dead, we'd have killed you long before now."

Her words aren't meant to put me at ease. We both know there are things way worse than death.

Not to mention, I don't know how much any of them knows about what happened, or my role in it, or the millions of ways I failed to bring about a better outcome. They're going to have questions about things I don't want to think about and absolutely don't want to talk about, and they aren't going to accept no for an answer.

The eldest uses this time to make silent appraisals that will no doubt affect how much longer she plans to let me keep breathing. With a satisfied nod, she stands up and smiles down at me, and once again, it's not a remotely reassuring expression. She turns away, stopping for only a moment to look back and give me the most terrifying look.

"My dearest Declan, yes, we do need to talk, and yes, I do expect answers," she says in perfect, unaccented English as she walks over to the bar and grabs a bottle of clear alcohol and returns to her seat.

I know I look stunned, and not just because the younger women have thick accents and she does not. I'm dumbfounded at how she's reading my fucking mind. There's no point trying to hide it, as no amount of bluster or bravado will change their minds. That's probably the only damned thing I *do* know.

"Declan, why do you look so surprised?" She cocks her head to the side, giving me an appraising stare before shrugging her shoulders and pouring herself another glass of what I assume is vodka. "You should know by now that we already know everything."

9

Keira

I'm woken up before the ass crack of dawn every day so I can help with chores for a couple hours before breakfast. With Emma down for the count until Declan returns, whenever the fuck *that* will be, I'll be expected to do double the work around here to pick up her slack. Forgive me if I'm wrong, but I was told when I was dumped here that I'd be expected to "help out." Instead, what they've got me doing is more like slave labor.

I don't mind some of it, but I rarely get to do the parts I like. Hunting, fishing, working out in the fields or in the orchards with the sun on my face and the wind in my hair—that's all considered "man's work." They keep me in the house as much as possible, either helping with the kids, cooking, cleaning, or whatever domestic drudgery Sarah can come up with to torture me.

I'm so done with this shit I could scream, so today, I'm getting the fuck outta here before my next round of indentured servitude begins. I'm going hunting.

Where I'm going I won't see anyone, so I put on my old, ratty jeans and a pair of ankle-high boots along with a boy's stained, wife beater undershirt I found up in the attic. I tie my long hair into a messy knot on the top of my head, despising the stupid braids the "girls my age" are expected to wear. The one time I did, Declan laughed and called me Pippi Longstocking, and even though I don't have a clue who that bitch is, I could tell by his tone that I wouldn't like her.

Some days when I head out super early, Gritty pretends to be asleep so he can stretch out on the cramped bed we share after I leave. Today he decides to grace me with his company, thumping out of bed as loudly as someone dropping a dead body on the floor. While I'm trying to sneak out, the lumbering ox taps as loud as he possibly can down the hall, making sure to hit every squeaky-ass step on the way down. I swear to God, he's trying to get us caught before I make my escape so he doesn't have to miss breakfast. He doesn't understand that I'm doing him a favor. If we stick around, we'll be trapped here all day.

We're barely off the porch when I see a light switch on in Emma's room. I know I should check on her before I go, but I just can't. I need my space. I race into the woods with Gritty on my heels, the huge Shepherd barking like this is some game we're playing and not our only shot at freedom for the day. I whisper-shout at him to shush but he only barks louder.

We run for a good quarter-mile before I see the small shed where we keep the hunting rifles, crossbows, and other crap we can't leave in the house because of the crotch goblins. I turn on the flashlight we keep out here and load my favorite shotgun before slinging the strap over my shoulder. I grab a backpack and fill it with more ammo, a water bottle I'll fill at the stream, and a few apples I snag off the lowest hanging branches as we make our way to the meadow where the wild turkeys have been chillin'.

Yeah, let them try to bitch about me goin' hunting when I come back with a nice, fat bird for dinner.

After another fifteen minutes the sun starts to rise right as I get to the stream. I take a minute to fill my water bottle and eat an apple as Gritty amuses himself by splashing in the water and barking at the minnows desperately trying to escape his snapping jaws. I smile when I remember how upset he got the first time he caught one, not understanding why it wouldn't play after he speared it on a tooth. But then he swallowed it, and I'm not lyin' when I say I saw the *exact* moment his remorse ended. Now that he knows they are tasty, my boy's not playing. He's in it to win it. Who knew a filthy, torn-up pooch from South Philly would become a sushi lover? Then again, I never thought I'd be getting up well before sunrise to shoot wild turkeys.

Country life has changed us both.

I get up and dust off my pants, calling Gritty who ignores me and trots off downstream to find more fish. *Whatever.* I just hope he doesn't scare everything away within a five mile radius before I bag myself a bird. I find the tree where I've set a short piece of wood about six feet up between two branches and begin to climb.

No sooner than I get settled, Gritty starts barking from somewhere a ways off, the sound one I know to be his special alert. As he's a particularly brave dog—and why not, as he's a 125-pound killing machine with a shitty attitude—the fact he's yapping like he's got a Supreme Archon cornered makes me curious enough to investigate.

The damn dog's probably barking at a raccoon or a fox, but I did hear Amos mention that someone's been stealing food out of dry storage rooms and spring houses. I hope it's not a burglar, as that's really gonna fuck up my day. As I get closer, I see whatever Gritty's cornered, he's managed to run up a tree. When I lift my gun to get a better look through the site, I nearly drop it in shock. It's not a possum or a fox, nor is it a raccoon. It's a boy.

I sneak closer, now able to hear a male voice loudly whispering for the dog to go away as Gritty leaps higher and higher in an attempt to snag the kid's dangling bare foot. "Please, dog, go away," he begs. "Please, I can't get caught!"

I step out dramatically from where I've been watching. "Too late, asshole," I say in my best tough-girl voice. "If you know what's best for you, you'll show me both your hands and then empty your pockets. Give me any trouble and I'll fill you full of lead. *Capisci?*"

He turns to face me, his face so sickly and thin under greasy, overgrown, brown hair that I'm not sure how he's still upright. He's sweating bullets, and after a few seconds he raises one hand in the air and croaks out in a raspy voice that he can't raise the other one. He turns a little further so I can see the thick, blood-soaked bandage wrapped around the biceps of his other arm, his wrist wrapped up in a sling made from a few knotted together pieces of his shirt. His hand is grotesquely swollen, his sausage-like fingers a freaky shade of purple.

The kid's in bad shape, but I know better than to underestimate him. Even a person on their deathbed can be dangerous. I tell him to climb down after getting Gritty to finally chill out and return to my side. It takes the kid a while, but he manages to get down without falling on his face. Once in front of me I notice he's wearing a gray and black striped uniform of sorts, the patch on the breast of his filthy shirt one I've never seen before. He's on the run from somewhere. Somewhere bad.

"Who are you and what are you doing here?" I demand.

"You're a girl!" he exclaims now that he can see me better.

"No shit, Sherlock. Now answer me before I get bored and shoot you just for fun."

"You wouldn't do that."

"Why? Because I'm a girl?"

He nods.

I unload a round about two feet from his right foot.

He jumps with a startled yell. "What in the name of God are you doing, woman? You could have shot me!"

I roll my eyes. "That's what I'm trying to tell you. Don't fuck with me."

He leans back against the tree. "Please," he whispers as he sways.

"I have no intention of staying here. I'm just passing through. The others I was with—I couldn't keep up and they left me behind."

I don't know what to do. The kid looks young and innocent enough to be incapable of lying, his light brown eyes imploring me to believe him. "Where are you headed?"

"Canada," he replies quickly. "There's a place in upstate New York with people who can help me get across the border. Please, miss, I give you my solemn word, I'm not here to harm anyone."

I look down at Gritty, wondering if my canine lie-detector believes him or not. I step closer to the boy, my weapon still poised to shoot, and give my dog the simple command, "Free." Gritty moves closer slowly, his hackles raised and his lips pulled back in a snarl as he prowls forward and sniffs at the terrified boy. Now that I'm closer, I see he's not as young as I thought. He's about my age, maybe a little older, and the lankiness I had assumed was due to a recent growth spurt, is instead from months, if not years, of starvation.

"Please," the boy begs as Gritty stands within inches of his groin and menacingly licks his lips. "Please don't let him hurt me. And whatever you do, please, please, tell no one that I'm here. No one can know. Promise me!"

Before I can tell him everything's okay, that he's actually passed all of Gritty's threat tests faster than anyone he's met before, the kid's eyes roll back in his head and he crumples to the ground. Gritty looks back at me with an expression that asks, "What the hell just happened?"

Well, dog, fuck if I know.

It takes what feels like ages to decide what to do, and then even longer to get up the courage to do it. Gritty stands over the boy and whines plaintively for me to do something, no doubt because it's no fun to terrorize the unconscious. I love this old fleabag to death, but sometimes he can be a real sadist.

I check the kid over while he's out, quickly realizing he's even sicker than I thought. He's got a raging fever, no doubt from what appears to be a bullet wound in his upper arm. Judging by how it stinks, it's infected. He's filthy and his clothes are threadbare, and his feet are thickly calloused and almost black with dirt. Because I'm not a perv I don't go looking for other injuries that might be under his clothes, but I don't need a medical degree to know that without treatment, he'll die way before he gets to Canada. Hell, I'm not sure he's gonna make it outta Lancaster.

I do what I can for him until he wakes up, grabbing my water bottle and tearing a chunk off the hem of my shirt to clean his face and cool him down before the fever cooks his brain. He stinks to high hell, the sort of putrid odor that someone gets after they've neglected themselves for far too long. I sit down next to him, the shotgun far enough away from him so if he's playing possum, he can't just reach over and shoot me.

After debating for a few minutes, I unbutton his pajama-style shirt. He's covered in bruises in various stages of healing, and as thin as he is, I can even tell where he'd broken and displaced ribs that didn't heal properly. I try to imagine what this boy's been through and how he managed to survive as long as he has, but even my imagination's not that sick.

When I start to unwind the sling from his damaged arm, he wakes with a start. He's disoriented and thrashes about a bit, but I subdue him quickly, telling him that he's safe and I'm going to help him. He licks his horribly chapped lips, his mouth so dry it does nothing. He croaks out a word that it takes a few tries for me to determine is "water." I help him sit up and give him the last of my water bottle, instructing him to take small sips.

"You need help," I tell him. "Your arm is badly infected and you have a high fever. I know someone who can help you—"

"No!" he all but shouts before breaking into a mucousy cough that steals his breath. "No matter what happens, no one can know I'm here. Promise me, please. You must promise!"

He's so upset I nod quickly, not wanting him to use up what little strength he has left by getting upset. I try to think where I can hide him until I can come back with supplies when I remember the old spring house I passed that's part of a farm no one lives in anymore. When I checked it out once before it was dry inside, and being partially underground, definitely cooler during the day. It takes so long for him to limp over there that I'm sure Sarah and Amos have probably sent out a search party for me, the sun now high enough in the sky to be somewhere around late morning. He lies down on the cool soil with an exhausted sigh and tears in his eyes.

"Thank you," he croaks. I stop him before he goes on, pretending like I do this sort of shit every day and it's no big deal. I refill the water bottle and grab a few juicy apples for him off a nearby tree and bring them back with me. The look of gratitude on his face makes me want to cry.

"I'll come back either later tonight or tomorrow," I tell him. "I have to get that bandage off and see what's going on underneath, and I don't want to do that without clean stuff to rewrap it. I'll bring you some food. Clean clothes. Oh, and some soap, because damn, you stink..."

I stop talking when I realize he's crying and I don't know why. Is he in pain? Is it his arm? His feet? Is he hungry? What?

He wipes his fist across his eyes and gives me a watery smile. "I'm just grateful that your scary dog found me." Then he laughs, a sweet, pure sound that shouldn't come out of someone who's both as weepy and as close to death as he looks. It throws me for a loop, cracking the thick layer of ice around my heart that I swore long ago I'd never let break.

I smile back. "Me too," I answer honestly. I pat his hand, swearing again I will return as soon as I can before racing back to the farm with a gleeful Gritty barking at my side.

10

Louise

There once was a time when I loved the spotlight and I lived for parties. Back in the days when I was young and foolish, I believed that a Friday night without an event to attend was a calamity of the highest order. I thought my life would always be like this, just one glamorous party after another. Never once did I imagine that just the thought of leaving my bedroom would one day make me break out in hives.

I reminisce about those early years a great deal, but not in the way most people do, with wistful smiles and glittering eyes. I rehash mine brutally, ripping the memories apart and searching for the signs that I missed. If there's nothing I've learned from my years of reading Shakespeare, it's that there are always signs before a tale turns to tragedy. Apparently, when it came to the story of my life, I somehow missed them all.

For the most part I was a good kid. I did whatever I was told until I was in my teens, and then my friends and I rebelled the way most kids our age did. But aside from weekend drinking parties when someone's parents went out of town, or the occasional drug use that rarely consisted of anything aside from some particularly good weed or an occasional line or two of coke, we never did anything too terrible.

I was among the most popular girls in my high school; the clique I belonged to included only girls from the wealthiest and most influential families who were all close friends of my parents. We were adored by our teachers, envied by the rest of the student body, and eagerly sought out by boys who would willingly cut off a testicle for the chance just to hold our hand.

But my girlfriends and I only ever hung out with the same boys we had since we were young, all of them also children of our parents' elite social circle. They were trusted to keep us "pure," all of them threatened within an inch of their lives to keep their hands, and other body parts, to themselves. Yet the threats weren't enough to stop them from playing *spin the bottle* or *seven minutes in heaven* with us.

My girlfriends and I all received our Purity Rings when we were thirteen, the ceremony presided over, of course, by my mother. We wore white dresses and veils and were accompanied by our fathers who beamed at us and told us they loved us—with the unspoken threat they would stop if we failed to remain virginal until our wedding night.

The highlight of the ceremony was when we each got an identical ring as a token of our pledge. We thought the rings were gorgeous, spending the next few weeks showing them off to everyone we met. We thought they made us special, and anyone who dared to make jokes about them we believed were jealous. About a year later, one of my friend's older brothers laughingly pointed out that it looked like a vulva with a giant pearl clitoris, and when we realized he was right, we were mortified. It wasn't until we were old enough to prepare for our coming-out parties that we girls got drunk one night and confessed that the fact we had to get on our knees and pledge our undying purity to our fathers—while face-level with his dick—was some seriously fucked-up shit.

Yet as far as I knew, by the time we turned sixteen, none of us had gone "all the way." I think that was more due to still believing in being swept off our feet by our yet-to-arrive Prince Charming than the promises we made to our fathers. It probably was also due to not finding the boys we grew up with remotely exciting or sexy. It's hard to feel passionately about a boy you once saw snort soda out of his nose.

It was during that same year that my mother found a new money-making venture in my friends and me, a private "social club" of sorts designed for the "budding Young Evangelical Ladies of the Lord," or YELL. To this day, that silly acronym makes me laugh. The classes were designed to brainwash us into becoming perfect little future wives and making as many little congregants as our poor uteri could handle. If we didn't bear enough kids to make nice, big Christian families, my mother was more than happy to arrange adoptions of "suitable children," who would inevitably be white, and more than likely, blonde.

My mother would love for everyone to think she did everything for the glory of God, but even back then, I knew that was bullshit. She got into religion for the money.

My father was a popular TV evangelist with a knack for turning atonement into cash long before they even met. Although my mother came from old money, and plenty of it, she was always looking for more. Their marriage was a match of convenience, as he wanted her society connections, and she wanted to be famous.

Yet the more they earned and the more famous they became, the more they wanted. Each year saw expansion in the form of new churches, and with each new house of worship, their wealth increased exponentially. They acted as if Greed wasn't one of the seven deadly sins. Instead, they nurtured it like a virtue.

I know I sound jaded, and admittedly, I am. From my earliest memories, I knew something was off about their "church" by the way people who didn't belong talked about it. As I got older and was able to understand more, I realized my parents were nothing more than talented grifters, and as I was often used in their schemes, that made me one, too. I hated them for that.

From the day I was born, I was a part of their show, the pretty, blonde-haired and blue-eyed child taught to say adorable things at exactly the right moment to make the congregation dig deeper into their wallets. When my mother realized I could carry a tune, I was enrolled in voice classes, and then became a part of the junior choir. When the church's marketing department determined I was drawing younger generations to services, I was elevated to a soloist and given a new hymn to sing each week. By the time I was twelve I was a household name across America with modeling contracts, the occasional magazine cover, and a handful of Christian-based product endorsements.

With the eyes of the nation upon me, every detail of my life was scrutinized, and I quickly grew to hate that. I despised that every piece of clothing I wore had to be modest, but not too modest; trendy, but not too trendy. There were whole teams of people who managed my image, and focus groups weighed in on everything from if I was old enough to wear a two-inch heel to the length of my hair.

Nothing about my life was ever left up to me, and my coming out party was no exception. This event was supposed to be my introduction to society, which was a laugh, because I already met every single prominent person invited at least twice. The guest list was a veritable who's who ranging from religious leaders to pop-stars, high-ranking military leaders to high-priced call girls.

I had always been a good listener, and an even better rememberer, which is never a good thing when a mother is a gifted and vicious gossip who never realizes how well her voice projects. I was often forced to attend to her friends when she hosted teas and brunches, and during those, I got quite an education completely unbefitting a young woman of my status. At a charity dinner benefiting some inane cause I long ago forgot, it took every ounce of my strength to not let it show that I knew Senator McWilliams enjoyed golden showers and

General Forthwith was a favorite exhibitionist sub at the local kink club. Both attended my mother's church every Sunday looking so pious they could have easily been mistaken as candidates for sainthood, and we always knew when they were being particularly "naughty" based on the size of their donations.

My debut was by far the largest production of my mother's where I'd be the star, and the pressure was on. I'd hardly eaten in weeks, as my mother was beyond determined that I have an eighteen-inch waist, just like Scarlett O'Hara did in *Gone With the Wind*. I must have practiced descending the grand staircase a hundred times before my mother deemed it graceful enough. We must have tried fifty hairstyles before my mother finally found the one that didn't make my cheeks look chubby.

Despite all the pressure on me for everything to go perfectly, I also can't say that I wasn't excited for the party, because I was. But I was also very, very nervous. When the day of the party dawned, I woke up anxious and sweaty, freaking out over all the things that could go wrong. The more I tried to calm myself, the worse it got, and less than an hour later, disaster struck. My boyfriend, Oliver Whitmore, called to say he was sick with a raging case of strep throat and would not be able to escort me.

My mother went ballistic, demanding he come anyway despite his 103 degree fever and a throat that felt like he swallowed razor blades. His parents eventually got involved, telling my mother he could barely stand and he would not be attending. Period.

She'd been so pissed off she demanded I break up with poor Oliver immediately. My mother ranted and raved for the next fifteen minutes, becoming increasingly more dramatic and ridiculous. I'd never been happier than when my cell phone burst into song.

"Hello? Is this Louisa May Cavendish?"
The voice on the line is deep and confident, the tone I would imagine

of the poised gentlemen in the Regency romances I read when my mother thinks I'm memorizing Bible verses.

My heart beats faster as I politely answer, "Yes, I am she."

"My name is Edward James Bellamy. I understand you are in need of an escort for a party this evening?"

I remember thinking that if this guy was even remotely as good looking as he sounded that strep throat just might become my new favorite disease. I remember how my cheeks warmed as I laughed at his jokes, and my heart beat faster with each clever response to my flirtatious banter. He sounded so much more like a man than the boys I was used to, and because I was a girl desperate to become a woman, I longed for the things he could teach me.

I was entranced by the delicious timbre of his voice, the spell he placed me under not even dulled by my mother's loudly whispered, intrusive questions. Unlike her, I didn't care who his parents were or what his father did for a living or to which country club they belonged. I was simply looking for someone I could have fun with on the most important night of my young life.

He knew nothing about "the social event of the year" as it was being billed by society reporters, and I found his lack of experience with debutante balls refreshing. When I told him so, he paused for a beat, and I worried he took my words the wrong way. But then the moment passed, and he spoke again, his voice dropping in octave and volume. He asked me if I believed in Fate, and when I told him yes, he claimed that these strange, last-minute circumstances could only be Fate bringing us together. I was besotted before the call ended.

After an afternoon of primping and prodding, I donned my white gown, slipped my feet into my low heels, and watched the clock as it slowly ticked closer to showtime. I was sequestered in a room above the ballroom until what I laughingly called "the big reveal" in front of nearly eight hundred guests, society reporters, and countless photographers. Everything from how I wore my hair to the designer of my gown were as closely kept secrets as nuclear launch codes. This was the moment my mother was determined would make me a star.

Occasionally, an outer door would open and let in the sounds of the guests below; the tinkling laughs of society ladies and hearty guffaws of their overweight, pompous husbands making me itch to be downstairs. As the time for me to descend the grand staircase came and went, I began to panic, suddenly afraid they were having such a fabulous time they forgot about me.

I hear my mother's voice as she opens the door, the saccharine sweetness of it belaying that something isn't just wrong, it's monumentally wrong. Whoever is with her she instructs to go back downstairs, that it will be just a matter of minutes before I will descend, and she has everything under control.

Whoever's there probably believes her, but something has her panties in a twist, and as usual, if I'm somehow not to blame, she'll find a way to place it on me. When she enters the room, she waits for the door to snick shut before stomping towards me and grabbing me roughly by my arms.

"Where did that boy come from?" she spits.

I shake my head in confusion. "What?"

"Don't act stupid, Louisa May. You did this to vex me, didn't you?"

I have no clue what she's talking about, but I still take satisfaction in whatever I'd supposedly done. I have so few chances to see the usually unflappable woman lose her shit that watching it when it does is one of my guiltiest pleasures.

I smile sweetly just as she taught me, using the demure voice with just a touch of Southern charm and fitting an evangelist's daughter that she demands of me in public. "Why, mother dearest, whatever is it that you're goin' on about? I assure you, I have no clue." Then I bat my eyelashes.

"That boy," she roars, "is not pure."

"Pure what, mother?"

I can tell she doesn't even want to say the word, afraid that somehow, she'll be overheard and the rumors about her, and about her church, will begin again.

Her face is so pinched, and she's so pissed, that I can't help it. I begin to laugh. I laugh so hard that I think I just might pass out, and considering how tight my corset is, there's a damn good chance of that happening. My mother's acting like Satan himself is going to escort me down the stairs tonight in all his bright red, eighteen-foot-high, horned glory. Then again, she's also a raging racist, so maybe she's somehow equated the two in a way I'll never understand.

She glares at me so fiercely that if I didn't need to be downstairs imminently, I know she would have slapped me. Instead, she tightens her grip on my arms, crushing the imported lace dripping off my shoulders.

"Listen to me carefully, young lady," she rants through gritted teeth. "You are going to mind your manners, be polite, but spend as little time as possible with that boy. You will dance with him only for the opening waltz, and that's it. I've already arranged to have your dance card filled with more appropriate young men, and hopefully, before the night ends, everyone will forget about him. Do you hear me?"

"Yes, mother," I whisper back. Appeased, she lets go, fluffing the smushed lace and frowning at the red marks her hands leave on my starkly-white skin. We both know they will bloom into bruises tomorrow, because they always bloom into bruises the next day. She turns towards the full length mirror and checks her reflection carefully, taking a deep breath to steady herself as she smoothes the skirt of her long, pink gown and straightens the pearls around her neck.

If only I had done as she asked. If only I had heeded her words, not because he wasn't "pure," but because I'd been too young and naive to see the evil lurking behind his piercing eyes and confident smile.

A few minutes later, the string quartet ceases playing, and my name is announced by the bandleader. My belly flutters with nerves and my face flushes. When the doors are opened with a flourish by two liveried hotel workers, I am the picture of everything a debutante is expected to be. Beautiful. Sweet. Poised.

Pure.

Flash bulbs burst, one after another, blinding me to such a degree I want to shield my eyes with my hand, but I don't dare. Thankfully, I've practiced the descent so many times that I don't need to see—I have the steps memorized. I gracefully slide one opera-length-gloved hand down the carved banister as the other gently gathers my skirts to keep me from tripping.

The music accompanying me is all but drowned out by the applause. I continue to smile and pretend I can see, but as I near the end where the banister thickens and the red carpet ends at the beginning of the smooth marble floor, I lose count. Is this step 23? 24? Dear God, is it 22?

In my panic, my foot slips off the step and I start to fall. There's nothing I can do; the railing is so thick with intricately carved flowers that my satin glove slips right off. I close my eyes as I await impact with the floor, but instead, I crash into the hard chest and waiting arms of the young man waiting for me. He swings me around gracefully, my arms looped around his neck and his strong hands around my waist. My skirts flare beautifully before he puts me down as gently as if I were made of spun sugar. His dark eyes glitter, his lips quirking in a half-smile he's trying, and failing, to hide.

"Well, that was quite an entrance," he whispers conspiratorially as he backs away, taking my hand in his. I curtsy elegantly to him as he bends gracefully to kiss my hand, and if I was the sort of girl who swooned, I would totally be on the floor right now. Everyone applauds as I stand and smile like a fool, all of them believing my stumble was actually some sort of highly choreographed entrance.

Everyone claps, and for a moment, I think everything will be alright. My father sips from his glass of Scotch as if watching his daughter nearly face-plant in front of the highest of society and have it end up alright is a daily occurrence. Only my mother's pinched face lets on that my fall was nearly a catastrophe of the highest order.

When Edward looks up from my hand and smiles, I'm a goner. I have never seen such a handsome man in all my life. His dark eyes shine as he rises to his full height, his perfect posture in his dress blues making him appear more intimidating than I expect. His thick black hair lies perfectly under his uniform cap, and even though I can see only a bit of it, I feel the strangest urge to tangle my fingers in it as I kiss his soft, full lips.

My tummy flutters, a strange warmth running through me that makes my heart beat faster and my brain empty of thought. "You're gorgeous," I blurt.

He smiles widely, his straight, white teeth even whiter against the deep tan of his skin.

"That's my line," he laughs as he leads me to the dance floor, the orchestra beginning the opening waltz.

I never thought to ask if he knew how to dance, but when he takes me in his arms, waits for the perfect moment to begin, and we take our first steps, I'm amazed at his skill. He spins me gracefully, beautifully, across the marble floor, our eyes never leaving the other's and our smiles never wavering. When the song ends and everyone claps, he again presents me, stepping back so I can accept the accolade alone even though he'd been the real reason I'd danced so well.

It had been a glorious night, the two of us joined at the hip as I introduced him to the most important people in the room. He treated me like a princess, attended to my every need, and frightened away the other boys who wanted to dance with me. Although I could see my mother's fury building, I didn't stop him.

I fell in love with Edward before the night even ended. As we danced to the final slow song of the night, my cheek resting on his chest, and his heart thumping steadily as we swayed, I was certain that I'd found my prince.

I look up at him as the song ends, his dark eyes hooded as he drops his mouth to mine. His kiss almost knocks me off my heels, the passion in it something I've never felt before. When the kiss breaks, we smile at one another, him a little deviously, and me, with the bashful desire to do a lot more kissing.

As if he read my mind, he whispers, "Want to get out of here?"

I nod quickly, taking his hand as we all but run for the exit. A number of my friends and their dates are headed out to a club that doesn't card, and as I had earlier told my mother a well-conceived lie about what she would consider an appropriate after party plan, there's no reason to not go. But as we near the exit, she grabs me, her hand a talon's grip around my upper arm as she drags me away from Edward.

"You're going home. You've spent more than enough time with that boy," she hisses even as she tries to smile and say goodnight to our departing guests.

"Mother, I told you earlier that I have plans. . . ."

She cuts me off angrily. "Now listen here, missy. . . ."

"No, you listen, mother," I retort angrily. "He's been nothing but sweet and respectful all evening. I'm not going to let your petty prejudices ruin my night."

As I pull out of her grasp, I spin so quickly I crash into his broad chest. I can tell by the look in his eyes that he heard every word and he is pissed.

He silently helps me into my coat, hands me my purse, and leans over to kiss my cheek. He raises a questioning eyebrow at my mother as he stands to his full height, glancing between me and a group of guests who are also leaving and will soon be close enough to hear our every word.

It's as if he's asking her to make a choice, to either bite her tongue or to make a scene. A few of the people around us are well known liberals, a word my mother spits with as much venom as she does Black, Hispanic, and abortion rights. Anything she would normally say right now she has no choice but to choke down.

With a final glance at my mother's irate face, I loop my arm through Edward's. As I turn away she grabs my arm and whispers into my ear that we will regret our disobedience.

At the time I thought it was just her petty prejudice talking, but it wouldn't be long before I'd learn what those words really were—a threat.

11

Keira

By the time I get back to the house it's almost eleven, and everyone's fit to be tied. Sarah was called to a neighbor's for some urgent matter shortly after breakfast, and with Emma on bedrest, Amos had no choice but to watch the munchkins. Although he doesn't say a word about the hours I was MIA, it's the first time I've seen him look pissed. I'm sure it doesn't help that Anya was wailing so loudly I could hear her cries when I was still a quarter mile away.

I make Amos a quick sandwich so he can take it with him to the fields. When he asks me where I've been, I babble about losing track of time while out hunting. His disbelieving eyes follow my every move until he rises from the table, and as if on cue, Gritty rips open the screen door and lets it slam behind him. The dog is filthy, pooling nasty-smelling pond water all over the floor I scrubbed yesterday. I drag his ass back out to the barn and tie him to the hitching post all the while cursing under my breath and wondering what the fuck else will go wrong today.

When I return, Amos gives me a long, hard stare, the same one Brother Love often gave me when we were in Philly after I'd fucked something up. It's the one that means he has an awful lot to say but is wondering if it's worth the effort. With an exhausted sigh he shakes his head, mumbles something I don't catch, and heads out the door without a second look. Up until now, I was purposely doing things to piss him off hoping he'd kick me out, but until I see things through with the boy...

Fuck. I'm being ridiculous. Despite knocking on death's door, he's probably long gone. When you fear for your life, a person can be capable of amazing feats. Trust me, I know. But if I leave, and later I find out someone stumbles over his corpse, I'll never forgive myself. When I was a kid, Brother Love took care of me when he didn't have to, so I feel now like it's cosmically my turn to return the kindness. Karma's been a real bitch lately, and the last thing I want is to end up on her shit list.

I hurry through my chores, check on Emma a few times and bring her some bone broth soup and a book from downstairs, one to bolster her body and the other to occupy her mind. She's still super pale but looks way better than yesterday, her demeanor surprisingly alert, and her shrewd eyes narrowed as she watches me tidy her room. No doubt she wonders why I'm being so nice. I take her blood pressure, which is still a bit high, as is her temperature, but it's also a million degrees in here. I get her a glass of cold lemonade and a second one of water and tell her to drink them both. The last thing she needs is to get dehydrated.

Sarah's three little ones are shockingly well behaved while I work. The six year-old twins, Samuel and Eli, manage to entertain their sister, Rachael, and keep an eye on Anya while I mop the floor. The last thing I want is for the kids to get filthy playing in whatever nastiness Gritty tracked in. It's bad enough I'll have to shampoo the damn dog before he can re-enter the house. I've got far too much shit to do to add bathing three wriggly kids to the list.

As I do the dishes and prep the sourdough for the preheating oven, all I can think about is the boy. I know he doesn't want me to tell anyone he's here, but I'm positive he needs surgery. At some point, I have to tell Declan, and he's gonna kick my ass for not telling him immediately. But I made a promise, and good, bad or indifferent, I'm going to keep it. Members of the BSB don't break promises.

The sound of tires crunching on the gravel drive wakes me from my thoughts. A rapidly approaching white van is heading towards the house, and knowing all the neighbors either drive horse-drawn buggies or plain black cars or trucks, this is not a social visit. There isn't enough time for me to get the kids out into the woods, and with Sarah gone and Amos in the fields, I have to deal with whatever fresh hell is headed for us alone.

I race up the stairs and help Emma hide in the small, airless space behind the armoire in her bedroom. She looks terrified, almost as if she thinks I'm going to turn her over to whoever's here. I'm not gonna lie—that hurts my feelings.

"I've got this," I tell her. "Just remain quiet. I'll come get you when they're gone."

I race back down the stairs, realizing only now I'm still in my jeans and stained sleeveless shirt, my hair a tangled mess. I only have time to throw an apron over my pants and swipe at the sweat beading my forehead and upper lip. Gritty is barking his fool head off out in the barn, and for once, I'm glad he's tied up. Say what you want about the fleabag, but he can sniff out an enemy a mile away. I have no doubt he'd try to take a piece out of them and the fuckers would shoot him. I wouldn't be able to handle that. Gritty's my best friend.

I peek out the window, trying to catch a glimpse as doors slam and voices grumble. I take a few deep breaths and quietly instruct the boys to stay silent while the strangers are here.

Two men in drab green uniforms come to the door and block the light coming through the screen. I gulp down the lump in my throat and try to look like I'm a good girl.

"How may I help you, good sirs? What brings you to us on this hot summer day?" I'm doing my best imitation of Sarah's style of speech and somehow end up sounding as Irish as my former Philly bunker mate, Paul O'Dougherty. Oh well, I've got to commit now.

One of the men has a tablet in his hand, his finger swiping along the lit screen as he searches it. He sees something he doesn't like and frowns. "We are here to see Sarah and Amos Zook. Where are they? And for that matter, who are you?"

"I'm Sarah's cousin from Ohio. I've come to help with the children for the summer. Both of them are working in the orchards today."

In all honesty, I don't have a fucking clue where they are, but the orchards are the furthest piece of property from the house and encompass a huge amount of ground. It will keep the men busy for a long while looking for them, and hopefully prevent them from returning anytime soon.

"Are you here alone?" the bigger of the two men asks as he steps towards me.

I swallow hard as I nod. "Yes, sir. It's just me and the children."

"Do you mind if we take a look around?"

Oh, fuck...

"Please, be my guest. You will see that what I say is true."

I open the door for them and they stomp in, their eyes flitting disinterestedly over the children as they open closet and pantry doors, check under the sofa, and root around in the basement. They help themselves to the oatmeal raisin cookies, the one guy spitting a mouthful of barely-chewed cookie on the floor and cursing when he realizes it isn't chocolate chip. Fucking douche noodle.

When they head upstairs I start to panic, my heart thumping a mile a minute as I call up to them. "See? It's as I told you. It is just myself and the children here."

The bedroom doors open and close, the closets get rooted through, and then the men stop in Emma and Declan's bedroom, their voices coming out in harsh whispers as they open the closet and armoire doors, the metal hangers screeching as they rub against the bar they hang on.

Fuck, I need to get them out of there...

My eyes land on Anya, who for once in her life, is sitting quietly as she gnaws on one of the boy's toy blocks. Although I know I'm going to regret it, I pick her up from her place on the floor and give her chubby thigh a harsh pinch. The ensuing scream is enough to wake the dead and does exactly what I hope—it brings the men racing down the stairs before they can notice the door hidden behind the armoire.

"Hush, child, hush," I croon as I bounce her on my hip. "I know you are frightened, but these men will not hurt us. There's no need for tears."

The one man looks a bit guilty, the band on his left ring finger giving me hope that he's not just a husband, but a father. Preferably, a kind one.

"You must forgive her. We get few visitors who aren't part of our community, and I dare say, the last uniformed men who were here gave her quite a fright. They were not nearly as friendly as you."

Now the one guy looks really guilty, but his buddy doesn't. He narrows his eyes at me and demands to see my papers, which I dutifully produce. He checks the picture against my face, the thick black bonnet I wore in the photo intentionally hiding most of my red curls. It's an identifying feature as there are few redheads out here, and the last thing anyone on the run wants is to be memorable.

Just when I think they're about done and are finally going to leave, the one guy starts up with fucking tablet again, types something in, waits, and then scrolls some more. He frowns as he looks over at the children, and I see him adding them up in his head and coming up with an extra.

Fuck, fuck, fuck!

"Who does the screamer belong to? I'm not seeing a child fitting her description registered to this household. It says here the Zooks still have at home two boys, age six, and a girl, age four."

I stutter and stammer, knowing if I produce her papers, they will see she belongs to Emily and David Hertzler, and then want to know where they are. It's not like I can go upstairs and produce Emma from the hidey-hole and all of us not end up with bullets in our brains. Including the kids.

"She's mine," I blurt, the men looking at me with wide-eyed surprise. "She is, um, the product of an. . . an unlawful, um, union. . . between myself and a. . . a. . . member of the Purity Patrol. He refuses to acknowledge her, so she has yet to be given papers while everything is sorted. We were shunned by our family, as having a child out of wedlock is, um, against our ways. Sarah and Amos took pity on us and let us live with them. I do not know what we'd do without their kindness."

I try to summon tears, but I'm a much better liar than actress. My story accomplishes its task, making the men uncomfortable with the thought of a Purity Officer raping a girl who, on a good day, barely looks fourteen. "I know it was wrong of me to leave my community without notifying the local patrol, but I was desperate. Please, kind sirs, I am very sorry for causing trouble."

"I see," the solemn one says, making a note in the file that I can only pray doesn't come back to bite us all in the ass one day. When he stuffs the tablet into his back pocket, I think they're finally going to leave, but they don't.

"Tell me, girl, have you seen anything strange going on around here? Is there anything we should know about? Other strangers. . .visitors. . .*cousins*. . . who have recently come to visit? Especially young men about your age, maybe a bit older? If you have information like that and aren't telling us, that could pose a very big problem for you and your bastard."

He looks at me with suspicious eyes, then reaches forward and grabs my left arm. He roughly runs the heel of his palm over the skin like he's trying to rub away dirt that isn't there. His partner scoffs. "I could have told you that she's not inked. She's skinny, but otherwise looks too healthy. The ones in the Carolinas all look a half a day from death."

I'm far too scared to ask what I look too healthy for, and now I have the added discomfort of how this asshole is looking at me. I try to pull my arm from his grasp, but he refuses to let go. He tightens his fingers around my wrist, causing me to cry out as the bones crush in his grip. "She knows more than she's letting on. I think we should take her in for questioning."

I swear to fucking Christ, my heart stops. I'd rather die than be taken to an IC. Bad shit happens in those places. I'd heard what happened to Emma in one of those, and she was not just the Governor's daughter at the time, she was engaged to the next Supreme Archon. What chance would someone like me have there?

Absolutely none.

Tears prick my eyes and threaten to fall. "Please, stop! You're hurting me. . ."

"This is nothing compared to what I'm going to do to you if you don't start telling me the truth. . ."

"Please, let me go. I don't know anything! I swear!" I'm crying and trying to pull away while not dropping Anya on her head as she screams bloody fucking murder. The guy with the wedding band takes Anya from me and puts her on the floor with the boys who silently crowd around her and Rachel, protecting them.

Even though it's clear that neither man bought my story, the hard slap across my face still comes as a shock. Within the span of a moment, my arms get pinned behind me, and no matter how hard I thrash, I can't get loose. The guy with the wedding band has me restrained, and no matter how hard I kick, he won't let go. As I continue to piss him off, his grip tightens as his partner beats me within an inch of my life.

This is it. They're going to kill me.

The guy behind me places his hand over my mouth to quiet my screams, and for some reason that pisses me off. I bite him as hard as I can, removing a chunk of skin that I spit onto the floor. He hollers as he pulls his hand away, now every bit as pissed as his buddy who punches me so hard in the stomach I feel like I'm going to pass out.

But then I remember the oath I took when I turned twelve and became a member of the Broad Street Bullies. Bullies don't back down, and we sure as shit don't give up. I never had any intention of telling these motherfuckers shit, and now, I'm even more determined. Fuck them.

The asshole punches me in the mouth and splits my lip. Instantly, blood is running freely down my chin and staining my apron—and out of everything he's done to me, this is the final straw. I suck my wounded lip into my mouth and lick the blood from it, and just as his eyes drop down to mine, I spit a giant wad of blood and saliva into his face.

I realize only after I do this how colossally stupid that was. He grabs me by the throat, cursing angrily as he lifts his arm higher and higher like he's trying to lift my body off the ground by my neck.

My lungs scream for air, my head throbs, and my neck feels like if he pulls any harder, he's going to do some sort of irreparable damage. My feet scrabble against the wood as my vision starts to darken, and I tell myself over and over again that I can't pass out. I have to stay conscious, if not for me, for the children. . .

Then I hear the most beautiful, unmistakable sound of a gun being cocked, the noise loud enough to be heard over my gasps, the children's tears, and the men's snarls. The way they swing their eyes to the source of the sound and see the rifle trained on them would be comical if I wasn't so damn scared.

"Let her go. Now."

With her big, pregnant belly and in her voluminous white night-gown, Emma looks like a vengeful ghost, her white-blonde hair loose and wild and tangled about her shoulders. She's lying on the stairs, the rifle in her arms at the perfect angle to kill them both without hitting me, her finger on the trigger. We both had the same training, so I know she's got the shot. We only put our fingers on the trigger when we're ready and capable of a clean hit. I give her a tiny nod, telling her to go for it.

The bastard with his hand around my neck is so surprised he loosens his grip, allowing my feet to hit the floor. I inhale a few much-needed breaths and my head begins to clear. Emma speaks a steady stream of soothing words, telling the children to hurry to the barn, that everything is fine, and we'll be out shortly to collect them.

Once they're out, she continues in that same calm voice, saying I'm going to be fine and that the man is going to let me go, even though I'm pretty sure that's not gonna happen. He feels twitchy, like he might go for his gun, his hand shaking against my throat. He and Emma are in a standoff with me squarely in the middle.

Emma drops her eyes for a split second, something I know she wouldn't do if it wasn't vitally important. When I glance down to see what she's looking at, I find the sharp knife lying on the table that I was going to use to score the dough before placing it in the oven. I blink once slowly, telling her I understand.

"Are you deaf, asshole?" Emma snaps. "Let. Her. Go."

Things happen quickly after that. Both men unhand me to pull their pistols, and when I duck to grab the knife, Emma shoots the man behind me. He falls to the floor just as I stab the man in front of me exactly like I'd been trained—under the right side of the ribcage with a vicious upper thrust. He screams as he lurches forward, but I stay with him, twisting the knife with both hands on the hilt. I use every ounce of my strength, inflicting as much damage as possible before wrenching it out and stabbing again. He drops to his knees as blood gushes from the wound.

His lips are moving but I can't hear what he says, the noise from the gunshot rendering me temporarily deaf. I can tell by the look in his eyes that he knows the knife wounds are fatal. I think I see the word *please* form on his lips, and for whatever reason, that breaks me from my stupor. How dare he beg now that our roles are reversed?

I rip the gun from his limp grip and turn it on him. The air suddenly smells fetid and nasty as the man, who just minutes before was ready to show me zero mercy, shits his pants as he begs for his life.

Well, ain't he just fresh fuckin' outta luck.

I grab him by the front of his uniform and shove the weapon in that sweet spot under his jaw and between his neck. He's gone terribly pale as shock sets in. The clinical part of me knows that he's going to die from blood loss, but that doesn't stop me from pulling the trigger.

I watch as life drains from his eyes as blood continues to pour from his wounds. Without a heartbeat, I know people can't bleed, but this guy's still bleeding. I fire another bullet, and then another, only stopping when I empty the clip. I scream as Emma comes up behind me, gently taking the gun from my hand, and wrapping me in a tight embrace. Her steady presence makes me realize how badly I'm shaking.

My mind is whirling, thinking of what we should do next, but finding a plan in the vast nothingness of my mind proves harder than wading through quicksand. My knees feel strangely weak, my whole body cold as Emma turns me away from the dead men. With her arms still around me, she ushers me slowly from the kitchen and out into the hot summer sun but it doesn't warm me. I'm so cold I'm shivering.

She takes me to the front porch swing and sits me down. Her arms are still around me, and mine are around her. Should I let go?

It's been so long since I've been hugged. Everyone knows that I don't like to be touched, but this feels kinda nice. Her hands are on my back, rubbing soothing circles like I've seen Declan do to her. She tells me that everything will be okay, that it's okay to cry. But that doesn't make any sense. I'm not—

Only then do I realize I'm sobbing.

12

Declan

I can't believe what I'm seeing.

"Hello, Declan." She takes a sip from her glass before placing it on the marble-topped table next to her. "It's nice to finally meet you. I've heard so much about you."

I know I'm gaping like a fool, but I was so convinced I was looking at a trio who could only be Anna's mother and sisters, that her British accent throws me for a loop.

"What? Is it my mother's accent that confuses you?" The woman on the right perches delicately on the thick leather arm of the chair and rolls her eyes at me. "Would you prefer we speak with Russian accent and bad grammar?" Her voice is not as deep as her mother's, not as yet thickened by decades of swallowing burning regrets, hatred, and loss.

"Or should we speak like you, in American?" The one on the left asks, mimicking my muddled accent. "Would you prefer the brutish dialect of the Philly people, or the quaint way of your new friends, the Mennonites? Or would you feel most at home if we spoke like your beloved Emma, with her polished, high-society voice?"

The way she easily slides in and out of each accent gives me the chills; the vicious glare in her eyes and the tension radiating from her body revealing she's absolutely the most dangerous of the three. She's older than the third woman, I think probably close to my age. The fine lines around her eyes are not as pronounced as her mother's, but more visible than her sister's.

"Why am I here?" I sit up a bit straighter, my shoulders screaming from the increased pressure of having my hands tied behind my back. "Who are you?"

"You know who we are," the oldest states unequivocally. "I saw it in your eyes. You looked at me as if you saw a ghost."

"She looks just like you."

"Looked." The single word is spit between gritted teeth, the unhinged one balling her hands into fists.

I close my eyes for a moment as my stomach clenches. "Yes. Looked."

"Sasha, my child, that's enough," her mother chides, never taking her eyes from me. "He suffers from her loss. I can feel it."

Her voice is quiet. Sad. Although she's lost a daughter, she seems almost sadder for me than for herself. She gives them some order in Russian, and the young one, the one whose name I still don't know, silently leaves the room. The older one remains until her mother looks up and gives an imperious nod. Sasha gives me a final vicious scowl before she exits.

With the door closed, Anna's mother rises and crosses over to me and uncuffs my hands. She steps back, watching me carefully as I rub my chafed wrists. As blood flows back into my hands, the tingling sensation is close to maddening as I clench and unclench my fists. I resist the urge to thank her for unbinding me, and I'm glad I don't after she steps around to face me, stares at me harshly for a moment, and then mercilessly slaps me across the face.

I don't have to ask why.

Before she returns to her seat, she heads over to the bar, grabs a glass and returns. She pours a healthy amount of whatever she's drinking into it and hands it to me before refilling her own. She settles down in her seat, crossing her long legs as she spins the vodka around in her tumbler.

I wonder if it's safe to drink, if there might be poison on the rim. But then why would they go through the trouble to drag my ass here just to poison me?

You never know. They are Russian.

The voice is right. In all the years I spent with this woman's daughter, if I've learned anything, it's not just that Russians are unpredictable, but that poisoning is historically one of their favorite ways to kill an enemy.

"I am Olesya Vasilieva, and as you guessed, I am Anna's mother. Sasha and Nina are my daughters. Anna's sisters. Despite Sasha's behavior, none of us harbor ill will towards you. In fact, our presence is just the opposite."

I almost laugh. I don't know how they treat people in the Motherland, but this sure as shit isn't how you treat a friend here. As much as I want to mouth off, the stern look she gives me is enough to keep me from pushing my luck. Instead, I sip from my glass.

"Anna died far before any of us foresaw," she begins. "There are things she had yet to teach you, things you must learn before you can lead your people to victory."

"Such as?"

She smiles condescendingly. "So impatient. She did warn me of that."

"There've been worse things said about me."

She narrows her eyes in disapproval. "Although that is true, impatience will get you killed."

"So can inaction."

"You aren't listening to me. Impatience *will* get you killed."

A chill races down my spine as she leans back against her seat. "You used to complain that Anna wasn't doing enough. That she should be doing more things. Bigger things. Things with more impact.

That is the thinking of a soldier, not a leader. A soldier thinks only from battle to battle, knowing if he doesn't survive this one, he won't need to worry about the next. A leader wants as many of his people, and yes, even his soldiers, to see the end of the war. If all of his people are dead, who will he have left to lead? Good leaders know that sometimes the right action is not to act at all."

"I don't want to be a leader," I grouse. "I fully intend once we get Bellamy and his cronies out of power to let someone else lead. I *am* a soldier, Olesya, not a leader."

"Then you should have made sure my daughter survived!" she roars, slamming her glass down on the table so hard vodka sloshes all over her hand.

I can't help it, I wince. I rub my hand over my eyes roughly, letting it rest over my mouth for a moment as I try to think of what to say next. I come up with nothing.

"I'm sorry for my outburst," Olesya sighs with a shake of her head. "But you aren't listening. Yes, you are a soldier. A very good soldier. I've seen few people in my lifetime with your level of instinct, ability to rally troops, and then effectively command them in such a short period of time."

I scoff at her words. "Yeah, so good I got forty people killed in a blink of an eye."

"What happened the other day was an unfortunate disaster, Declan, and one that had nothing to do with you. Someone else was responsible for that—someone from our side who wants to see you fail."

"That doesn't make any sense. Why would someone on our side want us to fail?"

"No. You're asking the wrong question. Try again."

I think for a bit. "They want *me* to fail."

She nods. "*Now* you are thinking like a leader."

I get up and start pacing, and she watches me intently as I walk back and forth, the only sound in the room my boots clomping across the tile. From somewhere deep within the building a clock chimes six times, and as if on cue, my empty stomach gurgles embarrassingly loud.

Olesya stands with every bit of grace as her daughter, the once prima ballerina. "Come. You must be starving. I have already made plans for you to stay here for a few weeks so we can finish your training. There are things you must learn and people to meet, and before you say that you cannot be gone that long, be aware that I have everything in hand."

"But—"

She places an outstretched palm on my chest to stop my pacing, and a finger on my lips to shut my mouth. "It's all been handled."

"How can you possibly know you've got everything handled?"

She smiles, and it's that same wicked smile Anna used to give me right before she delivered her favorite line.

"Don't you know by now, Declan, that I know everything?"

And for the second time in my life, I've found a person who I have no doubt does.

13

Emma

I hold a sobbing, bloody Keira in my arms, her heart pounding frantically as she weeps uncontrollably. Even though she acts like she's tough, she's still just a girl. As far as I know, she's never killed someone before, so it makes complete sense that she's traumatized.

I give her a few minutes to bawl before I pull away from her, placing my hands on her shaking shoulders and gently demand that she pull herself together. We have bodies to dispose of and a truck to make disappear, and for the life of me, I haven't the first clue how to make either happen.

Shockingly, Keira manages to get a hold of herself pretty quickly. She wipes at her bloody, tear-streaked face, her lip still quivering as her eyes leak a few last tears. She takes a few deep, shuddering breaths before letting out a long exhale, and then waits for instructions.

We head back inside, where I sit her down facing away from the bodies, then step over them to pour her a glass of water from the tap. But before I can get the glass to her, the screen door is torn open. Keira lets out a shriek of fright as Sarah barrels through the door, Amos' shotgun in her hands. "What has happened? Is everyone alright? I was just leaving the neighbors when I heard the shots."

She walks around the table and gasps at the bodies on the ground and the twin rivers of blood rolling towards each other creating a sticky pool of death. The copper pennies smell that accompanies it is beyond nauseating, and I swallow hard to keep from adding a pile of vomit to our very long list of things to clean up.

I expect her to be upset, or to demand to know what happened, but all she does is calmly head back outside and tell Eli to run to Adam and Dex's house and tell them to come immediately. Samuel takes his sister and Anya back to the barn and is told not to return until someone comes for them. Considering what he just witnessed, I don't expect that to be an order he'll disobey.

When Sarah returns she tells Keira to go to the basement and grab a few of the hefty tarps kept down there as well as a few of the old mops too gross for everyday use but kept "just in case." I'm certain that for whatever reason she held onto them, it never once crossed her mind they would be used to clean up a double homicide.

Just as Keira returns with her arms loaded to overflowing, we hear hoofbeats pounding down the drive. I peer out the window over the sink to find our neighbor dropping down off a sweat-soaked horse, a rifle strapped over her shoulder that she now takes in hand.

"Fuck," Keira whispers. "What do we do?"

"Esther will help us," Sarah replies far too calmly before she hurries outside.

We've met Esther before, the thin woman with a shrewd way about her having come to greet Declan and me shortly after we'd arrived. She'd been friendly enough the few times I've seen her, but I worry she knows who we really are. She's one of Sarah's closest friend's, the two of them often sharing looks that make me feel as if they're keeping secrets. Supposedly she's married, but rumor has it her husband hasn't been seen for quite some time.

When Esther's eyes land on the two dead officers, not a second's worth of shock appears on her face. She reaches for the tarp in Keira's arms and begins to unfold it.

Dex and Adam arrive minutes later, dripping with sweat and with weapons in hand. They must have sprinted the entire way.

"What the fuck happened?" Adam demands, flicking the safety on his Smith & Wesson before stuffing it into the back of his pants. I give him the abridged version as he and Dex lift the bodies onto the spread tarps and begin to roll them up.

"Thank God you're here," Keira says to them. "I don't know how we'd get the bodies out without you. These guys are really heavy."

"You'd be surprised what you can do when you must," Esther responds matter-of-factly. When Sarah scowls at her, she replies, "Sister, you know that is true."

Dex and Adam look at her questioningly, but she ignores them. "Tonight, strip the bodies and cut the men into pieces. You can dump them at the far edge of Kaufman's field in the farthest sty. I'll have the old man turn out the hogs before he goes to bed. They'll make short work of the remains."

Dex looks at her in horror. "Why does it sound like you've done this before?"

Sarah barks out a command to Esther in German, but the woman doesn't seem at all concerned with the harsh rebuke. "Sarah, you are harboring enough criminals on this farm to see us all shot, and yet you are worried about me telling them how we dispose of those who threaten us?"

She turns back to the men with a roll of her eyes. "Oh, and you must pull the teeth before feeding the heads. Pigs cannot digest teeth. We cannot afford evidence left behind."

"Oh, I'm going to be sick," Keira wails, as she runs from the kitchen and throws up right outside the front door.

Adam, Dex and I share a worried glance at one another, the three of us realizing at the same time that there's something very, very strange going on in this sleepy little town.

When Keira staggers back inside, she rinses her mouth at the kitchen sink, then resumes cleaning without a word of complaint despite continuing to gag every now and then. She's probably wondering what I'm wondering—do our pork chops and bacon come from this same macabre farm?

After the men load the bodies in the van, Dex and Adam decide on a course of action that may, or may not, involve feeding giant, man-eating hogs. I don't have it in me to ask. And when they return a few hours later, they build a large fire outside for us to dispose of all of our bloody clothes, cleaning implements, and even the thick, braided wool rug from under the dining table that is now irreparably stained.

Adam works pulling up the bloody, bullet-splintered floorboards and burns those too while we wipe everything down with bleach. At some point in his life, my brother apparently picked up some wood-working skills, because he, Eli and Samuel replace the floorboards in record time.

By the time day turns to night, we've set everything back to right; the only reminder of today's horror being the lighter color of the new floorboards and the scent of fresh-cut lumber and bleach. When we are finished, we all head to the stream to wash, the current not just removing all traces of blood and gore from our bodies, but also cooling us down after an afternoon's hard labor. We burn our bloody clothes and shoes, changing into fresh dresses that Sarah somehow always has in endless supply in the attic. When Esther heads home to tend to her own farm, she leaves dressed in different clothes than when she'd arrived. How exactly will she explain that to her husband? I mention that to Sarah, and she waves off my concern. She explains that Esther's husband travels a great deal for work and is rarely ever home, and then promptly changes the subject.

When my belly begins to cramp on the walk back from the stream, I forget all about the many questions Sarah's very obvious lie brings up. The moment she notices I'm feeling poorly, she orders me to rest on the sofa. She makes dinner as Keira watches the children, the poor girl still dabbing at the blood dripping from her split lip with an old kitchen towel. I'm pretty sure she needs stitches.

When Amos returns from wherever he's been all day, he talks in rapid, furious-sounding German, as he gestures to the floor and the walls and to Keira. Sarah, who usually isn't one to raise her voice, yells right back, the two of them stomping off to opposite sides of the house where they remain for the rest of the evening. For once, I'm glad I can't understand them.

I check my phone, just now remembering I never received a message from Declan. He's normally really good about checking in unless he's somewhere too dangerous to call or where signal blockers are being used. But my phone shows no missed calls, no texts, no nothing, and I can't help but worry that things are as fucked up where he is as they are here.

14

Trinity

I've never seen Louise like this before. There's a spring in her step and a light in her eyes as she plans an elaborate party for her husband's birthday. She handles everything by herself, only occasionally asking staff members to help her find out little details, like Edward's preferred Champagne or what brand of cigars the men in his social circles smoke. I would find it sad that a wife of so many years doesn't know these things about her husband, but for all intents and purposes, the less time he spends here the better.

With the social event of the decade only weeks away, Louise is damn near manic as she attends to every tiny detail. I'm not talking about if the napkins coordinate with the tablecloths level of insignificance—I'm talking about making sure the waiters and waitresses have every button on their uniforms sewn perfectly so they aren't crooked, or God forbid, come off as they pass around polished trays of hot hors d'oeuvres. Every day she thinks up a new potential catastrophe that, in her mind, will ruin the entire evening, and inevitably, her emotions spiral until she dissolves into hysterical tears. It's making for some enormously long days for me.

Today's crisis is the invitations. She insists they must go out *immediately,* but before she can choose the style or the wording, she must pick a theme. I almost laugh, but stop myself just in time. Does she honestly believe that choosing the wrong theme will ruin the evening before it even begins? Doesn't she know by now that she could finger-paint the invitations with human fecal matter and people would still show up for a chance to rub elbows with the Supreme Regent?

I'm only half listening as she prattles on, and I nod and smile when it seems appropriate. That she's twisting herself into knots to make this party exceptional for a man who won't appreciate her effort sets my teeth on edge. Yes, I admit I'm being petulant, but I can't help it. I hate this man with a bloody passion.

But my purpose is to make Louise's life easier, not harder, and being a grumpy cow about things will only hurt her. So I swallow my hatred and do my best to guide Louise into making appropriate choices and keep her as level-headed as possible in the process. Yet I can't help but worry over her obsession with this event. There's nothing specific I can pinpoint; it's just a gut feeling I have, and my gut is never wrong.

Louise has been in and out of Edward's office at least ten times today despite knowing she's not allowed in there. A few times I only had seconds to disrupt the security feed to keep her from getting caught, and what would happen to us both should that happen makes me cringe. At night she goes to bed early despite never looking tired, and when I check on her before I retire for the evening, she's either pretending to be asleep or sitting up in bed reading some inane Universal Church-approved book. She nods and smiles and wishes me sweet dreams while looking guilty as sin.

I want to tell her that whatever she's plotting, she needs to stop, but for once in all the years since I've known her, she's genuinely excited about something. With eyes that glitter with purpose and a flush of color on her usually pale cheeks, she looks twenty years younger. She's seen so little happiness in her life that I can't bear the thought of dampening her flame even if whatever has ignited it scares the crap out of me.

So the next day at breakfast, where she actually eats her bacon and toast as she prattles on again about possible themes, I do my best to not be bitchy. Although it's eight a.m. and I rarely drink, I really wish we had a pitcher of mimosas on the table.

"So? What do you think?" Louise frowns when she realizes I zoned out again. Her smile dims, and I feel guilty that I was dreaming about getting hammered and not listening.

"I was just thinking it would be fun to do a costume party. Why not have everyone dress up? Everyone must be so tired of wearing tuxedos and ball gowns to every event."

I catch the lilt of sadness in her voice, the fact she said *everyone* and not *we*. I can't remember the last time Louise was on Edward's arm at an event, well, aside from that sham of their daughter's wedding.

"You should throw a masked ball. You know, like they had back in Henry VIII's time," I suggest, realizing I've hit the nail on the head for the theme when Louise's eyes widen with excitement. "Have everyone dress in old-timey garb, and during cocktail hour, you can have the sort of entertainers they had back then mingle with the guests. You know, have acrobats and aerialists set up in different places, and if we can find it, maybe have some small exotic animals and their handlers come from the zoo. During dinner, you can hire a comedian to play the fool. Hell, if we can find enough virgins, they can do some sort of sultry dance for Edward, like Anne Bolyn did. I bet he'd love that."

I didn't mean to say that last part out loud, but it somehow slips out. I cringe, expecting Louise to get upset, but she smiles broadly, jumping up from her seat so quickly that it tips over backwards. With no small amount of horror, I realize she *loves* the idea.

Oh, so, so, so no bueno.

"This is brilliant!" she exclaims, clapping her hands as she jumps up and down excitedly. The two members of the House Guard stationed at the door startle at her outburst. They share a concerned look before deciding to not intervene.

"Yes, we'll do a medieval ball! We'll all dress in period costumes and I'll decorate everything with flowers and greenery like they did back then. Everyone will dine at long tables, and the food will be brought in and presented. We'll have an enormous roast pig with an apple in its mouth, and giant slabs of beef and lamb, and we'll eat with our hands and drink lots of wine and beer and that other stuff, what's it called, with the honey. . . um. . . MEAD! Yes, we'll have mead!"

She paces the breakfast room, rambling on and on, her excitement building to the point I'm now concerned she'll hyperventilate. "Oh, and we'll all wear masks—great elaborate ones, with feathers and jewels, well, maybe not *real* jewels, only Edward will have real jewels, and a crown! Yes! He must have a crown!"

I wave my hands in front of her to get her attention. "As the Queen, shouldn't you have a crown, too?"

She stops to think. "Yes, I imagine so. I think the King and Queen used to coordinate their clothing, too, but I'm not sure Edward would like that. He may prefer to coordinate with someone else. . ."

I slap my palm down on the table so hard Louise flinches. "No, he will *not* coordinate with someone else," I demand. "Louise, you are his wife. You have a position of power as his Consort. Don't you see that? It's time you take that seriously."

"I do take it seriously," she retorts, the hurt evident in her tone. "I've never taken anything more seriously in my life."

"I know you do," I respond softly, my voice full of contrition. I want to make sure she understands that I'm not angry with *her*, but she has to start standing up for herself. As proof of the sincerity of my apology, I spend the rest of the afternoon paying special attention to every detail she mulls over until it's time to get ready for dinner.

"I think tonight I will invite the young woman in the west wing to join us," she says slowly. "She must be so lonely locked in there all by herself."

The look on her face tells me not only that she's been thinking about this for a while, but that her mind is already made up. I wouldn't be surprised if the dining table is already set for two.

"I'm sure you think inviting her is a bad idea, but I feel sorry for her," she murmurs. "I know how she must feel, being cast aside, when once she'd been the center of his world."

I watch as her eyes fog over as she loses herself in a memory she'll use to flog herself with for God only knows how long. . .

15

Louise

The whole glorious evening felt like a fairy tale, but it's our time together after the ball that seals the deal on my feelings. At the dance club on the opposite side of town, I'm finally out from under my mother's disapproving glare. I don't have to laugh quietly or flirt covertly, nor do I have to steal glances at my date. I can now stare directly into his dark, walnut-hued eyes without worrying about her reproving remarks. I relish every second of holding his hand and love the feel of his arm wrapped around my shoulders or my waist.

My girlfriends are so envious of how attentive Edward is, always making sure I have a drink in my hand, or joining me on the dance floor whenever I squeal that the song the band's playing is one of my favorites. When we are overly warm and our feet ache from dancing, we all shove into a large booth and laugh and joke as we pop open another magnum of champagne.

After the club closes, we all pile back into the limo and go to my friend's estate whose parents aren't home. All of us girls are now happily coupled up either with our dates from my party, or with a young man they met at the club who proved to be better company. We immediately hit the liquor cabinet, not that any of us need more to drink. We're already quite hammered.

Edward brings me a glass of something strong but sweet, instructing me to sip it slowly. He watches the other boys with a look of haughty disdain as they pound beers and let out great, loud belches, the alcohol now making them behave like fools. They have all removed their jackets and ties, their shirts in varying stages of pulling free from their pants with only their cumberbunds holding the pieces of their tuxedos together. I grin up at Edward, who is still as tidy as he'd been when I first laid eyes on him. He doesn't have so much as a wrinkle in his uniform.

He takes my hand in his, leading me away from the chaos and into the library, as if he somehow knows how much I adore libraries made of wood the same dark hue as his eyes. In the low light I wander along the rows, running my fingers lightly over the leather bound spines. Each book in here has some special significance to my friend's parents to have necessitated being purchased as a first edition. It's truly an amazing collection.

I glance over at Edward, who's staring at a book locked in a spotlit glass cabinet atop a wooden pedestal, his fingertips hovering over the protective cover. At first I believe he's keeping his distance because he's afraid of setting off an alarm, but that theory doesn't fit with the look on his face. He behaves as if he feels unworthy to touch it.

I join him, both of us staring at the extremely rare, first edition English translation of Machiavelli's **The Prince**. It isn't in the best of shape, as centuries of careless handling and misuse have stained the pages and weakened the binding, yet the print is still dark and mostly legible. I tell him that it's one of the last remaining English translations to still exist.

"Extraordinary," he whispers. "I would give anything to own this."

I smile indulgently. "Well, unless you've got an extra hundred grand or so lying around, you're outta luck. Kelly's dad shelled out a hefty sum for that little piece of history, but won't tell anyone exactly how much. I think he's afraid his wife's gonna kill him if she finds out."

He flashes a disapproving glance, one so caustic I find myself breathless. I don't know what I said that upset him, but when he turns his face *back to the book, his agitation softens. After a few more seconds he turns to me with a smile as if the moment didn't happen.*

He gathers me in his arms, his hand reaching up, those same finger-tips that had been afraid to touch the glass now grazing my temple, my cheeks, my lips. He bites his lip gently, then releases it, his eyes glittering in the light illuminating the coveted book. Then he kisses me.

With no one around to see us, this kiss isn't the soft, gentle meeting of mouths we shared when others were present. This is different. It's hot. Lustful. Demanding, and almost a little mean. It steals my breath and makes my heart hammer as he snakes one hand into my hair, holding my head in a tight grasp, and ravages my mouth with his tongue.

I feel owned. Possessed.

And God help me, I love it.

He doesn't take things far, and when he pulls away from me I sigh, my lips stinging a bit from Edward's teeth. Heat flares in my cheeks, a few tendrils of my fancy updo having come loose and bobbing in the periphery of my vision. I hope I don't look as rumpled as I feel.

"I better get you home before you turn into a pumpkin," he jokes, taking my hand and leading me out of the library. Had this exchange happened earlier in the night, I would have teased that Cinderella didn't turn into a pumpkin, the carriage did. But now that I suspect how much he hates to be corrected, I don't. The entire night has been so wonderful that I don't want to say anything that might make him decide to not see me again. So I bite my tongue and tell myself that I'm overreacting.

It takes little convincing on my part to let him kiss and fondle me again when we're back in the limo, and when we reach my house, he kisses me one last time on the stone steps and informs me that he must see me again. Soon. Any lingering misgivings are wiped from my mind, and I respond to his demand with an enthusiastic kiss.

I'm sitting at the enormous table in the Residence's dining room wondering not only how I got here, but just how long I've been here.

Have we already been served the soup? The salad? The napkin is in my lap and all of my silverware is still in place, so I imagine the food has yet to be served. Thankfully, my lapse hasn't been too long.

I hate it when I lose time. Sometimes it lasts for only a few minutes, whereas others, it can go on for hours. Years ago, when I was very ill, it often lasted for days. It makes me sad, as it's time I'll never get back.

Back in the days when it was still an allowed field of medicine, a few of my psychiatrists said that I suffered from a variety of mental illnesses that stemmed from years of trauma and abuse. But now that mental illness has been declared by the Universal Church to be a corruption of the soul, I don't dare bring that up. My nurse made sure that any paperwork associated with my past episodes "disappeared," which is a good thing. As miserable as I am here, I'd be a million times worse off stuck in a filthy State asylum.

I do my best to remain agreeable, non-threatening, and most importantly, an amnesiac. I know a great deal of things about many powerful people, and they are all things they want to keep deeply buried. If they know I remember, I'll be in for a world of trouble that even being the Lady Consort can't save me from.

The double doors to the dining room open, the two servants charged with that single job pretending as if what's happening isn't something they're going to gossip about for the next year. The two patrolmen flanking my guest bow to me respectfully, and when their charge doesn't follow suit, they tug her down with them. When the three of them rise, the heavily pregnant blonde stares at me with daggers in her eyes.

I give her a friendly smile. "Please, sit." I scrutinize her appearance, noting the healing green and gold bruise on her cheek and the more recent blue and purple handprints decorating her bare arms.

I frown. "Officer, can you please explain to me why my guest is sporting bruises? It wouldn't be because you or your men are being unduly rough? I hate to think you could condone such unconscionable behavior, especially with a woman who is expecting."

I may not have the power of my husband, but I am respected in this house. Nobody wants to assume that if push comes to shove, they won't have to answer to my mother or Edward.

"No, ma'am, I can't say how she came to be bruised," he lies, his defensiveness giving him away. "I can tell you it wasn't me." The pointed look he gives Caitlin is one that dares her to contradict him, and although she stares at him quite hatefully, she swallows down the mouthful of words planning to do just that. Apparently she's smarter than I was led to believe.

I dismiss them just as the servers come in with our soup, the guards reminding me they are only a shout away should I need them. I'm not afraid of the blonde woman in her navy pregnancy dress embroidered with little pink whales and with her makeup and hair styled to perfection. Although I've heard stories of the terrible things she's done in the past, I think she knows better than to try to hurt me.

"Miss Brown," I begin as I pick up my spoon. "Would it be alright if I called you Caitlin? If you like, you may call me Louise."

The young woman looks a bit shell shocked but manages a quick nod. "Yes, ma'am, that will be just fine."

"Wonderful." I smile again as I sip delicately from my spoon. I feel Caitlin's eyes on me as she mimics my motions. By the time our main course arrives, I could tell you exactly when she will lift her napkin to tap at the side of her lips, or how long it will take to catch herself after she's thoughtlessly rested an elbow on the table.

We chit-chat idly, the time passing faster than when I eat alone, but more slowly than if I share company with someone I truly like. I stand when the meal is over, sending the servants into a flurry of activity as I head to my rooms for the night. The patrolmen stride over to us the moment we exit the dining room, but one sharp glance from me keeps them from grabbing her arms.

I stop next to Caitlin, placing my hand on her arm gently. Even my slight touch makes her wince in fear. "Tonight was quite enjoyable, as it's rare for me to have dinner guests. While you remain in this house, I hope you will continue to take your meals with me."

I can't imagine why, but Caitlin looks more rattled than if I said I'd put poison in her soup. She looks down at the floor, and then up to me. "Why are you bein' so nice to me?" She doesn't say it like she's suspicious. She says it like she feels guilty.

I pat her arm gently. "Because we women need to stick together, that's why."

I think that's where we, as a gender, went wrong before. Women had once risen so far in this nation, having climbed our way up from no rights at all to being almost equal to men. For decades, our fight for equality had united women of all ages, races and beliefs. We came together to demand the right to vote, to have our own bank accounts and credit cards, as well as to have autonomy over our bodies.

We still had a way to go to achieve true egalitarianism when something about our gender changed. Instead of sticking together, we let our differences divide us. We became distracted with any number of hot button topics, hunkering down on our particular beliefs and refusing to see truth or merit in any others. By the time we realized we'd cannibalized our chance to create an indivisible nation with liberty and justice for all men *and* women, it was too late. The rights we had worked so hard to obtain began to be taken away, one freedom at a time.

I refuse to make that mistake again, especially within my own home. "I see no reason for us to battle, Caitlin. I have no idea what Edward has planned for either of us. I haven't been told for how long you will be my guest, but what I do know is that I'm lonely, and I imagine you are, too. I would consider it a great favor if you would share your company with me."

I pat her arm once again as I bid her good night and head for the stairs. She's walking slowly, probably wondering if the stories about me still fearing the steps are true. As if my thoughts summon him, one of the House Guard takes my arm, my other hand white-knuckling the railing. Smugness radiates from Caitlin as she watches my careful ascent.

I'm no fool. I know she cannot be trusted. If she thought it would bring Edward back, she'd push me down the staircase in a heartbeat. I've often wondered what cosmic reason prevailed to allow me to survive, and I can't help but think that maybe this is it. Maybe I am to be a light to Caitlin during her darkest hours in the same way my staff has been to me.

Or maybe I'm being naive, destined to be disappointed when my efforts inevitably fail. But tonight had been a good start, and so for now I will remain, as Shakespeare so eloquently said, "ever in appearance like an innocent flower, but being always as wary as the serpent under it."

But she should be forewarned. Should she do anything to harm those I love, I am prepared to strike.

16

Keira

I'm so pissed I can hardly see straight, and it's not because that son of a bitch blackened my eye so badly I can barely open it. I'm mad at myself. I'd been so scared when everything went down that I forgot my training. I basically just stood there and let that asshole beat the shit outta me. I proved that what everyone says about me is true. I'm nothing but a dumb kid. If Emma hadn't saved me...

I shiver just thinking about what could have happened. She'd been so cool and collected, with not even a note of concern in her voice. Her aim with the rifle was as straight and true as if she'd been in the middle of target practice and not in a life and death situation. Had she been off even the tiniest amount she could have hit me. If she hadn't fired a kill shot on the first try, I'm a million percent positive we'd all be dead right now. And aside from being very tired tonight, Emma hasn't shed a single tear or seemed at all shaken by what happened, only repeatedly asking me if *I'm* okay.

I honestly don't know if that sort of badass behavior makes me fear or like her more. I think it's both.

As I'd cried and snotted like the pussy girl I apparently am, Emma held me and petted my hair, cooing that everything would be alright. She swore to me that she'd never let anyone hurt me ever again, and God help me, I believe her.

Now, hours later, the house is quiet and I have time to deal with my injuries. My whole fucking body hurts, which is to be expected after being used as a punching bag. My stomach and torso are covered in nasty bruises, and I think I may even have a cracked rib or two. Earlier I took some anti-inflammatories which helped some, so I take a few more now before the others completely wear off. I have a feeling that tomorrow I'm gonna hurt like bitch, so there's a bunch of shit I need to get done before I feel worse. The top of that list is checking on the boy.

But before I can do that, I need to suture my lip. As much as I wish I didn't have to handle this myself, without Scott or Declan here, I'm my own best shot of piecing this together and not ending up looking like Frankenstein. I take the first aid kit out from under my bed and pull up a syringe of lidocaine and head into the bathroom.

I startle when I look in the mirror, the bruising, swelling and abrasions looking far worse than I expect. Upon closer examination, everything should heal on its own and with minimal scarring, so I take a deep breath and bolster myself for the repair ahead. The lidocaine stings like hell until the area numbs out, but then I sew up my lip without much trouble. I do a pretty damn good job, if I say so, myself.

When I'm done, I repack my kit, mentally taking note of what needs replacing as I dress for a trek into the woods. After shrugging into my jeans and a clean shirt, I grab a flashlight, and pack up a back-pack with all the stuff the boy might need and head out into the dark.

I'd just gotten to the barn where I plan to untie one very pissed off Gritty so he can come with me, when I hear a voice. "Child, haven't you seen enough trouble today? Why must you feel the need to find more?"

It's Esther, plopped onto a hay bale with a rifle over her lap, her dark clothes helping her blend in with the shadows. She's got Gritty laying at her feet, the traitorous pooch refusing to even look at me. I imagine it's because I'd left him tied up all day like, well, like a dog, and not because he actually prefers Esther's company. He gets really mad when he's treated like a pooch.

"I can't sleep. I need to go to the outer barn and get a fresh bottle of lidocaine for the first aid kit for the house. I just used the last of it piecing together my lip. I figured I'd go now while it's still numb. It'll get all throbby if I wait and hike out there after it wears off."

"I see," Esther nods. "But what is in the heavy bag over your shoulder?"

I think quickly. "I have a few things for Adam and Dex I need to return, and as I'm going right by their house, I thought I'd leave it on their porch. You know, kill two birds with one stone."

She knows I'm lying, but she only tells me to be careful. I'm so thankful she doesn't interrogate me further that I don't bother to ask why she's sitting outside in the dark at our farm.

By the time I make it to the barn where we keep the shit we can't keep in the house, I stuff a bunch of medical supplies into my bag and then head into the woods. Gritty's finally gotten off his ass and caught up, marching alongside me like my very own, very irritated, bodyguard. He's standoffish and snippy, the few times I reach out to pet his head he lifts his lip and growls. It's as he's saying he could have handled things with those fucking patrolmen if only *somebody*, meaning *me*, hadn't been dumb enough to tie his ass up.

When Gritty and I get to the spring house, there's a hunched figure sitting outside. Not knowing the kid's name, I resort to whispering loudly. "Hey there, boy. Is that you?"

The figure turns his head towards me and croaks, "Yes."

I accidentally blind him with the halogen beam of my flashlight that he lifts his good arm to shield himself from. He looks worse than he did this morning. I sit next to him, noting how he's hugging himself and shivering despite the fact it's at least in the high-seventies and muggy as hell. When I raise my hand to touch his forehead he flinches.

"Hey, I'm not going to hurt you." I drop my tone into as non-threatening a register as I can muster. "I'm just checking for fever."

I rifle through my supplies until I find my first aid kit. I hand him the thermometer, and he looks at it suspiciously until finally putting it under his tongue. I reach slowly to press the button to turn it on, but the quiet beep still startles him enough to make him jump.

I understand his wariness, but there aren't many people out there who look less threatening than me. He's gotta realize by now I'm not here to hurt him. The thermometer beeps and he flinches again, practically throwing the thing at me as he scoots away a few inches. When I shine the light on it I see he's hovering a little over 102 degrees.

"Okay, friend. Here's the plan. Tonight we gotta get you smelling better so I don't pass out when I work on your arm. I'm gonna help you to the stream so you can wash up. I brought you clean clothes, and then I can check out your arm. Once we get through all that, I brought you some food that you have to promise to eat slowly. If you scarf this all down, you're just gonna puke it back up. Capisci?"

He nods, looking embarrassed. "I'm sorry. . ."

His voice trails off and he looks away just as I screw up my face in confusion, realizing too late how badly that hurts. "What are you sorry for? It's not your fault that you stink. Stink happens."

He stares at me incredulously before breaking out into a toothy grin, and then gives a barking laugh that quickly turns into a hacking cough. He stands shakily, and I have to help him to the stream to keep him from toppling over. Once we're at the water's edge, I hand him a bar of soap and a towel, and leave some fresh clothes on a rock to change into after. But he just stands there, staring at me.

"Go on," I tell him. "Get washing."

He fumbles with the buttons on his shirt, and then stops once he manages to get them undone. He looks at me nervously.

"Do you need help getting your pants off? Is that the problem?"

He blushes.

"Please," I huff, gesturing towards his private parts. "Don't be bashful on my account. What you've got I've seen plenty of times before."

"You have?"

I can't tell by his tone if he's horrified or offended, but the lidocaine's wearing off on my lip, it's beginning to throb, and I'm getting impatient. I'm never my friendliest when I'm hurt, and this kid's got about ten seconds before I'm gonna go pull down his pants and shove him in the stream if he likes it or not. But something about how he looks at me, like a beaten dog being offered his first biscuit, takes the edge off of my irritation. "Of course I have. I'm training to be a doctor. I see naked people all the time."

Okay, that's a stretch, but he doesn't know that. When he doesn't move, I sigh heavily and turn my back to him. "If you fall in the stream and drown because I'm not there to help you, you'll only have yourself to blame."

It still takes him a while to drop his pants and wade into the water, and he lets out a strangled cry of discomfort as the water envelops his feverish body. I hear him splashing a bit as he uses the soap, and then a loud hiss and a pained moan, which I assume is from the water seeping through the bandage and into his wound.

"You okay?" I call over my shoulder.

He's shivering so hard his teeth chatter, his voice tight with agony. "The water burns my arm. Oh, God, I'm gonna be sick."

I hear an ungainly splash, and despite my earlier efforts to protect his modesty, I jump in and help him. When the nausea passes, I sit him in a shallower spot and help him bathe, his cheeks flaming with embarrassment despite the fact I don't even go near his boy parts. I wash his filthy hair for him, using my fingertips to give his scalp a good scrubbing while praying that he doesn't have lice for me to catch. It's too dark to tell what might be hopping around in that mop.

I'm just about to stop when he suddenly relaxes, letting out a long sigh as his shoulders drop and he moves his neck around, the bones cracking. He sighs again. "That feels nice," he whispers.

The way he says that makes me continue, even massaging his neck and shoulders. It's clear he hasn't been comforted in a very long time as every new spot I move to causes him to stiffen until he realizes I'm not going to hurt him. When I'm done, I help him up the streambank before I turn my back while he towels off and puts on clean pants.

When I'm allowed to turn back to him, he looks at me shyly before turning away quickly. God, I must look hideous for him to turn around like that. But then he surprises me, tossing me the towel "in case I'd like to cover myself." Only then do I look down and realize that I'm sporting one hell of a set of high beams, and I groan out loud. In my haste to get out of the house I hadn't bothered with a bra, a decision I seriously regret now.

After drying myself off and draping the towel around me, I set to work cutting off the bandage while he holds the flashlight. In the light he can now clearly see my face, the look of horror on his telling me it's every bit as grisly as I'd thought.

"May I ask what happened?"

I exhale grumpily, doing my best to concentrate on removing the filthy cloth around his arm without hurting him any further. "I got into a fight with two Ag patrolmen," I deadpan. "If you think I look bad, you should see them."

"Is that a joke?"

I stop cutting through the bandage mid stroke and fix him with a frosty stare. "No, it's not a joke. Two assholes stopped by today when I was home alone with the kids. Things got ugly real quick."

He places his good hand over mine, his fingers as thin as chicken bones as they clench mine. "How did you get away?"

"I killed them."

He stares at me incredulously, I think trying to figure out if I'm fucking with him. He drops his hand from mine when he realizes I'm not. "Who *are* you?"

"If I tell you, I'm gonna have to kill you. Now sit still." I smile at him, making sure he understands I'm joking. As the bandage begins to give way, the stench of putrefying flesh makes my stomach churn and my eyes water. Even the slightest motion makes him cry out or inhale sharply. I'm so afraid he's going to pass out that I help him lie back in the grass.

Fuck, this is going to be worse than I'd thought. The cloth is stuck to the wound, and even the gentlest tugs are making him scream. "Look, I know this hurts, but you can't holler like that. I can't risk someone hearing you."

I give him a few minutes to calm down before telling him to brace himself. Sweat beads his forehead and his eyes frantically dart about, almost like he's gonna bolt. So I tell him that on the count of three I'm going to remove the rest of the bandage, but on two, I slap one hand over his mouth to muffle his screams and give the cloth a yank. To my relief, he promptly passes out.

Using the flashlight to get a better look, I stare at the wound. Not only is the injury far worse than anything I've treated on my own, I'm pretty sure it's beyond even Declan's scope to fix. There's no exit wound, and after giving it a quick palpation with my gloved finger, it's clear the bullet fractured the humerus, and fragments of bone have penetrated the muscle. How the brachial artery wasn't severed is a goddamn miracle.

I have no idea how he's managed for as long as he has. Images of Anna and the agony she suffered from her burns sneak into my thoughts and I promptly push them away. I refuse to let him die.

I clean his arm as best I can, working as quickly as possible before he comes to. I'm just finishing rolling the thick bandage around his arm and working the shirt sleeve over the gauze when he begins to mumble and thrash. I try my best to soothe him with murmured platitudes and outright lies that do nothing to alleviate his pain but make me feel marginally better about the torture I just inflicted.

When he manages to open his eyes, I smile. "Hey there, welcome back," I whisper gently as I push a few sweaty strands of hair off his forehead. "You did great. I got everything cleaned up and rewrapped while you were out. I swear, I'm done hurting you. At least for today."

Christ, do I suck at small-talk. "When you feel like you can sit up, let me know, and I'll help you. I brought you some food if you think you can tolerate it."

God, now I'm *babbling*. What is wrong with me?

He lays there for a long while, staring up at me with his chest heaving. He's in a fuck ton of pain, and I try to think of ways to distract him, but if I were in his situation I'd want to just be alone. Since I don't want to leave just yet, I sit with him in silence and wait for him to tell me what he wants.

When the color returns to his face a bit, I help him sit up and give him some water from my bottle, and a few antibiotics and anti-inflammatories to hopefully bring down the fever. I feed him small pieces of bread torn from the loaf and only a few small bites of ham, just enough that I hope it will buffer the drugs so they don't make him sick. The last thing he needs is to start puking or get the squirts.

I want nothing more than to bring him back with me to the farmhouse, but he got so agitated the last time I mentioned it that I don't bring it up again. He's been through enough for one night. I'll try again tomorrow.

As the night sky turns to the first light of day, I help him back to the springhouse. I lay out a clean blanket, wad up a second clean towel to act as a pillow, and lower him to the ground, being careful to not jostle his arm. I give him his instructions for the day, which are pretty much to keep drinking lots of water, try to eat a bunch of tiny meals, and rest. I leave the antibiotics, which I now know are woefully inadequate, and the pain meds, which are probably even more worthless, but I pretend, for his sake, they will be enough to help him begin to heal.

Through it all, he keeps staring at me, his big brown eyes still full of pain, but maybe, just maybe, a touch less glassy from fever. It makes me feel slightly better about leaving him for the day.

When I'm finally ready to go, I'm surprised to find Gritty standing guard right outside the door, an alert, silent sentinel watching over us. I lean over and give him a firm scratch behind his ears, which he likes, and he rewards me with a long, drippy lick to my cheek, which makes me laugh. I'm glad to see he's finally forgiven me.

I turn back one last time to the boy with a smile on my face. "So, anything else you need before I go?"

He briefly closes his eyes, swallows hard, and finally speaks in a wavering voice. "I want just one thing. Your name. I need to know who to thank God for when I say my prayers."

I don't even know how to respond to that, so I give him what he asks for in the only way I know how. "I'll tell you mine if you tell me yours," I reply in the most smart-assed tone I can muster, but it comes out sounding flirty instead.

What the hell is wrong with me?

"I'm Micah," he offers with a shy smile. "And you are?"

"Keira. My name is Keira."

He repeats my name, and I swear on all that's holy, I have never liked the sound of it nearly so much as when uttered by this poor, sweet boy's lips.

17

Declan

I spend the evening with these three weird women, saying little as I watch their interactions. They seem more like one person split among three bodies than three separate individuals, everything about them freakishly similar and yet different enough to not be perfect copies. They compliment each other, each woman showing off not only her best attributes, but making the others shine as well.

They give me a tour of their grand home, an abandoned mansion far from civilization. Nina apologizes for drugging and abducting me, claiming that their safety is in large part due to the fact only a select few know where this place is. As we wander through the rooms, she points out the artwork on the walls, noting which ones are real and which are incredibly good fakes. Glass cabinets throughout the building house one-of-a-kind trinkets ranging from Fabèrgè eggs to a one of a kind Patek Philippe watch that Sasha knows every detail about, including what it had last been sold for at auction and when it had "gone missing." There are tiaras that once belonged to Queens, and prized jewels that once graced the fingers, ears, and necks of the wealthiest people in the world. I don't have to ask how they came to be here. Their smugness is so thick it's actually hard to breathe when I'm with them.

"They are so proud of their little collection," Olesya smiles as she opens her arms and gathers her daughters for a hug. They pout at her mocking tone before all three of them laugh. Nina boasts that she's responsible for the most stolen pieces only for Sasha to add that the pieces she stole may be fewer, but worth more.

Yet it's Olesya who holds top honors for the most difficult heist, managing to liberate *The Joy of Life*, painted by Matisse, out of the Supreme Pontiff's heavily guarded home office. A particularly paranoid fucker, his homes are secured about as well as those belonging to the Supreme Archon, so how she managed to sneak out the nearly six by eight foot painting is beyond me.

When I tell her I need to hear how she did that, she smiles coyly. "That story, my friend, is far, far above your pay grade." She tortures me further by adding that she managed the heist while it was still framed.

This is my first real art appreciation lesson, the women proving to not be just fantastic thieves, but also extremely knowledgeable. It's clear their work is far more than a way to earn money, it's a passion. Their eyes light up, their gestures become more animated, and their laughter grows more buoyant as they tell me stories of past artifacts they have since "rehomed," all at an astounding profit with much of it used to aid our war effort.

We end the tour on the top floor, an enormous loft-style space where Olesya and her daughters work when not on a mission. The floor to ceiling windows provide stunning panoramic views of thick trees with mountains in the distance. Nina points out the high stone walls topped with shattered glass and razor wire in the far distance, just as Sasha leans in and whispers that is just the tip of the iceberg when it comes to their security. She says it like a warning, that even though they have removed my cuffs, I'm still their prisoner.

After the tour, we head down to the enormous professional kitchen more suited to a high-class restaurant than a home. The daughters decide on the menu on a whim, calling out ingredients that they gather from refrigerators, freezers and pantries and place aside large pots and pans their mother places on the stove.

"Filet of steak—seared, not baked—"

"With sea salts—pink! And those peppercorns, like pine. . ."

"Yes! That will go well with that last bottle of wine—"

"In the pan there, pour in the oil. Sister, turn down the heat, do not let it boil!"

"Chop up the veg—now in the pot, toss them in; then puree the tomatoes, ah, they're so fresh it's a sin!"

They weave and duck out of each other's way as they wield knives and spoons, a few times nearly nicking one another and grinning deviously when they check and find nary a scratch. Flames shoot up from the gas stove and then gentle, the scents of herbs mixed into vegetables and sizzling steak so mouthwatering it becomes a form of torture.

I am bewitched, staring at them the way I imagine Herod watched Salome dance with her veils, except these women are seducing me with caramelized onions and a fine cut of meat. They inform me that the steak will be cooked how it should be eaten—rare—and I can "go fuck myself" if I want it more cooked.

I offer to help, but they say no, that I'm their guest, and I'll just get in their way. Olesya pours me a glass of wine and tells me to sit back and relax, so I do. When everything's done and the food is on the plates, they drizzle some sort of divine-smelling sauce over the meat, and add just a bit more butter to the tops of the piles of smashed potatoes to make them glisten. They even put some sort of green, leafy garnish on the plate to make it prettier, and then they tell me to take a seat at the table.

When I sit next to Olesya, she shakes her head, instead gesturing for me to take the seat at the head of the table. The moment before I touch the gleaming silver utensils or lift the crystal goblet of rare, expensive wine to my lips, I wonder what's really going on here.

I've somehow gone from prisoner to guest in a matter of hours, my suspicious nature kicking in once again.

I think of all the ways they still might kill me, wondering about the sorts of poisons that could be mixed into food so as to be undetectable not only to the diner, but later, to a coroner. But they're eating and drinking the same food and wine, so I tell myself to stop being so paranoid.

I try to follow their conversation, nodding here and there, but my gut is still telling me something's wrong. The hair on the back of my neck is standing up, goosebumps raising on my arms as I occasionally turn to look over my shoulder towards the door. My earlier distraction led me to stupidly be seated with my back towards it, and as any person who's seen one of those old mafia movies will tell you, you should never let yourself be seated with your back to the door.

The women lapse in and out of English, their faces revealing nothing about what they are discussing, although Sasha occasionally looks amused when she gives me the side-eye and then peeks over at her sister. I'm nearly finished with my dinner when Nina rises to refill my wine glass and I decline, already feeling a bit tipsy and thinking it wisest to keep my wits about me. She refills it anyway.

My caution comes too late. Cool metal digs into the back of my head, the distinctive sound of a gun being cocked making me cringe. I swallow hard, the last bite of steak I swallowed sticking in my throat.

These women played me for a fool, and the worst part about it is that I knew this was a possibility the entire fucking time. Am I really that desperate to find good somewhere left in this world that I let them set me up?

Yeah. Yeah, you are, asshole.

Great. On top of everything, even the fucking voice in my head is mocking me, not that I need him to. I'm doing a bang-up job kicking my own ass right now. The women stare at me with looks ranging from disillusionment to disgust, but I can honestly tell you that none of them are as disappointed in me as I am.

Olesya stands from her seat and folds her napkin neatly before she places it aside her plate. She shakes her head with a few disapproving clucks, before turning to her daughters and whoever is holding the weapon to the back of my head. "What is the one rule to follow above all others that I know Anna taught you? The one rule to remember above all others?"

"Trust no one," I mumble.

She nods imperiously. "And what did you do wrong today?"

"What didn't he do wrong?" Sasha scoffs.

"Silence!" Her command is thunder and lightning, a proclamation of a wronged deity, and one that makes even her usually unflappable daughter look cowed. She grips her steak knife in her hand and walks slowly towards me. She places the blade against the throbbing artery in my throat, letting the blade sink just enough into my flesh to draw blood.

"We have less than four weeks to train him well enough to keep him alive for the next eighteen years. Do you think it can be done?" She's not looking at me now. She's looking at whoever's holding the gun.

"We better," the unfamiliar voice mutters.

She drops the knife onto my empty plate, the blood on the blade splattering into the remains of my meal. When the gun is pulled from my head and the cartridge removed from the chamber, I stand quickly, facing the tall, broad-shouldered man in a military uniform who I immediately recognize from his eye patch and facial scars.

I glare up at him, once again furious that I'm so fucking short in a world where every man has apparently been created at least half a foot taller. "So tell me, Cyclops, what happens in four weeks if I don't get my shit together to your particular level of satisfaction?"

"Then we're fucked."

* ★ *

A few hours later, we're still sitting around the table, the remains of dinner cleared and only glasses for our whiskey, wine and vodka that have been refilled numerous times are left as a testament to our discussion.

"I know this is a lot to take in," the soldier named Cassiel James adds after a long silence. I'm still reeling from what they've told me, and yet I know there's more they haven't. All of it proves what I've been saying since day one—I'm not the right man for this job.

With someone else driving the ship *could* their plans work? Yeah. Maybe. But not with me. Their plan for the future of the resistance, and its success, requires a clandestine collaboration between a number of desperate foreign nations, a few infuriated billionaires, a couple of irate trillionaires, and me.

Me.

What the fuck are they thinking?

For once, I agree. They've lost their fucking minds. There's no way I can pull off what they're asking, and once I find my tongue, I plan to tell them just that. Yet Olesya remains certain that their plan will be successful if I only believe it will, and it's this idiotic statement that finally shoves me over the edge. I start to laugh. When she asks what's so funny, I sarcastically ask her if I clap my hands and wish really hard, can I bring Tinkerbell back to life, too?

She gives me a dirty look, telling me that we've no time for sarcasm. She asks me again. Will I do it?

I don't answer right away. I've already told them I see this plan blowing up in our faces, and as I'm the one who needs to pull it off, it'll be *me* that gets vaporized on live television, not them. If just one tiny detail gets flubbed, there's no telling how many people will go down with me. I've done plenty of stupid shit in my life, and going along with this plan easily ranks in the top three.

Yet Olesya and Cassiel are sure it's going to work. One might think some godly actuary worked up the numbers and gave them the thumbs up. I want to ask them where their crystal ball's hidden, or which of the mirrors in this place is magic, as this plan they've come up with has to owe its success to the occult. It's far too fucking out there to have anything to do with God.

"How do we know that Bellamy won't just bomb the whole lot of us? You know he'll find out. He's got the weapons and could blow the whole lot of us before I've barely begun."

Olesya nods. "That's not a concern."

I roll my eyes. "Personally, I think it's a really big concern."

She stares at me knowingly, letting what I didn't realize until now sink in.

"Don't even fucking tell me—"

"Yes, Declan. He will be there."

"No," I shout, standing up so quickly my chair nearly tips over. "No fucking way. His goons will kill me on sight—"

"They can't," Cassiel argues. "It's neutral territory. Any aggression shown on neutral soil by its members is met with the highest consequences."

"Last I checked, we aren't members. They kicked us out after the Committee took power."

"That's true," Olesya states. "But Bellamy's trying to reform his image, and he cannot claim he wishes for peace and then shoot you five minutes later. Especially not with a camera pointed at him and a room full of delegates watching."

"So he'll have a member of his Goon Squad do it. They'll say they thought they saw me going for a weapon, or there was something in my hand, and oops! My bad. Declan's dead. I may be many things, but suicidal ain't one of them, lady."

"I'm in charge of Bellamy's security for the event," Cassiel states. "I will be right beside him at all times. I will be the one to make sure all his guards are unarmed before we enter the building, and once we get there, we are all checked for weapons by an independent security force. No one, not even Bellamy, can refuse. It's the perfect time for you to do this. It won't get any safer."

"Declan, if he is allowed to whitewash his sins to the world, the nation will be lost for good. Overseas, many people have already forgotten the atrocities of the war, and only hearing Bellamy's side is going to reinforce his position. We need outside help, and the only way to get it is to promote outrage. It's time to bring our message to the world. People need to see what is happening. They need to see you. They need to hear your voice. They need proof that Bellamy has not changed a thing about our nation except to make it worse. They need a flesh-and-blood leader to believe in, but right now, you're just a ghost. You aren't real to them, and you need to be."

I sit back down, close my eyes, and let my head fall into my hands. I thread my fingers through my hair and pull at the roots in frustration. I've argued over and over that I don't want to lead, but if I have to, I want to do it on my terms, and those have always included remaining in the shadows.

But no one cares what I want. I've argued that I'm not fit for this job—my temper's too volatile, my tongue's too sharp, and my hands are way too quick and willing to throttle people—and yet I'm told over and over again that it must be me. Yet nobody will fucking explain to me why. The last time I asked, Olesya promised that one day she will, but that day isn't today.

"Can you tell me just one thing?" I ask, my voice heavy with resignation. "You all seem to know so much about what's going to happen. Can you just promise me that my wife and children will be safe? I refuse to do anything that will put them in any greater danger than they're already in."

"I find it interesting that with just one question being asked, it's not to inquire about your future."

I frown. "You're a mother. At some point there also had to be a guy you liked enough to have three kids with. So don't tell me you wouldn't ask the same thing if you only got one question."

She smiles sadly, turning to her daughters and searching their eyes before she gives a nearly imperceptible nod. Time stands still, the room falling eerily still. Even the ticking of the clock silences as the air thickens.

I look to Cassiel, who is equally entranced. I somehow feel outside their circle looking in, both privileged to watch and yet wishing to be anywhere else but here.

"I can tell you this now, Declan Byrne, but nothing more," Olesya begins. "Your name will forever be tied to this land, but no divine title given."

Nina looks up from the floor and stares eerily at me. "You will be forever lesser than your children, yet greater."

"Your blood will not reign supreme, yet will be required for the one who will."

Their words make absolutely no fucking sense, and yet make all the sense in the world. I don't ask her to explain. It's clear they will reveal no more.

Olesya then turns her emerald gaze to Cassiel. "As for you, I can only tell you this: You will never wear a crown, but will one day wield immeasurable power. In your hands will one day be the clay, and if you do not mold it properly, everything Declan will sacrifice will be for nothing."

At the word sacrifice, I lift my eyes to find hers trained upon me. Although what she's said makes little sense, I know she's telling the truth, or she at least *thinks* she's telling the truth. Although I've been no stranger to touches of the unexplainable in my life, I'm not willing to leap off a cliff just because she thinks I can fly. Yet at the same time, if anyone were to have a link to the mystical, it would be her and her daughters.

Then, almost as quickly as the eerie mood began, it's over.

She asks me one last time if I'm willing to accept her help, and reluctantly, I nod.

"Excellent!" Olesya exclaims as Sasha chimes in with a caustic, "It's about time." Nina pours us more drinks, my conversation with Cassiel returning to mission logistics as the sisters listen carefully to me and whisper among themselves about diction and speech style. Olesya gives me detailed information on the high-ranking men and women I will meet, showing me pictures and videos on her tablet so I'll know them by sight. She tells me the names of the men and women most likely to give aid as well as instructing who to avoid.

As they rattle on, explaining the nuances of politics I never cared to learn and am now getting a crash course in, the daughters craft a persona for me. Their final recipe ends up being one part soldier, one part reluctant-yet-capable leader, and two parts rough-and-ready hero. Olesya reminds them to capitalize on the brand on my hand, reminding Sasha to show me how to clasp the podium so it's easily seen without looking like I'm purposely making it visible. Nina decides what I'm to wear and how I'm to look, whispering to Sasha that she's glad I'm handsome enough to make her job easier than for a few other leaders she's consulted for.

When I tell them there's got to be a way for me to have some form of weapon on me just in case things go sideways, Sasha chimes in to tell me about some of the hidden weapons she's created in the past. I ask if she wouldn't mind making me one of each, just so I don't feel quite so vulnerable walking into a room full of people where at least half want me dead. She gives me a wink, confidently stating she will outfit me well enough to make even James Bond jealous even as Olesya and Cassiel tell her no.

It's sometime in the wee hours when we finally call it a night. Olesya and her daughters head to bed after showing Cassiel and me our rooms, telling us to get some sleep before we start again in a morning that's only a few hours away. Before I enter my room, I shake Cassiel's proffered hand, looking into his deep sapphire-colored eye and startling at the vibrancy.

"Thank you for looking out for my wife on that mountain," I tell him with heartfelt appreciation. He looks at me a bit strangely before mumbling that no thanks are needed. He blushes when I thank him again, adding that if Emma were here, she'd be falling all over herself to find a way to make things right.

"Please tell her that I'm not angry," he tells me earnestly. "There was no way she could have known I wouldn't hurt her. Hell, I was lucky she didn't fuck me up worse. I was able to claim blood loss and pain for a lot of my actions that night, and as for me and Goodman getting into it in the truck, well, everyone chalked that up to the ongoing feud between the military and the Purity Police."

He chuckles lightly as he remembers something. "When the press made me the unofficial "hero" of Emma's "rescue," I heard from a number of people that really stuck in his craw. It didn't take much for me to use that to provoke him at Gregory's funeral. He's hot-headed and predictable, and just as I thought, I used his insecurities to get him to take a swing at me. Considering I was still gimping around, taking a potshot at the hero of the day made him look like a total asshole, and of course, I played up the "injury" to make things look worse than they were. Guy can't punch worth shit."

I chuckle as he grins, rubbing the spot on his jaw where Goodman's punch landed. "That hit barely even bruised me. I had to put makeup on it to make it look worse when I attended his disciplinary hearing and claimed to have no clue why he hit me. If only they knew what I said to him."

He laughs again, this time one of true mirth. "You'll be happy to hear he's been demoted, now overseeing some God-awful agriculture operation somewhere in the Carolinas. I like to think he's up to his elbows in shit, but knowing that fucker, he'll somehow manage to come out of being a pig farm security officer smelling like a rose."

"Still, Cassiel—"

"Please call me Cass. Only my mother calls me Cassiel."

I grin. "Okay, Cass. I know you don't want to hear it, but thank you, anyway. I owe you one."

"If it makes you feel better, I'll probably end up taking you up on that one day."

I slap him fraternally on the shoulder, not letting on exactly how queasy I'm feeling about most of what happened tonight. "You can bet your life that I mean it."

His easy manner falls, his face becoming serious. "Let's hope it doesn't come to that," he adds tightly before entering his bedroom and closing the door behind him.

18

Two weeks later. . .

Louise

The response cards are flowing in, and just as I thought, all of them are checked yes. I've been studying up on my guest list, as it's been a long time since I've seen most of these people, not to mention, there are so many new faces in society whom I was forced to invite, but I've never before met. I break out in hives just thinking I may somehow embarrass myself or my guests. I'm sure my staff will help me as much as they can, but when the day comes, I am determined to orchestrate the evening flawlessly. Because of this, my preparations feel endless.

When Edward was informed of my plans to throw a grand fête he balked at the idea. I must admit that my behavior hasn't always been exemplary at events, relying on drugs and drink to get me through long nights of watching my husband flirt with other women. He's undoubtedly terrified I'll embarrass him in front of all the men he's still so desperate to impress, having spent so little time with me to notice how much I've changed.

Even though I knew he'd be furious, I had my staff "leak" the event to the press, and with the invitations already mailed, Edward had no choice but to relent. After all, what sort of man would cancel a party his loving wife is going through all this trouble to throw? His only caveat to my continuing to plan the event is to make sure his social secretary is informed on all future party-related correspondence.

We were also instructed to tell everyone that Emma is far too late in her pregnancy to attend such a stimulating event. I almost wish I could get Edward on the phone to ask him what all this nonsense is about Emma living in our house. It's a deception that makes no sense, and I don't doubt that it's somehow tied to Caitlin being imprisoned in the other wing. Yet, I've been unable to tie it all together. It's as if my mind is blocking the link between them, a phenomenon doctors told me in the past is probably for my own good. Back then, I'd been okay with that. But now that I'm feeling stronger, I don't want to be protected. I'm tired of being afraid of what I don't know.

In many ways, I think Edward still lives a life of fear. Even after everything he's accomplished, I'm amazed that he is still more terrified of embarrassment than he is of death. If something goes wrong at the party, all he has to do is blame it on me and all will be forgiven. It's not like he hasn't done that before. Although most of his friends are monsters, even the worst of them are capable of forgiving an addle-minded woman for her occasional foible. It's only my husband who forgives me nothing.

When Edward and I first begin dating, he tells me we need to keep our relationship a secret. Not being stupid, Edward picked up on my mother's animosity and determined it best to avoid her wrath for as long as we can. At first I think it's sweet of him, thinking he simply doesn't want me to get into trouble, but as time passes, I realize that the only person he's actually protecting is himself.

My lies become a Friday night ritual, going to a "football game" or "out shopping" when really I'm out with Edward. We go on our date, doing any manner of fun things together, and almost always end up with the two of us fooling around in the cramped backseat of his exotic car. I usually make it home just seconds before curfew, rushing up to my bedroom so the staff won't see my kiss-swollen lips and rumpled clothes and report them back to my mother.

Back in my room, I jump onto my bed and pull my journal from its hiding spot and write down every detail before I forget even a second of it. I keep detailed entries, often writing for an hour or more before I fall asleep, blushing as I relive every kiss and touch.

Every Monday at lunch my girlfriends and I gossip about our weekends, howling with laughter over the boys my friends date who slobber instead of kiss and who can't unsnap a bra without a written manual. When I'm asked, I blush and say my weekend had been wonderful, but no matter how much the girls prod, I only divulge the barest of details. My girlfriends sigh over my stories of Edward's gentlemanly ways, wishing their boyfriends were less oafish and more refined. Kelly calls him "a real-life Mr. Darcy" one day, and the nickname sticks.

As the weeks of our clandestine relationship turns to months, I realize Edward never speaks about his family. He's always asking me questions about my friends and relatives, but when I try to learn about his, he changes the subject. Sometimes my questions put him in a foul enough mood that he ends our dates prematurely. I begin to wonder what's wrong with his family that he refuses to speak about them. Eventually, I stop asking.

Then, unexpectedly, one night he opens up to me. We'd been making out in the backseat of his car, and for once, he seems wholly distracted. Sensing something is wrong, I manage to wheedle out of him not only what's on his mind, but answers to questions that have been niggling at me for months.

He tucks me into his arms, and whispers about his pampered upbringing as if he's ashamed of it. I'd been certain he came from money, but when he tells me he's the sole heir to his father's oil-rich empire, well, you could have knocked me over with a feather. All the super rich boys I know are entitled assholes, constantly rubbing their wealth in everyone's faces. But Edward isn't. In fact, he is completely unpretentious.

His family owns numerous mansions around the world, all filled with fine art and priceless antiques. His mother wears jewels once worn by princesses and Queens, and he blushes adorably when he says that after we are married, I will get to wear those same baubles whenever I please.

He'd gotten self-conscious then, I think embarrassed to admit he'd been thinking so seriously about us. I pinch his chin between my thumb and forefinger and pull his face around so our eyes meet. Then I tell him that I don't care if he's penniless or richer than Cresus, that I love him, and he says it back.

After that, my virginity became little more than a technicality. I allow him more and more liberties with my body, craving his touch whenever we aren't together. I'd already given him my whole heart, and it seemed only natural that soon, my body would follow. After all, wasn't that the natural order of things?

But I was torn inside, the beliefs I'd grown up with regarding religion, sex and marriage not meshing with what I was learning from my friends. My mother refused to sign my permission slip to take sex education, so I relied on my girlfriends to tell me what they learned. They were learning more than just the names of the anatomy, the teachers also discussing things like hormones and the natural urges that came with them.

It all sounded so normal, so biological, that none of us understood why having a little careful experimentation was so against the teachings of the church. After passing around a particularly enlightenment-inducing joint one lazy Saturday afternoon, my girlfriends and I mused over what my mother preached and how it related to what they learned. If God made the clitoris and prostate to be pleasurable when stroked, why is it sinful to enjoy sex? If homosexuality isn't a choice, but the way a person is made by God, why is loving someone of the same sex wrong? If God never makes mistakes, why do many religions consider homosexuality an abomination?

Some of my friends sat down and talked through their questions with their parents, having open-minded discussions that encompassed religion and nature. When they told me their parents were more concerned with them having safe sex instead of no sex at all, I'd been honestly surprised. I had assumed everyone's parents felt the same as my own—that sex is for procreation only.

A few of my friends think it's worth me starting a dialogue with my parents, that maybe they will surprise me, but I know they won't. Even though we aren't Catholic, if I ask them questions about sex my mother will ship me off to a convent somewhere far away, or maybe even lock me in a tower, like Rapunzel.

I stew over when to give Edward "my greatest gift" and realize that until I am one hundred percent certain, I will abstain. But Edward is eager, pushing me further every time we make out. Exasperated, he tells me one night that he had needs as a man, and if I am too much of a child to understand that, maybe we shouldn't be together. He looked down at the gold and pearl purity ring my father gave me and scoffed, aloofly stating he should have listened to his friends who said I was too immature for a man like him. He dropped me off at my house early that night, not kissing me goodbye or even looking at me when I tearfully slunk out of his car.

I had once been so proud of that ring, and of the promises I'd made to my father and to my God. Now all I felt was heartache. Edward refused to take my calls for days at a time, the only time he answered he told me to stop acting like a clingy child and hung up on me. I'd cried so hard I made myself sick, curled up into a ball in my bed, unable to eat or sleep as I prayed for my phone to ring.

After ten days he calls me back, acting like nothing happened. My heart soars with happiness when I'm once again in his arms, and no *matter what he wants to do, I don't say no. I stop wearing my purity ring, and when my parents' eventually notice, I lie and tell them I'd lost it.*

Then one day, Edward really opens up to me about his relationship with his parents. This isn't his usual spiel about the well-educated power duo who wants him to take over their empire, but a story about an emotionally distant mother and a father who is never around.

He confides that his childhood had been lonely and unhappy, and how, if not for nannies and butlers and tutors, he would have been totally alone. He loved to play video games in his spare time, and more specifically, adored the action and strategy of games of war. Eventually, this would turn into his calling to protect and serve. I looked up at him with such awe when he told me that. He was the first person I'd ever met who was blessed with a calling. I couldn't help but wonder if someday I, too, might have one.

He thought his parents would be thrilled, but Matthew and June Bellamy were furious when they found out that he'd not only applied to Annapolis, he'd been accepted. They wanted their heir to go to Harvard or Yale, getting degrees in finance or business or maybe both. They wanted him to only do things that would expand their wealth and power, and couldn't see how a career in the Navy would be beneficial to their pursuits. They forbid him to go to Annapolis.

It has now been a year and a half since he'd last seen them, not having any contact with them since the day he left for school. He said that until they are willing to accept his choice, he has no interest in seeing them.

Oh, how I looked up to him for doing what I could only dream of doing! I desperately want to stand up to my mother and insist that what I have with Edward is special and beautiful instead of living in a state of our very own "don't ask, don't tell." My mother is growing increasingly suspicious that I'm still seeing Edward, and my father is simply too busy to care that I go out with "friends" but always return home in the same little red car.

As winter turns to spring, I become more and more emboldened by Edward's fortitude. His parents cut off his money in an attempt to lure him home, and thoroughly embarrassed, Edward admits that the car he uses for our dates actually belongs to a guy he knows at school who lets him rent it when he's not using it, himself. Although he loathes it, I give him money to help pay the car rentals and to help him get by, and I'm exceedingly careful to call the thick wads of cash "loans" to save his pride. He tells me how sweet I am to be so thoughtful, at times even using the money to buy me small gifts that I treasure. For my birthday, he gives me a gorgeous diamond and gold pendant that I never remove, not even when I shower. He'd asked one of the maids at home to take it from the vault and send it to him. He got down on one knee and said this was his promise to me, and once I was eighteen, he'd have it set as a ring, an engagement ring, if only I'd say yes. Of course, I said yes, and later that night, my virginity went from a technicality to nonexistent in the backseat of a borrowed car.

Shortly thereafter, I summon the courage to stand up to my mother. I am terrified as I knock on her office door at the church, praying that she won't answer. But of course she's there and tells me to come in, and to my horror, she has an entire group of her friends with her, all sipping tea and gossiping.

I immediately abort my mission. There's no way I can do this in front of an audience. After making a few pleasantries I am almost out the door when Mrs. Masterson, my best friend Kelly's mom, pipes up. "Louise, will you be bringing that handsome cadet to the benefit next week? What's his name again? Edward? Kelly told me so much about him. I'd love to meet him."

I spin to face my mother, who has the uncanny ability to glare furiously while smiling in such a way that no one else notices. She hadn't mentioned that I could bring a guest, and judging by the look on her face, she doesn't want me to.

Had I any sense I would make up an excuse, but I can't think of a reason quickly enough for Edward to not come. Instead, I pour myself some tea, pull up a chair, and tell the ladies how Edward is everything a mother could want for her daughter. The women sigh over the sweetness of our young love, a few of the ladies wishing their daughters could find a young man just like him. Through it all my mother says nothing, the only sign of her displeasure being the super-tight grip on her teacup that turns her knuckles white.

After I'm done prattling on about his wealthy family and showing them the pretty diamond pendant he'd given me that I wear under my clothes, my mother's friends switch to my side. Although Edward told me not to mention it to anyone, I explain how he'd felt so strongly about his calling to serve his nation that it caused a rift in his family. Even the most racist and classist woman at the table, aptly named Mrs. White, thaws at the mention of Edward's patriotism, giving my mother the coldest looks.

Regardless of her friends' reactions, I still expect my mother to give some reason why I can't invite him, but she doesn't. Instead, she smiles, and although it's brittle and strained, it's still a smile.

"Yes, Louisa May, I think you should invite Edward. I think it's high time we all get to know him better." She turns to her friends with a sly smile. "You were all young once too, my dears," she tuts to her friends. "But we aren't so old as to not remember our mothers were also the last to know all the details."

I am ecstatic. I can hardly wait to tell Edward that my mother will even send a car for him so he can arrive in style. We can now stop hiding our relationship, no longer Romeo and Juliet, but living out a different story, one where we will live happily ever after.

In hindsight, it's impossible to not see that my mother was up to something. I find it particularly apt that the words Shakespeare once said of Macbeth fit the tragedy my life would become so well. For I, too, had been cursed to be but a walking shadow, a poor player, doomed to strut and fret her hour upon the stage and then be heard no more. If my mother hadn't been so blinded by her bigotry, she might have seen how I would ultimately be the casualty of her dogmatism, and if I hadn't been so blinded by love, maybe I would have seen what my life was destined to become—"a tale told by an idiot, full of sound and fury, signifying nothing."

19

Trinity

Louise has been melancholy all week. It's hard for me to tell if this is an early symptom of another nervous break or just exhaustion caused by taking on too much. Either way, I need to tread carefully, because she cannot fall apart on me now. The wheels are in motion, and I will need her on her A game the night of the party. There is far too much at stake.

I'm tired and bitchy today, having spent last night watching over my charge as she suffered through one of her worst nights in recent history. She couldn't sleep, muttering *tomorrow, and tomorrow and tomorrow* as she wrung her hands and paced the hall by her bedroom. Occasionally she stopped to look down the curved stairwell that nearly took her life, each time making me more fearful she might throw herself down the stairs and end her misery once and for all.

She scowled as she swallowed the pills placed on her morning tray, complaining they will make her sleepy when she has so much to do. I told her I will take over her duties for the day, giving her time to rest and tend to her neglected orchids. That brightened her mood considerably, even if her eyes are now heavy-lidded with exhaustion and her voice raspy from overuse. I catch only occasional phrases that she whispers to her plants, realizing she's once again on a Shakespeare kick.

"Out, out brief candle!" she recites more loudly despite there being no candle in sight. Then she turns to me, her eyes cloudy, almost as if someone else is speaking for her.

"Tomorrow, and tomorrow, and tomorrow,
Creeps in this petty pace from day to day,
To the last syllable of recorded time;
And all our yesterdays have lighted fools
The way to dusty death."

Okaayy. . .

Then she snaps out of her haze, smiling as if her actions are completely normal, but that she finds the look on *my* face perplexing. Before I can address her questions, one of my maids comes rushing in, breaking one of my fundamental rules to never bother the Lady Consort when she's tending to her flowers.

"My Lady, hurry! It's Miss Caitlin. The baby's coming and she's asking for you!"

Louise drops her pruning shears to the floor, a wide smile taking over her face as her eyes glitter with excitement.

"Oh, how wonderful! I'm right behind you!"

The two of them race from the room as I silently pray for God to give me strength. I gave strict instructions when Caitlin went into labor last night that Louise was only to be told if everything is going as planned and when delivery is imminent. Not to sound like a bitch, but where Louise goes I too must go, and I really, really despise Caitlin. It's best for everyone that I spend as little time in her presence as possible.

Louise barrels through the door to the makeshift delivery room to find Caitlin in mid-push, her hair a mass of dripping, sweaty tendrils that stick to her ruddy cheeks. The room reeks of blood, shit, and sweat, Caitlin's loud complaints that she *can't, she can't,* turning to screams as another contraction hits. Everyone in the room shouts for her to *push, push now, push harder!!* until the monitor signals the contraction is over and the doctor orders her to stop.

Louise quickly washes the dirt from her hands before taking Caitlin's hand in hers. She demands the nurse grab her some clean cloths and cool water, and the second it arrives, she wipes down Caitlin's sweaty brow and cheeks. She encourages her through her next several pushes until the baby's head is out.

"The next push is it—you just need to pop those shoulders through and it's all over. You've got this, Caitlin!" Louise can hardly contain her excitement, her fatigue forgotten as she counts down to the next contraction.

The doctor is in position, yelling for Caitlin to *push, push, push,* but the baby doesn't budge. Two more rounds and the baby still doesn't move. I can't see what the doctor's doing from where I stand, but whatever it is, it's painful. Caitlin screams like she's being murdered.

A second doctor comes in to assist, muttering something about dislocating the shoulder, or maybe moving the baby, while a third doctor spits that whatever they do, they better do it fast. Alarms are sounding, the room now feeling smaller and tighter as barely-constrained panic sets in. A nurse points out that the baby's turning blue, and then everyone loses their composure at once. One OB doctor calls for instruments, the other for drugs, and the neonatologist, who had looked bored when we walked in, is now putting in his two cents now that he's got an investiture in the event. Every member of the medical team knows if anything goes wrong there will be hell to pay, and none of them want to find themselves on the receiving end of Bellamy's wrath.

I'm not sure what does the trick, but five minutes later the baby's out, the doctors leaving Caitlin to fend for herself as they work on the floppy, silent child. The head doctor's staccato commands tell us that the child is in a dire situation, a note of panic creeping into his voice as the minutes pass and the child doesn't breathe. A breathing tube is placed down his tiny throat, and IVs are placed that they give drugs through. Through it all, a nurse counts the time the child's "down," and with every minute that passes, we grow more fearful.

Sure, Caitlin may be a grade A cunt, and Bellamy, well, we all know what the child's father is, but this innocent child shouldn't have to pay for his parents' sins. Then miraculously, the smooth flat tone of the monitor blips once. Then twice. The doctors stand unmoving, one of them whispering behind his mask, "Come on kid, you can do it. . ."

Then the child begins to move, slowly at first, but each movement thereafter grows stronger. Caitlin is screaming, making demands and threats that, without the dire situation of the baby's health, would be comical coming from someone whose legs are still spread in the stirrups with her coochie visible for all the world to see. Louise tries to soothe her, still mopping at Caitlin's face until the new mother takes a swing at her with a furious, "Get the hell away from me!"

Louise looks absolutely stunned for a moment before she angrily tosses the cloth back in the bowl and strides over to see the baby. I can't say for sure, but I think she purposely stands where she can block Caitlin's view.

Caitlin better get used to this feeling, as the older this child gets, the less important she'll become.

It's a cruel thought, but it's the truth. She has to realize that at some point, Edward's going to kick her to the curb just like he has every other woman in his life. *She'd better watch her step, as better women have given Bellamy children. One of them is already dead, and the other one wishes, more days than not, that she was, too.*

"I think he's going to be okay," the neonatologist says, not to Caitlin, but to Louise.

"You *think?!*" Caitlin shrieks. "That's the next Supreme Archon you're talkin' about. You better do more than just *think* he's gonna be okay!"

"We're going to watch him very closely and run some tests, but he's breathing steadily and his APGAR was over a three by the nine minute mark. That bodes well for him. I'll know more in a few hours." Then he nods to a nurse who, along with the doctor, pushes the bassinet into an adjoining room and closes the door, ignoring Caitlin's furious demands to see her son.

Louise walks over to Caitlin but this time, stays out of arm's reach. She smiles as she tells Caitlin that her baby is beautiful, and not to worry, that she's going to go sit with him so he's not alone. When Caitlin begs Louise to stay with her instead, she tells Caitlin that I will stay with her. If this was a comedy skit on TV, everyone would be laughing at our twin visages of horror. But my job is to watch over Louise, not Caitlin, so despite Louise's request, I follow her into the baby's room.

Before I close the soundproof door behind me, Caitlin screams that the doctors "need to keep that crazy bitch away from my baby." I shoot her a taunting smile that silences her screams. I want to make sure she knows the only reason I've tolerated her entitlement is now gone, and if she ever raises a hand to the Lady Consort again, it will be *me* she will have to face.

20

Emma

It's been two weeks since my husband left, and I have no idea where he is or what he's doing. I've gotten a smattering of short, vague texts to let me know he's still alive, but nothing else.

The days I don't hear from him I worry he's been hurt, captured, or God forbid, dead. From experience, I know the lack of contact either means A) he's done something incredibly dangerous, B) he's in the middle of said perilous act, C) he doesn't want to worry me as he plans something life-threatening, or D) some combination of all of the above.

With no clue when he'll return, I slowly resume living like a normal person. After four days stuck in bed, I was so crazy with boredom that Sarah reluctantly let me get up and do some easy chores. The trade off was promising to nap with the children every afternoon like I'm some sort of overgrown toddler.

We're all on edge, just waiting for the day a busload of Ag police or Purity Officers swing by to ask what happened to the men Keira and I killed. Dex and Adam ended up declining Esther's generous offer to feed the dead men to the neighborhood body-disposing hogs, instead driving them a few hundred miles away in their truck. They strapped the men in the driver and passenger seats before setting the rig on fire and pushing it over a cliff with a known weak spot in the barrier. They made it look like an accident, and as long as the coroner doesn't look too closely at the remains, we will hopefully be cleared of any suspicion that they died here.

Yet, instead of life feeling like it's slowly returning to normal, things only feel more off. I can't really pinpoint any one thing; it's more like there are a lot of little things that are just somewhat askew. Esther starts coming over more frequently, and whenever she's here, Keira and I are almost always sent off on pointlessly "urgent" errands.

I must admit, I have other things on my mind and don't immediately put the pieces together, but underestimating Keira's ability to sniff out trouble proves to be a huge mistake. Tired of the wild goose chases we keep being sent on, Keira decides one afternoon that we should hold off on our town-bound errands and hide where we can watch them.

The first few times, Esther leaves with bundles of either clothing or bedding in her arms. On the days Esther doesn't come, Sarah often finds some reason to head over to her farm. We always know when Sarah's lying because she's a terrible liar; the one time Keira pressed her for a reason for one of her impromptu trips, she told us it was for a "canning emergency."

She's not the only one acting oddly. Keira has been going hunting a lot. That in itself isn't strange; it's the fact she keeps returning empty handed. For someone who usually takes great pride in her marksmanship, she's been unusually unbothered by her lack of quarry.

Keira's also been strangely distracted and exceptionally exhausted. I ask if she's feeling okay, and she says yes, even though she's still recovering from the terrible beating she sustained. Sarah asks her a few days later if she's sleeping alright, and Keira looks at her like she's gone insane and snaps out that she's "fine." That's when we know for certain that something's most certainly wrong.

Dex and Adam have practically been living here since Declan left. With little time to go before Amos must begin harvesting, the men spend long hours in the fields, the three of them doing the work normally an entire community would do together.

For the first time ever, all of the farms in our area were required to grow the same crop. The farmers told the Ag department that was a poor plan, as everything would ripen at the same time. For a community used to banding together to get work completed on time, this would cause a major dilemma. When everyone grows something different, the farmers and their families travel from farm to farm, picking the items when at their optimal ripeness. With enough manpower, the work can be done without exhausting everyone, and after each crop is picked, the workers then move as a unit to the next.

But with everyone's crops ripening at the same time, the system they've relied on doesn't work. With each farm owner responsible for only their own yields, and with their lives and land leases on the line, everyone stays at home. It's clear after the first day of harvesting that the community desperately needs help.

Just when we think there's no way we'll get it done, Adam pulls together teams of men and women from all over the tri-state area and beyond. Resistance members from Baltimore come by the van full; another good sized group comes all the way from the community in Ohio where Dex's family lives. When Brother Love and his cousin, Tim, arrive, flanked by Scott, Amy, and a small army of the New York crew, I cry with relief as I give each of them a tremendous hug.

"I always knew you loved me more than that scowling motherfucker you're married to," Scott jokes as he lifts me off the ground in a much-needed hug. The feel of his arms around me only now makes me realize how starved for touch I've been without Declan. Brother Love, not having seen me in months, marvels at how pregnant I look, and Tim asks me politely how I'm feeling before wrapping me in yet another warm, tight hug.

Despite the outpouring of help, it's still not enough people, but we hope we can gather enough for the farmers to at least not wind up homeless. We work day and night, the strongest of the men and women even working by lantern light. Our bodies bear the scourge of our labors, our fingernails caked with dry, dusty clay and our hands scratched and bloody. Our backs hurt so badly by the end of the day that most of us are in tears; even the pliant and ever-energetic children shuffle around like zombies.

The sun ruthlessly bakes us during the day, and our faces and arms peel to the point we look like lepers. At night, the mosquitos feast upon our exposed skin which quickly grows raw from scratching. A few people come down with infections and fevers that the local doctor treats from his dwindling supply of medications. I catch Keira handing some ibuprofen from the Bullies' stash to one particularly feverish-looking woman and I shoot her a chastising glare. It's not that I don't want Keira to help, it's that I'm terrified the sick woman will ask where the drugs came from. But she only gives Keira a few words of thanks before dry-swallowing the tablets and continuing to pick the row of beans they share.

I'm spared the hard physical labor due to my pregnancy, but it doesn't mean I'm idle. I spend my time either watching over an entire brood of children too young to join their parents in the fields, or cooking for the increased labor force who, thankfully, also brought food with them.

I hear from Dex and Adam that the volunteers are working every bit as hard as those who live here, a few of them even falling victim to heat exhaustion. I have no words to express the extent of my gratitude, and when I mention it to Adam, he nods in agreement. But then he bites his lip against words he doesn't want to say. After I prompt him, he tells me of the other groups he called who either didn't reply or flat out said no, one of them being a group of people formerly from Philadelphia who went their own way after the city fell.

"That Damien is a fucking asshole," Adam spits. "Declan's gonna have to do something about him. He's gonna cause trouble. I can feel it."

I agree. Damien has always been a loose cannon, pissed off beyond belief when Anna didn't choose him to be the next Commander. That he refuses to help a community who risked their lives for years to help the people in Philly is just additional proof that he's unfit to lead.

Over the next few days, I worry about Damien knowing as much as he does. Right now, he could get rid of a whole lot of us in one fell swoop if he were to rat us out. Sure, it would be too dangerous for him to collect the reward, but getting us all killed would certainly open the door for him to take over leadership. Just the thought makes me shudder.

Two days before the harvest is to be counted, our help heads home before the Ag patrols begin to arrive. I thank as many people as I can, hugging both friends and strangers and giving heartfelt wishes of safe travels. Everyone leaves blistered, burned and exhausted, with more than a few of them falling into the vans they arrived in and promptly falling asleep.

Over the next forty-eight hours, everyone remaining works nonstop. When it's time for the inspections to begin and everyone is required to congregate in the town square, Keira and I take Anya over to Adam and Dex's to hide. Their small home is terribly hot and stuffy, but we don't dare venture outside. The community is flooded with not only Ag police, but Purity Patrolmen roam the town and spot check farms for any number of infractions. Aside from leaving town, this run-down house in the woods is the safest place for us to hide.

When Adam and Dex arrive a few hours into our sequestration, they bring bad news. The heat is bringing out the worst in the Purity officers who wear their impractical wool uniforms with, not just pride, but sweaty discomfort. Already there have been more beatings than in past years, the officers taking out their irritation on the hapless farmers.

We wait in silence, all of us as undressed as possible to beat the stifling heat but still retain an ounce of modesty. The men lounge around in just their work pants, Anya clad in only a diaper, and Keira and I are in our thinnest summer dresses. Keira once again grouses why men can go without shirts and women can't, cursing the patriarchy and giving Adam and Dex filthy glares. Anya then proceeds to scream her head off for the next hour, apparently too uncomfortable to just cry like a normal child. I feel terrible for her, as not only does she have a terrible heat rash that nothing helps, she's begun teething. I try my best to soothe her but nothing works.

At times we wonder if we're smelling smoke, then the scent dissipates and we hope it was only our imagination. But when Esther finally comes cantering over on Marigold, her giant plow horse, it takes just one look at her face to know things had gone badly in town. The smell of smoke is stronger outside, and considering our distance from the neighboring farms, the fire must be huge.

Esther tells the men to run to Jacob Stoltzfus' farm, where a fire is threatening their home and barns. She tells Keira and me to come with her, gesturing for me to hand Anya up to her. Esther looks like some sort of Mennonite warrior Queen astride the chestnut war horse, the reins in one hand and Anya perched over her opposite shoulder. My daughter's eyes are huge as she takes in the world from a brand new perspective.

Keira and I climb onto Marigold's back, the two of us balancing precariously as we trot back to Amos and Sarah's farmhouse. Marigold spooks when we round the corner for home and encounters a field ablaze. The fire picks up speed as we ride past, and we helplessly watch it burn as the horse snorts and jigs. Marigold's eyes never leave the spreading flames that are, thankfully, blowing in the opposite direction from the Zook's wood-sided home and barn.

Esther swallows hard, clearing her throat before speaking. "Once it became clear that our community failed to produce what was expected, we were all called to the church to receive our punishment. We expected fines, and the owners of the farms producing the least to be evicted. If the head officer is in a particularly foul mood, maybe he would beat or lash a few men to make sure we are afraid enough to do better next year.

"We'd become accustomed to our usual officers, men who could be persuaded to be more lenient by giving them gifts. They were never shy about telling us what they wanted, and we always did our best to provide. They usually wanted things we could spare but that would be very expensive to buy in a city, like a side of salted pork or a loin of lamb. Those who raise grains and corn often made whiskey and beer. For years, these practices kept us from the worst of their wrath, and we found these 'gifts' to be a small price for us to pay.

"But the men this year were new, and much more demanding. As they read aloud the list of our deficiencies, it was clear there would be no real winners or losers, that we had all produced similar amounts. Instead of praising us for being so close to reaching our goals, we were met with suspicion. They claimed that the fields not yet picked had been planted late so we could keep a greater yield. I could understand that if we'd planted anything other than soy, but what do they think we're going to do with a surplus of soybeans?

"They were also unhappy with the beef and pork we produced. We explained that due to drought, much of what we grew was smaller and not up to their usual weight due to lack of forage. The heat baked the nutrition from what little grass managed to grow, with some farmers making the tough decision early on to cull weaker animals so the strong might grow to normal size. Additionally, this year brought more frequent issues with calving that resulted in the death of both cow and calf, and the size of the litters of pigs were not just smaller, but more frequently stillborn.

"But the truth fell on deaf ears. The few who dared to offer bribes were made a spectacle of by being publicly and soundly lashed, a few to the point of falling unconscious from the pain. Our elders went to the man who leads the new officers, he, himself the newly promoted head of the Ag office. This new officer is a particularly cruel man, with the sort of evil so deeply ingrained that he doesn't need to open his mouth for his viciousness to be evident. He sneered at our Elders, complaining that he couldn't understand their accents. With his hat in his hand, Elder Stoltzfus dared to step forward and begged them for just a few more days to finish the harvest."

Her tears break through, her voice filled with barely controlled fury. "That officer told our elders to kneel, demanding each to beg his forgiveness for not getting their work completed on time. They looked among themselves in horror and shame, and I could see in their eyes that they knew there would be no mercy if they did not. They looked out at the rest of us, nodded calmly, and fell to their knees. Some of these men were very old, and it was painful to watch them help each other to the ground. Together, they began to pray."

She stops speaking to wipe the tears from her face. "I prayed he wouldn't do what he did—"

Still seated behind her, I wrap my arms tighter around her waist, my own tears falling freely and dripping down the back of her dress.

"For the first time in my life, I saw peaceful young men creating fists from their hands, their eyes burning with fury, and may the Lord forgive me, I was glad for it. I wanted us to fight back, but it was already too late."

Esther paused to take a deep breath and let it out in a long, shuddering sob. "The officer smiled cruelly before giving the elders a choice. Their lives, or an "offering" of his choice from each farm. The way he looked at the wives and daughters, and even at a few of our boys. . ."

I gasp. "No—"

"Yes," she chokes out. "The men shared a single look among them, and then to protect us, to save us, Elder Stoltzfus lifted his head and told the officer they did not fear death; that if it would save the rest of us, they were willing to die. Then with that same cruel smile on his face, the officer shot them."

Keira slides off the back of the horse behind me, stumbling as she hits the ground. Her face is so pale I worry she's going to faint. "Why? Why would he do that?"

"Because he's a monster," Esther replies with an anger I'd never before seen in her. "And then, even after taking those innocent men's lives, he ordered his men to burn each of our Elder's farms. He decreed that anything we hadn't yet managed to pick, as well as anything we'd planted for our personal use, was to be either confiscated or destroyed. The patrolmen wasted no time setting the fires, and the dryness of the land is working against us.

"At the last farm I stopped at before coming to you, I heard terrible reports that once set loose, the Ag men did so much more. They raided pantries, and whatever they didn't take, they destroyed. A few men tried to reason with them, and were beaten nearly to death for their efforts. Their farms were also set aflame. They want to make certain that this winter, we will all starve. They are right now collecting the animals that are ours and are slaughtering them, taking what they want for food and killing the rest just for spite."

"Oh, my God. Where's Gritty?" Keira cries as she looks frantically about.

"Don't worry, child, the Stotzfus family sent their youngest out to warn as many of us as they could. Each farm they warned then sent out their children to warn others. It's a plan we've practiced many times, but have never needed until now. I was able to save most of ours and Amos' animals, and those I could not, I set loose. Hopefully other families receive their warnings in time to do the same. I got your dog out just in time and tied him out by the shed in the woods where your weapons are stored. He will be safe there."

Keira stares up at Esther in relief, and nods slowly. Then Esther clears her throat, wipes her eyes a final time, and squares her shoulders. "Emma, you stay here and watch the fire, and should it turn and come for the house, ring the emergency bell next to the barn and people will come. Unfortunately, there's nothing we can do to stop the fields from burning, so we are focusing our efforts on saving homes and barns."

Keira helps me slide off the horse as Esther kisses Anya on both cheeks and hands her down to me. I nod to them as Keira clambers back onto the horse, and they ride off. I sit outside with Anya and watch the fire devour everything in its path while doing my best to keep us out of the billowing smoke. I feel so incredibly useless, wishing I can help more than just by babysitting a raging fire that, thankfully, is burning its way further from our home.

I hold Anya to me tightly, trying to protect her as much as possible from the smoke and the heat. She fights me until I let her face forward so she can see, her eyes huge and round as she takes in the dancing flames. Her little mouth springs open into a tiny O of surprise every time a branch breaks and hits the ground in a shower of sparks. Despite the fact that fires normally instill fear in most people, what's choking me more than even the thick, acrid smoke is that Anya isn't afraid. Instead, she is silent and thoughtful.

"You're going to be a formidable woman one day, Anya," I tell her, dropping my lips to the top of her head, smelling the scent of smoke that has no place in a baby's hair.

She looks back at me crossly, as if to say, *you're just realizing this now?* And despite the horrors of today, I can't help but smile at her look of indignation.

* * *

By the end of the week, the community loses sixteen people, nine houses, fourteen barns, and countless heads of cattle, horses and swine. Acres and acres of farm and woodland have burned, the smoke still laying like a thick blanket over the valley. It blots out the sun, making everything seem even more gray and lifeless than we already feel in our hearts.

I finally hear from Declan almost a week after the massacre, and even though I'm furious at him for making me worry, I'm so relieved to hear his voice I don't have it in me to reprimand him. He mentions something about back-to-back meetings, and then something else about a time difference. That almost makes me smile, knowing how much he despises Daylight Savings Time, and how he grouses about it messing with his internal clock every time the topic is raised.

The reception on the call is terrible, his voice cutting out so badly that I'm catching only every third or fourth word. Right before the call drops, he leaves me with the most cryptic statement, something about going online and watching the international news. I can't imagine why, knowing in my heart that it can't possibly be for any happy reason. I can't imagine anything I'd like to do less than make room in my heart for more sorrow.

My husband knows nothing about what has happened here, and with everything he's got on his plate, I can't think of a good reason to tell him. Unless he's found a way to turn back the clock, there's no reason for him to come home. What's done is done.

I've marveled at how this community has pulled together over the past week, and despite their heavy sorrow, have already begun to rebuild. Families from nearby communities who've already finished their harvests have poured in to help any way they can; the men focusing primarily on construction, and the women banding together to cook, sew, and clean. Every person who arrives brings vehicles filled with food, clothing, and bedding. Livestock trailers arrive filled with pigs, laying hens, and a few cows, with one lucky family even given a new bull. Horses are donated to families who rely on them, their kind eyes taking in our chaos calmly, as if to say that now they have arrived, everything will be okay.

Our household does everything we can to help, fully understanding that our losses are nothing compared to those of others. We wake early to tend to our animals, Sarah leaving me in charge of the farm and the children for the day as she heads out to the neighbors. I have no idea what she's doing, as she's often too exhausted to rehash her day when she returns. Keira helps our overworked doctor treat the large number of injuries rolling in, everything ranging from hammer-smashed fingers to nasty cuts. She's been away a great deal of the time, often spending the night at Esther's and returning very early the following morning to help me and Sarah before heading out again. As exhausted as she looks, she never complains.

I'm busy from the moment I wake to the moment I fall asleep. After a few days of being alone with the children, I find myself so desperate for adult interaction that I take the children over to the neighbors and offer my help in whatever ways I can. I catch a few startled glances when I appear at the door to one home, but then they school their faces back to their usual, welcoming passivity. Even if they have recognized me, I feel quite certain that they will protect my identity.

I miss Declan's next call, but the smile in his voice message gives me hope. My mood lifts just thinking that whatever he's been up to, he has most certainly been causing some "good trouble," as Brother Love is fond of saying.

Today is our day to go shopping, and with Amos and the boys helping the neighbors with carpentry work, and Sarah and Rachael once again off with Esther, that leaves Keira to drive the buggy. Samuel and Eli have been teaching her, and she seems to be pretty good at it, urging their bay harness horse, Gable, into a steady trot. A few times we are passed by trucks zipping past, but even when Keira tenses up, Gable doesn't spook.

Armed with the long list of supplies that we need, we head into the heart of town. It's more crowded than usual, the number of farm trucks and hitched horses out during the middle of the workday making us wonder what's going on.

No sooner have we disembarked from the buggy and Keira tied Gable, Esther comes flying out of the mercantile, grabs me by the upper arm, and drags me through the empty store. Keira follows closely behind, voicing my thoughts about how strange there are so many vehicles on the street and yet no people inside.

"Wait, child," she huffs as she leads us through a curtain, down a narrow hallway, and down a set of steep stairs where almost all of the adult community is gathered. Every one of them is watching an ancient television that's been wired to an international transponder similar to the one I have hidden at the Zook's. A few turn briefly to see who entered and then turn back to the screen, a low murmur of annoyance letting us know our tardiness is unacceptable.

With no seats left, Esther, Keira and I stand in the back. The few young men who politely stand to give me their seat I wave away, wanting to see the television clearly without a head in the way. What's happening that's so important that we are taking the time to watch it live? Not to mention, where the hell did they get the parts to put this hard to come by, and highly illegal, technology together?

The footage cuts back from the studio reporter to a shot of my father sitting smugly in his seat inside a vast auditorium. The reporter whispers in her curt British accent that, for those of us just joining the live broadcast, we are watching proceedings at the U.N. building in the Hague, as they debate allowing America to rejoin. So far, several leaders spoke in favor, leading up to my father taking the podium and delivering a speech that was apparently well received. I have no idea what he said, but whatever it was, he'd obviously lied through his veneered teeth. I'd spoken to a number of ambassadors over the past months as I begged them for aid, and although most are not willing to risk my father's ire, they aren't leaping at the chance to become his new best friend, either.

There's a delay as the stage is prepared for the next speaker, the reporter unsure who that might be. The last minute change to the day's program had not been mentioned to the press until now, the event organizers claiming "security reasons" for the lack of notification. In the meanwhile, the cameras cut back to my father, who shakes hands and accepts words of congratulations from other men in the audience.

It makes my stomach churn to see him with his hair perfectly gelled and styled, and wearing a suit expensive enough to feed our community, and probably a few others, through what forecasters are already expecting to be a long, hard winter.

As if he knows the eyes of the world are watching, he looks straight into the camera, places a hand over his heart and dips his head, the words 'thank you' mouthed clearly enough for all to know what he said. The humble gesture spurs a few huffs of incredulity from our packed room, and a few words in German that make a few others titter disapprovingly.

The camera stays on him as the reporter mentions that a special security contingency for the next speaker has taken the stage, speculations now swarming between her and a senior news correspondent who has joined her. Until now, I had completely forgotten Declan mentioning something about keeping up with the international news, and I can only imagine this must be what he was referring to.

With the security team in place, the British Prime Minister takes the podium to introduce the next speaker, a male figure standing in the wings just enough offstage to be indistinguishable. The damn reporter won't shut up and let us listen to him speak, instead excitedly telling us there's a change in the energy in the hall, not that we need her commentary to notice. The camera pans the crowd; most of them looking confused, their brows knit in contemplation, where a few lean forward over their tables, their fingertips hovering over slightly smirking lips.

The reporter finally lets us listen, the Prime Minister praising the next speaker, calling him a "paragon of strength and courage," a "man of conviction," "a man who has come to speak despite the great danger he faces." He states that this man "has faced the worst punishment the current American administration can dole out, and despite the great odds has become, alongside his wife, the face of a revolution."

No.

The applause rumbles like thunder as the speaker is introduced, and when he walks out from the shadows and onto the stage, most of the audience, now shown on a split screen, leaps to their feet.

NO.

The camera flips from the prime minister back to my still-seated father, his earlier smug look wiped from his face. It's clear he's been taken by surprise, his mouth hanging ever so slightly open. He catches himself quickly, clicking his jaw shut so tightly I'm sure he's chipped at least one molar.

When the man of the hour reaches the podium, he shakes the Prime Minister's hand. The two exchange words that bring a smile to both of their lips, an air of familiarity between them that doesn't make any sense.

At first, I wonder if maybe they found a really good look-alike, someone they could use to stand in for him, but unless he's blood-related, I can't imagine someone looking that much like my husband without it actually being him. Sure, there are some minor differences; this man's hair is expertly cut, his beard fastidiously trimmed, and the tailored, black uniform he wears shows off his lithe, toned body, to its greatest advantage. But his dark eyes, thick, curly hair and wide smile are exactly the same.

Just when I think it must be him, I realize how comfortable and polished this man is as he takes his place behind the podium and soberly nods at the crowd still standing and clapping uproariously. He waits patiently for them to finish, as poised as only the very best career politicians are in front of a crowd.

No, that can't be my husband. He doesn't know the first thing about public speaking. . .

I'm still trying to convince myself that isn't my husband standing on a stage where anyone in that room can take a shot at him, when he finally speaks, thanking the crowd for their warm welcome. His voice is the one I know and love, a unique mixture of low rumble and yet clearly spoken, impassioned words. I never thought of him as eloquent, but then again, this is the first time I've seen Declan speak before a crowd.

Transfixed, I stare at the television, too afraid to even blink lest this be a witch's spell. I want this moment to be real as much as I don't, listening carefully as my husband throws down a carefully-worded, verbal gauntlet. With every accusation he makes against my father, the price on his head rises exponentially.

A white screen behind my husband's head comes to life as he contradicts my father's earlier statements that America, under his leadership, has reformed its brutal ways. He lists the atrocities committed by the first two Supreme Archons, a brutal refresher course for those who might have forgotten. There are pictures of the devastation shown on the screen behind him, many of them so shocking the audience gasps.

But when Declan begins to list the atrocities specific to my father's rule, the audience reacts more forcefully. The pictures that support Declan's claims are gruesome in their detail, the audience gasping as each ever-more-graphic photo is shown. The destruction of the Georgetown ghetto is exhibited as a series of increasingly zoomed-in shots both before and after the bombing, with the rubble of the church where Declan and I had been married among the landmarks he notes. A charred crystal rosary, somehow still intact lying among the rubble and ash, catches the sun in the last photo, emitting a starkly contrasting rainbow of light.

Other photos of that deadly night are shown; the pile of bodies lying where they died clawing at the gate, their mouths open as they screamed and begged for someone to save them. Vultures stand mere feet from the corpses, staring blankly at whoever took these terrible pictures, their eyes as void as those of the dead who litter the ground. The final shot of Georgetown is of an adult corpse using their body to shield a child from the flames, the two burned so far beyond recognition I can only stare in horror.

The destruction of Philadelphia is shown in shots taken from the river, the shoreline riddled with dead, pollution-deformed fish. A decaying sign prohibiting swimming in the murky filth serves as an unnecessarily redundant warning.

There are pictures shown from inside the bunkers prior to the Cyanide attack, of smiling men and women with their arms wrapped around one another. I recognize a few of them, but not many, as they were all people who lived in other bunkers. Declan tells the audience that every one of these people are now dead, courtesy of my father's command.

There are pictures of other communities in the midwest and the west coast, the quality of the people's clothing and housing a step above squalor and not in direct proportion to what my father claims are "determined by how well the people follow the law." Declan has the statistics and pictures to prove my father's statements are lies, somehow getting his hands on classified military documents showing how the hardest hit areas are always the communities with the highest number of minorities. He makes it clear this is yet another attempt to rid our nation of what our first Supreme Archon liked to call "the Brown Menace."

Declan pauses for a moment before launching into his next segment. His voice shakes for the first time since he took the podium as pictures of emaciated children wearing filthy, tattered, gray and white striped uniforms fill the screen. Their ribs show through threadbare clothes and their feet are calloused and black with filth as they stand in a cramped, razor wire-topped, dirt lot.

The last picture is, by far, the worst. Well-fed and impeccably uniformed men guarding the fence taunt the children from the opposite side with bits of food. Three boys are reaching through the wires, trying desperately to grasp the items held just out of their reach. The boys' arms are slick with blood.

Declan explains the imprisoned children have committed no crimes, but were taken from their families as punishment for their parents' "sins." Many of the children are the product of unlawful, mixed-race unions, taken from their families and sent to work camps where almost none live to reach the age of majority. Others may have been guilty of petty thefts of food or medicine, usually not for themselves, but for starving siblings or dying parents. Others were picked up off the streets of the ghettos for no reason whatsoever.

These children are given no opportunities for education and barely enough food to survive. A stolen report from the desk of the Secretary of Agriculture and addressed directly to Bellamy, claimed that "recent losses in profitability at several workhouses was a direct result of increased incidence of morbidity and mortality directly related to malnutrition and poor sanitation." Declan pauses for a moment to let that nauseating information sink in before adding that the officer who had written the report and advocated for reform was found a week later, face down in the Reflecting Pool.

The audience breaks their silence for the first time, the camera now spanning the room and focusing in on those who gasp, swear, or just look shocked beyond words. Many of the people surrounding me are sobbing, even normally unflappable Esther is teary-eyed as she holds onto Sarah, who is so beyond bereft, Amos leads her from the room. Keira has gone deathly white, one of the adults with a seat forcing her to sit when she begins to sway.

Declan takes a pause to let the General Assembly settle, I think realizing everyone needs a moment to process. He looks out across the room, then down at the podium, a self-deprecating chuckle leaving his lips when he looks up.

"I'd be lying if I said that, as a child, I dreamed of standing on this stage and addressing you. I will never be the sort of man who's comfortable in the uniform of a military leader, and most certainly not in the fine, tailored suit of a politician. I've not gone to college, nor have I served in the armed forces. I am little more than the mixed-race son of murdered immigrants who spent most of my formative years in a maximum security prison for crimes I did not commit.

"When I was twenty-one and finished serving my time, I had been so full of hate that I was willing to burn the world down if it meant I could get revenge. As I got older, and with the grace of God and an amazing community who took me in and loved me despite my many, many faults, I learned that I hadn't been put on this Earth to wreak havoc; I'm here to put an end to the suffering of gravely wronged people.

"You have no doubt heard the Supreme Regent call me a domestic terrorist and a dangerous traitor to his nation, and I'm sure that he believes there is truth in that claim. Yet he has never been more wrong. I never have, and never will be, beholden to *his* nation, as he, and the Archons who came before him, are usurpers.

"I was born a citizen of the United States of America, a Democratic Republic of the people, by the people, and for the people. I believe that all men and women deserve to be free to pursue life, liberty and happiness, just as the *Declaration of Independence* said. And just like our Founding Fathers did on July 4, 1776, I just declared the reasons why I, and those who feel as I do, wish to separate from a government who has shit all over our inalienable rights. And just as George the Third is called a "tyrant unfit to be the ruler of a free people," I assure you that the Supreme Regent, Edward James Bellamy, is far, far worse.

"Now, some of you may think that I will want to lead this nation should we prevail, and let me tell you, you couldn't be further from the truth. I have taken the position of Commander of the Patriotic Army with great reluctance, and if I could have found someone else to take my place, I would have begged them to take this duty from me. I am a simple man with very simple needs and wants, and at the very top of that list is my responsibility to my family.

"I initially declined becoming Commander because of them, but then, my wife made me realize I must do this *for* them. I want my children to not live in fear of ending up in a work camp because they are "tainted" with my Hispanic blood. I want my son and daughter to be free to follow their hearts and choose the paths in life that will make them happy. I want them to be free to love whomever their heart desires, no matter of ethnicity, gender, sexual orientation or social class. I want them to follow, or not, a religion of their choice. I want them to be able to vote for their leaders like we once did.

"It is for my children, their children, and all the children to come, that I have accepted the position of Commander of the Patriotic Army. It is because I am no longer willing to accept the things I cannot change that I'm going to change the things I cannot accept."

The slideshow ends with a black and white picture of what remains of the Lincoln Memorial—all that stands are the cracked and crumbling legs, the rest of the body blown apart and lying scattered around the feet. The figure's head lies sightless in the foreground, the background blurred, but clear enough to see where the word *resist* had been scrawled in red spray paint on the portion of the wall behind still standing with little more than a thought and a prayer.

The cameraman zooms in on my husband's face, accentuating the lines of concentration visible on his forehead, and the gleam of passion in his eyes. When the camera angle changes once again, it's a side view, clearly showing the large, poorly-healed X that had been burned into the skin on the back of his left hand not even a year ago. He grips the podium with his hands as he delivers his last comment, and now any thought in my mind that this poised, beautifully-spoken man is not my husband vanishes. The mark of the Black Card is one he will never shed, a cringe-inducing, death sentence we in our nation know to avoid like the plague. I doubt these well dressed men and women have any idea not only what it took for him to survive this long, but to have risen to the point he's addressing them. Hell, I don't even know how it's happened, and even though I'm terrified for him, for us, I'm so very glad that it has.

"Our once great nation needs your aid," Declan states firmly. "I ask you to not only denounce the administration of Edward James Bellamy, but to help those of us willing to give our lives in order to right the wrongs of the last few decades. As Prime Minister Winston Churchill once said, 'We shall not fail or falter; we shall not weaken or tire. Neither the sudden shock of battle, nor the long-drawn trials of vigilance and exertion wear us down. Give us the tools, and we will finish the job. It is evil things we're fighting against—brute force, bad faith, injustice, oppression and persecution—and against them, I am certain the right will prevail.'"

He pauses for a moment, taking time to look out over the audience, fixing his stare in that way only he has, that I'm sure has made every person in the room feel the depth of his sincerity. At one point a small smile graces his lips, one that's not congenial, but one that promises hellfire and damnation and threatens to topple a power so much greater than himself. It's the look I imagine David would have worn if he had mocked Goliath prior to battle, or if Moses had taken a moment to thumb his nose at the Pharoah. When the camera breaks to the audience, we are greeted to the sight of my father's ramrod-straight back as he hurriedly stands and climbs the stairs, retreating from the field of battle that, this time, is soundly won by the underdog.

21

Declan

Well, that was fun. . .

As much as I'd like to stick around and hobnob with the elite, I need to get the hell outta here before someone shoots me. It's all well and good that whoever designed my spiffy new uniform managed to fit a flak jacket under it, but that won't do shit if some fucker aims for my head.

The men surrounding me rush us back through the halls, shielding me with their heavily armored bodies. I feel significantly better when we get outside and they shove me back into the bullet-proof car that delivered me to the U.N. building. Without a weapon I feel naked, having had at least a shitty knife on me at all times since I got involved with Anna and John all those years ago. But based on what Olesya told me, it's a feeling I have no choice but to get used to. There are going to be a lot of events in the future when I'm not going to be able to carry anything more deadly than a pen, even if it's the kick-ass one Sasha made me that's got far more uses, and far deadlier ones, than signing my name.

My security detail splits into four groups as we head out into the same number of matching black cars. The soldiers who join me are armed to the teeth, each of them looking like they have done this job since the moment they were pushed out of the birth canal.

As our convoy speeds off, a steady chatter of voices checks in over coms. The nearly incessant back and forth of voices makes me feel surprisingly safe, a feeling I'm not remotely used to. I don't bother them as they do their jobs, instead, trusting them to watch over me as I lean my head back against the leather seat and use this moment to catch my breath.

I rake my hand across my jawline, startling at the feel of the shorter, coarser beard I have yet to get used to. Nothing in my life feels normal right now. Shit, nothing *is* normal right now. Even my body feels like it's no longer mine, clad in unfamiliar, tailored uniforms and shiny, leather dress shoes. I finally drew the line when Sasha tried to put a glob of gel in my hair so it wouldn't frizz up if it rained. After doing everything else they wanted, I felt I should at least be able to claim my messy curls as my own.

I had no choice but to learn quickly over the past weeks, and first and foremost, was figuring out how to negotiate with Olesya and her equally opinionated daughters. Each issue we tackled came with fierce opinions and pre-ordained gameplans, and although for most of them I would have come to the same conclusion, a few I was dead set against. We had a couple good arguments where I won a few, lost more, and even managed to negotiate a draw once, each time learning something new about the art of negotiation.

I've also met more people who are secretly on our side than I'd imagined. I was introduced to a few high ranking members of Bellamy's military, the men so disgusted with the orders they'd been given and the things they'd been forced to do that they practically ached to work with me. The ever-increasing power of the Purity Patrol has them gravely concerned, as the more money and weapons they're given, the greater the chance they might one day turn them on our ever-shrinking armed forces. There's been a great deal of talk about restructuring hierarchies of power, and along with it, a significant redistribution of assets within Bellamy's administration. Although there is a great deal about this I still don't fully understand, I know enough that increasing the size and power of the Purity Patrol is a large part of what Bellamy expects will allow him to stay in power until the Heir is old enough to ascend. But even then, he'll be the power behind the figurehead. I'm sure of it. He won't give up power until he's dead.

I rub my temples with my fingertips, trying to relieve the brain-tumor sized migraine all this behind-the-scenes shit is creating. Nothing is straightforward, every path circuitous enough to get even the greatest navigator lost. Sasha's number one piece of advice when I get lost in the loops of who's beholden to whom is to "follow the money, Declan. Always follow the money." Yet "money" isn't just cash and coin—it's who has food and who doesn't; who has clean drinking water and who's desperate for it. Resources are almost as scarce as cash, and medical care is becoming increasingly non-existent except for those with enough money to afford hospitals or black-market drugs.

As if this isn't enough to make my head spin, I have to figure in how China's going to handle having a resistance leader ready and able to keep fucking things up for them. They keep threatening Bellamy with annexation, beyond pissed we've welched on our debts for years. Yet no matter how badly we fuck up, they haven't yet pulled the trigger. According to Cass, after today they're absolutely going to wait and see what happens before they send over another delegation to potentially be blown up.

The more I learn, the more I think we're headed for yet another world war.

Although it's an incredibly naive way of thinking, especially after addressing the world stage with a speech modeled after the *Declaration of Independence*, I desperately want to have a diplomatic resolution and not a mishmash of spilled brains over a world-wide battlefield. Before I commit to that, I want to exhaust every other method of conflict resolution first.

I asked Olesya one night, as we sat doing shots of vodka in her office, if she thought there was any way possible for us to overturn Bellamy without killing a ton of people. For someone who normally speaks pretty quickly, she didn't say a word for nearly five minutes as she peered into the full shot glass before her like she was divining the future from it.

"Many people will die either with or without a war," she began. "I see no way around it except for one, and I'm not willing to go that route unless we must."

I tried my damndest to get her to elaborate but she refused, eventually getting snippy and going to bed. I can't imagine how awful that idea must be for her to not even want to mention it.

My phone vibrates in my pocket, breaking my train of thought. I fish it from my pocket to find the call's from a blocked number, which isn't unusual. I can only hope it's my wife. I've missed Emma so damn much over the past weeks, our few calls too short to even remotely satiate my daily requirement of her. I never expected to be gone this long, and every time I've closed my eyes to sleep, I've ached to hold her; every morning I've woken alone I've been disappointed to find myself without her. I told myself after we reunited in Philadelphia that I would never let us be separated ever again, but with the way things have progressed, we're spent more time apart than ever.

"Commander Byrne," I announce into the phone, the title beginning to trip more easily off my tongue.

"I finally got the number," Amy states matter-of-factly. "Are you ready to have me put the call through?"

I smile deviously. "Yeah, patch me through."

The phone rings four times before a furious voice demands to know what I want. He sounds more flustered than I imagined he would, and far angrier than I honestly want. Because what I desire most right now is for Edward James Bellamy to remember every word I have to say to him for a very, very long time.

22

Louise

The men assigned to the House Guard must think I'm either too stupid or too crazy to understand that if what they say has really and truly happened, we are all in very deep shit. They gossip among themselves, a few of them even pulling up video clips on their phones of the young Commander who took the stage and lambasted the ever-loving crap out of my husband. They seem particularly fond of rewatching the ending where Edward looks positively murderous before he storms out of the room.

Needless to say, the vote to allow our nation back into the U.N. was "indefinitely postponed." A formal inquiry was opened to check the validity of Commander Byrne's many accusations, of which state-sanctioned genocide is hardly the worst. Every single picture and document he shared was checked and double checked by the foreign press, and so far, every one of them has reported they are not only authentic, but that most of them can be sourced back to government servers. Unsurprisingly, the most damning reports could be traced back to his personal computer.

I feel a giddy, childish pleasure knowing Edward's probably beyond pissed to have been bested in front of every ambassador in attendance, but at the same time, I worry. I know how vicious an aggrieved Edward can be. He flew home within hours of Commander

Byrne's address, his latest in a string of press agents declaring a vague "personal emergency" as the reason for his hasty return.

I wonder if he'll use the baby as his excuse, but it's been a few days since he's been back, and almost a week since Caitlin's baby was born, and he has yet to even visit. Caitlin's furious that Edward hasn't been by to see his son, and I hate to tell her, but that's actually a good thing. All of Edward's plans were based on the assumption the baby would be healthy; the fact that he's not once again puts his regency in jeopardy.

Although the doctors have assured us the child is improving, he is hardly thriving. After two days on a ventilator, they did remove the tube, but his cries remain weak and desperate. There is still an IV placed in his teeny, tiny foot, an annoyance he barely even bothers to kick at except for the times the doctors and nurses specifically fiddle with it.

Edward must be worried what will happen if he presents the child to the nation and afterward, he dies. He won't be able to swap it out with another and have no one notice, especially now that the entire world is watching his every move.

Then, there's the entire Caitlin issue. Now that the baby's born, what happens now? Edward had been very clear to the doctors that he does not want the child to be breastfed, an order that, in my opinion, bodes poorly for the longevity of the young mother. Luckily for her, the child refuses to drink from a bottle, buying her at least a short reprieve.

If I were Caitlin, I'd be terrified, but with each passing day, she looks less and less concerned. There's a dazed look in her eyes when she looks at her son, one that, I must admit, frightens me terribly. She stares at him like she's plotting something, creating some plan that I should just tell her to forget, as it will not work. If there's one thing I know about Edward James Bellamy, it's that he's somehow developed a Teflon coating where nothing against him sticks, and all plans that might go even the slightest bit against him fail. As far as I know, it's been that way ever since the very first plot against him ended in absolute disaster.

The night of the benefit is one of those rare beautiful late spring evenings, where a lady in a ballgown can dance all evening and not break a sweat and yet not get chilled as she socializes while sipping champagne. The men don't fidget in their tuxedos and dress uniforms, not close to overheating under the layers of fine wool and crisp cotton as they will be just a few short weeks from now.

I check the wall clock for the thousandth time, wondering where Edward could be as he's over an hour late. My mother claims she sent the car for him, for whatever reason insisting I meet Edward at the ballroom and not arrive with him. With each passing second I grow more anxious, knowing Edward hates to be tardy. He will be furious by the time he arrives.

I remain as close to the entrance as I can without giving away that I'm anxiously waiting for my date. I fiddle with the pendant Edward gave me, rubbing the large diamond between my gloved fingers as if it will somehow summon him. My glove snags on a small rough spot in the setting, and I remind myself to take it to the jeweler on Monday to have it repaired.

The few young men who arrive alone, or with young ladies who aren't their girlfriends, chat with me politely, a few of them even asking me for a dance later in the evening. I politely decline them all. A few young men from Annapolis arrive a bit later, a crew of good looking boys I've never met. They leer at me rudely, like somehow they know what I look like without my gown. The tallest one elbows his buddy and gestures in my direction, the two of them smiling deviously as they whisper. I do my best to ignore them, but there's something about them that worries me.

Just as I'm beginning to panic, a black Town Car pulls up, the back door opening before the tires have fully stopped. Edward steps out, a scowl on his face and anger shining in his eyes. I don't dare ask him why he's late. Something tells me it's not his fault.

As the car pulls away, he checks that his uniform jacket is laying properly, and that the creases in his pants are straight. I've been with him long enough to know the extra pats to his pockets and a check to make certain that the hair under his hat is still gelled into submission are important rituals that center him. But tonight, they aren't working. He's so intent on getting inside, on making a good impression, he doesn't even notice me. I'd be lying if I say that doesn't hurt.

"Edward," I call out. He looks quickly around before spotting me, striding quickly to my side and giving me a perfunctory kiss on the cheek. He doesn't smile, nor does he say anything. I air kiss him as well, not wanting to risk leaving a lipstick imprint. The last time that happened, he'd been furious, accusing me of trying to sabotage his career. I ended up spending a lot of uncomfortable time on my knees making it up to him.

He gives me his arm and I loop my gloved hand through it, smiling up at him and telling him how handsome he looks. He nods distractedly, his eyes already skimming the crowd for people he wants me to introduce him to. He steers me over to a number of men in uniform, the fathers of friends I've known forever and with whom I quickly strike up an easy banter. I always know when Edward feels excluded as we talk of mutual acquaintances and events from the past, as he painfully tightens his grip on my arm. I'm glad I'm wearing long gloves to hide the bruises I'll inevitably have before the night ends.

When we sit down to dinner, I'm surprised that my mother has placed us at her table along with several of the unescorted cadets. Edward stiffens beside me, muttering "Fuck me," and rolling his eyes before saluting to the upperclassmen who look at him with revulsion. He reluctantly introduces them to me, and they all politely shake my hand. Well, all except for the tall one, a blonde brute named Bryce who takes a chapter from a Regency romance novel and kisses my hand. Edward stiffens, but says nothing.

Dinner is the typical, boring meal one expects at these events, but this one is made more painful by the company we keep. My mother entertains the charity director and her husband, with whom she's eager to make a favorable impression. She is an accomplished equestrienne who loves talking about her horses, so I can at least amuse myself by listening to her stories and occasionally chime in with one of my own. My father is in an animated discussion about antique cars with the two men seated next to him, the three of them discussing the ones they own and the ones they are eager to obtain. I smirk inwardly when my father calls over the event photographer and asks for a photo of the three of them. I'm certain he believes the men, who introduced themselves as "partners," are so in the business sense. I can only hope to be there to see his face when he finds out they are lovers.

The cadets next to me are bored out of their minds, resorting to filling their soda glasses with rum from a flask underneath the table to make the evening more bearable. The more they drink, the more Bryce flirts with me, and the more worried I get that he's going to provoke a fight. A few times I have to remove his hand from my thigh, but I do it as carefully as possible to make sure Edward doesn't see.

Edward acts strangely throughout the meal, the cadet next to him occasionally leaning over and whispering to him with a nasty smirk on his face. It's clear that Edward's doing his best to ignore him, but the pulse point at his temple is beginning to pound.

As dessert is served, the charity directors ascend the platform and take the podium, starting the program that will inevitably end with asking for donations. I'm embarrassed to admit that I have no idea what tonight's charity is, as I'm so used to attending these events they've all begun to blend together. I try to be polite and listen to the speeches, but the boy next to Edward is being increasingly rude, whispering louder than necessary, yet not loudly enough for me to understand what he's saying. Whatever it is has antagonized Edward to the point he's ready to explode, and having been on the receiving end of a few of those outbursts, I know things are going to get ugly very soon.

After the speakers end their spiel, my mother rises from the table, ready to take her place at the podium and perform her own song and dance. She's the picture of poise as she climbs the stairs, the grace she exudes an awe-inspiring sight for the parents with daughters vying for a spot in my mother's newest endeavor—deportment classes.

"Ladies and gentlemen, esteemed members of our military, and fellow followers of our Lord and Savior, Jesus Christ, I thank you for coming to tonight's benefit to support underprivileged young men and women who have joined our Armed Forces. . ."

I have no idea what's being said between the men next to me, but Edward hisses a particularly loud, "Shut up," to the boy next to him, who looks thrilled to finally be getting a reaction. I place my hand on Edward's knee, a subtle reminder that he needs to keep his temper in check, but in his fury, he swipes my arm away as if batting aside a fly.

I vaguely hear my mother droning on in the background, the predictable rise and fall of her voice almost soothing compared to the sharp consonants rising next to me. Every time I catch that other boy's eye he winks at me, something Edward failed to notice the first few times, but once he does, immediately ignites his suspicion of me.

"I'm out of here," Edward hisses. "I'm never going to forgive you for this."

And that's the moment everything goes wrong.

As he stands, I reach for him, imploring him to stay, but as I swing around, I knock over my glass of water which spills into his lap. Chunks of ice ping on the floor as he tries his best to swipe away the icy liquid before it soaks into the wool. He curses angrily as the boys laugh.

". . .We understand it's difficult for many of our underprivileged cadets to have a chance to go home and see their families during the year, and many can't even afford the expense to go home during holidays and summer break," my mother drones on. "With the intent to foster a program to allow those of limited means to see their families more often, we have a very special surprise for one of these deserving cadets this evening. Edward James Bellamy? Will you please join me?"

Wait—what?

Edward is still trying to staunch the water seeping into the crotch of his pants while everyone looks around for the lucky cadet. He looks up from the stain on his pants to the podium, his face turning a sickly shade as an elderly couple are shown their way to the podium. It's clear they're wearing their very best clothes by the way his father smooths down his cheap, rayon tie, and his mother checks to make sure her faded dress lays as best as it can over her lumpy frame. They look about eagerly with the sort of smiles I expect of mothers and fathers who desperately want to see a son they haven't set eyes on in years. And when his mother finally spots him in the crowd, she waves happily to him, pointing him out so his father can find him.

My mother calls for Edward again, and he scrubs harder at the stain that is only getting darker with each passing minute. He's sweating now, a drip running down the side of his face as he curses under his breath. Finally, Edward rises from his seat, the audience breaking into polite applause while the boys cackle with laughter. His face has gone from pale to scarlet in the span of a moment, but he pulls his shoulders back and strides up to the dias as proudly as any man can while looking like he just pissed his pants.

I'm so confused. These people can't be his parents. I'm waiting for Edward to state this is a mistake, that he's never seen these people before in his life, but then he stiffly envelops the woman in the ugly dress in his arms, and she breaks out into a loud sob. The man beside her thumps Edward on the shoulder, a huge smile on his face. At this moment, I don't believe either of them could look prouder.

Based on their reactions, there's no mistake. I try to come up with a reason for this moment of extreme cognitive dissonance, but aside from the simple fact Edward flat-out lied about coming from a wealthy family, what else could this mean?

When Edward is told to face the audience for pictures, the familial similarities are clear. He's unmistakably a blend of these two people, having won the genetic lottery to get all their best parts. He has his father's height and his mother's handsome features, including her thick black hair. What is undeniable is there is some sort of ethnicity involved in the darkness of his father's considerably darker skin tone, and most likely the reason Edward does his best to stay out of the sun as much as possible.

As I study their faces, the applause stops and now an uncomfortable silence descends upon the ballroom. Here and there, a few giggles erupt, and with each passing second, the titters grow louder. It isn't until I stop staring at his parents that I see the reason for the laughter is the growing wet patch on Edward's pants that his uniform jacket can no longer hide.

The look on his face as he's forced to endure my mother's obnoxiously long speech is a cross between murderous and misery. Edward's mother's proud tears punctuate my mother's smooth presentation with a few loud, snot-filled sniffs. More than one snooty woman comments loudly that she should show some class, while another society-wannabe claims the sound is making her ill. I give both of them scathing looks to shut the hell up, but they don't. It's clear they know he's with me, and because of it, any respect for me has also been lost.

I'm so shocked and angry that people who once told me how lucky I was to find a man like Edward are now disgusted by him that I want to go over there and slap them silly. It's not his fault he's poor. Sure, he shouldn't have lied about it, but considering how they are acting now, he probably felt like he had no choice. They never would have let him through the front door if he hadn't pretended to be someone he's not.

Just as I'm about ready to knock some heads together, my mother's speech ends and everyone rises to applaud her. I lose sight of Edward and his family, only catching them as they are escorted off the platform.

My mother catches Edward's arm in her tight grasp and drags him over to introduce to someone he looks like he'd rather die than meet as his parents are quickly escorted out one of the side doors by a security guard.

I try to intercept Edward before my mother can embarrass him further, but the room is packed, and it's hard for me to squeeze through the throng.

"So touching, isn't it, to see a young man so happy to see his parents? I dare say my darling Louisa May would never be so happy to ever see me as to lose hold of her bladder. . ."

Oh no. Dear God, please, tell me she didn't just say that.

There's a strange whooshing in my ears, the room both deafeningly loud and terribly silent as the blood drains from Edward's face. He turns to face my mother, giving her the most hate-filled glare I have ever seen. As if feeling his gaze burn her flesh, she turns to him, the two of them locking eyes the way I'd only seen once before in Barcelona between a matador and a bloody, spear-pierced bull. The poor animal had been taunted and brutalized, and with every sickening stab, the crowds had cheered. Yet the bull was determined to survive, and that meant destroying the man who threatened him for nothing more than sport.

I had thought what happened on the stage was the cruelest my mother had ever been, but boy, was I wrong. What she's doing now is so much worse. She never intended to use this night to welcome Edward as my boyfriend. She always intended it to mortify Edward to such a degree that he would never show his face in our social circle ever again.

The second Edward can, he wrenches his arm from my mother's grasp and bee-lines for the exit. I race after him, trying to make it to the lobby before Edward can leave, but the boy next to me grabs my arm and pulls me back to my seat.

"Let go of me," I spit.

"Are you seriously going to run after that lying Spic? He's nothing but trash, and not even the good kind. You know, the white kind. He's

done nothing but lie since the day he got here, and I don't doubt that he's gonna get kicked out of the Academy now because of it. Serves him right, too."

I jerk my arm from his hold and run for the door. I don't skirt the perimeter of the room, but head straight for the exits, bumping my way through the narrow spaces between tables. I know people are staring and whispering, and I don't give a damn. I have to tell him that it doesn't matter to me that he lied—

If he lied to you about his upbringing, what else has he lied to you about?

I try to ignore the intrusive thought, but it just keeps getting louder as it points out more and more things I now know aren't true. But I don't care that he lied. I even understand why he would. I need to tell him that I love him, and I'll always stand proudly by his side. . .

I burst through the double doors to see a commotion in the lobby, with Edward seething, his father hissing angrily under his breath and pointing an accusing finger at his son. His mother is crying, but her tears are no longer ones of happiness. There are three security guards trying to unobtrusively get them out the front door, and in my haste to put an end to things, I push my way between them just in time to catch the sharp shove meant for Edward right between my breasts. I fall in a heap of silk and tulle to the marble floor.

The security guard rushes to help me up as Edward storms towards the exit, his father keeping pace as he stage-whispers in furious Spanish. I assume by his tone that what he says are curses, but I don't have a clue what he's saying.

"Edward, please. What's going on?" I call over to him, trying to get his attention. When I walk up behind him and place my hand on his shoulder, he shrugs me off. "Please," I beg. "Talk to me."

There's a subtle shake in his shoulders, his hands clenching and unclenching so tightly his knuckles have turned a mottled shade of furious red and frigid white. When he turns his eyes are red rimmed and *his face is so, so pale. His lips are drawn so tight across his teeth it's as if they aren't there at all.*

"I have nothing to say to you."

"Edward—"

"Louise, I swear to God, if you don't get out of my sight right now, you are going to regret it like you've never regretted anything in your entire fucking life."

I step back, stunned. His mother gasps, equally shocked, but Edward's words are the last straw for his father. He slaps his son across the face as hard as he can. "We did not raise you to be an animal," he spits. "What is wrong with you?"

"I told you to never come here! Never! What part of that didn't you understand? You have ruined everything I've worked for. Everything!"

A taxi pulls up outside, the security guards breathing a sigh of relief as Edward storms towards the revolving glass door. I chase after him, begging him to listen, to understand that I had no part in tonight's plot to humiliate him.

But no sooner than I make it through the door, I'm grabbed by the brute that sat next to me at dinner. He pulls me into his body, wraps his arms around me and crushes his mouth to mine in a painful, brutal kiss. I try to pull away, but he's too strong. I finally manage to turn around to face away from my captor and call out again, but Edward won't even look at me.

"Please, Edward, let me explain—"

"Yeah, Louise, let's hear this great explanation," Bryce taunts. "Do you really think he's going to want to be with you after he hears what your part was in tonight's events?"

I stare at him in horror, but before I can say anything, he continues.

"I gotta admit," Bryce laughs, "I always thought you were a nice girl, but damn, you're one cold-hearted bitch. Not only did you dupe him into thinking you loved him, you set up this whole night to get back at him for lying to you about being rich. Not only have you proved him to be a liar,

but the way you went about it? Well, fuck. Color me impressed. Oh, and the water dump in his lap? That was fucking priceless."

The guys laugh like this is the funniest thing they've ever heard, and now I'm so upset I'm clawing at Bryce's arms to get free, but he still refuses to let me go. It's not until he places his hand over my mouth to keep me from screaming that I can inflict some real damage by biting him. Hard. He lets go with a hiss as he shakes out his stinging palm.

I race over to Edward. "What he said—it's not true—"

He raises his palm to me, motioning for me to not come closer, but it's the look on his face that stops me.

"Fuck you," he enunciates coldly. "I never want to see you ever again."

He spins on his heel and gets into the cab, not once looking back at me no matter how loudly I scream his name. As the cab pulls away I slam my palms against the window and beg him to let me explain. . .

But he refuses to even look at me, and the taxi doesn't stop. I stand in the portico and watch the tail lights drive off into the night as the boys congratulate one another on a prank well played. I reach to touch the diamond necklace around my neck and panic when I find it's gone.

"Looking for this?" Bryce asks as he dangles the pendant in front of me. As I reach for it he drops it to the floor where the large stone cracks audibly. But before I can retrieve it, he grinds it into dust with the heel of his shoe. I'm so stunned I'm afraid I'm going to faint.

"What? Don't tell me you thought it was real?" he laughs before realizing that the fake diamond isn't the only thing of mine that has broken tonight. "You'll thank us for this one day," he tells me more gently before allowing himself to get pulled away by his friends.

I bend down to retrieve the mangled chain and fragments of glass but only succeed in cutting my fingers before a member of the custodial staff races over to sweep up the mess. I stand slowly and peer around the empty lobby, searching for Edward's parents, but they too have vanished.

When the shock wears off and the tears come, I'm inconsolable. Not wanting anyone to see me break, I flee into the bathroom, locking myself into a stall where I remain for the rest of the night.

I'm sitting with Caitlin as she breastfeeds her still-nameless child, taking my turn to watch over them so the nurse can take a break. Unable to handle any more of Caitlin's inane, intrusive questions about my husband, I've resorted to reading out loud from my large tome of Shakespeare's tragedies to keep her quiet. The words roll smoothly from my tongue as I have most of it memorized, allowing me plenty of time to keep both eyes on mother and child.

With as much attention as Caitlin pays, I could probably break into a jaunty recitation of *Green Eggs and Ham* in the middle of Lady MacBeth's famous soliloquy and Caitlin wouldn't notice. Since I began reading, she's been staring off into space, a creepy smile playing at the corners of her mouth. Occasionally she looks down at the child and sweeps a perfectly manicured finger across his cheek. Although I'm unsure exactly why, the tender, motherly movement feels like a threat.

It's very warm in here, so we've propped open the door to Caitlin's room to get some fresh air. Just as I pause to pour myself a glass of water, we hear the quick opening and slamming of a few doors, and then a mad scramble of leather soles on marble floors. When I walked in here less than an hour ago, the guards had been sitting on their rear ends playing cards, so I assume the noise is them trying to hide the evidence. I really can't fault them for trying to alleviate their boredom. Rarely does anything exciting happen here. Their furious-sounding boss apparently doesn't feel the same, berating them with sharp words that sound much more frightening than if he just yelled. Then, the door is thrown open and Edward's personal Chief of Security storms in. He checks the room before shouting, "Clear," and then two more officers, both heavily armed, take their position at either side of the room.

The sharp staccato of a single set of footsteps forewarns that Edward's in a dangerous mood, the sort of humor where, in the past, not only jobs have been lost, but lives. The neonatologist rushes in from the adjoining room set up specifically for him and the baby, and based on the way his hair is disheveled and his scrubs rumpled, he'd been asleep. I can't blame him for napping, as the child is up all hours of day and night, and cries for much of it. The poor doctor looks exhausted and frightened, no doubt wishing he'd been given a few more days to bolster the child before his powerful father dropped in without warning.

Edward stalks over to the doctor and demands a report, his eyes fixated on Caitlin and the child. The doctor concisely explains that the umbilical cord had wrapped around the child's neck during delivery, and although the situation was remedied quickly, there is some concern that the child may "develop deficits." He says there is room to hope the child will suffer no ill effects, but the look on his face contradicts his words as he explains "we'll just have to wait and see."

Edward has never taken kindly to bad news or to waiting, so this statement does nothing to improve his mood. There's a wildness in his eyes, a feral glint that I've only seen a few other times, and it frightens me so badly I can barely breathe. He's so furious at everyone and everything that he does what he always does when unhappy — he lashes out. I'm probably the only one who doesn't gasp when he threatens to kill the doctor and his family if the child doesn't end up perfect.

I feel terrible for the poor man who remains silent, only bobbing his head once to show he understands. There's no point in reiterating that the problems during delivery weren't anyone's fault. Edward doesn't want the truth. He wants someone to blame.

"Give me the child," Edward demands of Caitlin. She has the baby over her shoulder, patting his tiny back with its protruding spine until he emits a faint burp. There is no reason for her to not comply, and yet she tests Edward's patience by making a show of caressing the child's back and whispering words to him we cannot hear. She gently scrapes a red, talon-like nail against the most vulnerable part of her child's head. Everything about her fills me with fear.

"Don't make me ask twice, Caitlin."

She looks up at him, her eyes glittering menacingly and her lip curling into a sneer. I know she thinks that now she's born him a child—a *son*—that she's somehow become the Queen of this God-forsaken castle. I think she's gone more than a bit mad since her incarceration, imagining herself as something other than what she is—just another one of Edward's broken, misfit toys.

I want to beg her to behave, not because I want to see her humiliated, but because I want her to be safe. I'm not sure she understands how perilous is the tightrope she walks upon, and how with each passing day, I grow more afraid for us all. As if she finally understands she's on thin ice, she hands the baby over to his father.

Edward takes him silently, studying the child wordlessly, his eyebrows knitting as his disappointment grows. The child stares back fiercely, his blue eyes scrutinizing his father's face every bit as hard as his father stares at him. I get the general impression that the son is every bit as disappointed in his father as his father is of him.

As if the baby reads my mind, he opens his mouth and spews the most rancid smelling breast milk all over his father's chest, the sheer volume seemingly more than the boy has probably drank since he was born. I vaguely remember a movie where something like this happened, except the child's head had spun in a full circle at the same time. The curdled-milk odor permeates the room, the mess dripping off Edward's clothes in steady rivulets that puddle on the floor.

We all stare in shock, even Edward stunned into immobility. It wouldn't surprise me that he never imagined this could happen, as he never learned from his other children how volatile an infant's tummy can be. He would have needed to have even a fleeting interest in them to have had the opportunity to learn.

The moment is broken when Caitlin bursts out in a loud guffaw, the sort of laughter that is impossible to stop, even when it becomes painfully obvious that it's dangerous to continue. With a sharp glare at Caitlin, Edward hands the child off to me despite Caitlin's outstretched arms, the threat to take the child from her permanently clear in his eyes. She tries to get herself under control, wiping the streams of tears from her eyes but wholly unable to remove the smirk from her lips.

Without a word, Edward grabs the towel the doctor hands him and mops at his suit while striding from the room. I breathe a little easier as his hand wraps around the doorknob, glad that he's leaving.

Then Caitlin calls out to him, calling him "sweetheart," and he stops as if frozen.

"Edward, darlin', I still need to give our boy a name, but I wanted to talk to you first. Baby, I want to name him after you."

You could have heard a pin drop in China, the room becomes that silent. When Edward turns, his face is a mask of fury. "That child will *not* be named after me," he seethes. "That sickly, pathetic mistake doesn't *deserve* to be named after me."

I gasp, his eyes swinging to take in my shocked face. "Let it be known, that from here on, that child is not mine, nor is he yours, Caitlin. He is the son of my daughter, Emma, and the former Supreme Archon. He is the Heir. My job, as Regent, is to ensure his survival until his twenty-first birthday when he will take the Throne under my guidance. His name will be Ryan Caine Gregory, and anyone forgetting this, or anyone saying otherwise, will be guilty of treason. Am I clear?"

We murmur our assent and avert our eyes, well, everyone except for Caitlin. She grins deviously, the wheels of her mind spinning as she contemplates what I can only assume will be her next, and probably final, colossal mistake.

"Whatever you say, baby," she drawls, her smile widening as she leans back into her pillows and fluffs out her hair as if she hasn't a care in the world. "Whatever you say."

23

Keira

"Why didn't you tell me who you are, you dumb fuck?"

I blow into the darkness of the springhouse as if propelled by a tornado, the only light the fading beam of my weak-batteried flashlight. I'm so furious, I can barely keep myself from giving the boy lying at my feet a good hard shake.

Micah is lying on his good side, his body turned away from me and a quilt pulled over his body and up to his neck. He sits up slowly and turns to face me, his hair a disheveled mess, his sleepy eyes straining to adjust to the light shining in his face. As he repositions he winces, momentarily closing his eyes against the pain. "What time is it?"

"It's time for me to kick your ass, that's what time it is," I grumble as I drop the heavy bag from my shoulder and let it thump to the floor. I flop down beside it, pulling out a few slices of thick bread slathered with butter and a wax paper-wrapped plate with leftovers from tonight's turkey dinner with everything already cut into bite-sized pieces. I hand it to him gruffly along with a fork, but he doesn't take it.

Sure, the gravy is in a congealed glop atop the turkey, and the mashed potatoes are cold, but I've brought him much worse looking food that he's gobbled up like a starved pig at a slop-filled trough. Something's wrong.

"Look, I'm pissed at you, but I swear I didn't poison your food. Come on, eat up. I went through hell to shoot that bird, cook it, and make sure I saved some for you. With everything that's happened you have to realize we're watching every bite at the house right now."

He looks guilty as he takes a forkful of potato and lifts it shakily to his lips, but when he tries to put it in his mouth, he gags. Micah drops the fork, turns his head to the side, and retches into his hand, but nothing comes up. When he's done dry-heaving I hand him a fresh water bottle, which he also refuses.

Scooting closer, I peer at him more closely while silently cursing myself for not remembering to charge the batteries in the dying flashlight. What I had at first taken for sleepiness is actually the off-focus stare of mild delirium, and the sweaty brow and flushed cheeks aren't signs of guilt or bashfulness, but of a raging fever. I place my hand to his forehead, the heat radiating from it hot enough to scorch.

"I'm okay," he slurs as he closes his eyes. "I'm just feeling sick to my stomach, is all." He's quaking under the blanket that he tries to tug closer around himself as a violent chill dislodges the fabric from his clammy grasp. It falls to the ground, the mere touch of the fabric falling against his bad arm causing him to cry out.

"What the fuck, Micah?" I hiss as I leap forward to get a better look at his grotesquely swollen arm. It's clear to even an untrained eye that the infection I'd managed to keep at bay for the past few weeks has, in the span of a day, grown life-threatening. Red streaks race angrily from the festering bullet wound towards his heart, and when I peek under the far-too-tight bandage, I catch the whiff of a scent I'd only smelled a few times before, but will never forget. Gangrene.

"When did this start? Why didn't you signal for me? Or better yet, why didn't you just come to the house? Your family wouldn't have turned you away!"

He slumps forward, his forehead thunking against my shoulder and becoming the only thing keeping him from face-planting to the ground. I raise my fingers to his neck and find his pulse racing. He needs help, and he needs it now.

I help him lie back, and he mumbles deliriously as I wrap him in quilts and blankets. He tries to pull loose, shaking his head from side to side, moaning the word *no* over and over. I'm not sure what he's objecting to, but I'm way past the point of caring about what he wants.

"Look, I have to get help or you're going to die. I can't let that happen. I just can't. . ."

My eyes fill with tears that I quickly wipe away. I don't have time for theatrics, and more importantly, neither does Micah. I reach for the flashlight that promptly dies in my hand, and the overcast night gives me no moonlight with which to help me navigate the uneven ground. I set off at a run, my footfalls beating to the voice in my head, the one telling me that I should have told someone about him the minute I found him and not tried to handle this on my own.

Stupid, stupid, stupid.

After the third time I fall and end up with something sharp slicing through my skinned palms, I am forced to slow down. I've twisted my ankle to the point that every step hurts like the devil, but I can't stop. I limp through the pain, occasionally crying out when an awkward step sends bolts of agony shooting up my leg. I sob and gasp, no longer careful to remain quiet or make sure to not leave a trail that could lead back to Micah. After tonight, Micah won't spend another minute in that spring house.

About halfway to the Zooks, I realize I can't go there. Right now, I need someone with a cool head, as there is no time to waste with emotions in the middle of a medical emergency. Although it's another mile to Esther's, I know the extra time it will take for me to get there will be worth it in the long run.

Sure, that's why you want to go there. . .

My conscience berates me for the lie, forcing me to admit I also don't wanna explain why I kept Micah's secret despite knowing I shouldn't. By the time I arrive I'm a complete mess, having spent the whole mile both cursing myself and trying to not pass out from the pain. Every muscle in my body aches, and any healing my poor body's managed after the beat down I got feels like it's been completely undone.

Surprisingly there are lights on in Esther's house despite the hour, so I don't feel bad for banging on her front door with a heavy fist. I call out her name so she doesn't shoot me by mistake, but even so, when she opens the door there's a shotgun in her arms. The second the door closes behind me she hands off the weapon to a young man wearing all-black military-grade clothes who I've never seen before. Even as he takes the shotgun from her, he keeps his handgun trained on me.

"Keira, child, calm yourself. What has happened? What is wrong?"

Deciding that I must be okay, the guy holsters his weapon and hurries to the kitchen. He returns with a glass of water, the look of questioning concern in his dark brown eyes matching mine. Something's going on here, and I have a very strange suspicion it's somehow related to what I'm about to confess.

Esther helps me to the kitchen table, my legs suddenly as shaky as those of a newborn lamb. She pulls out the long bench and helps me sit so I don't fall and crack my head open on the floor. I reach for the glass gratefully and take a quick sip that promptly goes down the wrong way. Esther pats me gently on the back as the guy heads back to the sink and dampens two dish towels he fishes from a drawer and brings them back to me. He moves easily about the kitchen, as if he's been here before. When he goes into her pantry and comes out seconds later with her first-aid kit, I know for sure that's the case.

He straddles the bench next to me, takes my bloody hand in his, and gently cleans my palm. "That one may need a few stitches," he mentions casually, his eyes never leaving his work. I start to splutter words that make little sense, the guy holding my hand squeezing my fingers gently and murmuring "shhh" just as Esther pats me on the shoulder and instructs me to breathe. She gets up and fumbles in a cabinet for a moment before returning, placing next to the glass of water with my large bloody handprint around it, a smaller glass of amber fluid that I'm instructed to suck down like a shot.

The whiskey burns and makes my eyes water, but it's not nearly as strong as the rotgut Brother Love makes. The fact that this stuff doesn't immediately make me worry I'm gonna go blind proves it's gotta be a better grade of booze. It does, however, calm me enough to make sense. Only then do I realize I'm still not right in the head, as I've spilled my guts without first demanding to know who the Boy Scout is.

Seems like today is just my day for making some serious fucking mistakes.

The man says something to Esther in a language I've never heard before, the words spoken so quickly I'm not sure if he spoke them as quickly in American if I would have understood any better. She looks over at him and nods, saying only, "We."

I look over at her in confusion. "We what?"

She shakes her head, saying something back to the man who has now moved on to clean my other palm. Esther heads upstairs for a few minutes and emerges with her hair back in a slick ponytail and dressed in a thin, long-sleeve black shirt and black leggings. She laces up her mid-calf boots quickly, taking the keys off the table and announcing she will drive.

"Stop! Somebody needs to tell me what's going on. Who are you?" I ask the man.

"I'm sorry, I've been very rude. My name is Isaac, and for the moment, all you need to know is that I'm here to help."

"Are you a doctor?"

He shakes his head and chuckles as he takes a few pads of gauze and tapes them around my still-bleeding palms.

"I'm something better than a doctor. I'm an Angel."

24

Declan

Since my address to the U.N., all I've done is fly from one country to another, meeting Presidents and Prime Ministers, Ambassadors, and military leaders. My days are filled with meetings that I handle well enough, but my nights are filled with private events where I'm forced to smile and schmooze, two areas where I fully admit, I suck.

Yet I've held my own, and so far, nobody's thrown me out on my ass, which I admit had been a major worry of mine. That's not to say I haven't made mistakes, but in the grand scheme of things, I don't think they were really that bad. Aside from accidentally addressing some English fancy-pants by the wrong title not once, but twice, and the time I dropped the f-bomb during a state dinner at some ritzy chateau in France, I've done pretty good.

Tonight's event is, thankfully, my last. I've been away from my family for far too long, and I'm not embarrassed to admit I'm suffering from a serious case of withdrawal. My bed is empty and cold without my wife to snuggle, and even when I do manage to sleep, I wake, still exhausted, in a bed that looks like I'd spent the night fighting for my life.

I should be kissing asses and shaking hands, but between the stress of this trip and lack of sleep, I'm too exhausted to care. To make things worse, I have a feeling that something is wrong at home.

Knowing that watching the clock won't make it move any faster, I try to mingle, seeking out the company of the few men I recognize who haven't been total twats, but it's not long before I find myself alone, staring out a window into the twilit city. My gut is telling me it's time to go, that I'm needed at home, and that fucker never lies. With each passing minute, the feeling gets stronger to the point I'm close to panicking. I bypass the hand shaking and pleasant goodbyes to people I'll probably never see again, and bolt for the door.

* * *

An hour later, I'm sitting in an airplane belonging to some Ukrainian billionaire, heading back to a Canadian airport close to the American border. I'm chasing the handful of Tums I chewed with a bottle of some sort of lovely Tequila, the unusual medicinal partners doing wonders to rectify my pissy mood.

I lean back in my seat and close my eyes, picturing Emma as she was before I left. I can't help but wonder what she looks like now, a month closer to her due date. Without having laid eyes on her for so long, I know I'll spot the changes in her body immediately, but what I really want is to feel them with every part of my body.

Fuck me, I wish this plane could fly faster.

I look down at the paper I've been absent-mindedly scribbling on, the list of potential names for our son still woefully short. So far, John and Andrew, both for my dearly departed surrogate father, are the only ones on the list. On the other side of the paper I've written the names that are a hard no, and that list is so long it overflows onto a cocktail napkin. I imagine anyone who spent six years in a maximum security prison would have the same problem.

What sucks is that I can't even rely on a good ol' family name. Like fuck either Emma or I want to name our boy after anyone from her side of the family, except maybe Adam. Although they're close, and the guy did save my life a few months ago, I don't think either of us are feeling the name. If we had, this decision would have been made months ago.

To choose a name from my family is almost worse. I don't mean because they were bad people, but because their names are damn near impossible to pronounce. My dad's full name was Tadhg Seamus Eoghan Byrne, and he fucking despised it. As a kid he was teased mercilessly, and as an adult, he grew sick of repeatedly correcting people. He'll come back from the grave and haunt my ass if I name my kid after him.

At this point, I've put off weighing in with a name for so long that if Emma's already picked one out, I have no right to complain. Well, unless she starts that shit again about making our boy a "Declan junior." I told her that even if I were to die before he's born, I'll come back and haunt her if she names him after me. She laughingly said that she would *absolutely* do that because it means I'll come back from the afterlife and be with her. Knowing her, she'll do it, too.

"Sir?" The flight attendant is standing next to me with a satellite phone in her outstretched hand. Shit, I must have been deep in thought to not notice until now. "I have an urgent call for you from a woman named Esther..."

I rip the phone from her hand and demand to know if my wife is alright.

"Whoa, slow down, my friend. Emma's fine, but we do have a medical emergency. Adam, Scott and Brother Love, will meet you at the airport. Although we hate to take the chance someone will notice activity over the no-fly zone, time is of the essence. I have someone willing to assist who has a medical background, but she's not comfortable doing the surgery solo."

"No problem," I tell her quickly. "Get Keira to do a full exam and have her call me with her thoughts when she's done. I trust her insights. Tell whoever's there if they have to start without me, the kid's actually an excellent assistant."

"I'm sorry, but we've already decided she can't scrub in for this one."

"Fuck—it's not her who needs surgery?"

"No," Esther says tightly. "But I suspect she has strong feelings for the person who does."

* * *

It takes a few more hours for us to reach the Canadian airport, where I meet up with Scott, Brother Love and Adam. Based on what I'm told, I'm probably doing a radical amputation of an arm gone gangrenous on a boy so sick he might not even be alive when we get there.

I sit in the back of the tiny plane with a flashlight and a few medical books Scott had been smart enough to bring. I've only done a few amputations in my short career, and none of them were remotely as complicated as this one. Even if I get the kid through the surgery, there's the infection to consider. I only hope, for both our sakes, that he either makes a miraculous recovery or dies on the operating table. I know that sounds awful, but my heart can't take a repeat of what happened to Anna.

When I'm so airsick from trying to read on the dipping and diving crop duster that I have to stop, Scott fills me in about everything I've missed. I feel particularly stabby after hearing what they all went through and I make it abundantly clear that I don't give a flying fuck what anyone thinks is "best," I *will* be told everything that happens from here on in a timely manner. *Everything.* They say nothing in response, the silence they should be filling with *yes, sirs* damn near deafening.

Then, of course, Scott tries to break the tension by bringing up the particularly forceful fart he had last week that nearly ended with him splattering his pants, and I'm torn between strangling him for being a smart ass, and hugging him for making me laugh. As I don't want to encourage any more inappropriate stories, and because I can't clock him because I'll need his help with this surgery, I settle for rolling my eyes.

This also proves to be the wrong way to handle him because he playfully punches me in the arm and laughs. "You've missed me something awful, haven't you, D-man?" He bats his eyes at me like a lovesick puppy and blows me a kiss. Dumb fuck can't take anything seriously.

It's mid-afternoon by the time we get to Esther's farm. Every muscle in my body's sore from flying like a piece of cargo and then being bounced around in the backseat of a rusted-out pickup truck. I'm going on thirty-six hours without sleep, and it's easily going to be a multi-hour surgery. Even then I won't be able to sleep until the kid wakes up, and only God knows how long that will take.

Christ help me.

There are a bunch of rusty trucks I don't recognize parked out back along with a few horses hooked up to buggies I don't recognize. Before Adam even shifts the truck into park, a woman races out the front door and heads full tilt for us. As much as I wish the first woman I see to be Emma, whoever's coming is far too lanky, and running way too fast, to be my pregnant wife.

When she gets to the car, she misjudges the distance and slams hands-first into my window. Keira looks absolutely exhausted, with deep, dark circles under her eyes, and her hair a rat's nest of tangles that sorely needs brushing. But then I see it's more than lack of sleep and worry making her look rough.

I get out of the car and take her chin in my hand and force her to stay still as I catalog the lip that had been recently stitched and the faded green and yellow bruises mottling her face and neck. Before I can ask her how she's doing, she breaks my hold.

"I'll fill you in later, but right now, we need you inside."

There's a level of panic in her eyes that almost always precedes tears or screaming and it makes my blood run cold; it's the same look I saw on Amy's face right before she asked me to euthanize her wife.

Just like that, I'm back in the small, airless room in the bunker, saying my goodbyes to Anna while Amy sobs uncontrollably. The syringes filled with lethal drugs are lined up in my lap, and even though I know it's too late, I beg God one last time to grant us a miracle. . .

Get your shit together, man. You can't afford to be flashing back when you've got a scalpel in your hand.

I snap out of the memory to find Keira's taken my hand in hers and is forcibly dragging me into the house. Inside, a number of people pray quietly, their reverent murmurs no louder than the purr of a kitten.

"Where's the patient?"

"He's in the bathtub. We're trying to get the fever down."

Wow. If this isn't turning into a fucking Greek Tragedy. . .

I take the stairs two at a time, the door to the bathroom congested with people waiting to do, well, I have no idea *what* they think they're going to do. They startle when they see me, but after a moment's gawking, they get out of my way. Inside, Sarah sits next to the tub with a washcloth in her hand, repeatedly dipping it into the water and wiping the unconscious boy's face.

"Sarah, I need you to move so I can look at the patient. . ."

She looks up at me, her eyes filled with confusion. I can't imagine the haircut and beard trim really makes me look that different, but when I catch a glimpse of myself in the mirror, I'm astounded at how much I've changed. In my spiffy new uniform, I fit in right now about as well as an alligator in Westminster Abbey.

"Micah," she whispers as she turns back to face the boy. "His name is Micah."

We don't have time for whatever this is right now, but I can tell that, like Keira, she's also about five seconds from completely losing it. It's painfully obvious that there's a lot more to this story I'm missing, but I also know this is not the time to ask.

I humor Sarah with a gentle smile and repeat his name. Micah. Knowing his name makes this surgery more personal, more real. Knowing that somewhere this kid probably has parents or siblings who love him and have no idea where he is guts me.

I kick everyone out of the bathroom except for Sarah, sending Keira downstairs with instructions for her and Scott to prep the kitchen table for surgery. Amos has already been sent out to procure as many bright lights as possible, and the only other doctor we can find, a local *veterinarian,* is on his way with an anesthesia machine.

Jesus Christ. Do they really want me to perform a surgery I've never done before on a septic kid with a veterinarian as an assistant?

Yeah, apparently that's *exactly* what they want me to do.

They had dunked the kid in the tub, clothing and all, Sarah saying they had no choice when he began to seize. Her voice is eerily calm when she explains that Keira had been the one to tell her to not use cold water, as the shock of it could kill him. Keira told her that was something I'd taught her back when we were in Philly, and Sarah whispers that she'll be forever grateful for us both.

Yeah, let's see how grateful she is if the kid dies...

I do my best to not let that thought show on my face, turning quickly back to the boy and beginning my exam. Every vital sign I take is more unstable than the one before, his pulse thready, his heart rate high, and his blood pressure frighteningly low. Keira brings up my bag and hands me a stethoscope, and when I hear his lungs are wet, I just want to cry. It's one thing to take an arm off someone who's otherwise mostly healthy, but this kid's so sick the only thing keeping him alive is the battle between his co-infections.

During the next half hour, we get the kid out of the tub, dry him off, dress him in a pair of clean, loose pajama pants, and arrange him on the scrubbed and draped kitchen table. I change into a pair of scrubs Scott brought for me, and start the lengthy process of scrubbing the shit out of my hands and arms at the freshly disinfected kitchen sink.

Amos shows up about the same time as the vet, who surprises me not just by being a woman, but by having a whole lot of tattoos on her arms and more facial piercings than I've seen on anyone in a long while. She's got long, dark brown hair that she fusses with incessantly until she finally gives up and gives it a good hard yank, revealing it's a wig. Underneath she has super short, spiky, red hair.

As if Scott's freak-o-meter summons him, he comes down from upstairs with a handful of clean towels, sheets and blankets, stopping mid-step on the stairs to gawk at the unconventionally pretty vet. He tries to cover up his gaffe after he clicks his mouth shut and continues down the stairs, but it's too late, and he knows it.

Scott and Amos help her set up her machinery as well as three stands of extremely bright lights. When her equipment's ready, she talks to Scott about gas and oxygen flow rates and that she thinks Propofol is probably the safest induction drug for someone so sick. He listens carefully to what she says, answering her thoughtfully and without his trademark silliness, and in no time, the two of them come up with an anesthesia protocol that, in theory, should be safe.

I can't tell if Scott's trying to impress her with his knowledge or simply has his game face on and isn't capable of slinging quips at the moment, but his oddly normal behavior's enough to make us all stare. Apparently he's made some sort of impression on the doctor, too, as I catch her stealing appreciative glances at the big doofus. Her cheeks pink adorably when she catches him doing it right back, and it makes me smile. It wasn't that long ago Emma and I had been just like them. . .

I finally get the vet's name, which is Rowan Zatara, but prefers to be called Dr. Z. I'd bet my left nut that's not the name on her birth certificate, but hey, whatever floats her boat. She snaps a few digital x-rays of Micah's arm with her portable machine, and Scott removes the disgusting bandage so we can get a good look at what we're dealing with. The smell is so foul that he runs outside to puke, the rest of us standing far enough back to be spared the worst of the initial blast of the God-awful stench. From somewhere in the depths of one of her bags, the vet pulls out a container of thick, stinky paste to dab under our noses, but it doesn't really help. Now it just smells like mentholated road kill in here.

With the injury now visible, it's clear we must amputate. Between the raging infection, tissue necrosis, and a lack of pulse in his wrist, not even the best vascular surgeon could fix this.

The only question now is where to make the cut. If I want to be cautious, I'd remove everything all the way to the shoulder, which is what I'm leaning towards. But that will make fitting a prosthesis incredibly difficult, not to mention, making it a much more difficult surgery. When the vet points out if the kid dies from sepsis a prosthetic will be the least of his concerns, I realize she's right. My primary concern must be his survival.

Scott, Dr. Z, and I scrub our hands a final time before gowning and gloving up, allowing Keira in only long enough to help us tie our masks and gowns before kicking her out again. I'm shocked she doesn't fight me, simply nodding at me before walking over to Micah and giving him a quick peck on the lips. She whispers something in his ear before ducking her head and walking outside without another word.

There's obviously a whole hell of a lot going on here that I've not been made privy to, but I shelve the thought as Doc. Z injects something in the IV in Micah's good arm. After his body visibly relaxes, Scott gently tilts his head back and deftly places a tube down his throat using a laryngoscope that she attaches to the machine.

She fiddles with a dial on one of the machines, turning it up a bit, and then back down, based on what she's seeing on the monitors. The rhythmic hissing sound is oddly soothing, the scents of antiseptic, and even the menthol, helping me get into the proper headspace for operating.

Just as I'm contemplating my first cut, Dr. Z bows her head and prays aloud. "Brigid, Goddess of Healing, Mother of all things, and Mistress of the elements, hear our prayer. Bless us with your gift of eternal light, and may it guide us in this, our dark hour."

Scott looks over at me, and even with half his face obscured with a surgical mask, I can still see the look of *what the actual fuck?* on his face. I shrug. One of the things I'm fighting so hard for is freedom of religion, so who am I to say she can't pray to whoever the hell she wants?

"Brigid, Goddess of Physicians and Healers, fill us, your servants, with your light. Inspire us with your knowledge, enlighten us with your spirit, and envelop us in your shroud of life.

"Brigid, Warrior Goddess and our beloved Fiery Arrow, manifest yourself in our patient. May the heat of your flames incinerate the infection and obliterate his disease. Bestow upon our patient, Micah Zook, your Divine gift of life. I pray for you to bless and watch over him as a cow to her calf, or an ewe to her lamb. Bestow upon him the gift of acceptance of his past trauma, and the courage to accept the changes ahead. Bless us, Goddess, with your power, wisdom and grace. So may it be."

She looks up at us with raised eyebrows. I look at Scott, who returns my shrug. We both repeat, "So may it be," which makes our new friend smile behind her mask, the crinkles around her eyes giving her away. Then she tells us it's our turn, so I say a quick Hail Mary and Scott says an even faster Our Father, and she replies Amen after each.

"What?" she asks when we look surprised. "What can it hurt? Between the three of them, one of them has to hear us, right?"

Although I'm pretty sure it doesn't work like that, we need all the help we can get. Scott then hands me a scalpel, and the three of us get to work.

True to form, Scott can't keep his mouth shut for more than five minutes, pestering the vet with questions about everything and anything his ADHD brain lands on. It's pretty clear that, in his mind, this surgery is their first date, as a few times I have to interrupt his questioning to get him to hand me things I need. I swear on all that's holy, when he tells me to *wait a sec* just as he asks the doctor not just which of her tattoos is her favorite, but where on her body it's located, I'm ready to punch him in the throat. Luckily for him, Rowan picks up on how pissed I'm getting, and steers the topic back to the surgery.

I need both of their assistance tying off a surprising number of bleeders, and I'm treated to a glorious ten minutes of near-silence before Scott starts with the questions again. "I know Zook is a popular last name among the Mennonite and Amish, but is this kid any relation to Sarah and Amos? Isn't that their last name, too?"

There's a beat of silence when I imagine he's asking Dr. Z and not me, but when she doesn't speak, I look up. Her brown eyes look confused, and then that uncertainty turns to concern. Even though she's wearing a surgical mask, I can see she's sucking on her lip piercing as she determines what to say.

"Did nobody tell you?" she asks with no shortage of confusion. "Micah is Amos' and Sarah's son."

25

Keira

They all hate you, and they have every right to.

I sit outside on the grass among the people who love Micah the most, all of them praying for him while surgery continues far later into the night than any of us expected. The voice in my head has been yelling at me the entire time that I should be praying, proving once again what a fuck up I truly am, and although it may be particularly brutal, it also isn't wrong. Micah's life hangs in the balance—a life that wouldn't be knocking on death's door if I'd only done something sooner.

As pissed as I am at him for not telling me he's Sarah and Amos' kid, I also understand why he didn't. He didn't trust me. In his mind, he was keeping us safe, but in reality, his secret could have killed us all. It was his escape that triggered the Ag officers to search his home, expecting pretty much any child escaping from the sort of hell he'd been in to bee-line for the last place they'd felt love and comfort. Had he told me the truth, that he was from here, that I was currently sleeping in his goddamn childhood bedroom, we could have prepared for the officers' inevitable arrival. Emma, Anya and I could have stayed with Adam and Dex. With us not there, the Ag men wouldn't have given Sarah and Amos much trouble. I wouldn't have gotten the shit kicked out of me. The children wouldn't still be having nightmares after watching two men get murdered right in front of them.

His desire to keep us safe nearly killed us all, and now I'm out here, getting more and more pissed at him even though he's fighting for his life.

My God, I am such a piece of shit.

The *woulda, coulda, shouldas* run amok in my mind, each one ringing so true, each one so accusing, I'm close to tears. I like to think it's the code of being a member of the BSB that would have kept my lip buttoned if he'd only trusted me, yet I know that's not true. For the first time in my life, I had someone all to myself—someone who looked forward to seeing *me*, talking to *me*, and sharing their company with *me*. For the first time in my life, I was someone's first choice.

Girl, you were never his first choice. Your relationship stems from nothing more than a lack of options.

That single thought hurts worse than a kick in the gut. I've come to love the boy I found in the woods, a boy who may not survive to see the sun rise because I'd been that desperate to keep him to myself.

The lump in my throat grows to the point it's hard to swallow, my eyes drowning in tears. I have no right to cry, especially not in front of Micah's parents, so I hightail it out to the barn to be alone. Despite the dimness inside, it's easy to make out Marigold's hulking shape in the farthest stall. She nickers quietly, shifting on her dinner-plate sized feet to pop her head over the door.

"Hey there, pretty girl," I whisper brokenly as I open the latch on the door and slip inside. "At least you're still speaking to me."

I wrap my arms around her thick neck, tangling my fingers in her mane, and hug her tight. When she dips her large, fumbling lips between my shoulder blades and gives me a gentle rub, I lose it, breaking into harsh, wailing sobs.

I will never forgive myself if Micah dies. He's kind, and sweet, and just so unbelievably *good* that I'd actually given up ever finding someone like him in this shitty world. Although we've both been through hell, it's clear he didn't let what he'd been through break him. He never complained, and was so nauseatingly grateful for even the smallest things that it makes me cringe as I regret my endless displays of ingratitude over the years. I feel terrible for never once telling Brother Love a simple *thank you* for everything he's done. Although I never wanted to admit it, I would have died if he hadn't taken me in.

And how did I repay him? By being a miserable bitch.

Marigold sighs heavily, leaning her weight into me as she lowers her head and shifts to cock her left hind leg, preparing her body for sleep. I tangle my fingers in her mane and inhale deeply of her clean horsey scent, and for the first time in my life, I feel truly at home.

Of course you only realize how good you've got it now that they're gonna kick you out.

That sets off a fresh wave of tears, and I cling tighter to the sleepy mare. Her breath comes out in the evenly timed, contented puffs that can only be made by a critter without a care in the world.

"Child," comes the deep voice in the dark. "I'm glad I've finally found you. I've been searching for you for some time."

I turn to see Brother Love standing in the aisle, his hands stuffed deep in his pockets. It's too dark to see his face, so I'm suddenly terrified of what he's come to say.

"I know how that mind of yours works, child. I promise, I don't know anything more than you do. I'm just here to check on you."

I wipe the tears from my eyes and try to take a deep breath, but all I manage is to burst back into tears. Without a moment's hesitation, Brother Love opens the door and envelops me in one of his amazing, heartfelt hugs that makes me cry even harder, and yet soothes me, all at the same time.

"Go ahead and cry, child. You more than deserve to," he whispers as he rubs my back. Somehow, knowing it's okay only makes me cry harder.

When I finally manage to calm myself, Brother Love leads me from the stall, latches the door, and sits us both on a straw bale set outside. We lean up against the weathered, wood-sided barn, the old man reaching into a pocket and handing me a handkerchief that I use to mop my cheeks and blow my nose.

"I really fucked up this time, haven't I?"

He folds his hands over his stomach and looks up into the darkening sky and sighs. He says nothing, not even looking at me until I turn to stare at him. He glances at me and then looks back up at the sky. "It's a pretty sky tonight."

I look up at the stars starting to emerge. He's right. It is pretty. But I don't want to talk about the sky. "Do you think Amos and Sarah will forgive me?"

His forehead creases in confusion. "Forgive you for what?"

"For not saying something sooner."

He pauses for a bit before speaking. "Keira, let me ask you something. Did you make Micah labor like a slave in the workhouse for years?"

"No," I answer timidly, looking down at my hands and picking absently at a scab on my knuckle.

"Did you chase after him as he ran for his life after he managed to escape?"

I frown as a drop of blood wells where I'd loosened the piece of dead skin. "Of course not."

"Did you shoot him even though he was unarmed?"

Now I'm getting angry. I look up to find his eyes trained on my face. "You know damned well I didn't."

He shrugs noncommittally, looking back up at the sky. "Then what's there for them to forgive?"

I roll my eyes. "I should have told them, or Declan, or you, that I found a boy in the woods. I should have known I couldn't treat that injury, but I let my pride get in the way. I let myself think

CHAPTER TWENTY-FIVE

I was a better healer than I really am. If I'd just said something sooner—"

"If ifs and buts were candy and nuts we'd all have a Merry Fuckin' Christmas," he huffs with no shortage of exasperation.

"But—"

"But what, Keira?"

"I just think—"

"That right there is your damn problem," he tells me with a finger pointed at my head. "You're thinking with your brain and not with your heart." He stops and shakes his head, giving me a look of consternation. "I swear upon the Word of the Good Lord and Savior Jesus Christ that you've been hangin' with Declan for too damn long. You, my child, have picked up a helluva case of the *woulda, coulda, shouldas* that rivals his, and trust me, that ain't one of his more admirable qualities. It makes him do stupid shit."

When it's clear I don't understand, he continues. "I'm gonna ask you something now, and you answer me honestly. When Anna died, did you think that was Declan's fault?"

I answer immediately. "Of course not. He did everything he could to save her. Doctors can't always save everyone."

"Okay. You know that. I know that. Fuck, *everyone* knows that—except him. He's still flogging himself because she didn't pull through. Truth is, she waited too long to get help. That was *her* decision. Esther tells me you said that Micah begged you to keep his secret. If that's true, and knowing how we members of the BSB keep our oaths, how is any of this your fault? That you kept your word and tried to save him all by yourself is all anyone's gonna remember. What you did was brave and selfless, and if anyone says otherwise to you, you send them over to me and I'll set them thinkin' right."

He stands up, stretches a bit, his spine clunking audibly as he tries to stretch it out. He stops for a second, looking down at me with kind eyes. "'Be kind and compassionate to one another, forgiving each other, just as in Christ, God forgave you.' That's Ephesians 4:32. But I'm gonna take that verse one step further. I say, 'Be also kind and compassionate to *yourself*, as we often sentence ourselves far harsher for our actions than our Lord and Savior ever would.'"

I think for a minute, nodding dutifully because I know that's what he wants. But I need to think about this for a while longer before I can decide if I agree.

"Come on, child," Brother Love tells me, extending his hand to help me stand. "Let's get back to the house. Declan's gotta be about done. Let's go pray with the others while we wait."

Hand in hand, we walk slowly towards the house. "Hey, Brother?"

He looks over at me, barely pausing his stride. "Yes, child?"

"Thank you," I tell him with every ounce of sincerity in my heart. "Thank you for everything."

26

Declan

I have never been more thankful for anything than when the surgery is over and the kid is still alive.

Don't get me wrong—it's not like he didn't try to die on us. *Twice.* But between Scott, the vet, and me, we somehow brought him back. Micah currently lies intubated on the dining room table, his bony body still surrounded by equipment in case I have to resuscitate him again.

We already cleaned up the tarps on the floor and removed the bloody towels, Scott quietly loading it into the truck parked out back to take elsewhere to burn. As someone new to parenting, there are few things I can imagine being worse than seeing the aftermath of my child's bloody surgery, and the three of us are doing everything we can to spare Sarah and Amos that horror.

I can't say this surgery is remotely some of my best work, as there wasn't much to work with. The rapidly spreading infection and rampant necrosis required removing not just the limb, but also the entire shoulder joint. Now that he's survived the surgery, I'm back to stressing over how functional he'll be once the site heals.

When we finally let his parents in, Sarah hurries through the door with Amos on her heels, the traumatized woman bursting into tears the second she sees her son lying on the table. We've covered him with a thick blanket up to his chest, but not high enough to give his parents any hope that I saved the arm. The amputation site is covered with thick, sterile cotton and gauze that's already seeped through in a few spots with blood.

"Oh Micah," she whispers hoarsely as she lays a trembling hand on his cheek. Her tears drip onto his face as she leans forward and kisses him on the forehead. She wipes them away carefully, and then plops heavily on the chair Amos brings over.

She speaks to Micah in German, and I would feel guilty for eaves-dropping if I had the first clue what she's saying. I prepare to leave them alone for a few minutes after taking one last look at the drip rates on the IVs, but Sarah stops me.

I'm prepared for all sorts of questions, and am ready to explain whatever she needs, but all she does is thank me. I can tell it's tor-ture for her to tear her eyes away from her son for even the briefest moment, so the ten seconds she takes to look me in the eyes is probably the most heartfelt gratitude I've ever received.

Amos pulls up a chair I thought was for him, but he motions for me to sit. I do as he asks, watching Sarah as she gently strokes Micah's hair in silence. I wait for them to speak, knowing this has to be an incredibly difficult moment for them and not wanting to babble through it just because I'm uncomfortable.

I look down at my hands, so fucking grateful that I still have them both and can use them well enough to operate. If John hadn't done everything in his power to save my hand back when I was in prison, if he hadn't done everything in his power to save my soul after I got out, this kid would be dead right now. I wish he was still alive so I can thank him again.

I have no idea how long we sit in silence when Sarah clears her throat. "Declan, can you please tell Keira to come in? I know she would like to see Micah now that the surgery's finished."

I nod, getting up slowly as every muscle in my back protests. I take a few, lurching steps until things begin to release and I don't look like Quasimodo as I reach the door.

Dr. Z is filling in the small group sitting outside on how the surgery went, the only bit I catch clearly being, "Please keep Micah in your prayers, as he's not out of the woods yet." When I don't see Keira among the group I head towards the barn, knowing that's most likely where I'll find her. I find her walking slowly towards the house, arm-in-arm with Brother Love, the two deep in conversation.

I clear my throat so as to not startle them, both of them abandoning their conversation to look at me. Keira races over to me as only the young can, her gangly, coltish limbs getting the job done where I would have probably face-planted into the dirt. She fires off questions faster than I can answer, and I simply tell her it's okay to go see him. If I were her, that's really all I'd want to know.

She tears off towards the house, Brother Love emitting an amused chuckle. Sensing I'm about to walk away, Brother struggles to follow me on the uneven ground. I offer Brother a hand which he slaps away.

"I ain't that old," he mutters indignantly just as his knees let out a chorus of loud cracks. "I can still walk in the dark by myself."

"Whatever you say," I chuckle right after I catch him by the arm when he stumbles. "I'm tellin' you right now, if you bust something falling on your ass, I don't have it in me to do another surgery tonight. I'm exhausted."

"Then go get some shut-eye. You look about ten seconds from fallin' over, yourself."

I roll my eyes. "You know I never sleep until my patients wake up."

"Why? You think it's bad luck?"

"No," I admit. "Just cautious."

He nods as he ambles along next to me. "Girl just made her first unofficial confession to me," he admits as he looks up at the stars. "I won't tell you what she said, but fuck if she ain't holding on to an awful lot of guilt. Reminds me of someone else I know." He knocks against my arm with his elbow.

"This your way of telling me I better make sure this kid lives?"

"No," he responds, swinging his gaze back to me. "It's my way of sayin' that, at some point, you both need to stop flagellating yourselves over shit that ain't your fault. I already told her that she's done nothing wrong. She just *thinks* she has because, once upon a time, she lived when others didn't."

I nod, understanding now why he's telling me this. "Anything else I should know that doesn't break your unofficial confessor/confessee privilege?"

"A few things," he adds evenly. "First, you need to know why she didn't tell nobody about the boy. It's because he made her promise. Now, I get that promises don't mean shit in the real world, but for a member of the BSB, those of us who ain't got nothin' but their word, they mean a helluva lot. She said she begged him to let her tell some-body, but he said no."

"At what point did she find out who he was? Just FYI, it's not a great idea to surprise a surgeon with that sort of info while he's actively operating. I didn't know until Dr. Z filled me in. Talk about pressure."

"I'm not sure, but not long." He pauses for a bit before asking, "You think he's gonna be okay?"

I shrug. "I hope so. We'll just have to wait and see."

"Yeah," Brother Love sighs. "That leads me to the other thing you need to know. Our little girl's in love with that boy. As far as I know he's been too sick and is too religious to have done anything with her, but my Lord, she's smitten. You're gonna need to talk to her 'bout that, too."

"Cut me a break, Brother," I whine. "Can't you do some of this? I've got too much on my plate right now to add a birds and the bees chat."

He slaps me on the back fraternally as he chuckles. "It'll be good practice for when your kids come of age."

"My kids are never having sex. Especially Anya. She's gonna be a nun."

Brother Love roars out a laugh right as we get to the door. "You speak like you've never met that child. She's more likely to end up the bride of Lucifer than a bride of Christ. I ain't never met a more ill-tempered child," he jokes. I flip him off, which only makes him laugh harder.

As I enter the house, I'm happy to see that Micah is starting to show subtle signs of coming around. Keira looks hopeful as she asks if we can extubate him soon, and although I'm usually all for waking people up as soon as possible after surgery, I'm in no rush this time. He's going to be in agony when he's conscious, and we're woefully short on pain meds. The best thing for him right now is to remain heavily sedated so his body can rest.

I consult with Dr. Z, and we decide to keep him sedated and on the vent, giving his lungs a rest until the I.V. antibiotics kick in. His heart rate is steady, his breathing okay despite the fluid in his lungs. After the additional sedation kicks in and Micah settles, Dr Z and I come up with a game plan for the next few days before she packs up the few things we no longer need and heads out. She plans to spend tomorrow hunting down more pain meds, and I ask her to tell me what I owe her for everything so I can repay her. She shakes her head.

"Esther's got it covered," is all she says as she climbs into her truck, slamming the door behind her. When it's clear I don't understand, she sighs. "I suggest you ask her what's really going on around here, Commander Byrne. You're not the only one harboring secrets."

I don't know why, but I'm honestly surprised when she calls me Commander. After the engine turns over, it's impossible to say anything else over the noise of the big diesel engine. She drives off with a curt wave that I return, her headlights catching on Esther and a young man wearing all black walking towards me. If it weren't for Esther's relaxed demeanor and their matching black attire, I'd be worried. But when they get closer, and the light from the open kitchen door illuminates them, I can only stare in shock at the embroidered logo on their shirts.

"We need to talk," Esther says before I can ask.

Jesus Christ. Ain't that the understatement of the century.

What the fuck else have I missed around here?

27

Louise

I stand before the mirrors on a small stool as the seamstress fits the pale blue gown to my body. She based my gown off of a picture of an old painting of Jane Seymour, the third wife of Henry VIII, and the one historians believe he loved the most because she was the only one who gave him a son.

It's an ironic costume, one that no one will understand, or if they do, they won't be dumb enough to admit. For the party, Edward will be dressed as the tyrant King, and I, as his devoted Lady Jane, and we will eat, and drink, and pretend to be merry. Then the next day things will return to normal with both of us hating each other as vehemently as before.

People often think there's not a point past antipathy, but I am living proof that humans not only have an infinite capacity to love, but also to hate. Every time I think back to the night my adoration of Edward turned to abhorrence, I hate myself just that much more for not having seen the evil within him sooner.

It's been a little over two weeks since the night of the disastrous charity event, and Edward still refuses to speak to me. I'm past the point of being distraught, but still harboring hope that if he'll just give me a chance to explain, I can make him understand that everything that happened at the event had been my mother's doing, not mine.

I'm home alone, watching yet another sappy rom-com and crying my eyes out when a friend of mine calls to tell me she'd seen Edward out at a seedy bar not far from home. I feel like this is fate giving me one last chance to make things right, so I grab my keys and quickly drive over.

It isn't until I arrive and look into the rear-view mirror that I see what a mess I am. My eyes are red and puffy, my hair a frizzy disaster, and I don't have a speck of makeup on, but I refuse to let that stop me.

The place is dark, crowded and smoky, and it's nearly impossible to work my way through the crowd. I don't apologize when I cause a few people to slosh beer all over themselves and me, continuing to search for Edward with single-minded determination.

Then I spot him. Even with his back to me, I know it's him. Over the past months, I memorized every dip and swell of his muscles, and every inch of his toned, lithe form. When someone calls his name and he looks over, I see the face of the pretty brunette he's chatting up, my eyes meeting hers over his shoulder.

They look quite cozy, with her back against the wall, his palm supporting his body as he leans over her to speak directly into her ear. But then she laughs tersely, as if what he says isn't remotely funny, and she's trying to not cause a problem. On second glance, she looks like she's been backed into a corner and is now trapped. I continue to gawk, not understanding how any woman wouldn't want to be the focus of his attention. I must make her nervous, as the girl finally says something that makes Edward turn around.

The look he gives me is cold enough to burn. He takes a single stride towards me, grabbing me by the arm hard enough to make me cry out. No one hears me, the sound swallowed by the loud music and raucous crowd.

"What are you doing here?" he shouts.

"Please, Edward, I need to talk to you." Despite my desire to remain calm, my tears begin to fall. He curses under his breath, his face growing

angrier with every passing second. The girl takes the opportunity to move, quickly coming over to the other side of me and placing her hand gently on my arm.

"Edward, who is this? Why's she crying?"

"She's nobody," he says, his eyes boring into mine. "She's just some dumb kid with a crush. I barely know her."

My stomach bottoms out like I'm on a roller coaster. I feel like I'm going to pass out.

"Go home, Louisa May. I've got nothing to say to you."

Using my full name hurts more than if he were to curse at me. Then he turns his back to me, cups the girl's face in his hand and drops a kiss on her lips exactly how he used to do with me. Although I'd give anything for him to kiss me again, her body goes stiff.

It's clear he's trying to hurt me by kissing this girl who, ironically, is clearly not interested in him. I'm sure he thinks that kiss will make me so distraught that I'll leave, but it doesn't. Instead, it enrages me.

I grab him by the arm and spin him around, a look of surprise shining in his eyes. Before I even know what I'm doing, I slap him so hard across the face that he drops his beer, the glass shattering on the sticky tile floor. There are a few shouts, a couple guys pissed their pants are now wet, but before a fight can break out, a burly, tattooed bouncer throws Edward and me out of the back door. Edward's supremely pissed off but says nothing, wisely not arguing with an employee who looks like he can bench press a Cadillac.

We stand in the alleyway out by the smelly dumpsters and stare at each other angrily. "Well? You wanted to talk to me? Talk."

Now that I have my chance, the words refuse to come. I stutter and stammer, and when I try to calm myself, I only make things worse by repeating that I'm sorry even though I've done nothing to be sorry for. I just know that's what he wants to hear.

Edward rolls his eyes at me and shakes his head. "You are such a fucking child," he spits. "You spent the past two weeks blowing up my *phone wanting to talk, and all you can do now is stand here and snivel and tell me how sorry you are."*

"I swear, Edward, I had no idea what my mother planned," I plead, finally finding a tiny bit of backbone. "It's not fair that you're taking it out on me—"

"Taking what out of you?" he fumes. "Do you really think I'm dumb enough to believe you accidentally dumped water all over me a few seconds before your mother called me up to the stage to embarrass me?"

"How do you think I feel?" I implore. "I love you, and yet it's never enough for you. Don't you know that I'd do absolutely anything to be with you?" I step closer, closing the distance between us. "I love you," I repeat, sliding my hand up the center of his chest until it lands over his heart. "I love you," I whisper as I lean in to kiss him.

At first, he doesn't kiss me back, and when I step back to look in his eyes, they are glittering with malice. "After everything that happened, you honestly think you deserve my love?" His lip kicks up into a violent smirk. "Prove it."

"What?" My heart thumps faster, something about the look in his eyes scaring me more than I'd ever been in my life. He grabs my arm roughly and slams me against the wall, my head knocking painfully against the bricks. His teeth bite at my shoulder and neck, his hands groping me violently. Every touch is meant to elicit pain, not pleasure, every action a form of punishment. When I try to push him away, he takes my wrists over my head with one hand, the other circling my throat tightly.

"You're hurting me," I squeak.

When he smiles wider, I know I'm in trouble. We're the only two out here, and the music inside is so loud, no matter how loud I scream, no one will hear me. The heavy bass pounds through the wall so hard that I feel the beat in my spine.

His grip around my windpipe is tight enough to make me woozy. I fight against his hold as he laughs, seriously afraid that he's going to kill me. I can't get my hands free, my brain begging me to come up with a good idea before he kills me. Knowing I have just one chance to take him by surprise, I take a step forward towards him and stomp on his foot as hard as I can. Surprised, he loosens his grip just enough for me to get a cursory swipe to his junk with my knee. The second he bowls over with pain, I run like hell.

My car is parked out front, the bar almost smack-dab in the middle of a strip mall. I put my everything into hauling ass, especially when I hear him scream "You bitch!" and the sound of his shoes slapping the ground as he chases after me. I don't dare look back, knowing that in the movies, that's when the girl always trips, falls, and, inevitably, ends up dead.

I'm close to rounding the corner to the front of the building when he tackles me. Gravel abrades my cheek, palms and arms, the cool night air stinging against my raw skin. Edward lays on top of me, grabbing a fistfull of my hair and slamming my head into the ground. Everything goes black.

I have no idea how long it takes before someone finds me, but I wake up in the arms of the pretty brunette from the bar. Some guy's with her who isn't wearing a shirt, and he's shouting into a phone, but I can't make out what he's saying. My head throbs. When I try to soothe the ache by pressing my hand against the most painful spot, it comes back bloody. When I look for somewhere to rub the blood off I notice I'm wearing someone else's shirt.

I try to sit up, but the girl holds me down. "You're okay," she coos. "Cash is on the phone with 911 and an ambulance is on the way. You just stay calm, and everything will be okay."

Everything sounds like I'm under water, and when the big guy comes over and kneels down next to her, he whispers something so quietly that I don't catch it. But I clearly hear her words when she whispers back sadly, "Yeah. I'm pretty sure she's been raped."

I stare at her blankly. Does she mean me? No, I would remember *if I'd been raped, wouldn't I? I still can't really remember much after getting thrown out of the bar, or even that much from before it, if I'm being honest. I'm not even sure where I am.*

My lack of memory terrifies me. Why can't I remember? Somehow, I manage to push myself off the ground despite her and Cash's protestations, and when I stand, I nearly fall flat on my face as my jeans pool around my thighs. I pull up my pants, my crotch tender when the fabric rubs against it. My thong had been torn, the thin fabric currently riding around my waist. I hastily tuck it into my jeans.

I hear the wail of a siren in the distance, the noise breaking through my foggy brain. "Look, you have to go to the hospital," the guy says as he jumps in front of me. "You were unconscious when we found you. You could have a brain bleed, or at the very least, a concussion."

"I'm fine," I shudder, an icy chill running down my spine. "I just want to go home."

"You're not fine," he insists. "Look, I know you may not want to admit this, but I think that guy raped you while you were unconscious. If you go home and wash off the evidence, you'll have next to no luck pressing charges. You have to get this on record."

I stagger around the front of the shopping center, the bright lights causing me to squint. I turn away from them and catch my reflection in the window of a clothing store and startle, coming to an abrupt halt. I step closer and press my hand to my split lip and the dark purple bruise staining my cheek. As I investigate the torn skin on my hands and arms, tiny pieces of gravel fall to the ground. I am completely and thoroughly numb except for the sticky, wet place between my legs that aches.

Then I throw up all over the sidewalk.

Cash and the girl try to talk me out of leaving, their tone urgent as I continue to stumble towards my car. He gently places a hand around my arm, and I scream at him so fiercely that he quickly lets go. I should feel bad for shouting at him, but I don't. I don't want to be touched. I start to sob when I finally spot my car, continuing to lurch unevenly until I get inside and manage to get the key in the ignition.

I peel out of the parking lot at a dangerous speed, nearly running over the Good Samaritans in the process. I'm beginning to remember, and I don't want to remember.

I stomp on the gas pedal, and even when the lights are red, I don't slow down.

I don't care if I wreck.

I don't care if I die.

I'm beyond thankful the house is dark when I pull in the drive. I tear off my clothes and get into the shower without waiting for it to warm up, turning the temperature up to almost scalding. I scrub myself with a washcloth until the torn skin bleeds freely and the rest of my skin is red and almost as abraded. When the hot water runs out, I sit on the floor in the shower and cry until I have not a single tear left to shed.

As bad as that night was, I had no idea things would only get worse. Twelve weeks later, I would take a pregnancy test. As I was on my knees, praying to the God I was rapidly losing faith in for the test to be negative, a bright pink plus sign formed in the results window.

My life, as I knew it, was over.

28

Emma

Sarah and Amos have been gone an entire day since Esther swung by with the truck in the middle of the night, woke us all out of a sound sleep, and then the three of them ran out of here like their hair was on fire. Amos stopped just long enough to shout for me to please watch their children, and then, they were gone.

I couldn't get back to sleep after that, the thoughts of everything that might be wrong riling me into a state of near panic. All the shouting and slamming of doors had woken Anya, and at that point, any chance of sleeping was lost. I thought that last night the exhaustion I felt would have knocked me out, but once again, I slept horribly. I eventually gave up and began my day somewhere around three in the morning, getting breakfast together for the children, and putting on a kettle for tea. I honestly can't wait to have this baby so I can have coffee again.

The screen door opens with a creak, nearly scaring me to death. Esther comes in with a basket of eggs in one hand and a steaming silver travel mug of coffee in the other. She's wearing fitted, black tech gear and has a big-ass rifle strapped across her back, and the picture before me is so bizarre that I wonder if I'm actually still asleep and this is all a dream.

She starts cracking eggs one-handed into a bowl while chugging coffee out of the mug with the other. I'm getting oatmeal ready for the kids, so after she beats the eggs into a froth, she pours me a cup of tea and motions for me to sit while she takes over stirring the gluey mess and scrambling a pan full of eggs. She takes a long sip of her coffee, then takes a longer moment to savor it with closed eyes. She doesn't open them when she speaks. "Did you sleep okay last night?"

Not only does she look different, she sounds different. "No," I answer, but it comes out sounding more like a question.

She takes another big sip of her coffee and swallows appreciatively. "Normally I'd say for you to go back to sleep, but I need you at a meeting at ten. Just FYI, the cat's not just out of the bag, it's run for office, and has been elected Mayor."

When it's clear I don't understand, she finally replies. "Everyone knows who you and Declan are. It's now time you find out about us. I'll help you get the kids together and morning chores done and then I'll drive us over to my place to drop off the kids. Keira and Sarah can watch them while we're in town."

"You've really missed a lot, haven't you?"

She laughs as she looks down at her clothes. "Shit, I forgot to get changed. No worries, I'll grab something from the attic and then I'll fill you in. I don't want the kiddos getting confused and asking the wrong people questions as to why Auntie Esther is dressed like an American." She's barely reached the second stair before she calls over her shoulder, "Oh, and you need to bring some clothes for Declan. He can't go into town wearing his uniform."

"What?" I squeak. "He's here? Where?"

"Yeah, sorry for the late notice, but as soon as he got here, he went into surgery. Things are still pretty touch and go with his patient, so I told him I'd come get you so he can stay with Micah."

Now I'm really confused. "Who's Micah?"

She turns around and smirks. "You really have missed a lot, haven't you?"

* * *

It's almost eight a.m. before we get back to Esther's. My head is still spinning from everything Esther told me, and I have so many questions that I don't know where to begin. Micah is extubated but still lying unconscious on the dining room table. Sarah sits by his head, loving stroking her fingers through his hair while Keira's at his side, holding his hand.

It's silent inside the house, but not uncomfortably so. Not wanting to break the silence, I tiptoe over to Sarah and give her a hearty hug, and then do the same for Keira. Both of them hug me back tightly, their emotions so big that words can't begin to express them.

I hear the shower running upstairs, and after Sarah tells me Declan's in the bathroom, I decide to bring his clean clothes up to him. I ease my way up the creaky stairs just as the shower shuts off, and I'm so happy to see my husband after being gone for so long I can barely contain myself. I try the knob on the bathroom door and find it unlocked, so I slip in the tight confines of the room with his clean clothes tucked under my arm and wait to surprise him when he finally pulls the shower curtain back.

"You know," he says from behind the fabric," It would be a *much* better surprise if I open the curtain and find you're naked, too." He pulls back the fabric just enough to stick his head between it and the wall and waggle his eyebrows at me. I laugh. So much for my surprise.

He sees the clothes in my arms and scrunches his face in annoyance. "Aw, come on. You know you want to. . ." He opens the shower curtain and invites me in, but I shake my head.

"You know I would love nothing more than to get naked with you right now, but the rebellion waits for no man," I quip, then add, "Or woman."

He quirks an eyebrow at me and grins saucily. "What about for an orgasm?"

I return his request with a look of mock disdain.

"Alright, fine," he grumbles as he gets out of the tub and reaches for the towel I hand him. I get an eyeful of my beloved before he covers up, and he grouses that it isn't fair for me to ogle him if he can't do the same. I roll my eyes.

Before he does anything else, he takes my hand and pulls me into his body, wrapping his arms around me. He feels like he's put on muscle, his shoulders and back wider and harder. I graze my short nails lightly over his skin the way he likes, and he groans quietly as he drops gentle kisses on my neck.

Oh, holy hell. . . .

"You're not playing fair," I whisper just before he takes my mouth with his, kissing me with an entire month's worth of pent-up passion that leaves me breathless.

"My God, I've missed you," he whispers as he backs me up against the wall and cages me in with his arms. He drops his scarred hand to my belly and gives it a gentle rub. "I missed you too, little man."

He drops his head so his forehead meets mine. "I'm sorry—"

I place two fingers on his lips and shake my head. "No. There's nothing to be sorry about. You were working. Now, just shut up and kiss me, Commander Byrne."

His tired eyes light up, but he pauses. "First, tell me you are alright. Tell me you've been behaving yourself."

I smile as I lie to him. He nods slowly, fixing me with a hard glare that makes me squirm, and when he pulls me against him and smacks my ass with the flat of his palm hard enough to make me yip, I'm not surprised. I'm a shitty liar.

"Try again. I'd like the truth this time."

"It's been hard to rest with everything going on, but I listened to my body as much as I could. I did my best."

"Well, I guess that's better than nothing," he says as he leans in for another kiss. "But from here on, I really need you to be careful. I know we have this fucking meeting to go to, otherwise I'd give you a *very* thorough exam right now," he says huskily as he slips his hand down my belly and cups me between my legs over my skirt. "And you better believe checking out every inch of you is the first thing on my to-do list when we get home."

He takes my mouth with his, his hand sliding up my body, over my belly and up to my breast, which he squeezes gently before tearing himself away with a labored, "God, I missed you so fucking much."

"Me, too," I whisper back with a smile. He comes back in for another kiss, the towel dropping from around his waist, and wholly unable to help myself, I grab two handfuls of his firm ass and squeeze. He groans as he presses himself against me, his desire evident.

But before we get much further than him untying the apron from around my waist, we hear the screen door close and the unmistakable sound of feet pounding the floorboards as Esther shouts our names. I pull away reluctantly, pointing to the clean clothes I'd dropped on the floor. "You better get dressed before Esther drags us out of here. I have a feeling that you being naked won't deter her."

He huffs out an amused breath as he tugs on his pants, groaning as he tries to arrange himself in the least uncomfortable position. "She's always seemed rather tough compared to most Mennonite women. I have a strong suspicion we're gonna find out why at this meeting."

When we get downstairs, Declan takes a few minutes to check his patient and give instructions to Keira and Sarah, but then Sarah tells us she's coming with us. With a smile to the rather surprised-looking girl, Sarah says she believes Keira can handle things just fine on her own, and should there be a problem, Amos is in the barn and will know how to find us.

Esther drives us in her truck past town and out to a remote farmhouse where at least ten buggies and trucks are lined up outside a barn. As soon as we park, we are crowded by a number of ladies who rush out to hug Sarah and ask about Micah. Their show of love and support is astounding, with every woman having brought food or baked goods, and most of them offering to watch the little ones whenever needed. It sets her off crying again.

We eventually make it inside where seats have been arranged in a circle. Esther points to where she wants us to sit, with me next to Declan, and Sarah and herself on his other side. Lastly, a petite young woman takes the final empty seat, her red, spiky hair and copious tattoos and facial piercings, and floor-length, black dress making her stick out like a sore thumb. She leans forward to tell Declan she will have the drugs he needs by late afternoon.

In any other context I'd probably be concerned, but I'm fairly certain she's the vet who assisted during Micah's surgery that Esther told me about. Although she's not part of their community, she's obviously not a stranger, as the women greet her with shy smiles. She smiles back but blushes hotly, obviously uncomfortable being the focus of a group.

I'm surprised that she's as comfortable showing her true self among us, as her appearance alone could get her in a whole host of trouble if seen by the wrong person. Wasn't she worried she'd be seen driving over here? After all, it only takes one watcher to end a life. When she leans over to shove her large bag under her chair, I see the ends of a brown wig sticking out of her bag. I still can't imagine that's enough to keep her safe.

Esther rises, and the people around us fall silent. When she opens her mouth, long gone is the quaint speech and soft voice of the woman I thought I knew. "My friends, we always knew there would come a time when we would need to get our hands dirty. I'm here to tell you that time is now."

Almost all the ladies either bob their heads in agreement or murmur words of assent, and that's when it hits me. Except for Declan and the vet, almost every head is covered with a bonnet, save for the couple of unmarried women with their hair pulled back into tidy braids.

"What we've accomplished over the years has been no small task," Sarah chimes in. "Giving food to the starving, sheltering the black-carded, and clothing the threadbare as they flee those who chase them." She stops for a moment, looking around the room and meeting eyes with a few women before turning to me and Declan. "These acts of service fall within the realm of acceptability of our Faith and we were pleased to be of assistance.

"Our men have aided outside communities, especially ones in the most dire need, like Philadelphia. Food, clothing and medicine were just some of the many things we provided for quite some time, and we felt good about our contributions. Then a few years ago, something happened here that changed us. It's something we don't discuss, not just because it's a rule handed down by the Purity Police and Ag Officers, but because it brings back a time so painful we often cannot bring up the words."

Sarah takes a hard swallow, and when she tries to speak, she has to clear her throat a few times before she finds her voice. "A little over five years ago, we failed as a community to meet our summer yields. That year, we lost much of our crops to the cicadas, and what little we salvaged was then lost to a warehouse fire caused by a lightning strike.

"Of course, the Ag police were furious. They claimed we set the fire on purpose, and were determined to make us pay."

Sarah takes a deep shuddering breath but is unable to stop the tears that fall from her eyes. "They waited over a month, just long enough for us to think maybe this time they would see reason and not punish us. Maybe this time, they would show mercy.

"I remember it had been a beautiful Sunday morning, with big, puffy white clouds in an otherwise clear blue sky. I was sitting next to Amos, with my three eldest lined up next to me, and the twins, being only a year at the time, being held and entertained between them.

I'd been so happy, surrounded by my beautiful family and singing the hymns of my Faith, that the crash of the door being blown open and what felt like an army racing in scared me so badly that I screamed.

"The man in charge pushed his way to the front. He was furious that we weren't following the State faith. So for that crime, as well as for not meeting our yields, they punished us by taking away any child they considered capable of a day's labor.

"I held onto my sons with everything I had, but the officers tore them from my grasp." She looks up at Declan, her eyes so glassy and wet I doubt she can see how broken hearted he looks. "Micah, who you operated on yesterday, was twelve at the time, and Levi, was only nine. They went quietly with the officers despite being terribly, terribly afraid.

"My eldest, Ezra, was fourteen, and he was one of the few who dared to resist. As a result of his insolence they beat him badly, and when they threw him on the truck he was so still I feared him dead. A horrid part of me wondered if maybe that was a better outcome than what my other two would face inside a labor camp."

She breaks into wracking sobs. I rise from my chair and pull her into my arms. I hug her with every ounce of strength in my body, letting her cry out her pain. Declan turns to Esther, asking her something I don't catch.

"It would be nearly three years before they would find out what happened to the children," Esther continues, picking up the story. "Jonah, one of Ezekiel's and Elizabeth's boys, somehow found his way home, but he was so thin and sick they feared he would die. They didn't dare go to our local doctors, or even our local vet, as at the time, everyone was still so afraid. We knew some of our neighbors were watchers, trying to save themselves by reporting on others. No one knew who was safe to turn to, or who could be depended on in a crisis.

"Not knowing what else to do, Elizabeth took a chance and traveled to a nearby village rumored to aid those on the run. They were not Mennonite or Amish, but a community of bohemians, pagans, and other nonconformists. As an act of desperation, Elizabeth drove right into the middle of town and started banging on doors until one finally opened. She told them her plight, only to be told they had no doctor, but they did have Dr. Z."

A woman, whom I presume is Elizabeth, takes over the narrative. "The woman took me to this small, peeling, wood shack, and when the owner opened the door to greet us, I got on my knees and begged her for help. She told me to stand up, and I thought she was going to make me leave, but instead, she pulled me inside and locked the door. She motioned for me to follow her to a small kitchen where she poured me a glass of cold water, brought me a damp cloth to clean my dust-covered face and hands, and told me to sit.

"I told her everything despite not knowing her. When I was finished, she went into a back room, pulled out a large satchel filled with supplies, and went into a locked room in the back filled with boxes and bags that boggled my mind. She loaded her things in my truck and stayed with us for well over a week. She only left once to go back for more supplies, and one other time, to help another critical patient.

"When it was clear Jonah was on the mend, she made me swear to not tell another soul about her. She told me that it would not be safe for Jonah to stay, as eventually, the patrols would come looking for him. That was when she told me she could arrange transport for him to leave the country. It broke my heart the day the young lady knocked on our door, but I knew I had to give him a chance at a better life."

Esther sighed. "Jonah was my first mission as a runner for Angels of Mercy. I knew nothing about the Amish, the Mennonite, or the Pagan communities, never having met anyone of their beliefs before. During the long trip back to the Canadian border, Jonah taught me almost everything I now know. When I handed him off to my colleague in New York to handle the actual crossing, I promised to keep in touch. I'm pleased to say he's currently studying medicine, a calling he felt after a certain doctor saved his life."

I peek over Sarah's shoulder to find the doctor looking horribly uncomfortable. When a few women reach out to grasp her hand, to thank her for her work, she waves away their touch. It's clear she doesn't do this for the thanks.

"As time went on, more and more people came through this area," Elizabeth continues. "We rarely saw them, mostly only knowing anyone had been through based on the things that went missing or were lost for a time only to be found in the strangest of places. For a while, we blamed the thefts on raccoons, but tell me, what raccoon has ever stolen soap and then actually used it?"

The ladies titter and nod their agreement until Esther begins again. "When another young man made his way back not long after, he carried with him a letter. That was how we learned that Sarah's eldest, Ezra, had earned a position of authority in the workhouse that enabled him to occasionally sneak children out. He wrote us a list of the names of all the children from our community who he had liberated, and at that time, he was already into the double digits. But at that point, we'd seen only two make it here.

"That was when I knew I had to set up some sort of trail for the escapees to follow. I talked it over with those who ran the Angels, and they determined I should integrate myself as a part of the community here so I could oversee this critical work and root out those who cannot be trusted.

"While I worked on this, we sent someone inside the camp to meet with Ezra. They labored over the logistics of getting the children out of the camp, as well as how to mark the trail to make it easier to follow. Since then, we've managed to get nearly three hundred children over the border. All but fourteen have survived."

Declan emits a long, low whistle of appreciation that pulls me from Sarah's arms. I look at her carefully, silently asking if she's okay, and she nods as she wipes her eyes. I sit back down next to my husband and watch him as he thinks, but before he can say anything, a young man strides forward to stand before Declan.

"We haven't met yet, but I'm Isaac. I am also a runner. I've been meeting with Ezra as often as I can over the past year. I've delivered medicine, vitamins, and vaccinations that he distributes to those most in need. We've set up a way for him to get urgent messages to me, and one came through last night. There are plans for the entire camp to be 'liquidated and repurposed.' I do not know what that means for certain, but it cannot be good."

He hands a folded piece of paper to Declan, and he flips it open, reading the few lines before crushing it in his fist. His eyes harden. "How long do we have?"

The boy shrugs. "I'd say a week, at most. We're watching the situation closely, but we don't have an actual date."

He pauses for a moment, taking a deep breath before continuing. It's as if he's summoning the courage to tell us what's coming next. "I think that whatever they are doing at the camp has something to do with the fête for Bellamy's birthday. So far, both the Canadian and British Prime Ministers are expected to attend, as well as the French President and a few European ambassadors. Bellamy plans to show the world that what you've accused him of is false. But to do that, he has to get rid of the evidence."

Declan stands. "I want to make sure I understand what you're asking. Are you asking me to liberate a work camp with almost 3,000 children in it in less than seven days? Is that what you're asking?"

The women look between themselves. Isaac looks at me intensely, and nods curtly. "Yes, that is what must happen or they will all die."

Jesus Christ.

"Where did this intel come from? How do we know any of this is true? How do we know this isn't a trap?"

Isaac pales. "I cannot tell you."

"What do you mean you can't tell me?"

"It's a secret I cannot divulge."

"So you want me to put my life on the line, the lives of these people, and the lives of your people, all on a piece of information given to you by who? The Holy Fuckin' Ghost?" Declan looks about ready to explode.

The kid stands firm. "I may be many things, but I am not a liar. If I say the intelligence is good, then it is good."

"Bullshit," Declan spits, striding over to the boy and grabbing him by the shirt. "Tell me or this whole mission gets scrapped right here, right now. Tell me who else is involved?"

"It came from my father, okay?! The intelligence came from my father."

"Oh, that's great. Just great. And just who the fuck is your daddy that I should give two shits about what he has to say?"

"He's the Canadian Prime Minister, you fucking asshole!"

Oh, shit.

Declan's still got him by the shirt as all the blood drains from his face, and when he suddenly lets go, they both stumble.

"You should have just said that, son," Declan tells him as he offers to shake the younger man's hand.

"Do not call me son," he hisses before breaking into a smirk and joining their hands. When he pulls away, my husband ruffles Isaac's hair despite the fact the boy's a good four inches taller. Isaac scowls.

Esther comes forward with a set of maps and blueprints, the four of us coming up with the beginnings of a massive plan with more moving parts than Declan can possibly oversee alone. He's going to need help, and he knows it, turning to the ladies who have been talking quietly among themselves.

"Look, I get why you ladies have kept what you've done quiet, just as I don't doubt your husbands, fathers, and brothers have, at times, kept things they've done from you. But if I'm to break these children out of a heavily guarded camp and get them to safety, I'm going to need the help of your *entire* community. We're going to need a lot of people, and a lot of supplies, to make this happen. I can't guarantee our plans will work, and I don't expect every group will make it to freedom. There will be losses. Both adults and children could die. You need to know that up front."

No one says a word until Sarah stands up. "I'm sure Ezra felt the same way when he sent that first child out into the unknown. But we are people of Faith, and we do not fear death.

"You should know that we saw the speech you gave to the U.N. The picture of the three starved boys reaching for the food with their arms bloody and torn—they are my boys, Declan. Mine! After the shock of seeing them so thin, so sick, we women met again. We held a community meeting, and talked it over with our families. We are ready to help however you need. Tell us what to do, and we will do it. We want our children back."

29

Declan

No sooner than we get back to the farm, my phone starts blowing up. I'm beyond exhausted and absolutely starving, but before I eat, or sleep, or even take a piss, I check on my patient, first. Whoever's calling can wait.

There's a small group of men and women sitting on the blankets in the front yard, and a table is set up with all sorts of food that smells incredible. My stomach has been trying to digest itself for hours now, and as much as I want to dive in and eat everything I see, I've got work that must come first.

My phone rings again, so I set it to vibrate. I check to see who's calling, and I groan out loud when I see it's Olesya. I've already ignored the first ten or so calls from her, so a few more won't kill her. I head inside and get the most thorough patient update imaginable from Keira, all of it coming in a no-nonsense tone without even a hint of sass. Could it be that our little girl is growing up?

Micah's hanging in there, which is about all I can hope for. We decide to start weaning off the sedation a bit, changing things up just enough to start bringing him around. I think Keira's going to argue with me at one point, but then thinks better of it. She tells me that I know best, and writes down her new instructions without a word of dissent.

I totally see now that what Brother Love said is true. She is a whole different person when she's with Micah. She's watching over him like some cross between a dedicated hospital worker and a guardian angel with OCD, with a whole lot of Momma Bear energy thrown in for good measure. It's the jumble of emotions only possible when you've got hard-core feelings for someone.

I'm pretty sure this is the first time she's loosened the reins on her heart, and if Micah doesn't make it, I don't know what will happen. So far, the surgery site isn't bleeding excessively, and tomorrow, when we remove the bandage, I'll know more. His fever is still high but his vitals are steadier, but infection cases have a habit of shitting the bed within a matter of hours. I know better than to think he's out of the woods.

Although I tell myself to not compare his case to Anna's, I do. It's *all* I've done since I laid eyes on him. Flashes of the mess of necrotic skin, melted sequins, and lace that I removed from Anna's back pop into my brain, the images as clear as the day I operated on her. My gorge rises as I remember the stench not that different from what exuded from the boy. I break into a sweat, unable to pull myself out of the flashback as I continue to stare.

It takes Keira physically shaking me to get me out of my head, and when she asks if I'm alright, I nod and shake my head at the same time and beat feet out of the room. She kindly lets me go without comment.

When I head back outside, Emma's waiting for me on the porch swing. Just as I reach her side, my phone begins to buzz again. I try to take a deep breath and not curse too loudly, but all I manage is an anemic wheeze.

Em sees that I'm not alright and jumps up to guide me to the swing. My legs feel weak as I fall back into the seat, and without letting go, I pull Emma into my lap and wrap my arms around her. I bury my face into her neck, grounding myself in her lavender and honeysuckle scent and the weight and warmth of her body.

Realizing I'm having a panic attack, I shockingly remember to use the grounding techniques Brother Love taught me specifically for when this happens. I think of five things I see, four that I hear, three I can smell, two I can feel, and although not technically part of the technique, I end the exercise by sharing a passionate kiss with my beautiful wife. When I finally manage a deep breath, Emma's body melts into mine, bolstering my strength exponentially.

The phone starts up again, but now that I'm no longer agitated, I realize how very, very tired I am. Emma gives me a wry smile as she tells me I better call back whoever is turning my phone into a vibrator before they come find me. I roll my eyes, and she gives me a quick peck on the lips before standing. Knowing I need the incentive, she tells me she'll fix me up a plate of food and will have it ready for the moment the call's over. I tell her it's a deal.

I walk out towards the barn before I call Olesya back, having a gut feeling that things are about to get heated and not particularly craving an audience if I explode. She picks up immediately, and the first word out of her mouth, well, the first one that isn't some sort of caustic, Russian vulgarism, is "no" spat so forcefully it too sounds like a curse.

"Great hearing from you, too, Olesya," I quip. "Having a nice day? What's new with you? How's the weather wherever the fuck you are?"

Either she doesn't get my sarcasm or she's ignoring it, so either way, this conversation's destined to be a doozie. "You already have a mission next week. You cannot be in two places at the same time."

"I can do both," I retort. "As of right now, it doesn't look like everything's going down the same day. They are going to need to get the kids out before the night of the party."

"Of course it's happening the same day! How stupid can you possibly be to think otherwise?"

"Okay. Spell it out for me like I'm five, Olesya. Why does it have to be the same day?"

She sighs heavily, then proceeds to talk to me in the most demeaning tone imaginable. "Because luck is not on our side."

I roll my eyes. "Fuck luck. Luck has never been on my side, and I've done just fine, thank you very much."

"You don't understand," she tries again. "With the plans we have set, I can *almost* guarantee—"

"No, you don't understand," I say, losing all patience. "There are no guarantees in life. Oh, I take that back. If you don't let me get some food and sleep before getting into this with you, I *do* guarantee we're gonna have a big fucking problem."

"Listen, Declan. I know I'm not always up front with you, but please believe me, you cannot take on the work camp. If you don't go through with our plans for the night of the Gala, there won't be another chance to get rid of Bellamy for over twenty years. Are you listening to me? Twenty years!"

"Nope. I'm done listening. I'm not going to let 3,000 children die if there's even the slightest chance I can save them. And it's not about the numbers, either. If I can help it at all, I won't let 300 children die, or 30 children, or even three! Now, you can either get on board, or get fucked. Help me find a way to do both, or you can count me out the night of the Gala. I've got my priorities, and I know I've got them straight."

"No, you don't understand, Declan," she tries again, but this time, a hint of panic seeps into her voice. Olesya sounding flustered ranks right up there with an airline pilot saying both engines are on fire and we're going down, so I listen carefully to her cryptic explanation.

"Spit it out, woman," I hiss. "Either tell me right now why I should let those children die, or I'm scrapping the Gala mission altogether. Your choice."

She remains silent.

"Nice talking to you, Olesya," I reply wearily, raking my hand over my scruffy jaw and bleary eyes. "Have a good night."

And I hang up on her.

30

Louise

With the party just days away, the house is a hive of activity. It's impossible to escape the swarms of people hired to do a million different tasks, with each and every one of them thinking they are the most important person in the room. They hiss and bark like cats and dogs as each demands their way, a few nearly biting my head off before realizing who they were addressing. Then they fell all over themselves apologizing. It would have been funny if they weren't so incredibly terrified, I imagine expecting me to react as cruelly and mercilessly as my husband. For some reason I'm not sure of, that they think this of me makes me very sad.

Between the noise and the crowds, all I want is to escape. Normally, I'd lock myself into my beloved conservatory, but despite my insistence that it be kept closed for the party, someone determined that my beautiful sanctuary should be used. Gone are my tidy rows of exotic orchids and the comfortable, thick-cushioned chairs I love to snuggle into to read. Instead, my precious blooms have been integrated into a wild, tropical oasis that will be open to everyone's enjoyment.

A variety of exotic plants and large, burbling fountains have taken over the room; the tile floor thickly covered with dirt and mulch to make the plants appear as if they've grown out of the floor. A meandering walkway made of stone and açai wood has been created through the foliage, a pathway designed to promote flow and to keep expensive shoes clean.

When I first saw it, I hated it. It felt chaotic and disquieting with its tall tropical trees brushing the glass ceiling, and their broad leaves casting ominous shadows that unnerved me. Many of the plants are too large and vividly colored for my taste; the bright corals, deep purples and stark, white flowers even more dramatic against foliage that ranges from so light it's nearly white, to shiny, decadent black.

After taking a few days to mourn the loss of my conservatory, and my staff reminding me a few million times that as soon as the party's over the space will be reverted to its original form, I again *try* to like the space. Someone put a great deal of energy and effort into this, and I at least owed them more than a quick glance before declaring it a travesty.

As I follow the path, I realize I don't know most of the plants. I'm not a botanist by any stretch of the imagination, but I can usually hold my own in discussions about gardening. My curiosity piqued, I take my tropical botanical atlases from the library and fetch my rarely-used gardening gloves; I know better than to handle unknown plants without protection. I spend hours determining which species the unusual flowers and strange leaf shapes belong to, occasionally needing other books from the library to make identifications. I'm truly surprised to see they are from all corners of the world, and although most of them are true tropicals, some are not. Some of these could easily be grown on our own grounds.

I lose myself in my analysis, realizing this may be my only chance to examine these species up close. What I at first had seen as chaos was, in actuality, incredibly well thought out. This is no mere garden, but an extravaganza of the senses designed to lure visitors into its depths with its vibrance, then seducing them with its scent. Every plant begs to have their silky petals caressed by manicured fingers, or their heady perfume rubbed on bare skin, allowing the wearer, and those in intimate proximity, to enjoy their delicious scent for the rest of the evening.

I camp out in the room, taking time out of my busy day to identify the plants as best I can. Many of them are easily discernible by their flowers alone; Angel's Trumpets of all sizes adorn the room, their colors ranging from pastel yellow to the deepest reds. Dark blue-purple spikes of Aconitum are placed throughout, as are the stark disc-shaped flowers of White Snakeroot. Ten foot tall trees of Castor Bean lend shade to the various nooks left open for either entertainers to perform, or later in the night, for secluded trysts. There are a shocking number of places to hide within the glass-enclosed walls, and when evening falls, the thousands of fairy lights and a few dimly spot-lit areas will turn this tropical oasis into a wonderland of sin.

It's not until I find in my atlas that the flowers I admire the most, the bright pink of the Nerium Oleander placed copiously throughout, that a long-forgotten memory returns.

As soon as I realize I'm pregnant, I know I have to get rid of the baby. Although I've been taught that abortion is a sin, the last thing I want is to bring a child into the world under these circumstances. When I think about it, it isn't just carrying my rapist's child that chills me to the bone. It's the thought of him growing up under the influence of my hypocritical parents and their morally-void religion which make me that much more determined to end the pregnancy.

I tell no one, not even my closest friends, as I try method after method to lose the child. I exhaust myself through exercise, and exist in a state of dizzy semi-starvation. I sit in hot tubs and saunas long enough to nearly pass out, dehydrating myself to the point I'm close to blacking out. I even tried eating the leaves and flowers of plants known to be toxic, stopping just short of the white Oleander my mother loves in her flower arrangements. Nothing works.

Despite starving myself, when I'm in my fourth month, I begin to show. I'm frantic when my clothes stop fitting, my mother incensed that I gained enough weight that I can no longer squeeze into my couture gowns. When the girls at school notice the changes in my body rumors begin to fly. It's then that I know I'm out of time.

The day of my appointment, I disguise myself as best as I can. I wear a dark wig and pull the hood of an oversized sweatshirt over that, and the ripped-knee jeans and cheap, oversized sunglasses are a far cry from my usual preppy outfits. The entire way there, I give myself a pep talk to bolster my ever-waning courage. As afraid I am of the procedure, I'm more terrified of the harrowing journey between the parking lot and the front door.

The anti-abortion freaks are always out there, harassing anyone attempting to get inside. They call the doctors and nurses 'baby murderers' and block the way of the women needing the clinic's services. Although only a small percentage of women go there for abortions, the protesters harass everyone, and they enjoy doing it. I know this to be true, because many of the protestors are parishioners from my parents' church. They love to sit around and chuckle about the girls they made cry, or high-five over the ones they successfully prevented from going inside. I can't help but wonder if it were their daughters who had gotten pregnant through rape if they would still be as steadfast in their anti-abortion views. Sadly, I believe they would.

I'm terrified they're going to recognize me, but it's a risk I have to take. The next closest clinic is hours away, and they don't have an available appointment for another month. I cannot wait that long. This is my one and only chance.

The morning of the appointment, I park blocks away and walk quickly through the crowd with my head down and dark glasses on. The women carry signs and shout "Shame!" and "Whore!" as I force my way through their ranks. Someone grabs my arm and spins me around to lecture me, but I manage to pull free, shrilly screaming, "Don't touch me!"

The woman grabs me by the hair as I turn to run, my wig slipping and exposing my blonde hair underneath. When I grab her wrist and squeeze it as hard as I can until she lets go, I look into her enraged eyes and realize I know her. She's the lead soprano in our church choir.

I run before I can determine for sure if I've been recognized. I race inside, searching for the nearest bathroom and barely make it inside before I begin to retch. Nothing comes up, not that anything should. I haven't eaten in days.

I shakily manage to pull myself together, going inside and giving the receptionist the fake name I made the appointment under. She asks for ID, and I tell her I forgot it at home, which I can tell she doesn't believe. She gives me an incredulous look, but still hands over a sheaf of papers and tells me to fill them out. I don't know how to answer even half of the questions. I know that little about my body.

I'm terrified as I'm led back to a clean, but well-worn room. The walls are scuffed and the furniture outdated, and everything looks just a touch dingy. For some reason, it makes me want to cry.

The nurse who comes in is kind and sympathetic, asking me all sorts of questions about my pregnancy, to which I give short, tight-lipped answers. She can tell more has happened than I am telling her, especially when she asks about the father. At that point, she stops asking questions.

She pulls a paper gown out of a drawer and tells me how to put it on so the doctor can examine me, and as I'm getting changed, I hear her list her concerns to the doctor through the paper-thin walls. The one she seems the most concerned about is that I'm underage. God only knows what she'd think if she knew how the child had been conceived.

I don't remember much of the exam, my mind floating off into space the second she touches me. Although she's gentle and very kind, explaining everything carefully before she does it, I'm so tense she can barely complete the internal exam. The nurse remains in the room and holds my hand through the entire thing, cooing for me to relax and instructing me to take deep breaths. The second the doctor finishes I burst into tears.

"So, so—can you do it now? I didn't eat anything today, so you can do it now. Right?" The doctor and nurse share a look that makes my heart stop. It's clear that nothing will happen today.

I begin to sob. They try to calm me down, explaining why it cannot be done today. First off, the procedure is going to cost $600. I tell them that's fine, producing a thick roll of twenties I'd been pulling out of every ATM I could find in the area over the past few weeks. It was really little more than I'd have taken out normally, except this time I hoarded it instead of blowing it on clothes, makeup, and meals out with my friends. I now had a few thousand dollars, and I told them they could have every penny if they could do the procedure today. Preferably, now. Right now.

But money isn't the issue. The problem is I need someone "responsible" not just to drive me home afterward, but to give consent because I'm under 18. I try to lie, to tell them I'm nineteen, but I'm a lousy liar. The fake ID I attempt to pass off as real is even worse.

Realizing I'm screwed, I panic. I quickly get dressed and run for the exit, but when I reach the lobby, I see there are now twice as many protesters outside. The receptionist is kind, escorting me through a doorway that leads us into the building attached to ours, which has an unmarked door that exits on a different street. She asks me if I'm okay before I leave, and I shake my head sadly before heading out into the sunshine.

I'm so lost in my misery that I don't pay attention to where I'm going. I wander aimlessly around the unfamiliar neighborhood for hours. Of the people I pass, nobody asks why I'm crying. Once I realize I'm lost, the people I stop to ask directions from pretend to be in a hurry and refuse to stop.

It begins to rain, and soon I'm drenched through. Night falls, and the wind picks up. I'm so, so cold. The part of town I'm in is the roughest I've ever seen. The few people who approach me ask if I'm looking to buy drugs or how much I charge for a blow job. They laugh when I run away.

I try to find a pay phone, but all I find is a filthy strip club. Knowing they must have a phone, I slink inside. But the place is packed, the men leering at the half-naked women on the stage. When I finally make it to the bar, I ask the bartender if I may use the phone and he tells me to get out. I beg him to please, let me just make a quick call, but he says no, calling over the bouncer who tosses me out into the street.

With no other options, I sit under their small overhang to get out of the worst of the rain. I'm so frozen and miserable that I can't even think. It's then that I give up, escaping into nothingness as I let my mind go blank. I don't hear the men stumble out to their cars when the place closes down shortly before dawn, and I can't answer the concerned questions asked by a few of the well-meaning dancers when they walk out to their cars. Eventually, everyone leaves.

By the time the sun rises, I'm numb in a way I've never felt before. When a pair of huge, black shoes come into my line of sight, I ignore them the way so many people ignored me. The man wearing all blue crouches before me, and talks to me gently, but I can't understand him. I can't even look at him. He places his hand under my chin and raises my face, but I can't meet his eyes.

"Come with me, child," he says soothingly. "Let me help you."

He tries to help me to my feet, but my legs buckle. He sits down next to me, and when I scoot over as far as I can and yet remain under the overhang, he frowns. He calls someone on his radio and requests an ambulance. I wonder who he thinks needs to go to the hospital.

The ambulance people are a lot more demanding with their questions until the man in blue tells them I don't speak. I try to tell them I don't want to go to the hospital, but the man in blue tells them to take me anyway.

At the hospital there's a lot more of everything. More people. More questions. More hands. It becomes too much. They start to cut off my clothes, and next thing I know, I'm back in that smelly alley.

I remember I have to fight.

When they manage to tie my arms down, I resort to biting. Then a needle pricks my arm, and, within minutes, my body becomes heavy and sinks into the mattress.

When I wake, it's to shouting. My fuzzy head is unable to make sense of things until my mother blows into the room. She's wearing lilac, her favorite color.

I wipe the sleep from my eyes just before my mother's palm cracks across my face.

"How could you do this to me?" she roars. "How?"

I open my mouth, but nothing comes out. Two nurses run in and pull my mother away. She screams and wails, the security guards now restraining her in the hallway where a small crowd gawks around her. Realizing she's making a scene, my mother calms quickly, at least on the outside. When she humbly apologizes for being "distraught," they reluctantly allow her back in my room.

"They tell me you're pregnant." She spits the word like it's the worst possible thing in the world. "I also heard you were spotted yesterday going to one of those, those—abortion places." She pronounces the word as if it truly tastes nasty in her mouth.

"Well, I contacted the doctor there, and she said you claimed you were raped. It was that horrible boy you insisted on seeing, isn't it? Isn't it?"

I stare at her blankly.

"I told you he was no good, but you refused to listen. He was the reason you were all banged up a few months ago, wasn't he? Well, I don't know what you did to deserve it, but I'm sure that you did. You do know that's what everyone will say, don't you? They will say you deserved this. Now I have to find a way to get you out of this mess, as usual. You never think about anyone but yourself, do you?"

She grabs her purse and hurries from the room, nearly knocking over the nurses trying to listen in. They come in quickly and close the door behind them, one of them handing me an ice pack for my cheek. They ask me questions that I understand, but can't answer. I stare at them blankly.

"Louisa May, I don't know what happened to you to make you incapable of communicating, but we want you to know—we believe that you were raped. Will you please talk to us? Can you tell us anything that we can use to help you? Did anyone see anything who can come forward on your behalf?"

I sit back against my pillows and burst into tears. It was just as the boy outside the bar had said. I should have gone to the hospital. I should have gone to the police. I should have at least bothered to remember the kind boy's name. Did it start with a C? Chip? Chuck? I wrack my brains, but the name's gone.

Over the next few days, I eat nothing. I drink nothing. All I do is cry, and when I run out of tears, I just lay in the bed and stare at the ceiling. They eventually place a tube up my nose and down into my throat and feed me that way, the doctors convinced my desire to starve myself is an eating disorder that needs treating. But with each passing day, I lose more and more control over my body. I can no longer even get up to go to the bathroom, the nurses now diapering and changing me like I'm an overgrown infant.

Eventually, the doctors discharge me to the care of a psychiatric hospital. Although I hear the ambulance driver say to one of the nurses that he's driving me to St. Francis', he doesn't. He takes me home. My mother fusses over me, pretending to be a model parent, but the second the transport people leave, my mother locks me in my room. I don't know why—I haven't moved on my own in weeks.

At first, it isn't so bad. I don't mind the silence. I make up stories in my head to pass the time, some of them good enough that I think if I were to ever regain use of my hands, I'd like to write them down. But then my mother decides my cataplexy is the work of the devil, and decides my "cure" will come from watching endless hours of her past televised specials.

When she's home, she subjects me to hours of her wild rants, claiming I have ruined everything she has worked so hard for. Apparently, word had leaked about my "shameful behavior." She's losing sponsors at an alarming rate, which means she's losing money. Her followers cannot understand how she can preach abstinence and purity and yet have a whore for a daughter.

From what I understand from the gossip I overhear from the staff, my mother is now using my claim of rape to make herself look better. After all, how could she be a shitty mother if her daughter didn't consent? That earns her back some sympathy, and a few new sponsors, but she loses them again when a liberal group accuses her of lying, saying the claim of rape is coming at a "convenient time."

Just as I'm wondering what Edward's doing during all of this, he makes a statement to the press. He has no lawyer—he's too poor to hire one. He says that none of what he's being accused of is true. He's articulate, relatable, and thoroughly believable to the point even I wonder if I'm remembering things wrong.

He does admit to getting angry and "pushing me around a little" outside the bar, but that's it. He says that anything else that happened must have been done by someone else after he left. He chokes back his tears as he looks straight into the camera and tells me he loves me and how much he regrets leaving me outside after our fight. He begs me to forgive him, not even caring if the child isn't his, that he wants to be a part of its life.

Every word out of his mouth is a lie. He doesn't love me. He doesn't want this child. And I certainly do not want anything to do with him. If I never see him again, it will be far too soon.

The public doesn't know him like I do. They don't know how he can twist the truth and masterfully manipulate any situation until he is the one in the right. He always gets his way. And he doesn't care who he hurts to do it.

During the course of his ten minute broadcast, the court of public opinion turns against me. I become the villain. I'm called a liar. Everyone now thinks I'm just some privileged girl willing to ruin a young man's life simply because I was too afraid to tell my wackadoodle mother I got myself knocked up.

After a few weeks of the press demanding I give a statement and getting nothing, they move on to other stories. In the end, Edward comes out of everything smelling like a rose as I rot away in my bedroom, forgotten. I've become little more than a human incubator, everyone checking on the baby, but never on me. They all assume I'm not "here" anymore, believing if I don't speak, I also can't hear or understand.

But we all know what they say about those who assume, don't we?

It wasn't that I couldn't comprehend what was happening around me, it was that I didn't want to participate in a world that gave me no say in anything, not even what happened inside my own body. So, if they wanted to accuse me and then forget about me, then I would forget them, too.

But the thing about being forgotten is that at any point, you can also be remembered. Often at the most inopportune time.

When I'm just shy of eight months pregnant, I'm unexpectedly awakened early one morning. My nurse enters with a maid, a hairstylist, and makeup person, which sounds like the beginning of a bad joke, but sadly, isn't.

I'm washed and waxed, my lashes curled, and my hair styled. The feeding tube is removed from my nose much to my nurse's consternation, as well as mine, as after whatever event happens, they will just have to put it back in. It leaves my nose raw and achy, leaving it to drip and cause the makeup artist to swear. When she lifts up a mirror and calls me "every bit as beautiful as before," we both know she's lying.

I have to admit, she's done a decent job making me look healthy, if still tired. The grand finale is when they cinch me into a pale pink maternity dress and slip my feet into a pair of ridiculous pink heels.

I'm arranged into a wheelchair, my dress smoothed over my knees and each curl of hair arranged as if I'm going to a photo shoot. My nurse pushes me down the hall to an elevator that must have been put in sometime since I "became ill." My father, who I haven't seen in months, arrives to push me the short distance from the elevator to my mother's office. He doesn't say a word, only sighing heavily right before he reaches the open door.

She's seated at her desk, not bothering to even look up as she says, "Come. Sit." I hate how she commands my father like he's a dog. My father stations my wheelchair between the two chairs facing my mother's desk, then sits in the one to my left. I cannot see who sits to my right. The few other people in the room are out of my line of sight, so I'm not sure who else is here.

"So, what do you think?" My mother asks the person seated to my right.

There's a pause before he growls, "I think this is fucking bullshit."

My muscles clench involuntarily, my broken fight or flight reflex not knowing what to do.

"It's this or prison," my mother shrugs. "Make your choice. I will not ask again."

I want to know what's happening. I want to know what's changed. I want to know why he's getting choices when I've been given none?

"I'll take my chances at trial," he drawls cockily.

My mother frowns. "Alright. And just say that, somehow, you are found not guilty. You will be kicked out of Annapolis, as your behavior is hardly becoming of an officer. This incident will be a black mark against your character that will follow you forever."

She pauses for a moment, but I know there's more. She always has more.

"Tell me—do you think you will be happy being a gardener, like your father? Or maybe a lifetime working in fast food would suit you better? How do you think you will feel after the stink of hot oil is so embedded

in your skin and hair that no amount of scrubbing will remove it? How will you feel when the men you went to school with come in and laugh at you? Will you look back on this choice with regrets, then?"

She sits back in her seat, her hands folded, right over left, on the top of her desk. She's almost smirking as she prepares to squash him like a bug beneath her shoe.

"If you decide to go to trial, the prosecutor will seek maximum sentences for statutory rape, as my daughter is not yet eighteen. You could be facing a sentence of up to twenty-five years. When you get out, the best years of your life will be over, that is, if you manage to survive. From what I hear, prison is a truly terrible place for men who rape little girls."

Although I can't move, or speak, it doesn't stop me from feeling his anger grow. Although the night of the attack is still fuzzy, I remember how his rage burned so fiercely it singed my skin, and I feel that same rage burning in him now. It makes no difference to me that we're in a room full of people. I'm terrified.

My heart races and my muscles bunch up to the point they twitch. I'm so close to breaking through this block that keeps me from being able to use my body, but my mind ignores the demands I give it to stand or speak. I beg it to work, to do something. Anything. This moment is clearly a turning point in my life, and one I need to gain control of immediately or bad things, worse things, are going to happen. I know it. I can feel it.

For the first time in months, I actually care about what's happening. For the first time since my shot at an abortion failed, I want to be included in making plans for my future.

I want out of this fucking house, and out from under the thumb of my controlling mother.

I want to press charges against Edward. I want him to pay for what he did to me.

I want justice.

I want revenge.

And I'm so fucking furious I want to scream.

How dare my mother dress me up like a doll, bring me in here, and sit me down next to my attacker? How dare she make deals with the man who raped me, beat me, and left me for dead? Why is he being allowed a choice in his future and I'm given none?

I tell myself to open my mouth, to speak up, but my body refuses. I try over and over to mouth the single syllable that can halt these proceedings, but my mouth refuses to form it. I try and try, but my face is frozen, my painted lips fixed in their customary grim line.

I'm screaming inside, but no one hears me. I'm trying so hard to break the spell keeping me frozen that I'm sweating.

I need to be heard. I need them to know that, once again, I. Do. Not. Consent.

Edward sighs resignedly, leaning forward and motioning for my mother to hand him the paperwork. "Give it to me," *he snaps.*

She smiles condescendingly before handing over the pile of documents sitting on her desk, as well as a pen. He scoots forward to sit at the edge of his chair, and scribbles his name and the date on a few dozen of them, and then pushes them to me.

For a moment I think I'm off the hook. I've done nothing voluntary for months. There's no way I'm able to sign my name.

"Give them to me. I will sign for her," *my mother states.* "It amazes me how you keep forgetting she's a minor."

My mother rifles through the papers carefully, checking each signature and date, and adding her own in a few places. With the papers signed, she stands up, reads off a few Bible passages, and then reaches into her top desk drawer. She places two plain gold rings on the edge of the table.

Oh, no. No, no, no, no. Fuck no. She's marrying us?

She reads the vows for Edward and makes him repeat them. She uses his full given name and enunciates each syllable with a nasty smirk on her face. He spits his "I do" *at her, adding a muttered,* "What fucking choice do I have?" *My mother omits the questions for me.*

She skips over most of the rest of the ceremony, declaring us husband and wife, claiming "that who God has united, no man may put asunder." She informs Edward he may kiss his bride, but thankfully, he doesn't. The minute it's clear that business has concluded, she hands him a sheet of paper and informs him she wants it memorized and delivered word-for-word at his press conference tomorrow. Only then will she clear his name.

"You've gotten what you want. Now give me what I want."

He looks absolutely furious when my mother reaches into her desk and produces a small slip of paper that he snatches from her hand. He storms from the room, but before he can make his exit, my mother calls out to him.

"Remember, Eduardo, should you do anything to invalidate our contract, it will mean long, miserable years in maximum security. I suggest you make good choices."

He slams the door behind him. My mother lets out an aggrieved sigh as she collects the papers and puts them back in their file, and places them in the bottom drawer of her desk. She fixes me with an exasperated glare, and then glides over in front of me, placing the gold band on my left ring finger.

"If you remember nothing about this day, Louisa May, you must remember that everything I've done was only to protect you." She says nothing else as she, and the rest of the people in the room, leave.

My father returns me to my room. My nurse smiles and tells my father she can take care of things from here, but he instead asks for a moment alone with me. He sits on the edge of my bed and faces me.

"I don't know if you can understand me, but I want you to know that I didn't want this to happen. I know he hurt you, and he deserves to go to jail. But Louisa, we also have a business to protect. This was the only solution we came up with where everyone manages to come out okay in the end."

I'm gobsmacked. How can he say this deal protects everyone? He claims to believe me, and yet he just sat there while I was married off to a monster all for the sake of money.

When the first tear falls from my eyes, my father looks shocked. He knows I understand. He mumbles a guilt-laced apology before leaning over and kissing my cheek. "This will be okay, I promise. And if things are hard, just remember, this is the best thing for your child."

How exactly is this the best thing for my child? Who cares if I'm unwed? In this day and age, six years into the 21st century, nobody gives a shit if there's no father in the picture. I think that, given the circumstances, it would be hard to find anyone who believes it's better for a child to have a violent, rapist father in the picture than not.

Suddenly, the things I do, and do not, want for my child become clear. I don't want Edward to have anything to do with my child. In fact, I don't want my child to have anything to do with my family, either. I don't want my baby to grow up anywhere even close to here, destined to be yet another prop in my mother's grand play.

I have to get out of here. Now.

When the nurse comes in, she sees I'm crying and frowns. She sits on the same spot my father just vacated, and looks at me closely. She places her hand over mine, her eyebrows knitting together when she sees how tightly my hands are clenched around the armrests.

She leans over and whispers in my ear. She says she wants to help me, but I have to be willing to put in the work. She tells me if I work very hard, she will find a way for me to escape, but this must remain our secret.

Over the next month, this one nurse increases my physical therapy. I regain the use of my limbs, and not long after, the ability to walk unaided. When anyone aside from this one woman is around, I continue to pretend I'm in the same semi-catatonic state, but I'm not a great actress. If anyone spared me more than a single glance, they'd see the return of mischief in my eyes. I create a plan to escape; all the episodes of crime dramas the nurses and I watched over the past months helping me hone it to the point it won't fail.

Now that I can feel my body, the NG tube has become a nuisance. I force myself to "improve" enough to eat. I'll need as much strength as possible for the upcoming weeks.

With just two weeks before I'm due, I make my escape. My parents are out at some event, so there's minimal staff on duty. The nurse who is supposed to be watching me is instead downstairs, fucking the security guard. I sneak out of the house, getting in my car that's, thankfully, full of gas. It's all so shockingly easy that I don't know why I didn't do this sooner.

I drive for miles, avoiding interstates and staying on roads unlikely to have cameras. I follow traffic laws carefully, knowing the last thing I need is to be pulled over. I drive until I'm so tired I can't go any further without risking an accident. I drive to a small airport in West Virginia and leave the car in their lot, only to then take a taxi to the bus station the next town over. I give the driver an extra $100 to keep his mouth shut.

I have no way of knowing if an Amber alert has been issued, and although I've disguised myself with a short brown wig and a pair of oversized sunglasses, the fact I'm mute unfortunately makes me memorable. I communicate when I need to with pen and paper, pretending that I'm deaf to keep people from asking too many questions.

I end up in Philadelphia, just as I planned. I'm exhausted, the trip taking way more out of me than I expected. I find a shitty-looking hotel and pay cash for a room, hoping the place isn't infested with bedbugs. The room itself is outdated but clean, and I fall on the bed and sleep a full twelve hours without moving.

By the next morning, I feel refreshed, but somehow different. My belly shape has changed, now a more rounded bump. The baby has been especially active since we'd begun traveling, and I'm ravenous all the time. I eat in cheap diners, sticking to foods that are as nutritious *as possible, but occasionally giving in to the lure of French fries and cheesesteaks.*

During the day, I wander around town, getting a feel for the different neighborhoods. There's a rich diversity to the population, the streets alive with people of different cultures who speak all sorts of languages I don't recognize. It's as far from my parent's all-white, all-rich, neighborhood as one can imagine. I love everything about it.

It's during one of these strolls that I begin to feel sick, a wave of nausea overtaking me that nearly brings me to my knees. I stagger over and sit on the stone steps of a bank, clutching my belly and doing my best to breathe deep. I'm only there a few minutes when a pair of leather-soled shoes hurries towards me, and a huge black man wearing a clerical collar squats down in front of me. I feel terrible when I startle at the horrible scar running down the side of his face that barely misses his eye.

"Can I help you, miss?"

I shake my head. He sits down next to me, calmly asking me a few more questions. I again shake my head.

"Should I call an ambulance? Do you think you're in labor?"

I look at him in terror, and shake my head again. I don't think I'm in labor, but now that he says it, I'm not sure.

"Come with me," he says, helping me to stand. He continues to talk to me in that same soothing rolling tone, like we've got not a worry in the world. It feels so very nice.

He leads me to the steps of a beautiful, old, stone church and ushers me inside, taking me past a few elderly black women who look at me with blatant surprise. He whispers to one of them who nods quickly and then promptly departs as he leads me over to sit down on a pew.

"Child, I can tell you've been through somethin' awful. What I want you to know is that I will help you any way I can. But I need you to talk to me."

Footsteps hurry up the aisle; the sound of heels clicking and the swish of a full skirt heralding the arrival of a woman. She crouches down so her face is in my line of sight. She's really pretty, with wide, dark eyes that look kind, but shrewd. She sweeps her long, black hair off her shoulders, and quirks her full lips which are painted a deep rose. She smiles at me, then takes a seat on my other side.

"I'm Effie, the Reverend's wife. We're gonna take good care of you, honey. Can you tell me your name?"

I shake my head.

"I don't think she speaks, but she ain't deaf. She understands just fine, too. I think she might be goin' inta labor, but I don't know for sure."

Effie rolls her eyes at him, and when she speaks, it's full of sass. "Ain't you got something you should be doin' right now? Or are you just gonna sit here and tell us both how you 'don't know nuthin' 'bout birthin' no babies?'"

I burst out laughing for the first time in months. Effie's a hoot and a half.

"Woman, are you ever gonna show me a moment's respect?" the Reverend says, sounding thoroughly affronted.

"I dunno," she questions. "When you plannin' on doin' something worth respectin'?"

He tries to look stern but fails, his mouth curving into a bright, beautiful smile. "Have I told you today how much I love you, you vicious, sass-mouthed goat?"

She pretends to be annoyed, and fails, smiling back. "You just did, you bull-headed baboon. Now, scoot on out of here. We ladies have things to discuss."

He stands to leave, but before he does, he asks me if he can say a prayer for me. I nod.

He places his enormous hand on top of my cheap wig, and I bow my head and clasp my hands together. So does Effie.

"Heavenly father, watch over this child. May she find fortitude in Your name, and favor in Your grace. Bless the child she carries; may *he, or she, grow happy and healthy, and may they praise You for Your blessings. In Your name we pray. Amen."*

Before I can mouth the word, he speaks again. "Oh, and if you can help the Eagles beat the Cowboys on Sunday, I would be most appreciative. Amen."

Effie smacks her husband on the arm playfully, telling him to get lost as she laughs. For the first time in my life, I'm witnessing a truly happy marriage, and my God, does it hurt to think I will never have that.

My resolve strengthens further, knowing that what I'm planning is absolutely the right thing to do no matter how much it's going to hurt.

Three days later, I dropped my beautiful, newborn son on the rectory's doorstep and rang the bell. I crouched behind the tall bushes, my hand over my mouth to stifle my sobs. A teenage boy answered the door, and then screamed for his mother. Effie came quickly, picked up my son, and read the note I pinned to his blanket.

Thank you for your extreme kindness.
Please, for the safety of this child,
don't try to find me.
His future happiness depends on it.
Please find him a loving home.

"Oh, sweet Jesus," Effie cries as she hugs my son to her chest. I want to rip him from her arms, to scream I made a mistake, and I want him back. But then the big, scarred minister comes running, and he and Effie begin a heated discussion about what to do. The note pinned to my baby's blanket slips free and floats to the ground, their son picking it up and reading it.

"Ma," he calls, pulling on her sleeve, but she and her husband are too wrapped up in their conversation to hear him. He repeats it a few more times before finally shouting it, getting both their attention.

"Didja see this?" He holds out the note to her, flipping over the folded piece and showing her the last thing I wrote.

His name is Cassiel.

"Cassiel—He's the Angel of temperance," Effie states, sounding a bit confused as she looks at her husband.

"No, I don't think that's why she's naming him that. Cassiel's also known as the Angel of Tears."

"But why would she name him after someone terrible like that?" their son asks.

"I s'pect because giving him up is probably the hardest thing she's ever done in her life."

He leans forward and touches Cassiel's face with an outstretched finger. He's gentle for such a big guy, and when he looks at my son, all I see is love and concern in his eyes. I know that of all the places where the state's Safe Haven laws allow people to drop babies, that I chose the perfect one. Even if they don't keep him, there is no question in my mind that they will find him only the most loving home.

With tears blinding my eyes, I run away before I change my mind. I run until I can't take another step, and then I sit on the curb and cry until I have not a single tear left. Then I begin the long, convoluted series of bus rides home.

I have just one last thing left to do, and then I can begin the arduous task of trying to forget. It's the middle of the night when I walk up the driveway, awakening the sleepy-faced butler who answers the front door. "We've been looking all over for you! Where have you been?"

I don't answer him. He grips my arm, dragging me into the sitting room before going to fetch someone. Probably my mother. When she comes running down in her nightgown and robe, she doesn't look relieved that I'm home. She looks pissed.

"Where have you been? What have you done?"

When I don't answer her, she slaps me as hard as she can. I lose my balance, falling to the carpet and narrowly missing hitting my head on the coffee table.

"Where's the baby?" she screams. "What have you done?"

I look up at her, a cruel smile forming on my lips, my unused voice thick, raspy, and unrecognizable, even to me. "He's dead."

"My lady?"

A voice breaks me out of my memories. It's one of my maids, coming to fetch me for an appointment I've no doubt forgotten. I slide from the platform and drop to the ground, smoothing my wrinkled dress and attempting to smile at the young woman who looks surprisingly anxious about disturbing me. When she tells me that my mother is here to see me, I understand completely. They hate her as much as I do.

"I'll be right there." I smile. I look back at the plants, remembering every detail I learned about each one. With my gloves still on, I pad over to the trees, taking a moment to admire the enormous, lobed leaves, the flowers, and most particularly, the fruit. It takes little effort to remove a few and place them in my pocket, all sorts of thoughts rolling through my mind.

They say revenge is a dish best served cold.

I smile at the thought, a plan forming in my mind.

Oh, yes, I most certainly agree. And on the night of the party, I know exactly what just deserts to make for a few of my very special guests.

Then I smile in a way I haven't smiled in over twenty years.

31

Keira

The next day, after everyone gets a good night's sleep, we transport Micah back to his parents' house. We lighten the pain meds and sedation, and by mid-afternoon, he's mostly awake.

I'm sitting at the edge of his bed, holding his hand, when he mumbles sleepily and rolls over a bit towards me. He's confused, not yet remembering how he came to be in freshly-laundered clothes with a soft mattress under him. He looks around, and I gently say his name, trying to get him to focus on me before he panics.

"You're home, Micah. You're home," I whisper, giving him a wide smile.

He looks like he doesn't remember me, but then smiles back. "What time is it? Have I missed breakfast?"

"Are you hungry?" He nods, and I smile again. "That's a good sign. You've missed breakfast, but I'm sure Sarah, I mean, your mom, or even I can make whatever you're in the mood for."

He scowls, a little more of his surroundings seeping through the haze of sedation. "Wait. How did I get here? I can't be here. It's too dangerous!"

"Shh, it's all okay—"

That's when he looks down at himself and sees the bandages wrapped around the amputation site, and begins to scream. I have no idea what it must be like to wake up an arm shorter than when you fell asleep, but I imagine it's terrifying. He begins to thrash, trying to get away from me, and he screams again when he bumps the surgery site against the mattress. This time it's in pain.

"Easy, easy there, Micah," I soothe. "Everything's gonna be alright-"

"What did you do? What did you do to me?"

Although I know it shouldn't, his words hurt my feelings. "You got really sick, don't you remember? I found you burning up, and then Esther helped me get you—"

"Who the hell is Esther?"

He needs to understand I didn't do anything to hurt him, and that everything that happened had been a matter of life and death. "Listen to me, Micah. You were going to die. I didn't have a choice—"

"You should have let me die!" he bellows.

Sarah arrives at the door, staring bug-eyed at her son. "Micah, I never want to hear you say that ever again! Do you hear me!"

She rushes to his side and takes him in a huge hug that makes him cry out in pain even though she's holding him nowhere near the incision areas. He bursts into tears, hugging his mother back with his one arm.

"I'm here, Micah. I'm right here," she whispers back. The whole scene is so heartbreaking, I can't stop crying. I try to tiptoe out of the room, but Sarah's voice stops me, and I venture a glance over my shoulder.

"Micah, Keira saved your life. If not for her, we would have lost you. You cannot be angry with her."

He pulls back, wiping his hand over his face. He says something to his mother in German that I don't understand, and she replies with another long hug when he begins to cry again. This time, I escape.

I put some chicken broth on to boil, planning to make Micah a little soup with some rice in it. He hasn't eaten anything for a few days now, and he's going to need to take it easy starting to eat again or he'll get sick.

After a while, Sarah comes downstairs, looking absolutely drained. She comes over and gives me a big hug.

"What's that for?" I ask after she pulls away.

"For bringing my son home."

I pause before asking her the question weighing on my mind. "He hates me, doesn't he?"

She shakes her head. "Do you want to know what he just asked me?" Without waiting for my response, she continues. "He wanted to know if you might learn to love him with only one arm."

My jaw drops. Sure, he's been super sweet, and I'd flirted with him a bit, but I thought my feelings were wholly one-sided.

I smile broadly. "Really?"

"Yes, child, that's what he asked. I told him you were far too sensible a girl to stop loving someone for such a superficial reason."

"You knew?" My voice sounds both shocked and accusing. "Why didn't you say anything?"

"'Tis not my business, aside from wanting you to court wisely and for some length of time before getting wed. You both are still so young."

"Wed?! I'm sixteen! Of course I'm not ready to get married!"

Sarah laughs. "I'm happy to hear that. Now, you'd better take that soup up to Micah before you boil it to vapor."

I put two slices of bread thickly slathered with butter, as well as the soup and a glass of water on a tray, and carefully maneuver it upstairs. Micah looks a bit sheepish as I place the tray over his legs and help him get situated, but when it becomes clear that he's not quite up to feeding himself, I spoon up some soup and bring it to his lips. He sips it gently, letting out a small groan of approval after swallowing. He thanks me after every bite until I tell him to quit it. He nibbles at the bread and butter as I take the tray from him and start downstairs to help with dinner. I'm just about at the door when he calls my name.

"Thank you, Keira," he says with tears choking his voice. "I just want you to know I don't blame you for anything. I'm sorry for earlier—"

"I told you to cut that shit out," I say gruffly, my smile ruining any chance of him thinking I'm truly annoyed. "Get some rest. I'll come up and check on you in a little bit."

Downstairs Scott, Declan, Emma and Adam are sitting around the dining room table pretending to look at a map. They all sport amused expressions, Scott all but biting his damned tongue off to keep from saying something snarky that Declan will probably cuff him for. I put the tray down next to the sink and wash out the bowl, noting how intently Dex is concentrating on the cooking lesson Sarah's giving him. The way his brows are knit together you'd think he was learning quantum physics. I think that for now, it's best they eat here before Dex accidentally poisons both himself and Adam.

I join the crew at the table, staring down at the map of buildings that makes up the compound where Micah was. The place is huge, with three buildings that act as dorms that are far too small to house the number of inmates who live there. Declan asks me if I think Micah's up to talking, and I ask him to at least give him a few hours to get some sleep, as he's pretty worn out. Of course, Scott asks what I was doing up there to tire him out, and just as I expect, Declan nails him with an elbow to the ribs. I scowl at Scott and flip him the finger, but deep down inside, I don't mind his teasing. The big doofus just can't help himself.

Declan crankily tells us to focus. They have a lot of issues to overcome before he's going to feel remotely comfortable with their plan, the biggest obstacle being how once we break everyone out of the camp we can keep them from panicking. There's no doubt in anyone's mind that once those doors open, those kids aren't gonna hang around and ask questions. They're gonna run. I mean, who can blame them?

"If Ezra's been able to sneak kids out all this time, they obviously don't do headcounts that often," I think out loud. "Who's to say they would notice someone new?"

"No," Declan firmly states. He gives me his best no-nonsense glare, and I roll my eyes.

"Seriously, Declan. I can do it. I just need a pair of those nasty pajama uniforms they all wear and rub some dirt into my face. No one will notice. I'm even skinny, so I'll blend in."

"I said no," he says again. "I need you here to keep an eye on our patient. I'll ask Esther when she gets here if they have someone other than Isaac who can go."

"Oh? Why's Isaac sidelined, too? Don't you trust him?"

Declan slaps his palm down on the table. "What am I going to say to the Canadian Prime Minister if his kid dies down here sneaking *into* a workcamp? It's bad enough he's been doing all this cloak and dagger shit for Christ only knows how long without my knowledge. And if I find out Anna knew and condoned it? I swear to God I'm gonna resurrect her ass just so I can bitch her out."

"I'd like to see that," a lightly-accented male voice says as he approaches the open screen door. "That could be a very useful interrogation tool." Behind Isaac is Esther, the two of them sneaking in despite their heavy boots that normally make a ton of noise.

Isaac sits down next to me and gives me a wink. "Just so you know, I think you could do it. I've gone in a few times, and nobody noticed me at all. The hardest part is dealing with the smell. They've all been there long enough that it doesn't bother them, but it's the sort of stink you cannot prepare for. Whatever you do, never mention the smell. It'll give you away."

"It doesn't matter, because neither of you are going," Declan declares. "Last I checked, I'm still in charge around here, and I'm telling you, my mind's made up. The answer is no."

Isaac shrugs, wisely not pushing the matter. After dinner, Declan goes upstairs to talk to Micah and change the dressing on his arm while I stay downstairs and wash dishes. Isaac grabs a towel and begins to dry the ones I hand him. He doesn't say anything until the rest of the crew ends up loudly discussing the pros and cons of a new plan.

He moves closer to me, his arm all but brushing against mine. He quietly asks, "Can you defend yourself?"

I look over, surprised. "Yeah, I can."

"Can you shoot? How are you with a knife?"

"I'm awesome with a rifle, and even better with a crossbow. I'm okay with a knife, but not a fan of them," I admit. "I hate that feeling when you end up squishing through an organ. I'd rather fix them than rupture them."

"So, you can administer first aid, too? That's cute," he mocks.

I flip him the finger, and I realize that between Isaac and Scott, it's been getting one hell of a workout today. "Fuck you, asshat," I hiss. "I'm a surgical aid, so I can do a hell of a lot more than just slap on a Band-aid."

He laughs. "I like you. You have spirit."

"Fuck you," I spit back. "Let's see how much you like it when I knock you on your ass."

He tosses his damp towel at me, and I bat it away before it can hit me in the face. "I'd like to see you try," he says flirtatiously.

Furious, I head outside to blow off some steam. Gritty comes running out of the woods with a rotting deer leg in his mouth. He drops it at my feet like some sort of offering, looking pleased as fuck with himself. I pat him on the head and call him a good boy like I know he wants me to, and then he picks it back up and trots off with it. No doubt he's gonna get the shits from eating that. Dumb dog.

With the sun going down, I start my evening chores. I lock the chickens in their coop, and check on the horses, making sure Marigold has enough water in the paddock she stays in when she's here. The hose doesn't reach out that far, so I fill a few buckets of water and use them to top off the trough. The whole time, I'm still stewing over what Isaac said.

"Just so you know, when I said that I like that you have spirit, that was a compliment," he says, startling me enough I nearly lose my grip on the bucket. "You really need to work on your sense of humor."

"What's your problem?" I demand, putting the bucket down and getting in his face. He acts like I unjustly accused him of murder, a *who, me?* look transforming his pretty face into one of mockery.

"I just want to know if you're serious," he says, lifting the bucket and dumping it into the trough like it weighs nothing.

"Serious about what?" I ask defensively.

"About helping liberate the camp. Do you really want to help?"

I don't miss a beat. "Fuck yeah!"

"Then we leave tonight. Be ready at midnight. Make sure no one sees you leave."

32

Trinity

With less than a week to go before the gala, my meticulous plans begin to unravel.

At first, I hadn't been concerned, as the problems that cropped up were of little consequence and easily rectified. Some of the hundreds of many strands of twinkling lights in the ballroom ceiling short out and must be replaced. A few of the plants in the conservatory have wilted due to lack of humidity, so we bring in extra humidifiers to perk them back up. The pastry chef is delivered rotten strawberries for some super special dessert Louise requests, and when all we can find on short notice are blackberries, she grumbles angrily at the last minute change despite the chef claiming she can make do.

These are what we once called "first-world problems" back in the days when we'd still been a first-world nation, and for the most part, I handle them without needing to get others involved. Everyone is putting in their best efforts, as there's not a single person involved in the preparations who wants to be held responsible for something going wrong on party night.

But as the day comes closer, and with time no longer on my side, the things that do go wrong that I have to deal with become increasingly harder to rectify. When a shipment of the Supreme Regent's favorite Cuban cigars fails to arrive, there is no time to reorder. When a case of 100 year-old champagne is dropped and all the bottles shatter, we are forced to serve a lesser vintage.

Louise set up some truly splendid entertainment to be held throughout the evening, the sort of acts that guests will talk about for years to come. But then the famous Soprano comes down with a terrible case of antibiotic-resistant Strep and cannot sing. An incredibly talented ballerina twists an ankle and can hardly walk, nonetheless dance. It's a scramble to fill their slots, but one of my contacts is able to send me two young women with an act that sounds intriguing. All I have to do now is make sure Louise is on board with the changes, as the last thing I want is for her to have a meltdown the night of the party.

When I don't find her in her office, I know she'll be with Caitlin and the baby. They have taken to calling the child by his middle name, Caine, as neither have fond memories of his supposed father. Most of the time I find the child in Louise's arms; when he's awake, she smiles and baby-talks to him, doting on him like she's actually the child's grandmother. When he's asleep, she marvels at his tiny features, often pointing out how much he looks like Edward, much to Caitlin's irritation.

I've taken to studying Caitlin carefully, and with each minute in her presence, I dislike her even more. I see how that woman's mind churns, and when she believes no one is looking, she stares at Louise with hate-filled eyes. I imagine Caitlin still thinks that if Louise was out of the picture that Edward would take her as his wife, when actually, nothing's further from the truth. I've heard that more than a few women have shared his bed since Caitlin's been imprisoned here, each one of them younger, prettier, and considerably less difficult. Her time is clearly over, the only things left to be seen are when and how she will exit this house.

I don't wish to discuss any of this in front of Caitlin, so I wait for Louise to be alone to advise her of the party changes. She frowns, unhappy that I took on this task without consulting her, but other than that, she's actually thrilled with a few of the substitutions. There's a hint of mania about her mannerisms and a glimmer in her deep sapphire eyes that worries me. It's not to the point where I think an increase in medication is in order, but it's still enough to concern me.

She hums to herself as she sits at her vanity and retouches her makeup, both things she hasn't done in a long time. She's surprisingly happy, laughing as she takes pieces of her hair she wore down today and plays around with ways she might wear it the night of the party. She talks about maybe adding a few braids, or strands of pearls, or even fresh flowers, forgoing the traditional hood Jane Seamour would have worn so she can show off her splendid golden mane. She wistfully sighs as she pokes at the wrinkles bracketing her mouth and the crows feet around her eyes, whispering to herself as she gently tugs at her skin to make it taut where it sags ever so slightly. I tell her she's still very beautiful but I don't think she hears me. I catch only a few words here and there that sound like regrets for not doing "something sooner."

But before I can ask her what that means, a knock at the door interrupts us. Her escort down to dinner has arrived. She's become even more fearful of the stairs this past week after a slight wobble descending them one morning brought back painful memories of her fall. The handsome young House Guard takes her arm and weaves it through his, escorting her like she's as fragile as a piece of blown glass.

He leads her slowly and carefully down the steep stairs, murmuring words of support as she tentatively tackles each one. When they reach the end without so much as a bobble, she lets out a relieved breath that she'd probably held the whole way down. She beams up at him when he tells her what a wonderful job she's done.

"I'm sure you think I'm being silly with all this, but I'm just so afraid that I'll take a tumble and end up missing the party. I've waited so long for this moment, and I can't bear the thought of not being there to see how my plans play out."

He smiles again, but his brows crinkle a bit at her choice of words. I must admit, so do mine. I'm beginning to think Caitlin isn't the only one plotting in this household, and that there are a number of plans currently afoot. I never thought my sweet Lou had it in her to take the reins of revenge in her own hands, but maybe I'm wrong. Considering what she's been through over the years, Louise has more reason than anyone to want to see this birthday be Edward's last.

I want to pull her aside and ask what she's up to. I had told her long ago to put her trust in me, and that I would see Edward punished. She said that she would, and I thought that she had, but something's changed. Maybe I've taken too long. Maybe she's lost faith in me. Maybe sometime between the day I came into her life and today she found a way to make thick her blood, stopping up the access and passage to remorse. Maybe her heart is no longer as pure as it once was.

Regardless of the whys and the maybes, the poor woman has suffered enough. I promised her vengeance, and there is still time for me to grant it. Until she actually steps in blood so far that she can wade no more, I still have the chance to do what I had promised. I can save her by taking the dagger from her hands and wielding it myself, like I'd been born to do.

For only by keeping her hands unstained can I prevent the need for all of Neptune's ocean to wash away her guilt. And by God, I will do that. Even if it's the last thing I ever do.

33

Keira

It was a long trip by car, by far the longest I'd ever taken in my life. Isaac laughed at me, saying that I was like a dog going on its first car ride, insisting I keep my window down so I could feel the sun and wind on my face. Even though I knew he had a point, I'd still flipped him off, and even when it became far too warm to continue to be pleasant, I kept the window down purely out of spite.

Isaac told me a lot about what he'd done over the years. He's not only worked in America, but also in a few other countries where extractions had to be arranged. He speaks four languages fluently, and two more well enough to get by in a pinch. He's been to London and Paris with his father, and vacationed on exotic islands with sparkling white sands and water clearer and bluer than anything he believed I could possibly imagine. Not to be outdone, I told him about the oil-spotted shores of the Schuylkill River and the dead, two-headed fish that wash ashore. Then we sat in silence for a long while. I guess he didn't know what to say after that.

I fall asleep for a while, only waking when we get closer to our destination and we have no choice but to take the interstate. Even though he calls ahead to his people to make sure it's clear of block-ades, I'm still scared shitless until we finally return to rural roads. It isn't until Isaac starts up another conversation that I notice he'd been clenching the steering wheel so hard his knuckles turned white.

By the time we get to the safehouse, it's mid-afternoon. I'm starving and sweaty and so ready to get out of the car. We're met by a few people who come out and hug Isaac, and they stare at me like he'd just brought home a kangaroo and asked if he can keep it. There are a few minutes of shouting in some shi-shi foreign language I think is French while I stand there and pretend to not give a shit what they're saying.

Isaac replies calmly to their statements, for all I know telling them I'm a sex worker he picked up along the way, until I realize I'm still in my farm clothes and my hair is in a braid. Standing here silently, I look more like a very young, and very pure, milkmaid than the menace to society I really am. So when one guy, who looks to be in his early twenties, reaches over and tugs on my braid, I grab his wrist and twist his arm behind his back. I make him tap out before I let him go. Only after he shakes out his arm and tells everyone he's okay do their looks of disbelief turn to respect.

Yeah, if there's nothing else I learned in Philly, it's that actions speak a fuck of a lot louder than words.

They welcome us inside the busted-up house, the crew of eight men and two women shaking my hand and introducing themselves. They bring out food and bottles of water, and although I'd never been a big fan of tuna fish sandwiches, I eat three of them after being told that once inside, there's no knowing when I'll eat again.

Most of the afternoon is spent going over maps of the building I'm going into and memorizing the facts of the identity I'll assume. I learn the names of the people I can trust as well as those I need to avoid. I'm disheartened to find it's not only the guards and patrolmen who have no problems taking advantage of a young girl, but quite a few of the inmates, too. By the time I'm done with their lengthy tutorial, I'm more than a little queasy, and it isn't because the mayo in the sandwiches went bad.

We all go to bed as soon as the sun goes down, and although I want nothing more than a shower before sleep, I'm told no. Apparently

I don't smell badly enough yet. Until I finish my mission, I'm not allowed to wash up or brush my teeth. Ew.

I'm shaken awake while it's still pitch dark outside. I'm handed a filthy, threadbare uniform to wear, and it stinks so badly that I don't even want to eat. Then they remind me I need my strength and I manage to choke down one tuna fish sandwich before climbing into one of the trucks with the rest of the undercover crew.

A number of them promptly fall back asleep, but even as exhausted as I am, I'm too nervous to nod off. When the truck stops, and everyone piles out, I'm told we have a five mile trek ahead of us through some thick woods, and to not make too much noise or leave too much of a trail. We break into smaller groups and spread out.

I'm assigned to Isaac's group, no doubt so he can keep an eye on me. We head out single file, working our way silently through the trees. It's as quiet out here at night as it was in Lancaster, minus the occasional mooing cow. I feel an unexpected pang of homesickness, wondering what everyone's doing back on the farm, or if they found the note I left for them tucked under Gritty's collar.

I'm sure Gritty's mad as fuck that I left him behind, not to mention, Declan's gonna kill me when I return. At the time, I thought it better to beg forgiveness than ask permission, so when Isaac asked before we left if Declan specifically permitted me to go, I lied.

"Thinking about backing out?"

The voice coming out of the dark scares the shit out of me, and I barely keep from yipping in fright. "Jesus Christ, Isaac. Tryin' to kill me?"

He's walking beside me, the moon illuminating him enough through the break in the trees that I can now see his face. He takes out a pack of cigarettes and offers me one, but I decline. He lights one up for himself and takes a long drag. "You know, you don't have to do this," he tells me gently. "You can still make it back to the truck before they leave. They don't go until we give the signal."

"I know," I say back snottily. "I'm not having second thoughts."

"No?" he asks, sounding surprised. "You're not scared?"

I think about lying, but he speaks before I can get out the words. "I was so scared the night before my first time that I threw up all over myself. I was imagining all the worst case scenarios and freaked myself out."

"Let me guess—then when you actually got there, it wasn't as bad as you thought?"

He takes another long drag off the cigarette and lets it out slowly. He doesn't look at me when he responds, "No. It was worse."

I swallow down the lump of sandwich in my throat that's now threatening a return trip. "Thanks. That's just what I wanted to hear," I rasp as I push a branch out of my way. "Oh, and a word of advice?" I add nastily. "If anyone ever tries to rope you in for pep talk duty, turn them down. You'd suck at it."

He reaches forward and grabs my arm, forcing me to face him. "I know now that I shouldn't have brought you. I thought you were older."

I roll my eyes. "Let me guess, you talked to Declan."

He winces. "Yeah. I caught Hell from him. I told him the truth, that I made a bad assumption and thought you were like me and just look young. I didn't know you really are young."

"How old are you?"

"I'm twenty-one."

"So? Age doesn't matter. It's what's in your heart that counts."

He scoffs. "You may think so because you're young, but there's a lot to be said for life experience. There's a big difference between sixteen and twenty-three." He pauses for a moment before continuing. "Why did you say yes when I asked if you wanted to come?"

"I dunno," I lie sulkily. "I just wanted to help."

"Don't lie to me," he says, annoyed. "Tell me the truth or I'll send you back right now."

I take a deep breath and let it out slowly. "I've been luckier than most people. I've always had someone help me when I needed it. After losing my parents, I was a wreck, but managed to survive long enough for Brother Love to find me. I spent years in Philly, and through everything from skinned knees to getting my period, someone's always been there to guide me.

"I talked a lot to Micah before he had his surgery. He told me stories about a lot of the people in the camp, and I just feel awful for them. They may be housed in a big group, but every one of them is really on their own. There's nobody in there to look out for them."

We walk again for a long while before he speaks. "Your heart is in the right place for our work," he says slowly. "Just maybe not for situations that hit you, as they say, quite so close to home. Inside the work camps is no place for emotion. Emotions will get you killed. Use your brain, and do exactly as we've told you, and no more. Remember that you can't help everyone, and not everyone in there is going to want to be helped. Do you understand me?"

I find it funny how, just a few days ago, Brother Love told me I needed to listen to my heart more, and now Isaac is telling me not to. "Yeah, I understand," I tell him, even though I really don't. I just tell him what he wants to hear so he won't send me back to the truck.

We say nothing else until the thick underbrush and trees begin to thin, allowing more moonlight to stream over us. The few people walking ahead of us stop, waiting for us to catch up. Isaac looks at his watch and motions for us to be silent and sit, flashing both hands twice and then pointing at his watch.

Twenty minutes to showtime.

34

Emma

Keira's gone.

She snuck out sometime in the middle of the night, met up with Isaac who I'm finding out now is twenty-one. If he were here, I'd slap his boyish face and demand to know what the hell he was thinking. She's not ready for something like this. She's too young. Too inexperienced. She's going to see things that will scar her forever, the sort of things that Declan experienced at her age and that, to this day, give him nightmares.

I'm furious with everyone. I'm livid that Isaac invited her to join them. I'm enraged at Declan for not instilling more respect for authority in her over the months we lived together. I'm fuming that no one else seems as upset about her skipping merrily off into enemy territory as I am.

I'm in the kitchen alone preparing lunch while trying to find the right words to convey that we need to go after Keira. Now. I'm thankful that Declan is the first to arrive, as it gives me the immediate opportunity to make my poorly-thought out demands without an audience. So even though he already looks grouchy enough to qualify as "slightly murderous," I launch into my ill-thought-out speech.

His eyes darken and his brow furrows as I ramble on, his body growing so stiff and still that he reminds me of a coiled snake ready to strike. I'm genuinely surprised when Declan says no, that he won't race down there and bring her home, and potentially jeopardize the entire upcoming mission. Not to mention, he believes he's already too late and she's most likely already inside the camp. He tells me that the best chance of her returning home unharmed is to make sure the overall mission is successful.

He measures his words carefully, delivering them in a way that practically screams there will be no further discussion on this topic. I know that deep inside he's angry and worried, but he simply can't jeopardize so many lives to race after a runaway teen with a good heart set on a very bad idea. I also know that if something does happen to her, he'll never forgive himself.

So I continue to badger him until he finally yells, "Enough!" so forcefully that my heart momentarily stops. I'm so angry that he just won't fucking listen that I burst into tears, the damn pregnancy hormones making me blubber on that he's wrong. When I'm no longer intelligible to even myself I plop down on the bench next to the dining room table and sob into my hands.

My husband mutters a particularly vile string of words and sighs heavily as he straddles the bench and tries to pull me into his arms. I slap him away, finally making how incredibly angry I am right now penetrate his thick, fucking skull. I demand to know that if our own child, his precious son, the one I will give birth to in just a few short weeks, were to do something like this in sixteen years, would he feel equally indifferent?

It's a low blow, and I regret it the moment the words leave my lips. He just sits there and looks at me, this strange expression on his face that's part fear and part something else that I can't quite figure. He rubs his palm over his stubbled jaw and tired eyes, squinting them tightly together for a few seconds before he emits a weary sigh. He takes my hand and once again pulls my back against his chest and encircles me with his arms. This time, I don't fight him, allowing him to flatten his palms against my belly and feel the child within me move.

He inhales quickly, I imagine once again surprised by the reality of impending fatherhood. Declan gently kisses the back of my head, nuzzling his nose against my jaw. He rests his scratchy cheek against mine and I lean into him, enjoying the bite of his beard.

He sighs heavily. "I asked Brother Love once nearly the same question. I asked him months ago, when we were still back in Philly, what should I do if someday I have to choose either my family or the cause? I told him I don't know if I have the strength to choose anything other than my family first, even when I know that's wrong.

"You know what he said to me? He said if that happens, if a choice has to be made, then I'll make one. He didn't say I'd make the *right* choice, he just said that I would choose. Is there a part of me that wants to go down there and drag Keira home? You bet your sweet ass I do. But there's nothing I can do now except pray that she follows whatever orders she's been given, doesn't do anything stupid, and manages to get out in one piece before someone notices she doesn't belong. Keira was trained well. We all knew that sooner or later, she was going to fight, and it just happens to be sooner than *we* are ready for. Just because we think she's not ready doesn't mean that's the truth."

He kisses me gently one more time, and I finally relax into his arms, knowing he's right. "I wouldn't be able to do what she's doing," I admit. "I don't mean because I'm currently the size of a house, but because this mission terrifies me. It's one thing to be caught outside of a prison, but to voluntarily enter one? Especially after you told me what prison was like for you?" I shake my head. "No. There's no way. I'm not that brave."

Declan scoffs, turning me around to face him. "Are you kidding me?" he asks incredulously. "You have risked more than nearly anyone else I've ever known. You dared to stand up against your father *and* against a Supreme-fuckin'-Archon knowing you would pay dearly for that. You've been beaten, brutalized, and intimidated, and yet you didn't back down. Even when you thought there was no way out, you *made* a way out. Does that sound like the actions of some pansy-ass princess to you? Fuck, you're even a better shot than I am now!"

I giggle as he lifts me from the bench so I'm now straddling him, his hands planting firmly on my hips. "You are one incredibly brave woman, and don't you dare think otherwise. That's an order." Then he leans in and kisses me with every ounce of passion in his soul.

Declan nips at my lower lip, demanding I open my mouth as he deepens the kiss. I'm breathless and nearly panting, my husband's hands cupping my ass as he grinds me against his erection. I let out a low moan, tipping my head back as he strings a row of tender kisses down my neck.

I open my eyes, intent to capture my husband's lips again, only to come face to face with three women standing just outside the screen door.

"Jesus Christ!" I shout, pushing away from Declan so forcibly we both nearly fall off the bench. He turns quickly, his gun drawn, but if they were here to hurt us, he would absolutely have been too late.

The eldest woman enters first, followed by two younger, but otherwise nearly flawless, carbon copies. I know I'm staring rudely, but I can't help it. It's not everyday that not one, but *three* ghosts walk into your kitchen.

"I am sorry to arrive uninvited," she says with a small smile gracing her wine-red lips. Her Russian accent is less pronounced than I expect, but otherwise her deep, throaty voice sounds exactly as I remember. "But a certain Commander hasn't been answering his phone."

"You can't be real," I whisper, getting to my feet and taking a step closer. I fully expect that upon closer examination, the similarities between them and my dearly departed friend will be fewer. Maybe what I'm seeing is a trick of the light, or maybe I haven't drunk enough water, and the high heat and humidity are making me hallucinate.

"I assure you, Emma darling, I am no apparition," she states as if she's read my mind. I gasp aloud, wondering how she knows what I'm thinking.

She smiles, the right corner of her mouth lifting slightly more than the left, giving a mocking edge to her words. "Sweet child, you should know by now that I know everything."

35

Keira

I'm gonna hurl.

I turn to my side and barf up the tuna sandwich when there's only five minutes left in the countdown. I'm as quiet as possible, yet I still feel everyone's eyes turn to me and glare. I wipe my mouth with the back of my hand, the smell making me retch again. I'd give anything to be able to rinse out my mouth or to chew on a mint leaf, but with no water and no mint, I'm gonna be stuck with this nasty taste in my mouth forever.

When Isaac gives the signal, we branch off into our smaller groups and creep through the gloom towards the tall fences surrounding the camp. Now that we're closer, I have no idea how we're getting in. The thick wire is run through with barbs, and even if we had gloves and climbed it, there's no way to navigate the razor wire at the top. That shit can cut through pretty much anything.

I look for a gate, but it's so dark out here I can't see far. With no lights shining this far out, I guess they think the security further in is tight enough that the fence makes better visibility redundant. I shiver at the thought.

After fifteen minutes, I'm getting worried. Anytime a twig snaps in the woods, I flinch. I imagine whoever is coming to let us in will come from that direction, as there's no way for them to get through the fence. When the fence rattles gently behind me, I nearly scream, stopping myself just in time.

Okay, Keira. Put on your big girl pants and get it together...

"Come quickly," the guy on the other side of the fence whispers. "We don't have much time."

Isaac pushes me forward, and I nearly fall flat on my face as I trip over a large, rotting tree stump. He squats down and uses every last bit of his strength to lift it just enough for me to shimmy under and drop into a hole. It's deeper than it looks, and I land on my ass with an audible thump.

"Follow this to the end. Someone will be waiting for you there," Isaac whispers. "I'll see you in a few days."

"Wait!" I whisper loudly. "You aren't coming?"

"No," he answers, truly sounding sorry. "Ezra will look out for you. Do as he says and you'll be fine."

The stump falls back in place, and I'm now enveloped in total darkness. The chickenshit part of me wants to lift the stump and go the fuck home, but it's too late for that. My choices are to stay here and absolutely die, or take the tunnel forward and *hopefully* not die. Great.

When what feels like a spider crawling on me breaks through my impending panic attack, I race forward while swatting at myself and trying to not scream like a little girl. I have to keep one hand on the wall as the tunnel is hardly straight, and even being as careful as I can, I still fall a few times. I eventually slam into the end of the tunnel, painfully bumping my forehead and nose against something rough and cool.

Maybe it's from fear, or maybe being underground is just that much colder, but I'm suddenly freezing. I try to warm myself by rubbing my arms with my palms, but it doesn't work. After a few minutes I begin to worry, wondering what I should do if no one comes. I feel along the dirt walls but find no signs of a door, and the ceiling is far enough out of reach that if I need to find a hatch, I'm screwed.

I'm so convinced I'm covered in creepy crawlies that I'm full on slapping at myself, and to keep from screaming, I'm biting the inside of my cheek so hard it bleeds. I was told to remain silent, but now I wonder if that command was wrong. I'm tempted to whisper, to quietly alert someone I'm here, but I freeze when I hear a noise. There's the sound of scraping, of something being moved, then a voice quietly cursing as something falls to the ground with a loud thud. A bit of light shines through some form of heavy utility grate. The person on the other side makes quick work of removing the screws and quietly lifts it to the floor. A hand reaches in and motions for me to come through.

They don't have to tell me twice.

I hurry through the opening, crawling out into a small, dimly-lit room. No sooner than I'm out, the stranger replaces the grate over the Shawshank-style hole and replaces the screws with quick twists of his fingers. I help him pile the rest of the shit in front of it, careful to not make a sound.

My rescuer stands at the door, listening intently for activity in the hall. It gives me a chance to get a look at him, and who I at first thought was a mid-twenties man, is really a guy little older than me. His hair is long, coming down a few inches past his shoulders, and it's clumpy with thick mats that suggest when it had been well kept, it had been curly. He's terribly thin; the threadbare uniform he wears hangs off his emaciated frame. His fingers look like they belong on a skeleton.

When he turns, he places a finger against his lips, then takes my hand in his. He listens at the door, and then cracks it open. Only after he's certain the hall is clear does he pull me through, and after silently closing it, he takes off running through the halls. I'm given no choice but to keep up or get dragged.

I'm so busy trying to keep up with his long-legged stride that I don't watch where we're going. I hope at some point my survival doesn't depend on back-tracking this journey as, within minutes, I'm completely lost. This building is not one they had me memorize plans of.

We finally make it out of the building only to enter the one directly next to it. The second the door opens I'm hit with the smell of something so foul I can't help but retch. The person I'm with grabs me by the hair and jerks me back painfully, staring down into my eyes angrily.

"Don't do that again. Do you hear me, princess?" he hisses nastily.

"Do I look like a fucking princess to you?" I spit back, doing my damndest to not let my eyes water from the combination of pain and stench.

"Compared to the other girls here? You look like a fucking *snack*." His dark brown eyes rake over me hungrily, his fist tightening in my hair a second longer before letting go. A single tear slips through my lashes, and I swipe it away angrily.

He groans. " If you can't handle a little hair-pulling without crying, what are you gonna do at night when the guys form a line around the bunker to take their turn with you? Don't think tears or begging will keep them from fucking you raw."

That's the last thing he says before I grab his arm and twist it behind his back so hard I'm close to breaking it. I shove his face into a wall that I'm pretty sure is smeared with shit, the satisfaction of proving him wrong making me more than a little giddy. "Where the fuck did you come from?" he pants through the pain.

"I'm from Philly, motherfucker," I spit. "That's where I'm from." Then I give his wrist another twist. I hear a pop and feel something give under my palm. Oops. My bad.

Someone claps behind me, the sound making me spin, taking my captive with me as a shield. As this new inmate strolls closer, my hostage begins to shake. He tries to break free of my hold, but has no luck.

What can I say? I've been taught *very* well.

"I think Princess here passed the test," my hostage rasps. "Mind callin' her off, boss?"

He grins. "Sure. You can let him go. Caesar won't hurt you."

Wow. He must think I'm especially stupid. "If I let him go, what's gonna keep you from both coming at me?"

"Good question. How about I give you my word? I've been told that for members of the BSB, that's important."

"How do you know that?"

"Because I've been there. I'd go with my father and supply them with food when the planes were unable to make the trip."

I feel like my eyes are gonna bug right out of my head. "Oh my God. Ezra?"

He nods. I let go of Caesar so fast he falls to his knees. He curses as he stands and shakes out his arm.

Ezra smirks. "If anyone finds out that she kicked your ass, it's gonna be open season on you. "If you really are hurt, I suggest you hide it. Now, go inside and make sure everyone's out on the floor. I don't want anyone missing our grand entrance."

"Yes, boss," he nods, before loping off down a long corridor and out of sight. Ezra takes his time walking, using the opportunity to tell me a few more important things that will hopefully keep me safe. He says that under no circumstances am I to let myself be separated from his group, but should it happen, I am to tell anyone who threatens me that I am under his protection.

We veer off the main hallway and down a narrower one until we reach a room at the end. He opens the door and pushes me through, pulling the heavy door shut behind us. Around us are a number of large, noisy machines that remind me a bit of the mechanical room we had back in Philly. Of all of the places for him to take me, this is not what I expected.

Ezra looks at me sheepishly. "I'm sorry for this next part," he yells over the din to me. "But if the guards don't believe us, we're fucked."

I want to ask him what he means by that, but he pulls a shiv made from some form of bone from inside his pants and clamps his hand over my mouth. "This room is pretty soundproof, but let's not press our luck. Try not to scream, okay?"

He sees the terror in my eyes, but it doesn't stop him. I try to fight, but he's too strong. The next thing I know I'm face down on the ground with him on top of me. His knee is in the middle of my back, and he twists my body so the outside of my left arm is up. He tears that part of my shirt open, and I scream as he carves into my arm. The second he's done, he leaps off of me so I can scramble to my feet.

"What the fuck?" I yell as I clamp my opposite hand over the wound. "Are you trying to give me Hepatitis or something?"

He doesn't say anything as he tears a length of fabric off the bottom of his filthy shirt. "Here, let me bandage you," he says.

He must think I'm stupid, but I'm not falling for that shit. He's not coming near me as long as he's got that knife on him. I tell him to toss the bandage to me, and when he does, I awkwardly wind it around my upper arm. I try not to think of all the germs I just introduced into my bloodstream and silently curse him again. I'm totally gonna haunt his ass if I die from the plague because of this.

"Let's go," he tells me before grabbing my other arm and hustling me out of the room.

Despite my many hissed questions, like *what the fuck was that all about?*, he remains silent as he drags me around to a set of huge double doors. There are four armed Ag patrolmen all armed with massive rifles guarding the entrance, the noise from within so loud we can hear it before they even open the doors.

The patrolmen look at us like we are dogshit under the soles of their boots. They ask Ezra who I am and where I'm from, and when he smirks nastily saying only, "I won her in a bet," they nod and leer back.

"She got a name?" the grossest of the guard says as he reaches for me. If there was a picture next to the word pedophile in the dictionary, it sure as shit would be his. I cower away, burrowing myself against Ezra in the process.

"I think I'm gonna call her Princess," he says with a lewd smile. "When I'm buried balls-deep inside her later tonight, I don't doubt she'll make me feel like fuckin' royalty." They all laugh at my expense, and despite being scared shitless, it takes everything in me to not kick them in the nuts until they sing Soprano. Fuckin' assholes.

We're finally allowed inside, Ezra whispering in my ear that I'm doing great, and just keep it together a little longer. The stench is much worse here, my eyes watering as I try my best not to retch.

There are ten or so inmates standing in a group, all of them apparently waiting for us. As terrifying as Ezra is, these guys are worse. They are the sort of men you'd see mugshots of on the evening news and not be at all surprised to learn were ax murderers. If I thought the looks I got from the Ag patrol were bad, these fuckers look like they want to carve off my skin and wear it as a suit. I do my best to not look afraid, but I'm failing miserably.

"This is Princess. She's mine. I've already put my mark on her, so spread the word that there will be no fighting over her. She's off limits. Anyone who touches her will have to deal directly with me. Understand?"

Most of them answer with a curt, "Yes, boss," but a few grumble under their breath that Ezra always gets the good ones. He glares at them until they utter their apologies, and then tells them to get the room ready for morning announcements. We move together as a unit to a raised platform, Ezra's men lining up below it as we stand behind them.

A painfully loud buzzer goes off and the room silences, the inmates below us lining up in rows. There are a few who don't—those giving and receiving painful-sounding beatings along the back wall continue, as do those engaged in sex that doesn't seem remotely consensual based on the screams.

Ezra drags me onto the stage with him, and it takes every ounce of willpower I have to not completely lose my shit. My heart's beating so hard I'm amazed they can't see it throbbing under my shirt, and the room's so quiet, I can clearly hear every grunt and sob from those being assaulted. I don't know why Ezra doesn't stop it, instead acting as if he doesn't notice.

"We will be given new assignments today. Everyone will report to their usual locations and await instructions. I advise that whatever they tell you to do, you do it. I will remind you that it only takes one person to not do their job, or to mouth off, for us all to suffer, and I can assure you, that if I have to suffer your punishment, you will most certainly suffer mine."

I can't believe what I'm hearing. How is this brute possibly related to my sweet Micah? How can he possibly think threatening these people with additional abuse is the way to get shit done?

I'm pulled from my thoughts when he jerks my arm and swings me to stand in front of him. He grabs my hair and forces me to look out in the audience, and I can't help but try to fight him. He wraps his hand around my throat and squeezes tight, and I'm so damn afraid, I go absolutely feral. Yet no matter how hard I twist and buck, he doesn't let go.

"Lastly, this wild, little filly is mine to break. You are not to touch her. Anyone not following this order will pay with their life."

He tears the bandage from my arm, and any clots that may have formed are torn off. The room goes wild, cheering and whistling, the masses stamping their feet in time on the filthy floors. He tosses the bloody bandage into the crowd where people fight over it as if it's a prize. I feel absolutely sick, but not nearly as ill as when I look down and see Ezra had carved his initials in my arm.

What the fuck have I gotten myself into?

36

Louise

I spend the morning doting on Caine while his mother spends an eternity primping and polishing herself as if getting ready for Prince Charming's ball. She ignores her son when he begins to whimper and even after he begins to cry. He sounds stronger, his little body finally putting on some weight. I hug him and croon sweet words, but nothing soothes him.

"I think he's hungry," I tell Caitlin. She ignores me, continuing to apply a thick coat of mascara that smears a bit under her eyes. I stand next to her and hold out the wailing child, making it clear she is to feed him now. She sighs heavily, annoyed at the imposition. I have no doubt if I wasn't here, she'd just let him scream.

She takes the child back to her bed and climbs in with another aggrieved sigh, as if I'd asked her to do hard manual labor and not breastfeed her child. She tries to catch a glimpse of herself in the mirror, but the angle's wrong. She lets out another long, mournful sigh. It's clear she wants me to ask what's wrong.

Although I really don't care, I know her pouting won't cease until I ask. She looks up at me tearfully, having called up an impressive amount of crocodile tears just in time to go with whatever speech she has planned.

"Oh, I'm just missin' the good days, when Edward and I used to go out and do things. He'd take me to parties and dinners, and I'd spend time with important people and wear all the latest fashions. I miss it."

I already know where this little speech is headed, as I've heard it before. She wants to go to the gala. She's hoping if she makes me feel badly enough, that I'll somehow overrule Edward and allow her to attend.

As we used to say back in my youth, she must be smokin' crack if she thinks she'll be allowed to step one foot in the ballroom. She can't be trusted to not create a scene, or to let Edward's enormous secret out of the bag. Every day, I wonder if this is the day he will come forward and tell the world about Caine's birth, but every night, not a word comes from the Executive Mansion. I can't help but worry what that means.

"Caitlin, stop. Just stop," I sigh with a shake of my head. "There's nothing I can say or do to convince Edward to let you go to the gala. Will you please just drop it?"

I'm uncharacteristically irritable today. I'm anxious and angry, my emotions flitting between wanting to verbally rip someone's head off and then worrying nonstop about being overly harsh. Right now, I want to slap Caitlin for flaunting the time she spent with my husband, yet at the same time, I feel sorry for her. I wonder if I can somehow get her out of here, to give her a wad of cash and tell her to run while she still can, but even if I did, I know she wouldn't heed my advice. She's deluded herself into thinking that once Caine gets stronger, he will welcome them both back to the Executive Mansion. It's when she says things like that when my pity for her hits the hardest, because once upon a time, I had thought that, too.

After I returned home without my child, I honestly thought my mother would push for an annulment, and I would spend the rest of my life pretending that the past year and a half never happened.

CHAPTER THIRTY-SIX

Oh, how wrong I was.

Despite how much she despised Edward, she claimed that, after much prayer, we should stay married. She cited the whole "what God has joined no man, or woman, may put asunder" bullshit and refused to hear another word.

You would think that after I got on my knees and begged her to change her mind, after I told her how he'd brutally raped me, that she'd feel different. Instead, she sighed heavily, looked down at me like I was the biggest pain in her ass, and told me to stop lying. When I looked at her incredulously, she spouted off that victims of rape cannot get pregnant, that she'd seen it on the news.

Um, excuse me—WHAT?!

For the next month, I brought her all sorts of credible scientific journals that proved her wrong, but nothing I said changed her mind. We were going to remain married, 'til death did us part.

The only saving grace was now that there was no child, there was no rush in telling the world about our forced marriage. I would still be allowed to go to college and study something suitable, but the summer after graduation, Edward and I would be wed, this time for all the world to see.

I cursed myself over and over for not going to the hospital that night. If I couldn't get my own mother to believe me, how would anyone else? That's when I remembered I did have someone to corroborate my story. Two someones. I just had no idea how to find them.

Luckily for me, I had plenty of time to hunt them down.

But fate was not kind, and time proved fleeting. I did everything I could to find them, but nothing I did led to their discovery. As days became months, and months became years, the circled day on the calendar grew closer. Through all this time, I never once heard from Edward, nor did I contact him. It was clear he wanted nothing to do with me, just as I wanted nothing with him.

Our wedding day dawns bright and clear, the sort of gorgeous June weather every bride prays for. Well, all except for me. In truth, there is no weather miserable enough to match how I feel. I even thought about running away, but my mother had me so closely watched I never had an opportunity.

I prayed night and day that Edward would leave me standing at the altar, but he didn't. When the double doors into the church open with a flourish and the string quartet launches into Canon in D, all I can think is how has my life come to this?

Each step down the aisle is another knife in my heart. Edward stands with his back to me, his posture forced and stiff, and even when my father places my hand in his, he doesn't look at me. It isn't until my mother pronounces us husband and wife that he turns to me, the look of sheer hatred on his face nearly making me faint.

At the reception, people stand to give speeches in our honor and toast us with expensive champagne. I am wished over and over again for the "joy of a honeymoon conception" and each time it's said, I force myself to smile when all I want to do is cry.

We barely say two words to each other at the reception, even our first dance together is stiff and silent. If anyone notices how awkward we are, no one says a word. Nor does anyone mention how much Edward drinks.

By the end of the night he can hardly stand. When he begins to get belligerent, my mother pours him into the limo that will take us to the airport, and then shoves me in after him.

I tell her I don't feel safe. I tell her he can't be trusted.

She tells me that I should have thought about that before I chose him all those years ago. Then she slams the door in my face.

The cabana in the Maldives where we stay is an absolute paradise. The luxurious surroundings are wonderfully private as it sits far from the rest of the resort, in the middle of crystal clear waters. We have a small motorboat that we can take to the mainland for dinner and dancing at night, but we never do. Every morning, Edward wakes before me, takes the boat and leaves, not returning until the very early hours of the morning smelling of women's perfume and sex. A few nights he doesn't return at all.

Most brides would be furious, but not me. I'm thankful he found a diversion. His dalliances leave me able to enjoy my time, the staff making sure I'm cared for and fed, bringing me mouthwatering meals that I thoroughly enjoy at my candlelit table for one. I lose myself at night in my books, often reading until I hear the distant hum of the boat and then quickly turn out my light, pretending to be asleep.

After ten days of this, I'm ready to go home. I'm eager to start my new job as an Information Security Analyst with the degree I'd earned alongside my one for English Literature. I only have a few days to set up our house before all my time will be spent learning the ins and outs of my new profession, all while pretending to be happily married. I'm still not sure how, but I'm determined to make my new life work.

I fall asleep quickly and easily after a full day in the sun and my third generously-poured glass of wine. I wake a few hours later to the sound of high winds and cool water dripping on me. Lightning flashes and thunder booms, the placid water under the cabana angry and churning. Yet the storm is not nearly as furious as the sodden man standing over me with his hands already formed into fists. I scream and stumble from the bed, tripping as my nightgown tangles between my legs.

To this day, I honestly believe I would have been less afraid if there had been a stranger in my room. That violent night was just the first of countless that I would endure. I never told anyone what happened, as I had no one to tell. After our marriage, none of my friends would have us in their homes lest Edward's *impurity* somehow soil them. If I invited them to our place, they always had prior engagements. I did make friends at work, but I wasn't allowed to spend time with them after hours. Edward kept close tabs on me, and the few times I did flaunt his rules, he somehow always found out. I learned quickly that a few hours of fun with my colleagues was not worth the week of aches and pain that inevitably followed.

After our honeymoon, Edward grew smarter with his abuse. He always made sure the bruises he inflicted were in places easily hidden, and the few times they weren't, he schooled me so well in the lies we would tell that even I no longer knew fact from fiction. He could twist any argument we had so that I was always wrong, even listening to just enough of my mother's Sunday sermons to be able to say I was a shitty Christian for not being more subservient.

The old me, the one who smoked weed, and drank, and stayed out all night with my friends, wouldn't have cared one bit what he, my mom, or even God thought about my actions. But over the years, things changed.

I changed.

I began to drink; at first just a glass or two of wine a night to help me sleep, and then it was three, and then five. After the number of empties became downright embarrassing to take to the curb for recycling, I switched to hard alcohol, only to start drinking that like it was water, too.

On top of everything else, there was the ever-increasing pressure for me to get pregnant. As much as Edward hated me, he still demanded sex regularly. Usually it was when he'd come home from a night out, reeking of cigarette smoke and strong liquor. He never talked about wanting children, and I never brought it up. I'd always dreamed of having a large family, but that was when I also thought I'd have a loving husband who yearned to be a doting father.

So, the day Edward came home and said I needed to get pregnant ASAP, I almost laughed. He made getting pregnant sound like just another chore, like picking up his drycleaning or cooking dinner. I asked him why now? What was the rush? He looked me straight in the eye and said the publicist he'd hired to get him ready for a Senate run in a few years claimed that he'd get more votes if he had a few small children to parade before the cameras along with his pretty wife.

But as the pages of the calendar flipped, my uterus remained empty. Edward made me feel like a complete failure as a woman, unable to do the one thing I was biologically designed to do. Of course, he also insisted it was my fault, so even after putting me through a battery of painful, invasive tests and being told there was no reason why I couldn't conceive, he continued to blame me.

Then, just about the time he was ready to give up, I missed my period. When I missed it the next month, too, I bought a test, but it took me another month to get up the courage to use it. When the little pink plus sign appeared in the window, my first reaction was it had to be wrong.

I told myself I would wait until I could go to the pharmacy and pick up a few more tests before I'd tell anyone, but even after they came back positive, I still told no one.

The very next week, a story about a pretty young woman who bled out from a rare, but almost always fatal, pregnancy complication was all over the news. Neighbors had heard her terrified screams and called the police, but by the time the paramedics arrived, she was dead. Knowing she hadn't been dead long and there was a slim chance the child might still be alive, the paramedics cut the child from her, saving his life.

I'd been initially so horrified by the tragic story that I immediately set up an appointment with my OB/GYN for the following week. I watched the news every night for word on the baby's condition, crying tears of joy when they finally reported he was going to be fine. I obsessed over the future of the sweet little orphan, reading every article about him I could get my hands on.

I still said nothing of my pregnancy, now telling myself I'd wait until after my first prenatal visit before breaking the news. I wanted to make sure my baby was okay before telling anyone. The last thing I wanted was to tell everyone I was pregnant only to be blamed later should I lose it. Despite my miserable marriage, I was growing okay with the idea of having a child. I told myself that maybe what Edward needed was a little boy, or girl, to break through the hard shell encasing his heart. Maybe once he saw me as a mother, he'd be kinder.

I also told myself that if he ever lifted a finger against our child, we would leave. Immediately.

That night, Edward came home so drunk he could barely stand. I hadn't seen him like this in ages, and I knew better than to ask what was wrong. He didn't go to work the next day, holing up in his office and speaking quietly, but urgently, on the phone until late into the night. He was hiding something from me. Something that worried him greatly.

I thought all the secrecy meant he'd found a new mistress, or when my bank statements came in at the end of the month, there'd be yet another large withdrawal from my accounts to pay an unwanted one to go away. But Edward had cheated on me through the entirety of our marriage, and used my private funds at his whim, and never cared if I knew. Whatever happened was apparently something much worse.

As I waited for him to come home that night, I became increasingly angry. Despite not having told him about the baby, I planned to tell him that his dalliances needed to stop. We needed to try to make our marriage work, if not for ourselves, for our child. When I tried to talk to him over dinner, Edward became so angry that he threw his plate across the room and stalked out. He got in his car and left. By the next morning he still hadn't returned.

Then, I found out why Edward was acting so strangely over the past few days. That afternoon, *The New York Times* broke the story that my husband, Edward James Bellamy, is the orphan boy's father.

Our lives become a media circus. I can't leave my house or go to work without being accosted by reporters. Late night comedians make jokes at

Edward's and my expense, the sort of tasteless quips people titter over water coolers at work the next morning. I never need to wear blush as I am continually red-faced with embarrassment.

Just when things begin to die down, a second wave of scrutiny hits. After somehow managing to obtain the mother's phone records, another newspaper reports that there had been a call of a few minutes' duration placed from the mother's apartment to Edward's cell phone during the time she would have been in labor. Although the contents of the call are unknown, it's long enough that he can't claim it was placed in error.

If I thought we'd been in the midst of a scandal before, I'd been sorely mistaken. What started as an embarrassing turn of events morphs into a full-blown criminal investigation. Edward remains silent at the insistence of his attorneys, a strategy that backfires spectacularly. In the jury of public opinion, Edward is guilty as sin.

It makes me sick to think him capable of what everyone is saying and what I know deep in my heart he is capable of. I worry for the child I carry, wondering if I find myself in the same situation, would Edward also let me die?

Unequivocally, I know the answer to be yes.

The day our financial records are hacked and printed for the world to see, I had enough. To see the vast sums of my money being transferred into her account over a period of nearly two fucking years is the final straw. I don't care what the church, my mother, or anyone else had to say about it, I'm done. I want a divorce.

I'm waiting for Edward in our living room when he rolls in about two in the morning. He barely spares me a glance before heading upstairs to the spare bedroom he sleeps in except when he wants me to service him. I follow him in and stand in the doorway, staring at him as he walks into the bathroom, turns on the shower, and begins to undress.

That he dared to ignore me set off something in my brain that, to this day, I don't understand. All the years of cowering from Edward fueled my anger, and for the first time in my life, I felt the true depth of my hatred towards him. To realize something like that for the first time should be a terrifying thing, but it wasn't. It *empowered* me. I'd been hurt enough, thank you very much. Now it was my turn to do the hurting.

"I want a divorce." My voice is calm but forceful.

He turns to me, his black eyes mocking as he smirks back. "And you think that I don't?" He walks over to me, grabs my chin in his fingers and pulls me closer. He reeks of whiskey and cheap perfume.

I don't know what snaps in my brain, only that it does. I slap him as hard as I can, breaking his hold on me and causing him to stumble backwards. I don't doubt it hurt me more than it hurt him, my palm burning from the impact with his rough cheek. He turns to me with the strangest expression on his face, his eyes piercing through to my soul, a small smile on his lips.

"So, you still have some fight left in you after all?" he chuckles before his face turns into the one I'll see in my nightmares forever.

The beating that follows is only second to the one that night so long ago in a dark alley behind a seedy bar. After he forces himself on me, he stands up and glares down in disgust at where I lay, sobbing in a curled up ball on the carpet.

"'Till death do we part, wife," he spits. "For this scandal to blow over, we need to present a united front. You will stand by my side, be a supportive partner, and say and do exactly as I say. You know what I'm capable of, and I suggest you remember that before you raise your hand to me ever again."

Two days later, I miscarried at home.

I was battered, bruised, and far too afraid to leave my house and get medical attention in my current condition. I stayed in bed around the clock, only getting up to get an occasional glass of water or to use the bathroom. I didn't return the calls from work asking where I was, nor did I answer those of Edward or my mother who demanded my appearance at events I refused to attend.

I prayed that I'd die, but of course, I didn't. After a week of barely being able to breathe from the grief, I forced myself to go downstairs. As a reward for my effort, I poured myself a drink. I needed to numb the pain or I was going to go insane. This was the only way I knew how.

I was thoroughly wasted when Edward came home that night and found me sitting on the floor in my dirty nightgown with a nearly-empty bottle of bourbon in my hand. He rolled his eyes and looked at me with scorching disdain before leaving me to my own devices.

The next morning, I had a screaming hangover and my body ached from sleeping on the hardwood floor. My mother stood over me, shaking me as she tried to rouse me.

"Louisa May, of all the days to indulge yourself, this is not it. Get yourself up and get ready."

I get in the shower and into a pretty lavender dress my mother brought with her. Although I look absolutely exhausted, with my hair styled and makeup in place, no one would have ever guessed I'd just lost a baby. I wordlessly climb into my mother's limo and we drive in silence. I don't even care where we're going when we pull into a gated community and drive another few miles until we come to a huge mansion surrounded by another imposing stone fence.

"Who's house is this?" I ask, knowing I've never been here before.

My mother titters before answering in her most sarcastic tone. "Your husband really should keep you better informed, Louisa May. It's yours, silly. A little gift for you for taking everything that's happened in such good stride."

I give her a scathing glare before glaring up at the imposing monstrosity of a home. "Edward bought this for me?"

Now my mother really laughs. "Of course not. It's a gift from one of his supporters. The only things your husband knows how to spend money on are whores."

I cringe at her crass language. The door is opened for us by a liveried butler who gives us a tour of the finely furnished home. It's stuffy and overdone, what my mother refers to derogatorily as "new money style."

There's only one room under construction upstairs, a guest room suite that smells of fresh paint and new carpet. The workers smile at us as we walk through, taking a moment to fluff out the navy blue curtains they're in the process of hanging. There's a small print on them that I step closer to see, and I gasp aloud when I realize what they were.

Little, yellow ducks wearing sailor hats.

Oh, dear God. No. Please, no.

I race into the bathroom and barely make it to the toilet before I vomit. I know what they're going to demand of me, and I won't do it. I can't do it.

My mother walks in moments later, her back ramrod straight and a frown on her face. I honestly don't remember any of the lecture except for the word "duty" being thrown around like she has any idea what the word means.

I am so broken that all I can do is cry. My mother sits me down in the library and gives me some sort of pill that thoroughly numbs me out. When it wears off, I ask for another, liking the feeling far too much to let it go so soon.

It's dark when the front door opens again, the sound of leather soles slapping the marble floors giving away that it's Edward before I even hear him call my name. I sit in the dark and continue to stare at nothing until he flips on the switch, bathing the room in light.

He's furious. Apparently, I was supposed to meet him at a press conference, but I honestly don't remember anyone telling me I needed to go to one. He continues to rant and rage, demanding that I look at him, but I can't. It isn't until I hear the strangest sound, like that of a kitten's cry, that I look up and see the baby in his arms.

I shake my head, mouthing the word no because it's all I can do. No matter how hard I try, I can't make a sound. Edward tries to hand the child to me, but I refuse to take him. He finally shoves the swaddled baby in my chest and lets go, forcing me to either accept him or drop him on the floor. Less than a minute later, the front door slams shut behind him, and I'm left sitting there, stupidly holding his child.

I stare at him blankly when he begins to cry. I don't even know his name. "You're not the only one unhappy about this," I murmur as I get up and lay him on the sofa and walk woodenly to the bar. I grab a bottle of vodka, but this time, I don't bother with a glass.

37

Keira

As promised, Ezra keeps a close eye on me. As the head inmate supervisor, he makes regular rounds of our workhouse, checking in with the guys under him to make sure everything's going as it should. Today's been nothing but one problem after another as the crews attempt to shovel piles of caked pig shit from the ground and then scrub the filthy floors and walls spotless without the proper equipment. When he has to leave, he puts Caesar in charge of watching me.

No one speaks to me as we work, although many stare. They all turn away when my eyes meet theirs, often looking around in fear to see if Caesar noticed the interaction. It's clear everyone in here's terrified of him, and yet I nearly took the punk down with a simple self-defense move. At least that thought makes me smile.

We get a five minute break every four hours, most of us opting to sit down, a few people lining up to drink from the hose we're using to clean the filthy building. I want to warn them about the dangers of coliform bacteria, but looking at most of the inmates, that's the least of their problems. I've never seen such a sickly looking group.

I worry that most of them won't be able to run as fast and as far as they'll need to get to safety, but their physical health is not my only concern. Many of them are so mentally checked out that they're barely aware of their surroundings, where others have lost touch with reality completely. Brother Love's gonna need a baseball bat and Jesus on speed dial when he works with the violent ones.

"Princess. Come here," Ezra calls over from where he's standing with a few of his crew. I've learned that here, nobody uses their real names. Whatever name Ezra and his thugs give you is what you're called, well everyone except for Ezra. I guess being the boss comes with privileges. So far I've heard of people named Shit Stain, Cum Bucket and Fuck for Brains, so I really can't complain about Princess, even though I hate it.

He wrinkles his nose as I approach. I know I stink to high hell, but there's not a damn thing I can do about it. He and his buddies are all supervisors, so they're cleaner and smell considerably better than the rest of us. "Before you leave tonight, make sure you hose off. I don't wanna catch some disease from you being dirty when we fuck."

Um, excuse me, but no way in hell is that happening.

I nod at him obediently even as my eyes shoot daggers at his face.

"You gonna let us have a turn when you're done with her?" one of the more unhinged of his group asks. "You keep telling us that one day you will, but you never do. You keep killing them before we get a chance."

I look up at him in fear before I school my features back to being angry, but not fast enough for them to not see. A couple guys snicker nastily, looking at me like they're ready to devour me. I doubt even they know if they want to bang me or actually take a bite.

"I don't know yet," Ezra says. "Depends how good she takes my cock if I let her go. This one's a virgin, or so I'm told. I might keep her to myself for a while. At least I know I won't catch a STD from this one."

A few guards enter the room, Ezra barking out that break time's over and for us lazy slugs to get back to work. He nods my dismissal as he walks over towards the guards. I steal a few glances at them as I work, the look on Ezra's face worrying me. Whatever they are talking about has him concerned, but he hardens his jaw, stands up a bit straighter, and nods.

The rest of the day is more of the same, and it's way past dark before the buzzer signals the end of the workday. I'm so tired I can barely stand, my palms blistered and raw. We all line up and wait to be marched back to the barracks, when the doors open and the guards march back in. There are more of them this time, and they are more formal, lining up facing us. Even Ezra and his men join our line, their chins tipped up and chests thrust forward. Someone should tell them they are far too thin to adopt such a pose. They all look like a strong breeze could blow them over.

A tall blonde guy marches in, his white uniform adorned with gold buttons an odd sight in a world where the authorities wear the drab green Ag uniforms. He's a Purity Officer, and based on the badges and medals on his chest, an important one. He stands before us, glancing over the line with an expression on his face I can't read.

"Ezra, step forward," he barks.

"Yes, sir!"

The officer strolls over to him, standing just close enough to give him a thorough once-over with his eyes. Ezra doesn't flinch when the lecherous bastard takes another step forward. They talk quietly for a few minutes, Ezra never once relaxing his stance. Although most of the guards around here seem to respect, if not fear, Ezra, this guy is a whole other story. This is the first person I've noticed Ezra's afraid of.

I'm nervous as hell when the officer strolls down the line. He stops in front of a few people to ask their names, nodding as if he's adding them to some list in his mind. When he stops before me, the clear blue of his cold eyes startles me. I've always prided myself in my ability to school my face into whatever it needs to be, but this guy catches me off guard. I inhale a sharp gasp as we lock eyes, the iciness of his gaze making me shiver.

My fear makes him smile. He takes his time looking me over, the sneer on his face making my stomach somersault. He reaches forward and takes a lock of my hair in his fingers and tugs gently on it, watching the curl straighten and bounce back when he releases it.

"I've always had a special fondness for redheads," he tells me in a throaty whisper. "What's your name, sweetheart?"

"Princess," I answer meekly, despite wanting to spit in his face.

"It suits you," he says, nodding his head. A wicked smile blooms on his face, the sort of smile that means he's thinking something really dirty right now. "I intend to see a great deal more of you in the near future, Princess."

Ugh, just the thought makes me wanna puke. He chucks me under the chin with his finger, and it takes every ounce of my willpower to not retort, "Over my goddamn dead body." Thank God we're only here for two more days. Hopefully he won't have time to summon me before then.

We're marched back to the barracks, and the second the guards slam the heavy doors shut and lock them from the outside, Ezra grabs my arm and drags me up several long flights of stairs and shoves me into a tiny cell of a room. "Stay here, and lock the door behind me. I don't give a shit if someone says the place is on fire, don't open that door unless it's for me or Caesar."

"What's wrong?" I grab his sleeve and try to get him to stay a moment longer.

"We have to move the timeline up. We've gotta be out of here tomorrow."

I frown. "I thought we had more time? What's changed?"

"That asshole being here," Ezra snaps, sounding exasperated. "Bad things happen when he's here. Really bad things."

For the first time, Ezra completely drops his cocky facade and looks truly scared. "The last time he was here, he pulled out a gun and opened fire in gen-pop. He killed a bunch of defenseless kids for no reason. One of the people he shot was my brother. I managed to get him out, but I have no idea if he made it."

I pull him in close, whispering in his ear. "He's alive. He was in rough shape when I found him, but he's going to be okay." I don't tell him we amputated Micah's arm. I don't know how he might react to that news.

"Oh, my God, thank you," he whispers back as he pulls me in for a hug, crushing me to his chest. "Thank you so much. When I get back, I want you to tell me everything, but for now, just lay low, and whatever you do, don't let anyone in. I mean it."

He steps out a second later, but waits for me to engage the crude lock before leaving. I peek through the tiny window and watch him meet up with a few of his guys before trotting down the stairs and out of sight.

Exhausted, I lie down on his tiny mattress on the floor and stare up at the ceiling. Not long after, the lights are shut off, and everything goes black.

I must have fallen asleep, because the next thing I know, I'm woken by the sound of frantic banging against the door. When I hear Ezra's voice, I fumble with the lock to let him in. It's so damn dark I can't see a thing, but I eventually wrench it open. Four or five guys push their way in, all of them hissing to hurry. Someone tackles me to the mattress, their hand pressed over my mouth to keep me from screaming. The sound of fabric hitting the floor fills the room, as more sweaty bodies land next to me.

"Just go along with this. Please," Ezra whispers before whipping his shirt over his head and telling me to hurry up and do the same.

I'm scared half to death when a few seconds later, footsteps race up the stairs. The guys are all over me and yet weirdly, hardly touching me. They make the sort of noises I heard back in Philly when a few of the guys watched old pornos together, and that's when, *oh shit,* I realize I'm in the middle of a pretend orgy. I understand we have to make this believable, but what the hell did they do that this is their first choice of alibi?

A heavy fist slams against a door, demanding we open up.

Ezra stands quickly and whips open the door, the guard's flashlight bouncing off Ezra's naked body. "Whadda you want?" he asks, sounding annoyed as fuck. "We were just getting to the good part."

I feel the guys shuffling around me, then something warm and wet drips down my side. Oh my God, if someone just jizzed on me, I'm gonna fucking kill them. . .

But then I detect the scent of copper pennies in the air and realize it's blood. One of them is bleeding. A lot.

After convincing the guard we've all been screwing around for a while, the Ag officer retreats. The second we no longer hear him in the hall, Ezra rummages around in the dark, coming up with a lighter in his hand. One of the guys moans, but it's not a sexual sound. It's pain.

I go into healer mode, demanding to know who's hurt and what happened. The guys scatter, leaving the injured one writhing on the floor. Ezra comes closer with the lighter, illuminating one of his buddies. His shirt is soaked with blood, and when I lift it to get a better look, more blood pours from the hole in his abdomen. I grab the blanket on the mattress and use it to put pressure over the wound, but it's soaked through within seconds.

"I can't fix this," I tell them. "He needs surgery. Even then. . ." my voice trails off. The guy moans louder, and one of his buddies slams a palm over his mouth to shut him up. Less than a minute later, he stops writhing.

"Fuck!" Ezra shouts. The room remains silent, all of us looking down at the body. A few of the guys are glassy eyed, and one of them wipes a tear from his cheek quickly, trying to not let the others see. Judging by how gutted everyone looks, nobody would have teased him if they had.

"Okay, we've got to get him out of here," Ezra states as he pulls on his clothes. Someone next to me sniffs loudly. "We don't have time for tears. We've got less than two hours before the morning alarm, and any trace of him being here has to disappear before then. When they see he's missing tomorrow, they're gonna search everywhere. Not a trace of blood can be in here. Got it?"

"Wait," I demand before the guys pick him up. "I have an idea. Ezra, I need your knife. If I can dig the bullet out, I can make this look like a stabbing. We can say he started acting crazy, and you all began to fight. He pulled the knife, but one of you got it from him. Then, somehow in the dark, he got his own knife in the guts."

The small flame flickers out, and when Ezra finally flicks it back to life, it illuminates his scowl.

"If we keep things vague, blame everything on him, and the fact it's so fucking dark in here, they might believe it."

Ezra thinks for a minute, letting the light flicker out. "I feel like shit about blaming this on him. Caesar was a good guy."

I flinch, realizing I'd been too in the "zone" to even see who'd been hurt. I'd only known Caesar a couple hours, but he did seem like a decent enough guy. "Look, Ezra, nothing we say or do can change the fact he's dead. I know that's harsh, but it's the truth. Someone's gotta take the blame, and they are gonna punish the shit out of whoever we point the finger at. I say we do this, and once we get the fuck outta here, you can build him a fucking monument if you want. Until then, I think this is our best chance."

The guys talk for a few minutes, and after giving me the green light, I tell them to turn around. There's no reason for them to watch me digging around inside their friend, but I do need someone to keep the lighter going while I fish around for the bullet. Ezra volunteers, sitting across from me as I work. I hope he can't see how bad my hands are shaking, my only consolation coming from my occasional upward glances at Ezra's face that looks equally shook.

"What were you doing that he ended up getting shot?"

Ezra swallows thickly. "We had to get a message out to our contact and let him know we've gotta get out of here tomorrow night. I had just picked the lock when we got surprised. We ran for it, barely making it back here when he started shooting."

"But you got the message out," I prompt hopefully. When he doesn't answer him, I look up at him. He looks away, never saying a word.

"Ezra—"

"No," he mutters.

"So what happens now? Are we still doing this tomorrow?"

"We have to," Ezra says. "They're bringing in more guards, and once they get here, we won't stand a chance. We have to run and take our chances hiding in the woods until someone comes to get us."

"We're gonna need a bigger diversion. Something to keep them occupied longer so we have more time. Something that's more important than chasing after us."

I stop talking so I can focus on my task, working in silence until my finger finally hits something foreign-feeling inside what I'm pretty sure was his spleen. I wiggle my finger to one side of the bullet and the blade on the other, and begin to slowly work it out. When I'm done, I place the bullet in Ezra's outstretched hand.

"They killed your friend. Honor him by one day taking one of theirs," I say as I fold his fingers over the spent bullet. I stand up, looking for something to wipe my hand on, but of course, there's nothing. Instead, I bloody up my other hand, kneel next to the dead boy, and press my hands over the wound.

"Everyone ready?" I wait for confirmation from everyone after they get into place, and then for Ezra to give the signal. He slips the lighter back into the deep pocket inside the mattress, the dark engulfing us all. Then when he tells me he's ready, I take a deep breath, and let out the loudest scream I can muster.

38

Emma

I must be dreaming.

There's no other explanation for what I see other than I'm in some fucked up version of *A Christmas Carol*. The three identical ghosts are dressed in long, flowing, black dresses with their blonde hair streaming around their shoulders. They look so much like my dead friend they can only be here to torment me.

Upon closer examination there are minute differences. A freckle or wrinkle, where one hadn't been, or the extra three inches of height that force me to look up into her eyes. But their color is exactly as I remember, the deep, vibrant shine of polished emeralds.

Declan introduces us, and I shake hands with the women. Nina seems sweet and almost a bit naive, especially when compared to her thoroughly caustic sister. Of the three, it's Olesya who reminds me the most of Anna, with her all-seeing, steady gaze and regal bearing.

I offer them lemonade, and when I pass out the glasses, I'm not remotely surprised when Sasha pulls out a flask of vodka and spikes everyone's glass except mine. We sit around the table in silence, each of us wondering who will speak first.

"So, what brings you three to our neck of the woods?" Declan begins lightly.

Olesya takes a sip of her drink, closing her eyes and savoring it as if it's the finest Champagne. "I already told you, we need to talk," she finally answers as she opens her eyes.

"Look, I'm not changing my plans," he responds wearily. "So if you came out here to try to change my mind, you've wasted a trip."

"What you do is, ultimately, up to you. You just need to know what you will be risking."

"I'm confused," I pipe up. "Is there something you aren't telling us?"

"I've been trying to get your husband to understand that we cannot change our existing plans at this late date. He and his team are needed elsewhere on another mission. I understand his great desire to save the children, but the lives he saves there are nothing compared to the ones that will be lost."

Declan slams his fist on the table, making me jump. "Stop speaking in riddles, woman, and tell me what you know!"

"I have already told you what I can," she murmurs. "You just have to trust me."

Declan stands. "Weren't you the one who told me *not* to trust you?" He drains his glass and thumps it back to the table. "Look, I've got things to do. If you change your mind and decide to tell me what you know, you know where to find me considering that you know *everything*."

The sound of his sneering voice is cut by the screen door slamming behind him. I sit with the women in silence, not having a clue what to say after that.

Luckily, Olesya fills the void. "You were close with my daughter. You know she was gifted in many ways far beyond those of a ballerina."

I nod, more than a little wary of where this conversation's heading.

"Ours is a gift the women in our family have had for centuries. There have been many names given to women with our abilities over the years, most of them derogatory. Many of our family have died because people believed things about us that weren't true.

"My daughters and I are past caring what people think of us, or what names we are called, but I draw the line when people think we can control things that we cannot. Our gift has a way and a will of its own."

She stops to take another delicate sip of her drink, Nina picking up where her mother left off. "I do not know if Anna ever mentioned it, but our mother had not just three daughters, but two sons," she says quietly. "One was older, and one came after me. Both died in infancy, both found dead in their cribs. When Nicolai died, I ran to my baba, my grandmother, sobbing loudly and wanting to know why my mother hadn't seen this coming. What was the point of the blessing of foresight if not to shield us from pain?"

She looks up and away from me, a sad smile on her face. "She asked me, 'Who ever said our ability is a blessing?'"

"So, you actually see things? Like in dreams?"

"Sometimes it comes in dreams," Nina responds. "But usually, it comes more as a feeling, a disturbance, that we cannot shake. That's when we consult the cards, or brew potions, or partake of herbs and mushrooms that allow us to clear our minds and become more receptive to the unknown. Then if we are meant to know, we are shown."

"Can you do this for specific questions? Or for other people?" I ask. "If I were to ask you something specific, would you be able to find the answer?"

Sasha scoffs. "We aren't fortune tellers, Emma, and what we're talking about isn't some parlor trick we use to entertain our friends. The things our family has seen through the years have influenced everything from weather patterns to revolutions. We are very selective about what we share, and trust me, we don't share even a fraction of what we see."

"There's a price to be paid when we share what we see," Nina chimes in, I think sensing her sister's growing irritation. "We always warn people of it when they ask us to look into things for them, and of course, they always say they will pay whatever they must at the time. They think it is *we* who demand payment, but the cost is not paid to us. The cost, in fact, has *nothing* to do with us. It's a payment to the Universe, to Fate, to the Gods and Goddesses who answer desperate pleas in the night that should never have been asked. One should never beg the unknown to change the trajectory of Fate. She is a cruel and vicious mistress, and one who should be respected only from a distance."

I'm almost tempted to think they're joking, but the reverence in their lowered voices, the way they almost whisper the name *Fate*, makes it clear that they are deadly serious.

"So, what is the cost for changing the course of Fate? Is it a soul?"

"Fate has no need for souls. What She wants is equilibrium," Olesya states as if it's the most obvious of answers. "People almost always ask Her for something that will benefit them, especially after something terrible has already happened. They ask Her to take away their suffering, but for that to happen, someone else must suffer. Sometimes you not only pay your price, but that of another, or ten others."

She stops for a moment to think. "The price is always higher than the ask, and one should know that the payment will be extracted when least prepared for. When it is time, Fate may come for you, or She may come for someone you love. She may even wait until you think She's forgotten, only for your bill to come due in a future generation—for a child or a grandchild. Those who have paid the price and lived to tell have always said that making a deal with Fate is as bad as dealing with the Devil. One never wins."

They stare at me as if they already know what I'm about to ask, so even though I'm afraid to, I ask anyway. "So, you saw something bad happen if Declan goes ahead with this plan to liberate the work camp?"

Olesya nods, looking sad. "Yes."

I glance away when I hear footsteps on the stairs, Nina coming down with my daughter in her arms. I'm amazed that I didn't see or hear her go up there, honestly willing to swear she'd been sitting at the table a second ago. Anya is transfixed with her, staring at Nina like she found a unicorn.

"I hope you don't mind, but I thought I'd save you the trip up the stairs and us listening to her piercing cries."

Olesya stares at the child, her eyes teary as she reaches for her. "Please, Nina, let me hold her."

The child is equally mesmerized, but not so much by the stately older woman, but by the pendant hanging around Olesya's neck. Anya grabs hold of the round, silver disc with a many-pointed star etched into it, and stares, transfixed, into the faceted diamond center. The pendant looks ancient but not worn, like a treasure that rarely leaves the safekeeping of a vault.

Olesya smiles when the baby tugs on the chain, bringing their faces within inches. When Anya tips too far forward and bonks her forehead against Olesya's, she gives the woman a broad, beaming smile and begins to laugh.

"She likes you," I grin.

"She senses kindred spirits," Nina responds.

Even Sasha softens, reaching forward and running her fingers through Anya's dark hair. She closes her eyes for a moment, not opening as she whispers, "This one is destined for greatness." The others nod their agreement.

After a few minutes more of cooing to my daughter, Olesya takes the pendant from Anya's hand and hands my baby back to me. I expect her to scream her displeasure, but she instead takes her chubby fist and puts it into her mouth.

The women stand. "Declan won't listen to me, so there's no point in us staying. I know that his mind will not change despite my warning. When he returns from pouting, tell him that he needs to leave now. Things have changed for the children he's so desperate to save, and not for the better."

She shakes out her long skirts and flips her long hair over her shoulder. "We must go now, Emma. The tides are already changing, and even as we speak, the skies are darkening as a great storm approaches."

Olesya walks around the table, as I stand to walk them to the door. "Emma, it was lovely meeting you, not to mention, to also meet Anna's namesake."

She stops for a moment, appearing almost as if she hears something the rest of us do not. She nods her head and smiles, taking off the pendant Anya is so enamored with, and places it in my hand, closing her fingers over my fist.

"This is very important, Emma. You are not to give this to Anya until she's eighteen. Understand? Until then, keep it safe. Under no circumstances, should anyone else put it on. Fate has dictated that Anya is to wear it next. No one else. Never anyone else."

She kisses me on each cheek and then a third time on the lips and turns away, her daughters trailing behind. Nina gives a small wave of her fingers and a smile as she departs; Sasha gives a perfunctory wave over her shoulder but doesn't look back.

Now that they're gone, I realize I still have so many questions. I slip the pendant into my apron pocket and hurry towards the door. I want to call them back, to ask them what everything they told me really means, but it's too late. The three of them have moved quickly despite looking like they are on a lazy stroll, already crossing over into the fields. They walk side-by-side through burnt rows, their fingertips grazing the tops of scorched plants that turn to ash at their gentle touch and are carried off by the breeze.

I don't call or chase after them. If there was more they could tell me, they would have. Anya and I watch them until they are out of sight, both of us more than a bit shell shocked by the visit that I now believe had nothing to do with my husband, and everything to do with my daughter.

39

Keira

A few hours later, guards haul us in front of the prick in charge of the camp, all of us reeking of sweat, blood and fear. We're lined up in an interrogation room, the guys pretending to not be afraid while I've been instructed by Ezra to act terrified to the point of blubbering. Their thought is that the guards won't want to deal with interrogating me if I'm already incoherent, leaving them to take the brunt of the punishment.

I don't get why they are even punishing us considering they treat everyone like they're expendable. Shit, what's one more dead kid to them when we're droppin' like flies already?

When the head fucker clomps in I turn up the sniveling, but it's hard to summon the tears. He steps towards us, staring closely into each of our faces as we look straight ahead, knowing better than to meet his gaze. I catch the glint of his gold name badge, the name Goodman engraved in black. It takes everything in my power to not roll my eyes at how inappropriately named he is.

"Whoever tells the truth first will be met with leniency. I want to know what happened and who's responsible. Now."

None of us speak, my sniffing sounding nauseatingly loud in the silence and drawing his attention. He strolls over to me, looking down his nose at my tearstained face, and how my uniform and hands are covered in blood.

"You have the most blood on you, so I suspect you had a rather large part in the festivities," he begins, sounding almost conversational. "Did you kill him?"

I look at the ground like I'm ashamed. "N-no, sir," I stutter. "I tried to help him."

"Help him? What? By stabbing him?" he laughs. Before I can say a word, he pulls an intricately carved knife from his belt and places the serrated blade to my throat. I inhale quickly, my eyes bugging out of my head as it draws a bead of blood. "Tell me, little girl, if I were to stab you, would you think I did it to help you? Or hurt you?"

I sure as shit hope he doesn't expect an answer, as I've got a feeling anything I say will be wrong.

"Sir, please," Ezra states quietly. "I mean no disrespect by interrupting, but I can vouch for her. She tried to help him after we realized what happened. She put pressure on his wound until help came. That's why she's so bloody."

He pauses for a few long seconds before withdrawing the blade from my neck and turning to Ezra next to me. "Ah, Ezra. Why am I not surprised that you are once again interceding for a weaker member of your crew?"

"Sir," he gulps. "I swear that the account I gave of last night's events is exactly what happened. I have no reason to lie to you. If anyone should take the blame, it's me. I should have realized Caesar was losing his grip on reality before he turned violent."

I chance a glimpse upward to find Ezra locking eyes with Goodman.

Oh, shit.

The crack of the officer's palm across the boy's face sounds more like a gunshot than a slap. Ezra loses his balance and stumbles into me, almost knocking us both to the floor.

"They can go," Goodman spits angrily. "If Ezra is so interested in protecting his charges, then he can take the punishment for them all." He stares at Ezra nastily, the glint in his eyes proving that whatever cruelty he plans is destined to be terrible. Before we can say or do anything, we're all ushered from the room and sent to our work assignments, but not before Ezra begins to scream.

It seems like hours pass before Ezra staggers into the room we're cleaning, his eyes red and swollen, and his face pale. He moves like he's in horrible pain, barely pushing one foot in front of the other. I drop my shovel and walk quickly to where he's propped himself against a metal railing, the agony he's in intensifying with each passing minute.

"Get back to work," he spits through gritted teeth.

"What happened to you? What did he do?"

"Don't worry about me. I'll be fine."

"You are *not* fine," I spit back. "Maybe I can help you. . ."

"Trust me, princess, there's not a goddamn thing you can do for me. Now, get back to work. I've gotta meet with my crew. Go to my room when you're done tonight. We're leaving at midnight. Make sure you're ready."

"Trust me," I deadpan. "I was ready to leave the second I got here."

* * *

With each passing hour, I'm getting more and more excited, or nervous, or maybe some combination of both. I manage to catch eyes with the guys throughout the day, all of them taking turns supervising so Ezra can get some much needed rest after his ordeal with Goodman. He's only gone a few hours before he limps back to the observation area with a vicious scowl on his face. A few times an hour he calls out names of inmates that his crew brings to him in a small room down the hall. The kids pulled off the floor look terrified, but return trying to not smile.

We have no choice but to let the inmates the guys trust the most know what's going to happen tonight. They, in turn, are to tell the people they trust the most. Everyone "in the know" is expected to help the young or sick as much as they can without getting caught, themselves.

By eleven thirty, I'm trembling with nerves as the guys and I say our farewells, everyone looking every bit as nervous as I feel. We check the halls and see no guards in sight, which I'm told is not unusual at night. The staff thinks we're all too downtrodden to attempt an escape and have gotten lazy, making tonight's job that much easier for us. Dumb fucks.

At ten before midnight, the fire alarms sound, the smell of smoke already reaching us inside our building despite the fire being a good distance away in the furthest barn. As the animals are far more valuable than us, the guards race to get them out of the burning building and herd them into the fenced overflow area. What the assholes running this place don't know is that the chain-link fence is rusted through, and it will only be a matter of minutes before the panicked animals break free. While the guards frantically try to corral the loose swine, the inmates will be running for their lives.

Our plan works beautifully, and we have no trouble getting out of our building. Ezra and his crew easily kill the few guards left to watch us and then use the dead men's keys to open the doors to the outside. We run along the edges of the fenceline where it's darkest, and sprint for the front gates that are blessedly wide open and unguarded. Halle-fuckin'-lujah.

A few kids panic, deciding to leave their groups and head off on their own. I guess they think they're safer that way, or more than likely, they're drunk on freedom and not thinking at all. If I didn't know we have trucks coming to pick us up, I might even think going solo is safer. We didn't tell anyone more than they needed to know in case someone gets captured and tries to cut a deal by snitching, so aside from where to meet the trucks coming for my specific group, even I know nothing else. Even though members of the BSB don't squeal, no amount of torture can make you give up information you don't know.

As I run my group right out the goddamn front gate, I can't help but think this escape went too smoothly. I hate to tempt Fate, but for the most part, this has been way too fucking easy. I managed to not only sneak into, but also out of a work camp where, except for those inmates Ezra managed to liberate, no one left unless it was zipped inside a bodybag.

Now all I have to do is get my group safely to the pick up site and hunker down until we're rescued. I smile widely as I think the hard part is over, and sometime within the next forty-eight hours, I'll once again be headed home.

40

Emma

Declan's in the barn stacking hay when I come in with our daughter perched on my hip. He's been trying something new to handle his fury, and that's to do something physically productive instead of exploding in anger. Brother Love taught him this during our months in Philly, and especially when you live on a farm, it's a very useful coping mechanism. Not to mention, it saves me from having to wrap his torn up knuckles every other week, so all in all, it's a win in my book.

I don't say anything for a while, taking a seat on an errant bale in the aisle and watching my husband work. Anya plays in a small pile of loose hay at my feet, grabbing tiny fistfuls and tossing them in the air and laughing happily when they fall back on her head. For a child who can scream louder than an airhorn when she's mad, she's also shockingly easy to entertain.

When Declan finishes his task, he rubs his shoulder while trying to stretch it. I wave him over and point to the ground in front of me, and he looks every bit as happy that I'm offering him a massage as if he just walked into our bedroom and found me naked.

I prod the muscles in his neck and work my way down to his shoulders, assessing how tight they feel and determining where he needs work the most. When I work on the tenderest spots, I can tell when it begins to feel better by the few low moans he lets slip.

"You keep that up and Amos is going to think we're having sex in here again," I laugh. Then my thumb slips into a particularly sore spot and he yelps in pain. I apologize when he shoots me a dirty look over his shoulder, but it doesn't stop me from digging into it until it finally loosens.

"He took Sarah and Micah into town to get some last minute things before we leave. I don't think the boy really wanted to go, but he needs to get out of his room and start living again. I get that losing an arm is hard, but moping isn't the answer."

"Oh, really? That's particularly rich advice coming from the guy who's perfected the art of brooding," I tease.

He looks over his shoulder and gives me an incredulous look. "You better watch it, wifey. You're still not too pregnant for me to spank."

I roll my eyes. "Oh, promises, promises." Then we both laugh.

After we sober up a bit, it's time to talk about what happened inside. I keep working the knotted muscles despite knowing that once we get on topic, they're just going to tighten right back up again.

"So, Olesya and the girls are. . . a bit strange," I begin, struggling to find the right word to describe them.

Declan reaches forward to grab Anya out of her little hay pile and pull her into his arms. She gives up her game without a fuss, instead amusing herself by running her hands all over my husband's short beard. He laughs when she tries to stick her hand in his mouth, and she joins him when he begins gently biting at her fingers with his lips pulled over his teeth and making silly noises like he's going to eat her.

He looks up at me, his big brown eyes soft and shining with the love he has for his daughter. Declan turns slightly towards me and rests his head against my knee, wrapping the arm not supporting Anya around my calf. The movement makes the necklace rattle in my apron pocket.

"What's this?" Declan asks, fishing the thick chain and pendant from my pocket.

"It's a gift for Anya from Olesya. She said she isn't supposed to have it until she's eighteen."

He raises his eyebrows in surprise and emits a low whistle of appreciation. "This thing is ancient, probably some sort of family heirloom. I'm pretty sure the center stone's real. Why'd she give it to Anya? Wouldn't one of her daughters want it?"

I shrug. "She said Fate told her Anya is to wear it next."

Declan nods thoughtfully. "Well, who are we to fuck with Fate?" He dangles the pendant in front of her and she grabs for it eagerly. When it's in her palm she stares at it intently, her eyes almost as big and round as the stone in the pendant. "She sure does seem to like it."

"Oh, Olesya also said something about if you are hell-bent on rescuing the kids, you better leave now. She said the kids will need you sooner rather than later."

He hands me our daughter and shuffles to his feet. "Did she say anything else?"

"Not really. Only that changing the plan and you not going on the mission at my parents' house is a huge mistake." I pause for a second, looking down at Anya before raising my suddenly teary eyes to my husband.

Ugh, fucking pregnancy hormones.

"Declan, what if she's right? What if something terrible happens?"

He smiles down at me sweetly, catching my first slipped tear with his thumb and cradling my cheek in his palm. "We can't spend our lives constantly afraid of the worst. Bad things are going to happen, but that doesn't mean we have to live our lives afraid of our own shadows. That's a shitty way to live."

He kisses me on the top of my head, taking a moment as if he's savoring the experience. "Just know if something does happen, that I love you very much. I love you more than I ever thought my miserable, old-ass heart was capable."

I laugh through my tears, loving how Declan always knows just what to say to lift my spirits. It sure isn't a Shakespearean sonnet, but his layman's words mean more to me than any posh recitation of poetry.

"I love you and your miserable, old-ass heart, too." I tilt my head up and receive the lips waiting to kiss me. And in that moment, there is no fear or worry in my heart. Only love.

41

Keira

We run as far and fast as we can, having no idea at what point the guards will notice we're gone. I try to give everyone enough breaks, knowing that years of near-starvation and lack of cardiovascular activity have made them weak. Some of my charges have thick, phlegmy coughs brought about by years of inhaling feces, strong urine and other contaminants, the extent of the damage done to their young bodies not to be known for years to come. I hate to think that at least some of them are risking a quick, sure death by a bullet only to suffer years' worth of misery coughing up what little's left of their lungs.

When we finally hit the edge of the woods that opens up into a wide, cleared field, we take a few moments to catch our breath and regroup. It takes a while, but I finally count everyone present. A few of the faster runners bitch about having to wait for the slower ones, and I make it crystal-fucking-clear that if they leave now, they're on their own for good. When they sass back, I add, "Oh, and good fuckin' luck getting out of this shitty country without our help." That shuts them up real fast.

We're lucky that it's only a crescent moon tonight, as a full moon would have made us easy pickings if we're spotted. I have everyone vary the paths they take across the field, not wanting it to look like a marathon rolled through here when the guards finally do come after us. I don't feel remotely safe until we're back in the deep woods on the other side.

The trees aren't as thick as they were, a sign we're moving into new-growth forest in previously developed land. It's slower going, with more underbrush to trip us up and less big trees to shield us from bullets. I keep us moving until night becomes day, everyone now thoroughly exhausted with even the frontrunners begging for rest. Yet as wiped out as we all are, I'm surprised to find most of my charges smiling broadly.

Then it hits me—most of them haven't seen the sun rise since they were imprisoned, and for many of them, that was *years* ago. That something so simple as watching the sun come up is this emotional for most of them makes me feel like the most selfish shit on the planet. I remember every time I bitched about living in the country and cringe at my thoughtlessness. I think about all the times I wandered the land and didn't notice the colors of the flowers or how the wind sang as it blew through the leaves. I took my freedom for granted even when I lived in the underground bunker in Philly, and I downright hate myself for needing to witness this in order to appreciate everything I'd been given.

I peer up into the morning sky, vowing to never take another moment of freedom for granted. Hell, for all I know, we might get gunned down in the next five minutes, or we may all live another fifty years, but this is a promise I intend to keep.

I don't even realize I'm humming an old tune we sang a lot when Brother Love concluded Sunday services until I notice the number of kids surrounding me. My face is beet red based on how hot it feels, and I promptly stop, feeling self conscious.

"That song sounds familiar," one of the older boys says. "Didn't they sing that back during the war?" I roll my eyes and smile at him, making it crystal clear there's no way in hell I'm gonna sing it for him. Brother Love always teased me that I sing about as well as a six year-old plays the violin, and I can't be mad about it because it's the truth.

Despite their pleading, I don't give in, telling them they've suffered enough without listening to me sing. Then that same boy picks up the tune, his crisp, clear voice so beautiful I can't help but stare at him in wonderment.

> *"When the last child cries for a crust of bread*
> *When the last man dies for just words that he said*
> *When there's shelter over the poorest head*
> *Then we shall be free."*

He stops singing, his face blushing beet red. "Come on, sing with me."

As much as I don't want to, I can't refuse him.

> *"When the last thing we notice is the color of skin*
> *And the first thing we look for is the beauty within*
> *When the skies and the oceans are clean again*
> *Then we shall be free."*

I laugh after finishing the verse, the boy smiling at me as he finishes the Garth Brooks song by himself. When he's done a few people clap, but I quickly motion for them to stop. We've already taken too big a risk by singing to make any more noise. I stand up and brush the dirt off my ass before telling everyone it's time to get moving. We still have a few hours' walk to get to the safehouse, and when I promise everyone food and water after we get there, they become a lot more motivated.

I walk next to the boy who sang, who introduces himself as Tony, and I can't help but grin as I think about the two brothers named Tony in Philly who were complete bad-asses, yet willing to shiv each other when it came down to who'd eat the last chocolate chip cookie. I tell him about them, and when he says he hopes he'll one day get to meet them, I tell him with absolute certainty that, one day, I'll make sure he does.

As the sun rises in the sky, it gets hotter. There's not a speck of water to be found out here, and a few of the kids are already feeling the effects of dehydration. We have to stop more frequently and for longer periods of time, the stragglers taking longer and longer to catch up. We need to keep going, but by mid-day, it's clear we've got a few who simply can't go on.

I search the area around us and although everything around us is mostly flat, I manage to find a section of thick bushes with a bit of a gully behind them that might cover them enough to avoid detection. If they come with sniffer dogs they'll be caught, so I send up a prayer that any troops following us are without a canine unit.

I think of Gritty, the pang of missing him making my chest ache. I doubt the big lunkhead even misses me, probably using my absence as an excuse to chase and kill Sarah's chickens to his heart's content. But then I think of all the times he let me hug him and cry into his scruff when I felt alone and then licked away my tears until my face was slimy with dog spit and I couldn't help but laugh. I'm surprised when my vision goes a bit blurry, a few stray drops of moisture clouding my vision. I laugh at myself as I wipe them away, knowing I'm being silly , but I love him and miss him with all my heart.

I also find myself missing Declan's annoying commands, and Anya's piercing screams, not to mention Sarah's gentle reprimands every time I fuck something up or accidentally drop an F-bomb. I even miss Emma's smiles and usually sweet mannerisms. Well, she's sweet until I seriously piss her off, and then she gives me Hell.

But of all the people from home, it's Micah I find myself thinking about the most. I wonder how he's feeling, and if he's following the strict schedule I wrote up for him to use to wean himself off the pain meds. I wonder how he's coping mentally, and although I'm not one to usually think about emotional shit, I wonder about his state of mind after everything he's been through. I remind myself that he's tough, that he survived a surgery that almost killed him. Twice. I'm sure he'll be coping just fine by the time I get home. . .

Then it hits me. In the span of hardly a minute, I thought of that beat-up farm in Bumfuck, Pennsylvania as home not just once, but *twice*. We're hardly a traditional family, with our mishmash of backgrounds, beliefs and ethnicities, but somehow we still came together and became a family. For the first time since my parents were murdered I no longer feel like an orphan.

I'm roused from my thoughts by the sound of a distant motor. It's far enough away that I don't waste time being quiet as I race back to the group. I tell them to run, giving them a few landmarks to look for to hopefully find the safehouse on their own, and they take off as fast as their exhausted legs can carry them. A few stumble in their haste to get away, the panic in their eyes as they look back at me before heading in the opposite direction chilling me to the bone. A few look over their shoulders, probably wondering why I'm not running off with them; then their self-preservation instincts kick in and they leave me alone with the three who cannot run another step.

"Come with me," I tell them gently. "I know where we can hide."

I know if Declan were here he'd tell me to run, and if he was here, maybe I would. But I also know he wouldn't leave these kids behind. He often told me that being an adult means doing things we don't want to do, and being part of a family often means sacrificing what we want as an individual for what benefits the family.

Do I want to get the fuck out of here? Hell, yeah, but not at the expense of those who can't come with me. Although I only spent a handful of hours with them, these kids are now part of my family, and if I've learned nothing else from my time with the Bullies, Byrnes, and Zooks, it's that family sticks together. And right now, I'm all the family these three kids have.

42

Declan

As most of our stuff is already together, it doesn't take us long to get on the road. To keep from attracting notice, we stagger our exodus and use different routes, but due to the fact we need to get there sooner rather than later, we double up on the quicker ways. We all have different stories to use if we get stopped; the trucks with trailers are going to pick up horses or cows from another community to replenish stock, and the ones without are on their way to pick up seeds or supplies or some other bullshit items. All of us have weapons stashed in various compartments in the vehicles, with all of us praying to not need them during the drive.

Amos drives as Scott and I keep watch, the three of us crammed shoulder to shoulder in the front bench seat with the back loaded to almost the ceiling with as much supplies as we can fit as well as one very large, and very pissed off, German Shepherd. Gritty refused to be left behind, standing in front of the truck and barking up a storm until I got out and tried to move him. Then he jumped into the truck through the open door and refused to budge. Desperate to get going, and really not wanting to get my fingers bitten off, we decided to let him come with us. I just hope he doesn't make us regret it.

We ride in silence, even Scott unusually quiet. Rowan had dropped him off at the farm right before we left, the two of them making googly eyes at each other but otherwise not showing any other signs of affection. If I wasn't so worried about the next twenty-four hours, I'd tease him about their budding relationship, getting him back for all the inappropriate shit he's said to me in the past. But right now, I've got too much on my mind to spare more than a thought to him and his pagan princess.

With the change in plans we're going to have losses. As a leader of a revolution, I know that there has to be a level of losses on any given mission that I have to believe is acceptable, but this one's impossible. They're *kids*, and in my opinion, it's never okay for a child to die. I think of my own children. Anya. My son. Even Keira and Amos' and Sarah's kids. I'd do anything to save them.

My phone rings, startling the three of us to the point we all jump, and I catch Scott's elbow in my side. I curse as I answer the phone.

"Okay, here's what I've found out," Cass begins, scrapping the social niceties to get down to brass tacks. "There was a fire in the back barn last night. When the Ag police tried to get the pigs out, they broke through the overflow lot barricade and ran out into the woods. While trying to corral the pigs, the kids escaped. I'm not sure, but I think all three thousand got out.

"Lucky for us, they didn't bother to concern themselves with the kids until shortly after sunrise. As soon as the Head Asshole realized he lost his workforce, he called in every Ag officer and Purity Patrolman in a fifty mile radius. He's sending in 500 armed troops on trucks to round up the pigs and kill the kids."

He pauses as I let loose a string of curses. "Look, this was going to be bad with just the local Ag police on this, but these kids can't outrun trucks fitted with assault rifles. There's nowhere to hide out there, so they'll have to keep moving. If they're smart, they'll be well past any set rendezvous locations we planned, so your teams are going to need to do a fair amount of searching to find them while not getting caught themselves."

He pauses for a second. "Declan, this mission has massacre written all over it. You're going down there with a bunch of farmers to try to round up scared kids in woods filled with heavily armed Ag and Purity Police. If you go down there now, it's gonna end up in a shootout, and I really hate to say this, but you're going to lose."

Okay. Now I'm pissed. "What are you saying? Are you honestly telling me to turn around and go home and leave these kids to die?"

"What I'm saying is things are bad with what we *know*, but what concerns me more is the shit we don't. I don't think you realize what you're walking into. The new guy running things down there is bad news. He's dangerous, Declan. Even though they were going to kill those kids anyway, he's now going to make an example out of every one he finds. If word gets out that a bunch of kids got the best of him, he'll be embarrassed and feel like he has to prove himself all over again. He's going to keep hunting them until he finds them."

"That just gives me more incentive to get down there faster."

"You aren't listening to me, Declan! Unless you can get trucks there within the next few hours and planes on the ground in the same amount of time, there's not a rat's ass chance of anything happening other than all of you dying."

Just as I'm getting ready to yell, "Then we're all going to fucking die!" another call buzzes on the line from another number I don't know. Without telling him, I click over to the other line, praying whoever it is has better news for me.

When I hear her voice, I smile, knowing in my bones that the miracle I've been praying for my whole damned life just arrived, and just in the nick of time.

43

Emma

I'm exhausted.

From the moment Declan left, taking almost two-thirds of the population of Lancaster with him, I've been on the phone with every person I could think of who might be able to help. I called every ambassador I had a number for and gathered additional numbers from both those who agreed, and even from a few of those who declined, to help us.

I waited for return calls anxiously, pacing the floor of the barn where I have my computer and satellite phone set up. I sent enough emails that my knuckles ache and my fingers swelled, but it's all worth it when I tell Declan that not only have I gotten the kids a way out, I found a way to do it without raising a hint of suspicion that foreign governments are involved. I smile every time I think I have my father to thank.

In a few day's time, the nation will be celebrating my father's six-tieth birthday. For much of my childhood, I remember him bitching about plane travel being a nightmare, and since then, it's only gotten worse. Much of the infrastructure that kept air travel safe and on time was destroyed during the war, and with our country's closed-border policies, it wasn't a priority to repair.

After the war, Americans became even more frantic to escape. Foreign comedians had endless fodder for material when, for the first time in history, Mexico reported having trouble keeping Americans from sneaking into *their* country. Canada was overwhelmed with refugees, their social services systems overtaxed to the point they were eventually forced to close their border.

The Coast Guard was busy fishing people out of the water as thousands of Americans tried to get to Cuba in leaky, overloaded boats and pathetic-looking rafts. Hundreds of people died after the Cuban government turned them away, the people escorted back to their flotation devices with barely enough food and water to make the trip back. Knowing they would be either shot for defection or sentenced to life imprisonment, many opted to die of dehydration and remained out to sea where they at least could die free.

The Canadian Prime Minister was the first person I called for help, and he was beyond sympathetic and exceptionally helpful. He contacted the President of Mexico, and between them and the British Prime Minister, we quickly figured out a plan.

The timing of my father's party couldn't possibly have worked better for us, as he was forced to shut down every other airport in the nation in order to have enough trained staff to safely land planes in the Premier City. This is a very lucky break for us, as we can use the empty airports however we need with no one there to notice. After a few more calls, I am besieged with offers of weapons, ammunition, and even vehicles from a few eager nations, as well as offers of food, clothing, medical supplies and other necessities not fighting related from several others.

As I scramble teams to meet the planes, I call everyone I have a number for and beg them to race to the various airports and help unload the items so the pilots can get back in the air as soon as possible. Dex and Adam are charged with routing planes to the airports capable of handling specific types of specialized aircraft while Amy stands by, waiting to scramble government radar and aircraft detection systems.

Although time consuming, it's fairly easy to pull off what we need for the evacuation of the children, and for that, I largely have Isaac and his father to thank. His father had originally not wanted to offer asylum to the children, hoping another nation, or nations, would be willing to bear the wrath of the Supreme Regent if word ever got out.

But when Isaac found out he dad said no, he apparently said something that made him change his mind. I don't want to be rude and try to pry the information out of the Prime Minister, so I don't ask. But Isaac is not a foreign leader, and when I see him next, I have every intention of prying.

By the time I finish everything I need to do, it's dark outside and the children are asleep. Sarah and I are enjoying a glass of lemonade on the front porch when my phone rings and Isaac's lightly accented voice advises us to not worry about the incoming vehicle, that he's on his way up our drive. Headlights flash around the corner a moment later, leaving both Sarah and I curious as to why he's here and not headed to Esther's.

He gets out of the car and comes towards us, the lights from inside the house illuminating his smiling face. He's again dressed in all black, the small, gold *Angels of Mercy* logo on his shirt glinting in the light. His dark, expressive eyes are bright and cheerful, his long, easy strides eating up the distance between us. He reminds me a bit of my husband, his skin too dark to be just tanned, but not light enough to be considered white by the new American standard. He's incredibly handsome, the sort of good-looking one would think would have landed him into a profession like modeling or acting and not rescuing at-risk children.

Isaac greets us with kisses on our cheeks and then casually plops down onto the wooden porch. He stretches out his long limbs, eliciting a chorus of creaks and pops from his body as he tells us how much he despises long car trips. Micah joins us from somewhere inside the house, shaking hands with Isaac before gingerly lowering himself to sit beside him on the porch.

It's easy to see Micah's still in a great deal of pain, not to mention, his balance continues to be quite precarious. Yet I have never once heard him complain, or be grumpy, not even when Rebecca accidentally bumped against his bandaged shoulder during dinner and he'd howled in pain. When she started to cry he did his best to soothe her despite him being the one speaking through pain-clenched teeth.

We chat for a while about mundane things, and at one point Sarah goes inside to grab the pitcher and two more glasses for the boys. Isaac drinks deep from his glass and promptly refills it, telling Sarah it's rare to find someone who doesn't put too much sugar in their lemonade. I'm sure her frugality is based more on the price of sugar than anything else, as she sure does enjoy her tooth-achingly sweet shoofly pies.

I finally ask Isaac why he's here, and he admits it's only for a brief stop on his way north, but he had something he wanted to ask me. When it's clear he doesn't want to say whatever it is in front of Sarah and Micah, they retreat inside the house. He doesn't speak again until it's silent inside the house for a few minutes, my interest piquing further with each passing minute. He pulls out a cigarette, lights it, and takes a deep drag.

"You do know those things will kill you," I scold gently.

Isaac exhales hard, careful to blow the smoke away from me. "So will a bullet to the brain, but that doesn't stop me, either."

"I understand your calling to help those in need," I reply. "But I don't see any reason why you have to smoke."

He cracks a smile, turning the cigarette to stare at the burning cherry for a moment before taking another drag. "I picked it up from the others. We do it to relieve stress. I think you can agree that what I do is pretty stressful."

I smile at him from my perch on the swing, patting the seat next to me in invitation. He unfolds his legs and sits next to me, careful to keep the smoke as far from me as possible.

"I wanted to talk to you without Declan here," he begins, looking out into the darkness as if I'm not sitting right next to him. That's when I realize he's not smoking out of habit, but because he's nervous.

"Okay," I prompt, my own anxiety rising.

"Why do the two of you do this? Almost everyone believes there's no chance another uprising will do anything aside from killing a lot of people. Your father's too strong, and even with help from my country, it won't be enough."

"Do you think I don't know that?" I reply wearily.

"No, I just don't see what is the point of dying when there's no chance of winning."

I know he's not trying to anger me, but I feel it building anyway. "Maybe we both think some things are worth dying for. Maybe it's because I don't want my son living in a nation where his very existence is illegal simply because his father's half Hispanic. I don't want my daughter to grow up to be bartered and sold like she's worth no more than a farm animal. I want them to know true freedom, and to have real rights. I want them to be able to choose their own paths in life, and not to have their futures dictated to them."

I pause for a moment, staring at him even though he doesn't return my gaze. "So, why do you do it? You could go to college and learn something a great deal safer, like business or medicine. You could even study to become a lawyer, or be a politician, like your dad. Wouldn't you like to be Prime Minister one day?"

He drops his cigarette to the porch and grinds it out with his shoe. He picks up the stub and examines it closely, as if he expects the secrets of the universe to be written in the charred end. "I can't imagine doing anything other than what I'm doing now. After all, if it weren't for the Angels of Mercy, I wouldn't be here."

I swear to God, my heart stops. "Are you telling me. . ."

"Yes," he says, diving into his pocket for another smoke. "I was born in America. My birth parents paid to have me smuggled out of the country. If I had stayed, I'd probably already be dead."

"Oh my God," I whisper. "How did you find out? From what I've heard, those records are kept in strictest confidence."

He lights another cigarette with slightly shaking hands and takes a deep drag. "I found out the way most kids find out their parents' secrets. I was twelve years-old, and I was snooping for Christmas presents in the attic. Instead of gifts, I found a box filled with papers, almost all of them with my name on them. I found that interesting, as why would official-looking papers be up here and not in the fireproof safe, or better yet, locked in the bank?

"I kept reading, not too surprised by what I found. I knew I was adopted; my parents never kept that from me. They were very open and honest about everything—well, everything except for the part about me being American.

"That news I found very upsetting. At the time, my father was a practicing lawyer who specialized in adoptions. He had just finished arguing a case in international court where a seven year-old child who had been rescued by the Angels and lived in Canada almost her entire life, was ordered to return to her birth parents. I don't remember now how it all came to light, but I do remember that the lawyer on the American side argued that because money changed hands, the rescue fell under child trafficking laws.

"My father pleaded his side, responding that the child was going to, at best, be sent to a work camp, or at the worst, be executed for defection the minute she stepped back on American soil. Tensions were very high between both nations that year, and the Americans were threatening war if our government didn't send the child back.

"The judge ruled in favor of the Americans, claiming that the contract between the parents and the Angels was void because of the money. The next day, my father accompanied his sobbing clients and their hysterical daughter to the border where the little girl was taken into custody, not by her birth parents, but by some pinch-faced government agent. She was headed to the work camp, her birth parents "recently deceased" and no living family members found to care for her. The only parents she ever knew begged to keep her, but then a few heavily armed American soldiers marched over, grabbed the girl, and pulled her over to their side. There was nothing that my father or anyone else could do. They tried for years to find out what happened to her, but it was as if she vanished. We all believe now that she's dead."

"My God, that's terrible," I breathe.

"I know. And imagine how I felt, only a few years older than her when she was taken, and now knowing that if anyone ever found out, that could happen to *me*. I closed the files and did my best to forget I ever saw them, but of course, I never did. It wasn't until I was eighteen that I told my parents I knew the truth, and that I wanted to skip college and go to work for the Angels. As you can imagine, they weren't happy, but they also knew they couldn't stop me. I have always been a headstrong child, and my stubbornness only grew worse as I aged."

He chuckles to himself, obviously thinking of something in his past. "My mother insisted on accompanying me to my first meeting, and I was furious. Who would take me seriously if I brought my *maman* with me? Although we don't share blood, she's always been a fierce protector. She was determined to know everything about the group who would take my life in their hands.

"So imagine my surprise when we met at a closed cafe at midnight and my handler greeted my mother like they were old friends. Apparently, she'd been working with them for years, quietly obtaining sizable donations to keep them going. You see, despite the Canadian government demanding the Angels of Mercy disband, because of my family, they only grew more powerful. Although told to disband, they never stopped smuggling at-risk children over the border. My father vowed that there would never be another child sent back across the border as long as he lived, and so far, there have been no more. Well, none except for me."

"If you're caught—"

He chuckles darkly. "Now you know why I smoke."

I smile sadly. "You're a good man, Mr. Charon."

"No, not *Mr. Charon*," he replies as he looks down at the ground and takes a deep, fortifying breath before looking up at me with tear-filled eyes. *"Monsieur Andrews."*

44

Keira

We hide for hours in the ditch behind the bushes listening to trucks drive by and men tromp through the underbrush. A few times they get close, but the four of us stay as still as statues, barely even breathing until we hear them move along.

We don't move until after night falls, all of us rested enough to trudge forward. We still have miles to go before we reach the safehouse, and I'm at the point where I'd do some seriously morally gray shit right now for even a sip of water. I think the kids with me would, too.

We stop often to rest, as every step gets increasingly harder for their malnourished, dehydrated bodies. I'm becoming more afraid that their bodies will fail before I can get them to the safehouse, and I'm not strong enough to carry them. I don't know what I'll do when they can't go on any longer.

In the meanwhile, I do my best to not think about it. I do my best to not think at all. We are still at least three miles away from our destination when we see the yellow orbs of incoming flashlights bouncing gaily in the distance. The underbrush is thin and the ground is flat, so there's nowhere to hide. If we run, we'll alert them to our location. Although I can climb a tree and hope the men don't look up, I know the kids with me can't. At this point, they can barely walk.

"Keira, go on without us," the eldest boy whispers. "It's no use. We can't go on much further, anyway. I'm going to count backwards from a hundred slowly, and when I hit one, I'm going to flag down the guards. I expect you to be far enough away by then to be safe."

"No," I hiss. "You will *not* do that."

As if to prove his point, he slowly starts counting backwards.

"Please, Keira, do as he says," the other boy adds. "Save yourself. You did what you could for us, but all we're doing is slowing you down. We'll cover for you. Now go. Run."

I look at the three of them, my eyes blurry with tears. "Come on, we can make it. It's really not that much further—"

"Over there! I hear something!" One of the men shouts as all of their lights swing in our direction. My heart is in my mouth, my muscles tensing as my body prepares to run even as my mind tells it to stay. My eyes flit from my three charges to the lights bouncing faster towards us, the men now running straight for us.

"Go, Keira. Now!" The boys nod and gesture for me to run, but when I look for the girl, she's no longer with us. She's running away from us and towards the men, waving her stick-thin arms in the air and emitting a haunting, keening cry. When their high-power lights hit her, she's somehow turned into the most frightening figure, becoming a living, breathing ghost eager to devour the souls of men paid to hunt children like sport. I have no doubt she will forever haunt whichever fool shoots her.

Although I should be running, my feet remain rooted. I watch in horror as gunshots interrupt her screams and the poor girl falls to her knees. I don't know how many times she's hit before she casts one last look over her shoulder and mouths the word *run* before falling to the ground.

I almost scream when a hand wraps around my wrist and begins to drag me away from where I stand. As if released from a spell, I run as fast as I can despite still being blinded by the lights. It's not long before I'm now dragging the boy behind me, the two of us stumbling and lurching through the brush with the other boy at our side.

It's amazing how much energy a person can summon from nothing after seeing someone get shot. I'm sure there's got to be a math problem in there, somewhere. *If Keira has only 25% of her energy left and needs to run four more miles at her top speed of 8 mph, how much faster can she run after Asshole X shoots at her?*

Okay, that's it. I'm losing my shit for sure if I'm trying to come up with unsolvable math problems while running for my life. Shots ring out again, and a pained, garbled cry is emitted somewhere to the left of me. I'm in full flight mode now, my inner desire to remain without extra holes in me keeping me from even looking for the other boy who now also won't make it home.

I have a horrible stitch in my side, and my feet hurt like you wouldn't believe as I race through the trees. I stumble over a root and land hard on my knees, the searing pain stealing the last of my breath as I nearly black out. Again, the boy drags me to my feet after I nearly pull him down on top of me.

We stumble along, the two of us hanging on to each other, too terrified to let go. Our breath comes out in loud gasps, my heart pounding so hard that I'm not surprised I can hear it over the racket we're making. My heart beats faster and harder and louder with each step as I await the bullet with my name on it that will be coming any second now.

I lurch forward when the hold on my hand suddenly disappears, the boy I ran with now sprawled on the ground. I narrowly manage to jump over his body to keep from trampling him and immediately slam on the brakes once I know I'm clear. I run back and grab his wrist, trying to drag him to his feet, but he doesn't get up. He's in a lot of pain, doing everything he can to remain quiet and not give away our location, but we haven't a moment to waste. He has to get up.

"Where does it hurt?" I demand as I dive to the ground beside him. He's clutching his left ankle with both hands as he writhes in agony. When I finally pry his hands away and give the bones a feel in the dark everything feels sticky. He tries not to scream as I fumble over the source of the blood—a jagged shard of bone protruding through the skin.

"Go," he manages to rasp out. "Save yourself."

I stare at him for another long moment, racking my brain for some way to get him back on his feet. It's not until he reaches over and grabs my hand, sliding something into my palm, that I'm broken from my trance.

"Do you hear me, girl. Run!" he hisses forcefully.

The sounds from the woods rush back into my awareness, the sounds of more feet thumping and more bodies breaking the dry underbrush underfoot, that I snap back into the moment.

If I don't leave now, I'm going to die, and goddammit, I don't want to die.

As much as I hate to leave him, dying next to this kid isn't gonna help anyone. I squeeze his hand, the rectangular item caught between our palms reminding me it's still there. I'm determined not to drop it.

"Burn their fucking world down," he says fiercely as I scramble to my feet and look at him one last time, searing his face into my memory before I haul ass out of there. I tell myself to not think about him, or what will happen to him when they find him, focusing on putting one foot safely in front of the other despite having very limited light.

When I'm about a mile away, I stop to take a breather. It's been some time since I've heard anyone behind me, and blessedly, there have been no more gunshots. I pray that I'm safe. I pray they didn't find the boy I was with. I lean up against a tree, my shirt and hair stuck to my back with sweat. I wipe my forehead and lift the hair off the back of my neck, letting the cool night air dry the stickiness below.

I unclench my fist and finally take a look, finding the boy had given me one of those old, cheap, disposable plastic lighters.

Burn their fucking world down. . .

Now that I understand, I have no intention of letting him down. If his last request is for me to start a fire to help cover our tracks, then I'm gonna set a goddamn inferno.

Filled with new purpose, I backtrack carefully through the woods, finding small outcroppings of dried brush and piles of old, crunchy leaves, and use the lighter to set them on fire. When the flames catch, they burn brighter than stars, illuminating my deepest, darkest desire to kill every man who dares to hurt my friends and family. And I have no interest whatsoever in blowing out the flame until every last one of these bastards are dead.

45

Declan

We spend the entire night wrestling groups of terrified children into our vehicles and get them out of the immediate area as quickly as possible. It takes longer than it should, as they are understandably terrified of us, and none of them are where they're supposed to be. Most of them continued to run well past their rendezvous points, the fear of being recaptured rendering them incapable of sitting and waiting for us.

I can't say I blame them. Had I been given a chance to run when I'd been incarcerated, I'd have run as fast as I could and never looked back. Even if I knew a rescue was on the way, there was no way I'd wait around with my thumb up my ass until they arrived.

Aside from our entire rescue timeline being fucked, we've run into another totally unforeseen problem. An out of control brushfire rages in the woods around the encampment, forcing us to reroute trucks and reconfigure the grid of men and women searching for runaways on foot. We don't know what started the fire, and quite honestly, we don't care. Luckily for us, it's bad enough that a bunch of Ag police are taken off of recovery duty when one of the fires burns its way back towards the camp. I can only hope it burns that shithole to the ground along with all the motherfucking guards inside it.

As we drive through deserted streets and empty fields looking for escapees, our headlights catch the eyes of a lost porker here and there before it takes off as fast as its little legs can carry it. I can't say I blame them, especially considering what we humans have put them through. These CAFOs are Hell on Earth not just for the kids forced to work there, but for the animals, too. From what Micah told us, most of the pigs are kept in stalls no bigger than they are, and they are forced to wallow in their own filth as they are force fed antibiotics to keep them from getting sick, and steroids and hormones to make them bigger and fatter faster. As soon as they reach a certain size they are sent to the slaughterhouse even if they show signs of sickness or are covered in sores.

For the first time in my life, I feel bad for every commercially produced slice of bacon and piece of sausage I've eaten. Even though my stomach aches from hunger, I'd rather starve than eat one of these poor animals. They deserve to be free.

Godspeed, piggies. May the rest of your lives be better than the beginning.

Before the sun comes up, we've delivered a little over eleven hundred children to various private runways and defunct airports within a hundred mile radius, with a couple hundred more kids laying low for the day until more planes can land tonight. We aren't sure how many have been recaptured, or how many are still hiding that we haven't found. In all honesty, we aren't even sure how many got out in the first place. Although Amy's tapped into radio signals inside the camp, she hasn't gotten much intel about the Ag officers' plans aside from being frantic to recapture their valuable four-legged food sources.

It's hard to figure a success rate for this mission without knowing if all the kids even managed to get out. There were three buildings designed to house them, and as far as we know, we've only found kids from two of them. I'm doing my best not to think the worst, but I've never been a glass-half-full kind of guy. Although I repeatedly tell myself that every child saved is a win, my heart aches for the ones who won't make it out.

With daybreak less than thirty minutes away, we head off to the safehouse where we'll hunker down for the day. The minute I get there I have a long call with Amy, and she fills me in on everything else she's learned. There's still no word that anyone's seen Keira, and I make it clear to everyone that I am to be told the second she's found. We drove past the safehouse she was supposed to bring her group to multiple times, but there's no sign they even made it there. I can't help but worry that something went seriously wrong.

We hunker down in an abandoned farmhouse about fifty miles from the work camp for the day. Almost everyone falls asleep the second their aching bodies hit the rotting floorboards, with me, Amos, and Gritty among the few who remain alert. I put my phone on vibrate so the million and one calls coming in don't disturb the crew who will be putting in at least one more long night, if not two, before finally heading home.

When the call comes in that Ezra and his group were picked up by one of our other crews just minutes before sunup, I'm relieved. After getting a rundown on what happened from him and asking him a million questions, I get father and son together on the phone. I allow Amos as much privacy as I can give him inside the small house filled with people, especially when he starts to bawl like a baby the second he hears his son's voice. They lapse into German, a few of the men from Lancaster peeking over when they hear. As soon as they figure out he's reuniting with his son they turn away, most of them falling asleep with smiles on their faces and dreaming of when it will be their turn to hear their child's voice.

After some heavy pleading, I give in and tell Amos he can take the truck and meet his son at a meetup point one of the Angels sets up. He hugs me so hard I think he's going to break my ribs before he dashes out the door. He returns a few hours later with eyes swollen from crying but a huge smile on his face.

When he finally steps away to find a place on the floor to sleep, he remains awake for a long time. I don't know if grief is setting in, knowing Ezra's soon going to be far away, or if he's experiencing the extreme anxiety of knowing his middle son is still unaccounted for. He starts to sob again, but this time, it's not from joy.

By three in the afternoon I'm so exhausted I can barely keep my eyes open. Scott takes over phone duty so I can get some sleep, but the moment I lay down, my mind is again off to the races, imagining every horrible, worst-case scenario for the night ahead. I get up an hour later, no better rested and twice as anxious. Scott's smart enough to not say anything about my looks or attitude, as both are particularly ugly at the moment. Instead, he brings me a cup of room-temperature coffee that tastes like caffeinated ass but does manage to perk me up a bit.

When I'm finally feeling a little more human, Scott hands me a piece of paper with a number scrawled on it. "What's this?" I ask.

"Someone you don't want to talk to, but I think you need to," he answers cryptically.

"I'm not in the mood, Scott," I snap.

"Damien called. He wants to speak with you."

"For fuck's sake," I grumble. "I don't have time for his shit."

"I tried to find out what he wants, but he'll only speak with you."

"Fuck him," I spit. "If he wants to speak to me so badly, he should've fucking met us here to help. Adam called and damn near begged him to help us with shit several times since we all left Philly, but he never does. So if he needs something now, fuck him. If he wants to be a goddamn leader so badly, he can figure shit out for himself. I've got enough to do right now." I stuff the paper in my pocket and stomp outside to oversee the distribution of ammo before everyone heads out for the night.

We've found the radio frequency the troops are using and have been listening carefully to their chatter all day. Tonight, there will be more troops to contend with, and already a few groups of kids have been rounded up and marched back to camp. The runaways are housed with those who didn't make it out to begin with, and I have no idea how many kids that may be in total. A rescue of a couple hundred compared to a thousand or more will require different methods. I don't know how I'm going to get it, but I'm going to need a lot more information before I can even think about rescuing them.

The planes coming to pick up the kids tonight are coming from Mexico, and Adam and Dex have their hands full relaying information to the pilots when it becomes clear they don't speak a word of English. How Tweedle Dumb and Tweedle Dumber managed to forget that I'm fluent in Spanish is beyond me, but by the time I get roped into the mess, they've found a translator and the planes are, thankfully, en route.

By the morning of day three, I'm almost delirious from exhaustion. I have no problem falling fast asleep when Scott gets back from wherever the fuck he's been with a duffle bag under his arm that he refuses to tell me what's inside. Seeing how bleary eyed I am, he offers to take the first shift with the phone, and I gladly turn it over. He lets me sleep most of the day, waking me from a sound sleep around four in the afternoon by dropping a wrapped sandwich on my chest. It startles me awake to the point I'm gonna need to check my damn drawers, but before I can even threaten the motherfucker with severe bodily harm, he hands me a giant mug of somewhat decent coffee. That's the only reason I don't clock him in the puss for waking me like a goddamn psychopath.

Tonight's the last night we can stay here before we have to head home, and there's a lot we still need to do. Scott begged me to let him run the operation to liberate the kids in the camp, and as he's got a lot more wartime experience than me, I gladly hand that responsibility to him. While I was asleep, Scott called in a bunch of his Marine buddies and some of the Philly crew, who show up shortly before six dressed like they're headed into a literal warzone. The two Tonys show up a half hour later looking like the cat that ate the canary with a trunk full of hard core assault weapons. I'm almost afraid to ask where they stole them from.

Scott rifles through the mix of weapons with his eyes all lit up and a smile reminiscent of a kid on Christmas. When he finds something that looks like a rocket launcher, he moans loudly like he's ready to orgasm. He does everything except make out with the weapon that he happily tells everyone he's so excited about firing that it's making him hard. Of course, after saying that, everyone instinctively looks, and then he rattles off a bunch of stupid quips that make me want to smack him for being a silly fuck at such a serious time. Luckily for him, I need him on his A-game, so I keep my hands to myself.

When he and his team get ready to head out, he pulls out the ratty duffle bag and tosses a number of Ag uniforms at the guys he thinks they'll fit best. The rest of the crew are now in civilian clothes, pretending to be rebels Scott and his "guards" have captured. Of course, everyone's wearing body armor under their clothes and are armed to the teeth, and the second they're inside, they're gonna kill anyone who gets in their way.

As they head out, my phone rings again. This is something like the twentieth time he's called this afternoon, and knowing the son of a bitch isn't going to stop pestering me until I talk to him, I answer. "What the fuck do you want, asshole?"

There's a beat of silence, and for a second I wonder if maybe it's not Damien, afterall. Then he laughs, that same nasally twang that will come far too soon even if I never hear it again.

"Well, ain't you just a ray of sunshine," he drawls.

"I'm a little busy right now," I spit out every bit as caustically.

"I can help you with that if you'll let me," he retorts, but his tone doesn't match his words.

"Every time we've asked, you aren't interested in helping. Last time we chatted, you made it pretty clear you won't take orders from me."

"I still won't take orders from you," he snipes. "I'm doing well out here with my own crew. My numbers are growing. People want to follow me."

"Well, good for you. Look, I don't have time to sit here and pat you on the head and tell you what a good boy you are right now—"

"Have you even bothered to look more into the people from Ohio who disappeared?"

Well, fuck me, he's got my attention now. "What are you talking about?"

"I'm sure you remember," he retorts cockily. "My IT team intercepted a message meant for you, and you were taking so long getting a plan together that my crew and I got there first. All those people I rescued were so grateful they follow me now. They're loyal to *me*, and now they're recruiting for *me*."

For one of the very few times in my life, I'm actually speechless. Olesya had been right all along. I'm being subverted by someone on our side.

After I don't say anything for a moment he asks, "Um, are you still there?"

Scott comes over to tell me they're leaving, but he backs away when he catches the look on my face. He gives me a two-finger salute before turning on his heel and walking out the door. The second he's gone, I panic, praying that's not the last time I see him. He may be a total goof, but he's probably the closest thing I've got to a friend since, well, ever. I'm never gonna forgive myself, or Damien, if that's the last interaction we ever have.

"Let me guess," I respond. "The bomb in the truck. You put that in there, didn't you?"

"Pretty smart, huh?" he chuckles. "I had hoped to see something on the news about it blowing up after being delivered to the IC, but of course they don't put that shit on TV. The last thing the Purity fuckers want is for the masses to think we have a chance against them."

I close my eyes tightly, barely containing my fury. He has no idea that his idea killed forty of my best people. I'm so enraged my blood turns to ice in my veins as I fill him in on what he actually accomplished. I swear to God I can hear him sweating through the phone.

"I—I didn't know you were going," he stammers. "I thought you were just going to let them die."

"When have I ever just let anyone die?" I yell, causing a few people to stare. I take a deep breath, trying to calm myself, but I can't get the furious tremor out of my voice. "Listen to me very carefully, Damien. You have thirty seconds to decide. You either fall in line and swear you will do everything I tell you from here on, or I'm getting off this phone and notifying the families and friends of the deceased that in your quest for glory, you are to blame for the explosion. I can promise you that you won't last the week before one of them hunts you down and kills you."

"I didn't mean for that to happen!" he yells, sounding truly panicked before hanging up without giving me an answer.

It's clear he's learned nothing. He's probably already trying to justify his actions by twisting this up in his brain to somehow be my fault. I don't doubt that at some point he's going to call and beg me to spare him, but it's too late. He can't be trusted. As much as I hate adding killing him to my very long list of shit to do, it's clear he's giving me no choice.

* * *

I join the men on the ground tonight, my nerves unable to handle another night doing behind the scenes shit. We're all dressed in black and carrying enough firepower to blast anyone coming at us straight to Hell. I'm amped up and ready, the rush of adrenalin juicing me up for the long night ahead. I've got my phone and radio on me and am ready to fuck some shit up.

Gritty is whining as he watches us prepare to leave. He's been pissed off since we tied him to a support beam after he tried to run off yesterday. "If I let you out to take a piss, is there any chance you won't take off?"

Gritty gives me his best puppy dog eyes, no doubt thinking *not on your life, motherfucker.*

I untie the rope, and wrap the loose end around my hand, not trusting a dog the size of a small pony to not jerk me off my feet if he takes off after a squirrel. No sooner than I open the door he bolts, but I'm ready for him. He looks back at me when he hits the end of his tether and lifts his lip at me.

"Come on, we both know you aren't gonna bite me. Now do your business so I can get on the road—"

As if he knows that means he's getting locked up, he lunges for me. He gets my forearm in his mouth and bites down hard enough that I instinctively let go of the rope and try to pry his mouth off of me. The moment the rope goes slack and I get my hand around his snoot, he jerks his entire body to the side and takes off running into the woods.

I expect him to run away, but he only goes about fifty yards and stops. He turns back to look at me and barks, turning back to face the direction he's dying to run off in. I check my arm, finding that although it hurt like hell when he bit me, and he ripped the shit out of my shirt, Gritty barely broke the skin.

The fuzzy fucker's up to something.

Then I remember Brother Love telling me Gritty had been a trained sniffer dog, even using him to search for people in Philly after one of the shelters collapsed. Sure enough, the dog's nose is twitching a mile a minute. "Do you smell something? Do you smell someone who needs help? Do you know where Keira is?"

He barks again when I say her name, bouncing in place as he determines how much longer he can stand to wait for me. The rest of my group is watching me, waiting for my order.

I roll my eyes and shrug after Gritty barks impatiently again. "Well, you heard him," I say to the men behind me. "Follow the fucking dog."

46

Louise

The night before the party, Edward comes home.

He requires a complete run through of the night's festivities to make sure there will be "no untoward surprises," and so far, the rehearsal has gone off without a hitch. When I meekly ask him if he's pleased, he nods curtly, not willing to spare a single word of praise. His entire demeanor is stiff and cold towards me, but thankfully, not mean. That's something he saves for when we're alone.

I zone out as I sit next to him at the banquet table even though I've been told to behave as if it's the night of the party. Edward wants to see how I plan to act during the festivities, occasionally breaking his silence to ask me questions that he wants to know how I will answer. He has me rehearse the stupidest things and repeat certain lines as if I'm going to be in a play and he's my director. He becomes angry when I don't play along to his liking, swearing if I don't act "normally" tomorrow night, or if I do anything to embarrass him, there will be hell to pay.

As if I'd expect anything else.

His threats cease when the grand dining hall doors open, and the first of the dinner entertainers glides in. I have told all of the entertainers not to tell him what they will be performing, wanting to keep it a surprise for the big night.

The heavyset woman enters confidently, stopping to bow to Edward and curtsy to me, even though I find the whole bowing and scraping thing ridiculous. She's a lauded Soprano who will sing the famous aria from *Madame Butterfly*, a not-so-subtle dig to my husband about his many infidelities that I doubt our guests will catch. She runs a few scales to check the ballroom's acoustics before saying she's excited for tomorrow night, and leaving us with a grand swish of her voluminous skirts.

Next, there's the lovely pas de deux from *Giselle* to be performed by the newest principal dancers of the National Ballet. The dancers are both very good looking, and Edward hasn't stopped leering at the ballerina since she walked in. The pair try a few steps together on the floor before quietly discussing how they will need to prep their shoes to prevent slipping. Edward all but humps the Prima Ballerina's leg in an attempt to woo her, and to her credit, she mentions that the man she dances with is her husband at least eight times. It doesn't stop him from slipping her a card with his private number on it, her husband seething, but wisely, remaining silent.

I'm sure by the third act, a beautiful, formerly-famous Broadway actress singing "Maybe This Time" from Cabaret, that people will begin to talk, so I switch up the next few entertainments to be more frivolous. A team of acrobats. A troupe of dancers in medieval garb doing an intricately choreographed routine. A comedian who will kiss Edward's ass with a "roast" that I'm sure won't even come close to being insulting. Much like the ballerina's husband, I'm sure he wishes to stay alive.

There will then be a soulful rendition of "Rolling in the Deep" sung by a new pop music princess who sounds shockingly like Adele from back in the day. She is the grand finale before dessert is served and the floor opens for dancing, so I'm surprised when, after the teen diva leaves, two young, beautiful blondes stride into the room looking around them as if they've never seen a room so grand.

"Can I help you?" I ask politely, fully expecting them to admit they're lost and scurry off to where they belong. Instead they slink forward, their bright, emerald eyes glittering, their cherry-red lips curling into dangerous smiles. Edward leans forward slowly, his own devious grin forming.

"We are here to entertain the Supreme Regent," the bolder of the two states while striking a seductive pose.

She has a strange accent, something exotic I cannot place. Two women couldn't have possibly been created more to my husband's taste, their unexplained appearance making me wonder if he invited them. I'm almost about to ask them if their talent is tandem cock sucking, but catch myself just in time.

Oh my God, where the hell did that thought come from?

"You have me intrigued," Edward states with a sly smile. "Tell me, how do you plan to entertain me?"

They giggle coquettishly, the less forward one breathing out in a sultry whisper, "We will dance."

I'm about to ask them their names, but Edward stands, quickly adjusting his dick in his pants, before walking around the long table to take each of their perfectly painted hands in his and give each of them a lingering kiss.

Oh, give me a fucking break.

"Why don't we go somewhere more comfortable? I'd love to hear more about your plans to entertain me."

They giggle and bat their eyelashes as Edward leads them out, the bold one laughing as she looks over her shoulder at me and winks. I'm not sure how to comprehend that.

She's either taunting you or letting you know she's going upstairs to kill him.

Oh, dear God in Heaven, *please* let it be the second.

When the door closes behind them, the crew practicing the procession of desserts enters. I watch them disinterestedly, my mind roiling as it tries to figure out why those two girls look familiar and what that damn wink meant.

Many years ago, this blatant display of Edward's infidelity would have crushed me, but through time and frequency, they've lost their power over me. One would think that after that horrid night when he'd dumped Adam in my lap and slinked off to a month-long stay at a "rehab center for sex addicts," that his inability to keep his dick in his pants would have improved. Maybe it would have if it had been a legitimate program, but the place was nothing more than an exorbitantly priced spa for wealthy men dumb enough to get caught doing dirty things. The only thing Edward learned there was how to better hide his infidelity.

Needless to say, the second he came home, he focused entirely on rehabilitating his image. He hired image consultants and PR specialists who gave him a detailed list of things to do and say to erase the stain on his reputation. Unfortunately for me, most of the things they recommended required my attendance.

It sickened me to be called into these meetings. I didn't have it in me to pretend I was okay with what we were doing, but I didn't have the strength to tell them to go to Hell, either. I sat stiffly and glared at everyone as I looked over the long lists of appearances I was to make both with and without Edward, but always with Adam.

I initially believed that these people were only here to rehabilitate Edward's reputation, but it was quickly pointed out that I was also being judged harshly in the court of social media. Many of the things said about me were far harsher than anything Edward was called; one liberal platform called me "a complete idiot" for not immediately filing for divorce, and another proclaimed that my subservient behavior was "consistent with those having been brainwashed by my mother's cult."

I wasn't surprised the liberals were bashing me for staying with my husband, but what did shock me was the things my fellow conservatives said. They were claiming that I was the reason Edward strayed! Me! They called me disinterested. Cold. *Frigid*. A lot of people went so far as to say they *felt sorry* for Edward for being saddled with a woman who obviously wasn't doing her duty to satisfy his needs. They fucking felt sorry for *him*!

The fact that I had become the villain incensed me to no end. I remember thinking to myself that if they want a villain, I'll give them a villain, but, back then, I didn't have it in me to do the things Edward did. As much as I wanted to slap him, I couldn't without him beating me, and even if the opportunity arose, I'm simply not the sort to cheat. I don't crave simple carnal distractions the way my husband does. I want true intimacy and a meaningful bond. I've only ever wanted to be loved, cherished, and above all else, respected.

Realizing that they had their work cut out for them, Edward's people enlisted another general in their crusade to sway me to do their bidding—my mother. She marched into my home one day and sat me down in the library and lectured me on what it meant to be a good Christian wife. She informed me that I was dropping the ball. She reiterated ad nauseam that regardless of Edward's flaws, we were married for better or for worse, and 'til death did us part. She told me it was clear Edward was, at least in the public's opinion, living up to his vow to become a better man, husband, and father. She told me it was time for me to do the same.

She gave me a long list of things to do, all of them distasteful at best and vomit-worthy at the worst. Between her and the PR people, my schedule was packed with luncheons, appearances, appointments and church functions. I gave speeches to all sorts of women's groups, denouncing women more interested in careers than having children, criticizing those who believed in a women's right to choose, and outright condemning those who had abortions. Every speech or appearance I gave saw my popularity rise, much to Edward's and my mother's immense satisfaction. It didn't matter to them that after every event, I came home, drank a bottle of whatever I first grabbed at the bar, and promptly tried to drown myself in it. My mother one day told me, "Louisa May, it doesn't matter if *you* believe the things you say. It only matters that *the public* believes that you do." But it did matter to me. It mattered to me *a lot*.

Edward and I went everywhere together, and despite the occasional catcalls and taunts I was told to ignore, I smiled and acted smitten with my philandering, abusive spouse and was the picture of motherly perfection to the bastard child I was forced to adopt. We went to church every Sunday and sat in the front row with Adam, using him as a prop that we passed back and forth as needed. I went to the church's Happy Wives and Mothers group, where various speakers were enlisted to teach us all the tips and tricks to keeping our husbands happy and fulfilled (in *every* way!) in a proper Christian marriage. I was shocked when, on the third meeting, my mother brought in a "famous" Christian sex therapist I'd never heard of to teach us how to keep things interesting in the bedroom. There was talk of wearing sexy lingerie and sensual perfumes, and being open minded enough to try any new or unusual positions our husbands wanted. We were told to always be properly groomed "down there," and to have our legs perpetually shaven and ready to spread at the snap of our husbands fingers.

Most of the women in the group nodded and agreed with everything these "experts" said, especially when they told us a good Christian wife never has "headaches," or are "too tired." Even if we're on our deathbed, this woman saw no reason we still couldn't be "of service."

I seriously thought I was going to throw up.

The next lecturer brought in puppets (*fucking puppets!*) to demonstrate different positions for us to "spice things up" if our love lives were becoming stale. For those husbands who needed a little help along with their little blue pills, our expert demonstrated how to "perform exceptional fellatio" on a banana. The only thing funnier than her demo were the faces of the horrified older women more likely to kill themselves than suck their husband's knob.

But by far, the most distasteful part of the long list of things required of me was one I was hell-bent not to do. Everyone was desperate for me to get pregnant.

It baffled me how they could forget Edward already has a son; a son whose existence has apparently threatened to topple kingdoms and sway elections and whose gall to survive has necessitated us hiring this entire team of assholes! When I said as much, although considerably more politely, they smiled at me like I was addle-minded. They told me that *we* still needed to have a child that was *ours*.

Preferably, a male one.

I honestly would have rather died, but by now, I'd lost all say in my life. We tried to get pregnant, or rather I should say, Edward fucked me regularly and with the sort of passion one would have doing only the most distasteful chores. For someone who enjoyed sex as much as he did, one would think he'd at least make it good for me, but our congress was every bit as boring, dry, and dissatisfying as filing taxes.

After two years passed, I was sent to a fertility doctor who ran a million tests and found nothing wrong. After another two years, Edward also underwent fertility testing, and his swimmers were reported to be in perfect health.

It was not long after that that Adam developed a particularly nasty cough that morphed into pneumonia, requiring him to be hospitalized. Although we had a nanny who cared for him, it was deemed "inappropriate" for the nanny to be at his bedside and I was told to go. My misery at having to attend to him when the child would have much rather had his beloved Belinda was luckily written off by the doctors and nurses as worry and concern.

Unable to sleep in the hard, faux-leather recliner pushed next to

Adam's bed, I finally crawl in with the restless child who hasn't stopped begging me to hold him since we got here. He's feverish and uncomfortable, fidgeting nonstop until I finally wrap my arms around his sweaty little body. He's shivering hard enough to make his teeth chatter, but within minutes of me pulling a blanket over him, he kicks it off, saying it's too scratchy. Eventually, he falls asleep, and shortly thereafter, I follow suit.

When I wake a few hours later, Adam's burning up. When I try to rouse him, he's listless and uncommunicative, and even when I frantically shout his name, he doesn't respond. When he begins to seize, I scream.

The nurses race in, taking him from my arms and begin to work on him. A doctor who looks not much older than me rushes in, giving quiet orders to the nurses who obey him quickly. I stand silently and watch them, their movements so precise and coordinated they feel almost choreographed.

It's not until after they stop the seizure that I realize I'm shaking and crying, my arms wrapped tightly around my torso in an attempt to comfort myself. The doctor takes the stethoscope from around his neck and listens to Adam's chest that's now decorated with sticky squares and lots of wires. Another nurse enters, telling him there's an available room ready in the PICU and they are ready to receive their new patient.

He nods, raising the railing on his side of the bed as another nurse does the same on the other side before they roll the bed out of the room and move as a unit quickly down the hall. He turns to me, his blue eyes concerned as he offers his hand and introduces himself, but I don't care who he is. I just want to know if Adam will be alright.

"We're taking Adam to the PICU, so, please, follow me, and I'll fill you in on what will happen next. I understand that what you saw was quite frightening, and I want to assure you that seizures in febrile children are not uncommon. We're taking him to the PICU because we'll

be better equipped to handle them there should he have another. I still believe that once we get his fever down, he will recover completely."

I breathe a sigh of relief. The doctor is so calm that even though I'm far past the level of freaking out, his demeanor puts me at ease. I swipe at the tears on my cheeks, embarrassed that I'd behaved as badly as I did. He pulls a wrinkled paper napkin from his white coat pocket and offers it to me. "It's a bit crumpled, but it's clean."

I take it from him with an awkward laugh and dry my face, trying as best as I can to make sure my mascara's not smudged all over my face without the aid of a mirror. When we reach the main doors of the PICU, the doctor swipes us into the locked area with the card dangling from a lanyard around his neck. He's left handed, and I can't help but notice no wedding ring on his finger.

Although this is absolutely not the time to be checking out Adam's doctor, I can't help notice that he's incredibly good looking. He has thick brown hair and light brown eyes with flecks of amber, his mouth set in a stern line at the moment, but I wouldn't doubt at all would be wonderful to kiss.

I school myself back to seriousness, afraid he'll somehow read my mind and call me out for being a terrible mother. I'm sure good Christian mothers never eye-fuck their kid's doctors.

We enter the room where Adam sleeps peacefully. A second IV has been placed, the fluids dripping rhythmically into his flushed little body. The doctor examines Adam carefully, orders more drugs to be given and schedules a few more tests before pulling up a much more comfortable looking chair next to the bed and motioning for me to sit. He sits on the edge of the bed, gently running his fingers through Adam's messy hair and smiling when Adam's eyes slowly crack open.

"Hey there, little buddy. How are you feeling?"

Adam looks up at him in confusion, probably wondering where the hell he is. He stares up at the doctor for a moment before asking hopefully, "Daddy?"

My heart breaks. Adam wants nothing more than to make his father happy, but he never can. Edward is always rough, and mean, and quick to discipline his son, and when Adam does something sweet or good, his father still refuses to say a kind word. Despite everything, Adam hasn't given up, instead continuing to try harder to make his father love him.

"No, sweet boy, I'm Doctor Rutherford. I'm here to make you feel better. I'd really like to be your friend. Do you think we can be friends?"

Adam looks over at me questioningly, and I smile and nod at him that it's okay. "I'll be your friend," *he says groggily.* "But only if you promise not to poke me with needles."

The doctor laughs, reaching over to boop the boy's nose with his fingertip. "Well, I'm not going to lie to you, little man. I can't promise that. But I can do something to make them not hurt so much. We have a very special cream here that we can put on your skin to make the needles not pinch. How about if I tell them it's okay to use that on you. Sound like a deal?"

"Really?" *Adam's face lights up for a minute before becoming distrusting again.* "You aren't fooling, are you?"

The Doctor laughs again, sounding truly amused and not the way most people do when placating children. If I didn't already find this man attractive, I sure do now.

"Nope, I'm not fooling. I wouldn't be able to fool a big, smart boy like you if I tried! Now, close your eyes and get some sleep, and I'll see you again before I leave at the end of my shift. Okay?"

Adam nods and gives him a grin before snuggling into his pillow and closing his eyes. I walk the doctor to the door and we talk for a few minutes about Adam's upcoming tests.

"You know, we'll probably keep him here for a few days. We're going to be watching him like a hawk while he's in the PICU, so if you want to go home and get some sleep and come back in the morning you can."

I look through the glass at the sleeping boy and am suddenly overcome by the urge to watch over him. "No, I'm going to stay here in case he wakes up in the middle of the night. I don't want him to need me and not be here for him."

The doctor nods. "I understand completely. I've yet to meet a mother who can sleep at home with a kid in the hospital. The recliners in this unit are pretty comfortable, and I'll get one of the nurses to bring you a pillow and a blanket. You can at least try to get a few hours of sleep."

I thank the doctor for his kindness, and when I look up into his eyes, I feel my cheeks flush. His brow crinkles as he looks at me, a strange look on his face. He takes my arm and steps us further down the hall.

"Um, this is a little awkward," he starts, a blush rising on his cheeks. "But there is something I do need to ask from you. I hope you don't mind." He reaches into his pocket, takes out a business card and a pen, and writes a number on the back of it.

"If your husband plans to visit while I'm on duty, can you give me a heads up?"

"Sure," I respond. "But may I ask why?"

He chuckles darkly, looking left and right to make sure no one overhears. "He beat the crap out of me once, many years ago. He said if he ever saw me again, he'd kill me."

"What?!" I gasp, looking horrified. "Why?"

"Because I knew what he'd done, and I refused to let him get away with it."

47

Declan

I don't know how Gritty does it, but we find more kids with his help than we ever could have on our own. Most of them are in bad shape, either too weak to run any further, or too badly injured to do much more than wait to die. Most of them tell me a red-haired girl told them where to hide, even helping some of them dig shallow holes under bushes or find a fallen tree to hunker down in until help arrived.

Our group dwindles quickly, as most of the kids are unable to walk and need to be carried out. Eventually it's just Gritty and me. After a few hours of chasing Gritty's ass through the woods, I'm exhausted, but aside from stopping to piss a few times, the dog just keeps trucking on like he's on a mission. A few times we hear patrolmen and Ag officers in the distance, but we're thankfully too far away for them to notice us.

As more and more kids are rescued, I realize why Gritty's soldiering on—he's latched onto Keira's scent. Each kid he unearths he jams his snooter in their armpits and groins until they squeal, only to back off and look at me expectantly and wag his tail wildly. I think he's excited each time he finds another one alive, but is eager to get moving again each time it's not Keira. I tell the kids to stay where they are and radio in their coordinates for someone to come get them. Although most of them beg me to stay, I gently tell them I can't. I have to keep moving.

With each kid I find, I worry more about Keira. I tell myself she's resourceful, that she's the sort to be in the middle of the worst sort of danger and manage to get out of it with little more than a few scratches and a sassy quip. Yet as the clock races towards daybreak, I can't bear the thought of not finding her and having to leave without her.

I'm so deep in my head that I literally trip over a kid hiding in the brush. He lets out a pained howl at almost the same time I fall flat on my face, my palms burning as they take the brunt of my weight. The kid does his best to crawl away from me, but the second he manages to stand, it's clear he not only can't run—he can't walk.

He's screaming for help, which is the last thing I want him to do. Although we're pretty deep in the woods, I've seen enough recent tire tracks that make me believe we aren't as alone as we'd like to think. When I catch up to him he's trying to climb a tree, but again, he can't. He ends up with his back against the bark, his eyes darting and wild as he begs me to spare him.

I tell him who I am. I gently tell him that he's safe and I'm going to get him out of here, but he won't listen. He begs me in increasingly loud and panicky tones to not send him back to the workcamp, and to please, please not kill him. I finally manage to get him away from the tree and grab him from behind with my hand clapped over his mouth. He thrashes against me and continues to beg for his life, and although he's not hard to subdue, he's still making far too much noise.

"Listen to me. Listen to me!" I whisper-shout in his ear. "I'm not going to hurt you, or send you back to the camp. Do you understand? I'm here to take you home. Home!"

His body finally goes limp. I manage to lower him back down on the ground, all the while speaking to him in soothing tones. I pull out my flashlight and take a peek at his leg, grimacing when I see the bone sticking through blood and filth crusted skin. There's no way he can walk on that, and he's heavy for anyone other than probably Scott to carry. I call in our location, telling them the kid needs a ride, and to ping my radio for our location.

Gritty has come back from wherever the fuck he trotted off too, and to say he's in a state is the understatement of the century. He barks at me sharply, takes a few steps away, then barks again. It's clear he wants me to follow him.

"Who's out there, boy? What did you find?"

He barks again and lopes off another few steps. Did he find Keira? Is that what he's trying to tell me?

I scramble to my feet. "Look, wait here. I promise I'll be right back."

The kid looks up at me, grabs my pant leg in his filthy hands, and begs me to not leave him. "Look, I need you to be quiet," I hiss. "I swear, I'm not going to leave you behind. I just need to see what this dog's going on about. I'll be right back. I swear it."

I manage to pry the kid's hands off me, and he crumples to the ground, sobbing. I promise again to come back before taking off at a run to follow Gritty. If this dog caught the scent of a pig and this chase ends up being for nothing, I swear to God, I'm gonna kill him. But Gritty's also pretty intuitive and he loves Keira with all his little doggy heart, so if there's any chance he's found her, I have to check.

My phone buzzes in my pocket, but I ignore it. Trying to run in the dark is hard enough to do without taking a call, and the last thing I need is to end up like that kid with a bone poking through my leg. Not to mention, I'm out of breath enough to sound like a total pervert if I answer, my breath now coming in short, choppy bursts. I spent way more time getting my muscle strength back after I was shot instead of working on cardio, and only now do I realize what a dumb mistake that was.

I listen closely to my surroundings, trying to be as quiet as possible while hauling ass as fast as I can. I'm headed uphill, Gritty having stopped to wait for me before mounting the crest. When I've just about reached him, he sits and stares at me like he's waiting for me to give him his next command. That's when I hear the voices.

I whisper for him to stay, and for once in this disobedient dog's life, he actually lays down and places his head on his paws. I creep up the hill, crawling along on my belly for the final few feet before peering over the edge.

There's a group of about ten kids down there on their knees and with their hands on their heads. They are surrounded by two Ag officers and a Purity Patrolman, two with their weapons trained on the escapees while the guy in white talks on a radio. The headlights from their trucks illuminate the area well enough that I have to squint to see until my eyes adjust. I quietly remove my rifle from where it was slung across my shoulder and set it up, adjusting the scope and praying I'm at a good enough angle to take the guards out before they can shoot me. I'm well covered, but I'm also alone against three well-trained officers.

I follow the one Ag officer with my scope as he approaches the kids, and I nearly stop breathing when I realize one of them is Keira. Unlike the others who look down at the ground, her chin is tilted up as she glares at the officer defiantly. Part of me is incredibly proud of her for being so brave, while another part of me screams at her to not provoke the son of a bitch.

As I set up my shots, I notice the guys keep turning to peer into the woods behind them. I can't hear what they're saying, but they're acting like they hear something. I listen carefully but don't hear a thing, so I doubt it's other people or incoming vehicles. I'm close enough that I'd be able to hear that.

The officer that was on his radio finishes his call, holsters the thing at his waist, and pulls out his handgun. He snaps his fingers to get the other guys' attention and points towards the noise. He's heading into the woods, hoping to catch whoever's out there unaware.

I just about have my gameplan set and have relatively clean kill shots on the two guys dumb enough to not be wearing body armor, when something happens. There's some sort of kerfuffle in the bushes that sends one of the men racing towards the commotion, the other guy stepping closer to the kids and telling them to not even think about running.

A minute later, I hear a loud scream, a piercing yelp, and two shots fired. There are a few shouts before the other guy who'd been watching the kids reappears, his entire focus on keeping the lunging, snapping dog from taking a chunk out of him.

I peek over my shoulder, and of course, Gritty's not there. I guess he thought I was taking too long and decided to take matters into his own hands—or would that be paws? When the Ag guy steps out into the clearing, I see that not only did Gritty nail this guy a few times, but a chunk of white uniform fabric also hangs from his growling, snapping mouth.

Good for you Gritts. I hope you bit the shit out of them.

Gritty has taken cover behind a large stone, snarling and growling like Cerberus, himself. As the men talk about what to do with Gritty, who is still trying very hard to eat them both, one of the assholes pulls a handgun.

Oh, fuck that shit. You are not gonna kill my dog. Not on my watch.

Even though I have no idea what happened to the third guy, I won't let them shoot Gritty. No fucking way. I take my aim and pull the trigger, the man falling to the ground after I place two quick shots in the center of his chest and one in his head. Not knowing where I'm shooting from, the other officer looks about frantically just before Gritty bunches himself up and leaps. He takes the motherfucker down easily, the guy getting one terrified scream out before the dog silences him for good.

I wait a few seconds, hoping that prick number three will come out of hiding, but nothing happens. No longer being held, a bloody-mouthed Gritty races to Keira and licks her astounded face as she hugs him tightly around the neck. The kids get up and start to run in different directions, but when they hear my shrill whistle, Keira yells for them to stop, and fuck me, they *listen*.

I race down the hill with my weapon at the ready, my eyes scanning the area for any sign of the third guy. Fucking coward is probably hiding somewhere licking his wounds. I motion for the kids to come to me, and when they do, I point in the direction they need to run. I tell them if they see an unmarked vehicle with men in black to not worry, that the men are with me and will help them.

Keira hangs back with the kids who are in bad shape and painfully slow at a time where speed is critical. A few of them even need to hold on to each other for support, their steps so small they could probably crawl faster. When they catch up to me, I hand Keira a loaded handgun that she expertly handles, racking a cartridge in the chamber and placing her finger next to, but not on the trigger. I'm glad the Bullies taught her well as this absolutely isn't the time for safety lessons.

Through all of this, Gritty hasn't left Keira's side, the joy at having his girl back evident in his big, brown eyes. I glance over him quickly, glad to see no evidence of bullet wounds, but I'm sure Rowan won't mind giving him a good once-over for me when we get home, just to be safe. Gritty jumps up a few times, demanding Keira's attention when she's talking to me, and each time she laughs and calls him a good boy, ruffling the fur on his head. It's the happiest I've ever seen the slobber monster, and in all honesty, I owe him a couple steaks or something as a reward when we get home.

"That was some damn good timing," she tells me, easily keeping stride beside me despite the fact she's now practically carrying a young boy. She's filthy enough that her red hair is a murky shade of brown, and there are bruises, cuts and welts all over her face and arms. Yet she's smiling like the cat who ate the canary, so for now I'll assume her wounds are superficial. "I thought I was headed to meet my Maker before you showed up."

"Yeah, me too," I admit. "But you have your dog to thank for saving you, not me. He's the one who found you. We've been hunting you for days."

"I know," she tells me with a sly smile. "I ran across your people way more often than the asshats from the camp. They almost caught me once, but I climbed a tree until they rolled. You really need to tell your people to occasionally look up when they're searching."

I'm ready to kill her, but I hold my temper, not wanting to scare the timid kids, but trust me, we're gonna have a whopper of a discussion when we get home. Had she told us she was out here, we would have known she was safe. We could have armed her.

We could have put her on a plane and shipped her off to Canada or Mexico.

"You thought if we found you, we'd make you go home, didn't you?" I ask when the truth hits me.

"Yup," she responds, popping the p for emphasis. "Fuck, Declan, I had to run off with Isaac because there was no way in hell you would have let me come. We both know that. All you've ever done is see me as a little girl, and yeah, I'm young, but I've been livin' the rebellion since I was just a kid. Most of the rest of you started once you became adults. Shit, I probably have more years of hiding out and raising hell under my belt than most of you." She stops for a second before adding with a laughing smile, "Not to mention, *'I'm West Philadelphia, born and raised. . .'*

I chuckle with her, vaguely remembering the words she raps as the beginning of the *Fresh Prince of Bel Air*. Knowing the Philly crew, it was probably taught to her as a form of poetry or to be used as a war cry. Maybe both.

"You did good, Keira," I tell her honestly, her smile widening further at my all-too infrequent praise, but she bristles when I lower my voice and continue. "But you're still in a shitload of trouble. You disobeyed my direct orders and went rogue, and those are offenses worthy of a Court Martial."

"No, I didn't disobey you," she retorts hotly. "I just went over your head. Isaac said I could go."

"Isaac is *not* my boss. Not even close. Did you tell him you were only sixteen?"

She's quiet for a minute before slyly answering, "He didn't ask."

Jesus Janet Jackson Christ, this girl's gonna be the death of me.

She quickly changes the subject while I curse under my breath. "Any idea what happened to the other guy? I'd love to add his name to my death list. Motherfucker was a real bastard, and far up the food chain. Let's just say," she nods her head in the direction of the child next to her, a cue for us to not be too blunt about things, "He 'really, really likes' little girls and boys. Although I think he also enjoyed Ezra's unconsenting company, too, if you catch my drift."

Just the thought of some sadistic pedophile being put in charge of a work camp full of kids makes me want to vomit. I quickly turn my revulsion to anger, knowing that's way better fuel for my current mission.

We walk a little further, both of us silent and wary. I've had the feeling someone's been following us for a while, and I think Keira senses it, too. I grab her arm and make a few quick motions with my hands that I hope she understands as we are being followed but to not say anything. She gives me the thumbs up.

A few times a twig breaks, or a stronger gust of wind rustles the leaves extra hard and we turn, weapons raised. Yet every time, no one's there. I try to get her to walk ahead, whispering to her that I'll stay behind and guard our flank, but she refuses. She says the BSB never leaves anyone behind.

When we catch up to another small group taking a rest on some rocks, we pass the stragglers off to them. We tell them not to dawdle and shoo them on, acting like we're going with them, but instead take up a spot behind some rocks and wait. I give Keira the rest of my water that she drains except for the bit she pours down Gritty's throat, and when she asks if I have any food on me, I give her a protein bar that she practically swallows whole. We sit in silence, listening to the wind blow through the trees, our ears trained for even the slightest noise that could be this guy.

"Okay, let's go," I tell her. "As much as I want to kill this mother-fucker, it's gonna be light soon, and we're leaving at dawn. We still have a way to go."

She rolls her eyes at me and sticks out her tongue, and any thoughts of her having matured over the past few months are wiped from my head. Just as I'm ready to tell her to get up and grab Gritty's rope, he spins his head, his ears perked. A second later, he emits a low growl, bares his teeth, and takes off sprinting back in the direction we just came from.

Fucking dog. . .

My radio suddenly begins buzzing loudly, and not wanting to give away our hiding spot, I fumble to silence it. I tell Keira to stay put as I scramble to my feet, and when she doesn't respond I look over to find she's already gone.

I am abso-fuckin'-lutely going to strangle that girl when I get my hands on her.

I run as fast as I can but the two of them are faster. Every time I take a turn or make a bend around trees or rocks, I think I'm catching up only to find them not there. I'm terrified that son-of-a-bitch is going to ambush her and I won't be there to save her just like I couldn't save Anna, or John, or Marta. . . .

Fuck. . . Fuck!!

I'm doing my best to drown out the intrusive thoughts, and stop thinking of everyone I've failed. Off to my right and down a steep slope is a truck parked with the headlights on and engine running. The driver side door gapes open, and there's no one inside.

In my haste I end up sliding most of the way down the hill, my legs burning with the demand I put on them to keep me upright. Gritty snarls and barks from somewhere behind the truck, but I don't see him or Keira. I don't dare shout out to them, hoping to surprise whoever's out here. As I run towards the truck, I'm momentarily blinded by the headlights. Gritty's frantic barking is so loud now that I know I'm close, but I still don't see them. Where the fuck are they?

That's when the scream pierces the early morning air, a sound so full of pain and terror that my heart stops. I run faster, my mind a jumbled mess of Olesya's warnings and terrifying predictions, and although I hadn't believed her then, I'm becoming more of a believer with each passing second.

She said bad things would happen, and sacrifices would have to be made.

Dear God, please, please, *please* don't let me be too late. . .

A massive pit forms in my stomach when Gritty stops barking. Then there's silence.

Behind me, a door slams and an engine roars to life. I skid to a stop and turn back, scrambling to get my weapon ready to fire just as the turning vehicle blinds me with its headlights. I shoot, having no idea if I hit anything of value, ducking behind a tree just a millisecond before the driver fires back. I return every shot of his with at least two of my own, begging my eyes to hurry up and adjust. Between us I have the superior firepower, and if I can just see clearly for one fucking second I'm sure I can get a kill shot. . .

But the driver must realize this too, because he suddenly veers sharply to the left and floors the truck, racing to put as much distance between us as possible.

Knowing he could return at any time with reinforcements, I

race around frantically as I loudly call out Keira's name. When she doesn't answer I holler for Gritty, who answers me with a plaintive whine.

Although I know it's a bad idea, I pull out my flashlight and wave it along the ground. I'm too afraid to be quiet, resorting to screaming Keira's name. My voice catches in my throat and my eyes fill with more and more tears with each unanswered summons.

I follow a path of broken twigs and bent branches to find Gritty's leash wrapped tightly around the root of a fallen tree, the dog close to strangling himself in his effort to pull away. He lunges at me before he recognizes me, and when I tell him to calm, he barks frantically until I untangle the rope. Once loose, he takes a few off-balanced steps before crashing through a bramble bush and racing behind a copse of trees.

I follow him closely, but he's quicker and far more agile. I'm winded from running and screaming Keira's name, and the few frustrated tears I'd shed at some point have now turned into panicked sobs. I scream and scream, my voice cracking and breaking as I try to catch my breath that's only coming in strangled gasps. My chest hurts from the effort, the pain excruciating as my overworked lungs try to catch up with my galloping heart.

Please, God, I will give you anything you want, just please let Keira be okay. If anyone has to die today, please, let it be me.

When I finally hear her voice I'm so relieved I cry even harder. The heat of panic and sweat of fear suddenly evaporates, leaving me chilled and so very cold. I stumble through the brush, looking everywhere for her, using my flashlight to peer in even the most unlikely places. I keep telling myself that as long as she can speak, she's fine; that whatever injuries she has, we can treat.

Once I find her, everything will be fine, I repeat over and over in my mind. I'm doing my damndest to convince myself everything is going to be fine, fine, fucking *fine,* that if I have faith in my belief, that I can make it true. Like in that story from my childhood, where Tinkerbell doesn't die because the kids believe in fairies and their faith brings her back to life.

I berate myself for thinking about fairies in this critical moment, then switch to cursing myself for being shitty at tracking. If I were the one lost, Keira would have found me by now.

Who the fuck am I kidding? She wouldn't have lost me to begin with.

It ends up being Gritty I see first, or rather, his rapidly swishing tail. He's standing overtop Keira, his ass to me as he vigorously laps at her face. I skid to a halt, my mantra still repeating in my head.

She's going to be fine, fine, fucking fine. . .

As I close in, I pick up an unnatural tang in the air, something metallic, a foreign scent that doesn't belong to the woods. I wipe the tears from my face as I pull myself together, still telling myself she's fine, fine, *fine*—until I get close enough to see she's not.

A chill runs through me, one icier and far more fierce than I've ever felt before. Time stops, as does my heart. I try to run to her, but my legs won't work. My knees buckle, dropping me to the ground where the smell is now much stronger.

I'm close, so I crawl to her, feeling like I've been switched into slow-motion.

This can't be real, this can't be real. . .

My brain refuses to register the entirety of what I see, only allowing snippets to register. . . Keira lying on her back, her small hand raised and tangled loosely in the thick fur of Gritty's chest. . .

weak, so weak. . .

Her pale fingers covered with dirt and rust. . .

not rust. . .

her voice so soft it's hardly a whisper as she speaks to her beloved friend. . .

her *last words. . . .*

I claw my way to her side. She's so still, so pale, that she could be a statue. I place my hand on her cheek and turn her to face me and she blinks once, trying to clear the tears from her eyes. Her lips are cracked from dehydration and beginning to turn blue, her face a frightening shade of gray in the scant rays of the moon and the insufficient illumination of a dying flashlight.

Fading away in the dimming light. . .

Fuck this shit. She's not going to die. I won't let her die.

I drop the flashlight, blaming it for Keira's unnatural color, blaming Gritty's shadow for the darkness around her eyes. I try to push Gritty aside, but he growls and snaps at my face, telling me in no uncertain terms he isn't going anywhere. I finally manage to push him aside enough to see her more clearly. Her chest convulses with a cough that she's too weak to cover with her hand, a fine mist of red coloring everything it lands on.

Oh God, this can't be happening. . .

"Oh, Keira," I breathe as I reach for her, gently smoothing a few strands of her hair from her face. There's a terrible gurgling sound coming from her chest, and when she tries to speak she coughs again, this time spattering small drops of blood over us both.

"Don't speak," I tell her. "Save your strength. Help's on the way."

I grab my radio and call for help STAT, not bothering to hide the panic in my voice. I toss the radio aside, only now seeing that I'm kneeling in a pool of blood.

I need to find where all this fucking blood is coming from and put pressure on it, but Gritty won't move. I beg him to move, wondering what the fuck is happening in this critical moment that's reduced me to arguing with a goddamn *dog*. Then, I swear on all things Holy, the dog turns and looks at me as if to say *how stupid can you be? There's nothing either of us can do.*

She's dying. . . even the dog can tell. . .

Gritty turns back to his best friend and gives her face one last lick. It smears the blood on her face, something about that making everything just that much more awful. I can't be here. I don't want to be here...

You were always meant to be here...

Keira untangles her hand from Gritty's fur and scratches behind his torn ear, but unlike every other time, Gritty doesn't take enjoyment from it.

He knows...

When Keira reaches for me, Gritty finally steps aside with a heavy sigh. He lies down next to her, his face so close to hers that his exhales ruffle her hair. Keira's lip curls slightly, the world's smallest smile on her lips as she turns her head to face Gritty and whispers that she will always love him. She brokenly tells him that when it's his turn, she'll be waiting for him at the Rainbow Bridge.

Oh fuck. Don't cry, don't cry, *do not cry...*

"He saved me once. It was my turn to save him."

I don't know what she means, I don't know what happened, and of all the things I don't know, the one thing I do, is that she's dying. There's nothing I can do.

It is as it must be...

I take her hand in mine, her grip so weak that I clutch her hand hard enough for us both. If I don't let go, maybe she'll survive, maybe I can ground her spirit to Earth and keep her from dying.

I think it may be working when she starts to speak softly, her voice quivering from the effort. "I never thought you'd be the last person I'd see before I die." She whispers so quietly that I have to lean over her mouth to make out the words. "But I guess it's okay. There's uglier people I could look at."

She smiles when I sputter out a laugh through my tears, but the moment of humor dies quickly when a thin stream of blood drips from the edge of her mouth.

Oh, no.. no! Please, God, give me more time!

I sit by her side, her hand clasped in mine, my body hovering over hers with my other hand gently rubbing her cheek. I should be doing things to ease her pain, and all I've done so far is piss off her dog and leak tears all over her. I'm being no good for her at all. Fuck, I should let Gritty take over. . .

As if hearing my thoughts, something cold and wet nudges my hand, and I look over to find Gritty staring at me like *get your shit together before I rip out your throat with my teeth.* I take my hand from her cheek and wipe the tears from my face, then wipe it all on my pants before replacing it. My leg is falling asleep under me so I shuffle myself just enough to bump the flashlight with my foot, the light bobbing for a moment before the beam illuminates the source of her injury.

Is that? No, it can't be. . . *Is that my knife?*

I shake my head, closing my eyes for a brief moment, giving my brain a moment to reset from its hallucination. There's no way. It can't be.

When I open my eyes again, the knife is still protruding from her chest, the handle towards my hand. Although it hasn't been in my possession since the night Emma used it to defend herself, I can practically feel the grip in my fist. I know how each and every intricately carved groove feels against my palm; where each and every design corresponds to the tattoos on my arms.

The knife that had been in my family for generations has no place being lodged in this child's chest. My mind is so befuddled, my heart bursting with such a terrible mix of emotions, that the most rational thought I can muster is that none of this is real. I'm either in the middle of a fever-dream, or maybe *I'm* the one injured and this is a final, fatal vision of my own.

Every time I blink, my heart leaps with the possibility my eyelids might wipe the sight away, yet every time, I'm greeted with the same. I tell myself this is all just a sick trick of my mind, but if this is indeed a ruse, my other senses are in on the tasteless joke. I feel her blood, thick and slippery against my fingers, as I wipe it away from her lips. I see her skin paling and her lips turning a darker blue, her injured body giving up the ghost as blood pools around her body. The distinctive copper pennies smell is overwhelming, mixing nauseatingly with the smell of our combined fear and a touch of recently burned forest.

Somebody, anybody, do something!

"I loved you, you know," she whispers, her eyes struggling to stay open.

I smile down at her, not caring how my tears drip off my face and onto hers. "I know," I whisper back.

"Declan, will you do one last thing for me? Please?"

I nod quickly, her grip loosening. *Oh my God, we're running out of time...*

"Will you kiss me? I don't want to die with my only kiss being from a boy who was unconscious."

Although I have more than a few questions about that, they will remain unanswered. There isn't time. She's fading fast. We have, at best, minutes left, but probably only seconds.

I nod quickly, licking my lips to get the taste of my tears off them, Keira's eyes barely focusing as I lean in and press my lips against hers. I kiss her the way a sixteen year-old girl should be kissed for the first time, in a gentle, respectful way I can only pray my daughter will one day be kissed by her first boyfriend. I keep it sweet and short, and when I pull away from her, I lean forward and place my hands on either side of her face. This time, I kiss her on the center of her forehead, and when I'm done, I drop my forehead to touch hers.

When I pull back to look in her eyes, I see that the blood from her mouth had transferred to my lips, leaving an obscene print on her forehead. Although it sickens me to see, I don't wipe it away. I don't want Keira's last sensation to be my fingers wiping away my kisses.

I don't want her last thought to be that I'm ashamed of giving her the last thing she'll ever ask for.

"Is it wrong that, just now, I pretended you were Micah?" she rasps, attempting a smile that looks more like a grimace.

I smile back through my tears, and shake my head gently. "No, Keira. There's nothing wrong with that."

She gasps quietly, her face scrunching in pain. She looks so afraid. "Will you s-stay with me?" Her voice is so soft and child-like that I'm gutted by her fear-filled request.

"Of course, sweetheart. I'll be with you until the very end."

Less than a minute later, she's gone. I check for a pulse, and find none. No breath comes from her slightly parted lips. Her heart has stopped, and with it, my own.

I rip the offending dagger from her chest with an agonized scream and throw it in the grass. I can't stand to look at it or even think about how it got here. It had been lost on the side of a muddy Virginia mountain, only to show up here, buried deep inside a sixteen year-old girl's chest. What sort of devilry made this possible?

No, I can't think about it. Not now. Not when her body is still warm in my arms. I wrap my arms around her tightly and clutch her to my chest, and in the silence of early dawn, I sob. I lose all sense of time and place, allowing every ounce of my grief to flow. I'm unable to do anything but grieve.

When a firm hand grasps my shoulder, I don't panic, or swing out. I don't care if they're friend or foe, here to help or to kill me. I vaguely register someone repeating my name, the voice male, the tone every bit as broken as mine. Whoever it is drops heavily to their knees by my side, and when I finally gather the courage to see who belongs to the hand reaching forward to pick the grass and leaves from Keira's curls, I realize Scott has come for me. I'm oddly comforted by his hand that remains clasped to my shoulder.

"D-man, I'm so sorry," Scott whispers brokenly. "But we have to get out of here."

The last thing I want to do is to move from this spot. Moving means taking her back to the safehouse. Seeing other people. *Talking* to other people. Answering questions and making plans, and then packing up to go home.

Oh, God. *Home.*

Where everyone else's eagerly heading, and for the first time in my life, the place I least want to be. I'll have to explain to Emma and Sarah and the kids what happened. I'll have to tell Brother Love that the little girl he not only saved, but nurtured, and cared for, and loved, is gone. I'll have to tell Micah the last thing she said before she died was for me to tell him that she loved him.

This train of thought starts me sobbing again, and when Scott reiterates we've gotta go, I shake my head. When he reaches down and asks if he can take Keira from me, it's not meant as a question, but to prepare me as he pulls her from my arms. I feel so weak, so broken, that I let him take her. She'll be safer with him.

Scott carries her easily to the truck and lays her gently across the back seat. I stare at my bloody hands for a long moment before wiping my palms on my thighs. The blood is mostly dried, and no matter how harshly I rub my hands on my clothes, it refuses to wipe away. I wonder if I'll look at them ever again without seeing her blood on them.

When I look up, Gritty's staring at me. He nudges my cheek with his cold, wet nose and whines, looking at the bloody ground, then at me, and then towards the truck. He nudges me once more, and trots off behind Scott.

Everyone is eager to go, and I'm holding them up. I stand stiffly, my joints cracking and every muscle in my body protesting. Everything about this moment feels wrong. Although I know the haze

I'm barely functioning in is from shock, I can't help but feel there's something else off.

I search for my things, grabbing my rifle and the long-dead flashlight from where I'd thrown them in the scrubby grass, their weight in my hands feeling strange as I secure them to my body. Just as I'm about to reach for the bloody blade, something else metallic catches the first of the early morning light. When I pick it up, something on it bites into my thumb.

I shake off the pinch, marveling at the bead of blood on the pad of my thumb that's blooming like the world's tiniest rose. I don't bother to wipe it away, instead examining the offending item like I'd never seen one before.

It takes a few moments for my brain to find the right words. It's a polished, brass name tag, the sort created for fancy uniforms worn by important people. A piece of bright, white fabric remains pinned in place, the color and fabric the same as those worn by upper level Purity Patrol officers. Keira must have ripped it off him when they fought, leaving me a posthumous clue to her murderer's identity.

The haze of grief I'm in evaporates the moment I see the name. I am left clear-headed and cold, and ready to respond to the gauntlet thrown at my feet. I pick up the knife from the ground and stare at it for a long moment, still praying it's not the one lost months ago, but a facsimile, even though I know it's not.

This knife still has another job to do. . .

The whisper on the wind calls to the simmering anger in my heart and fans the flames into a raging inferno. As if I just broke the surface from swimming underwater, the world around me clears, my focus sharp. The wind picks up and tousles my hair and ruffles the leaves. Color returns to the forest as a single ray of light breaks through the canopy of leaves, illuminating the blood-covered blade. My fingers wrap tightly around the carved hilt.

Oh yeah, this knife absolutely has a lot more work to do.

I look up at the early morning sky and make a vow to myself, to my wife, to Keira, Micah, and yeah, even to Gritty, that this son of a bitch will die by this blade, and I will make it every bit as slow and torturous as I can. I'm filled with renewed strength, a new purpose, knowing now exactly what I must do.

Quinten Goodman better watch his goddamn back. For someone wicked his way comes.

48

Emma

Sarah and I are just finishing the dinner dishes when Declan calls to say they're coming down the driveway. Usually he stays on the phone and chats until I meet him outside, so my first clue that something's wrong is when he promptly hangs up.

Sarah and I both know something's wrong before Amos even parks the truck. Declan is staring out the side window looking positively shell-shocked, and Amos and Scott don't look much better. When the door opens, even Gritty doesn't bounce out and jump all over us. Instead, he hops quietly out of the back seat and trots over to my side, slipping his head under my hand for scritches and pressing his big head tight against my thigh.

"Where's Keira?"

I wonder if she once again fell deeply asleep during the ride, the girl historically unable to stay awake in the car. Scott winces and Amos tears up at the same time Declan reaches me and envelops me in the tightest hug imaginable.

My body goes cold.

Something wet splashes against my neck, and the moment I register that my husband's crying, his entire body shaking, I don't need to hear the words to know what no one has the heart to say.

"Sweet Jesus, no," Sarah sobs as she falls into Amos' arms. Scott whistles to Gritty who trots over to him, and the two head inside the house. I hear him say something to the children, and then there's silence. I don't know what I expected of the children, as the lot of them are probably too young to understand death. But then I think of everything this community's been through, and I realize that maybe they do. Maybe they're silent because they are just as lost for words as the rest of us.

Sarah and Amos speak quietly together, but I manage to overhear him tell his wife that they already delivered Keira's body to the local funeral home. He asks about Micah, and I hear Sarah quietly tell him he's helping Dr. Z with something at her place and will be home tomorrow. My heart aches for the young man who has yet to find out his first girlfriend, if you could even call their relationship that of boyfriend and girlfriend, is gone. The thought sends a chill down my spine, prompting Declan to pull me even tighter against him. Amos and Sarah whisper quietly for a few more minutes before also heading inside.

I rub Declan's back as he cries, resisting the urge to soothe him with the words we use for the distraught. I can't say that everything's going to be okay, because *nothing* about a sixteen year-old girl being dead is okay. If there's ever a time for tears, it is now.

I have so many questions, not that I have any intention of asking them, as this isn't the time. Hell, I wonder if there's *ever* a time to ask the whys, whens and hows, especially when the answers don't matter. Knowing how she died won't bring her back.

It's well past dark when Declan finally pulls from my arms, wipes his face on his sleeve and looks up at the stars as he struggles to compose himself. When he speaks, his voice is hoarse. "I keep thinking I'm out of tears, and yet I am unable to stop bawling."

I nod, not having any idea what to say. I lead him to the porch swing, sitting down on one end so Declan can lie on his back with his head in my lap. It always soothes him when I run my fingers through his hair, and judging by how he looks, he's in desperate need of comfort. The only noises, aside from the swing that creaks under us, are the chirping crickets, the croaking frogs, and the occasional hoot of a barn owl. Their songs sound particularly sad tonight.

We stew in our grief, Declan's breathing hitching a few times as more tears fall, but eventually his exhales even out and the deep wrinkle between his eyes softens. Even though I can no longer feel my legs, I don't move. I'm afraid if I wake him, he won't fall back asleep. My discomfort is a small price to pay if it allows him a few hours of rest.

I continue to work my fingers through his hair, gently untangling knots and pulling small twigs and leaves from his messy curls. Eventually he shifts position, and I lurch to grab him before he falls off the swing, but I fail spectacularly. The two of us tumble to the ground in a pile of limbs, my skirt and apron flapping as Declan tries to untangle us. He's disoriented and still half-asleep, a tiny curl of his lips, the beginning of a smile, looking freakishly out of place on a face otherwise ravaged by grief.

When I place my fingertips to his lips he gives them a sweet kiss before the grief hits him anew and that wisp of a smile disappears. He rolls over on his back and looks up at the sky, the faint moonlight making his glassy eyes gleam. He doesn't look at me when he whispers, "Do you have any idea how much I love you?"

I nod as I brush my fingertips over his scruffy cheek and turn his question back on him. "Do you have any idea how much I love *you*?"

He turns to face me, giving me the tiniest nod. "Yeah, I think I do."

I almost think he's going to say something else but he stops, instead pulling me against him, my head resting on the groove of his shoulder, my hand lying over his broken heart. His shirt is stiff under my fingers, the fabric saturated with dried blood. I try to not think about it, to pretend it's not Keira's blood, blood that would still be *in* her if she just hadn't been so determined to prove she was all grown up.

That's the thought that finally breaks me. Declan holds me tighter, his hand rubbing soothing circles on my back as I sob. Keira had been so eager to be one of us, to be an adult, an equal, that it led to her death. I wonder if we'd maybe handled things differently, or given her more say in her life, if we could have prevented this. Or was her tragic death inevitable, something Fate had determined the moment she was born?

My mind takes me down a rabbit hole of *should haves* and *what ifs*, the train of thought so exhausting that the next thing I know, Declan's gently shaking me awake, insisting that we go to bed before the mosquitos suck us dry. He helps me up and we head into the silent house. I ask him if he wants me to make him something to eat and he shakes his head, holding out a hand to lead me up the stairs.

In the light of our room, I see he's got blood all over his clothes and sprayed and smeared on his skin. Some of it's transferred onto my apron, and I set it aside to soak in the morning along with Declan's clothes. Not wanting to dirty the bathroom, he tells me he's going to wash down at the stream, and he'll be back in a bit. He tucks me into bed, kisses my forehead sweetly, and promises to be back soon.

When I wake it's to the sounds of Sarah rattling around in the kitchen and the smell of fresh-brewed coffee wafting up the stairs. I roll over to find Declan's side of the bed empty and the sheets cold to the touch. I turn on the light and peer around, finding a note propped on his pillow.

I unfold it with trembling fingers, a sickening feeling forming in my belly as I pray it doesn't say what I know it will.

49

Trinity

Louise isn't well.

Those of us who compromise her most loyal staff all notice that as the day of the party approaches, her nervous condition worsens. Considerably. She's trying to hide it, but I've found her engaging in behaviors I thought were long behind her. Some aren't nearly as concerning as others, but the frequency, and now the severity, of the ways in which she soothes herself have me quite concerned. Not to mention, I have no idea how to hide them should she exhibit them during the party.

Already today, I have found her multiple times ensconced in what I call her "thousand-yard stare." She stands motionless, almost transfixed, peering off into the distance as if watching something very engaging. It's creepy to watch, and very hard to shake her out of, and when she finally emerges, she's disoriented and extremely emotional. Most of the time she needs to be sedated to prevent spiraling into either irrational anger or hysterical crying.

For the past hour, Louise has been talking to herself, mumbling things that make no sense. She's stopped only to make wild, unfounded accusations of the guards and the temporary staff. If I were to be kind, I'd call them the ramblings of a crazy woman, and if I were to be rude, well, there's no need to go there.

To say the least, this absolutely cannot happen during the party, not that any of us have any control over these spells, least of all, dear Louise. I don't know who would be more pissed off if she should break down in public, her bitch of a mother, or her evil, cheating husband. They take her mental illness as an affront to them, acting as if her suffering is a plague upon their household and not what it really is—the direct result of their years of mistreatment. If she embarrasses them, they have only themselves to blame.

I didn't know her when she was young, but after a few years of caring for Louise, she finally trusted me enough to tell me everything. It's become impossible for me to act as if I don't know what Edward and her mother did, so we decided years ago that I should remain out of sight when El Capo and the Evil Queen Mother are around.

With only hours before the party of the century begins, I've been in contact with my people as much as possible, updating them not only on the plans we've put in place for tonight, but on Louise's unstable condition. While Louise takes a few hours to get some much needed rest, I tap away on my laptop, updating everyone involved. I know it's probably too late to change what they've planned, but just in case they abort their mission, I tell them that no matter what, we must make sure that Louise escapes. Tonight.

I'm not surprised when there are a flurry of replies telling me no, but I insist. I worry that in her significantly more delicate state, she may accidentally say or do something that will implicate her for the things I've done, and I cannot have that on my conscience. I tell them if she doesn't go, neither will I.

A sharp rap at my door nearly scares me to death, my "Just a minute!" the sort of frightened chirp only those with something to hide can make. I unplug the computer and barely shove it under the bed before a member of the House Guard enters, telling me I'm needed. A quick look up at the clock shows I've lost track of time, and

CHAPTER FORTY-NINE

I am indeed late for Louise's appointment with the hair and makeup women.

I smile sweetly at the no-nonsense young man and fake a yawn. I thank him for coming to fetch me, claiming that I had laid down for a few minutes, and that I must have forgotten to tell someone to wake me. He grumbles something about how it must be nice to be able to nap in the middle of the day, to which I have an awful lot of things I'd love to tell him I wish *I* could do, but I stifle the urge. I can't risk my retort being reported, especially not on an important day like today.

The house is in an uproar, with florists bringing in the last of the enormous arrangements for the ballroom, and the aerialists setting up the rigging in the ceiling for the silks and ropes they will dramatically dangle from during the cocktail hour. I pass the enormous table of gifts in the hallway that's already so overladen a second had to be brought in. I'm sure more will be coming tonight, with each guest trying to top the others in order to gain favor with the birthday boy.

Some of the gifts, the ones that the most prominent people coming tonight demanded be opened and displayed, are set aside on separate pedestals for all to admire. There are priceless pieces of art, and sculptures that will most likely end up in a warehouse when they really belong in a museum. One of the bigger ass-kissers gifted Edward a Stradivarius violin that will never be played. A gold and jewel-encrusted *New State Text* arrived yesterday, given by the Supreme Regent's devoted servant, the Supreme Pontiff, a gift I would bet my left tit that my employer will never read.

Of the gifts displayed, the most heinous came, of course, from Mother Barbara. She had a life-size statue carved of marble depicting Edward in a Christ-like pose, in robes and with long hair I can guarantee the uptight motherfucker never had. It will be placed in the lobby of the flagship New State Church for all to see, forever blessing the masses as they enter. If you look at it at just the right angle, the figure looks a bit cross-eyed, no doubt done on purpose. The entire thing is grotesque enough to be comical, and I have no doubt at least one poor guest will end up rotting in the Reflecting Pool when they cannot contain their laughter.

When I finally make it to Louise's dressing room, the stench of hairspray greets me before I even open the door. She fidgets in her chair as the women work on her, both of them ignoring her as she complains when one pulls her hair too tight or the other uses a lipstick color that she flat out says she doesn't like. She immediately perks up when I arrive.

"Get out," she states so quietly that the women ignore her. A single glance at the mirror shows they've done nothing of what she's asked, instead patting her on the shoulder and telling her to be quiet, that they know better than she does what Edward likes.

I'm just about to step in when Louise stands up so fast the stool she's sitting on topples over. "Get out!" she yells with a ferocity I thought she no longer had. The women step back, their mouths hanging open, but they don't leave. It's not until Louise starts grabbing the pots of rouge and palettes of eyeshadows and throws them at the door where they shatter in a dazzling display of color, that they finally leave.

Louise looks at the mess and sighs, telling me to leave it, and that because she made it, she'll clean it up later. She rights the stool and sits heavily at her vanity, tears swimming in her overly made up eyes. She wants to look regal, and they made her look like a clown.

"Get me Caitlin," she whispers brokenly. "She always made Emma look so pretty. She'll know what to do."

I tell her it's a bad idea, but she won't listen. As her agitation grows, I know letting her volatile mood escalate further will prove disastrous for us all.

"Fine," I tell her. "But just for the record, I don't trust that woman any further than I can throw her. And if anything goes wrong, I'm throwing your ass under the bus."

I temper my words with a joking smile, and she sniffs back her tears, and smiles back. I help her get the half ton of makeup off her face and promise Louise that I'll make sure that no matter what, tonight will go off without a hitch. She smiles back slyly, but says nothing.

I now know without a doubt that, tonight, I'm not the only one who will be up to no good.

50

Louise

It's easier than I expect to get Caitlin up to my room, and when I tell her what I asked the stylists for and then show her what they used, she's downright horrified. She rifles through their boxes and bags while I brush out what remains of their ridiculous, poofy hairstyle.

For the first time in weeks, Caitlin's excited and animated. I think she's happy to have something to do, not to mention, to finally be let out of her room and away from the child she's clearly begun to despise. It's a pleasant few hours that we spend together as I am transformed, talking and laughing like I suspect she and Emma once did. As my hair and makeup come together, I'm amazed how her skillful hands make me not only look younger, but less tired, and more like the woman I was right before the accident that almost took my life.

While Adam is in the hospital I have a lot of time to think about my life, and in that time, I come to a few eye-opening conclusions. I'm drinking far too much, and taking way too many pills. I despise my parents and hate my husband, spending more time than is remotely healthy fantasizing about how to kill them and get away with it instead of leaving my husband and cutting all ties with my family.

But what I regret the most is how I've treated the little boy who is currently sound asleep, snuggled in my arms. I'd taken out my misery and frustration on this innocent child by rebuffing his pleas for attention and spurning his love. Yet, despite withholding my affection, he continues to love me with every ounce of his generous little heart.

I honestly feel like the worst woman in the world, and vow to change. Immediately. So while Adam remains in the hospital, I spend every waking moment with the little boy who has now stolen my heart. He eats up my attention the way a kitten laps up cream, asking me to read him book after book, or play with the plastic dinosaurs or trucks I bring over from the playroom. He fights sleep like it's the enemy, I imagine afraid he'll wake up and find the old, disinterested me, and that the past days had been only a pleasant, if feverish, dream.

A lot of what brings about my change of heart are the long talks I have with Adam's PICU doctor, a man in previous years I'd raised heaven and hell to locate only to now find completely by chance.

I'd only known him as Cash, so that's what I'd used to try to find him. I had no idea it was a nickname, his real name being Emmanuel Rutherford the Third. His college buddies jokingly called him Cash for the simple reason he was dirt poor but had been given a name worthy of a billionaire, and at some point the name stuck. Even now, he insists I call him Cash instead of Dr. Rutherford, unless, of course, should Edward or my mother be near, not that that ever happened. Neither of them has stepped foot in the hospital the entire time Adam has been admitted.

Ten days may not seem like a long time in the grand scheme of things, but it's long enough for three things to happen. Adam's condition improves dramatically, returning him to the bouncy, energetic boy I used to complain was too loud and now whose burbling laughter I cannot get enough of. I learn that good people still exist; the doctors and nurses are so kind, so thoughtful, that even their simplest gestures of care or concern bring tears to my eyes. Lastly, but by far not the least of what happens, I fall head over heels for a certain doctor with a billionaire's name.

I feel like a schoolgirl, all blushes and smiles when he's around. I hang on his every word, alternately praising and thanking him as

Adam's health improves. When we have less about Adam's condition to discuss, our tangential conversations grow longer and our questions more personal.

Cash never married and has no current girlfriend, and I assume it's because he put his career first. He'd accomplished a great deal at a very young age, and is now a greatly sought-after practitioner with a stellar reputation. I imagine when he settles down, he'll be able to have any woman he wants. I'm happy for him, and sad for myself, as I feel things for him I know I cannot have.

Then, the night before Adam is to be discharged, Cash confides that he remains single because the woman he wants is already taken—taken by the madman who once threatened his life.

I never once suspect that what Cash tells me are lies, as a more honest person doesn't exist. He's like me in the way we are both lousy liars, so we do our best to not put ourselves in positions where we need to lie.

"I knew you looked familiar when I found you in that alley, and the next morning, I realized from where. When my grandmother got sick and couldn't go to church, she used to watch your parents' services. Although I told her, no offense, that your parents were crooks, she used to watch because of you. She loved to hear you sing."

We're sitting in Adam's room, the lights dimmed because it's the middle of the night. We're out of the PICU and in a private room, and over cups of lukewarm coffee, I finally hear the truth.

"I bought a ticket and went to the church the following Sunday, fully expecting to prove myself wrong. I told myself that poor, battered girl couldn't have been you. When you weren't there, I started to worry.

"I found out where you lived. I went to your house and the maid refused to let me in. I asked to see your mother or father, but they weren't home. I tried multiple times, but each time, I was turned away. The last time I was there, I gave my name and number and asked the maid to give it to you.

"Then one day on campus, this guy came up to me and asked me if I was the one who kept trying to see you. He was pissed. My sister was the girl he'd been flirting with at the bar, the girl who was with me when you woke up, and this jerk getting in my face fit the description she gave me to a T. I knew I had to tread lightly, as he seemed more than a little unhinged.

"I told him I was just checking up on you, that I was studying to be a doctor and believed your condition to be serious. I told him I suspected you had been assaulted sexually. He told me your health was none of my business. We argued, and then he pushed me. Being young, dumb, and hot-headed, I threw the first punch, not realizing he brought backup. The next thing I knew, I got the shit kicked out of me. He told me if I ever came near you again, he'd kill me."

Cash crumples his empty coffee cup in his hand, the memory bringing back his understandable outrage. "About a week later, I was called into the Dean's office. He asked me if I'd been fighting on campus, not that he needed to. My face was still all swollen and bruised, and my arm was in a sling. He reminded me that brawling was an offense that could get me expelled, as they had a zero tolerance policy for violence on campus.

"I'm not proud of what happened next, but you have to understand something. My family was dirt poor. I'd gotten into school on a full-ride scholarship, and if I got kicked out, it was unlikely I'd get in anywhere else. My future was on the line. I tried to explain what happened, but he wouldn't listen. Then your mother walked into his office like she owned the goddamn place."

"What?" I forget I should whisper, my shock overtaking me. Adam rolls over in his bed, and I hold my breath. I need to hear the rest of the story, and I know I never will if he wakes up.

After a few minutes when Adam doesn't wake, Cash continues. "She'd written out a check for an obscene amount of money that would pay not just for medical school, but for some additional 'spending money' to help me through my internship and residency. She said she was more than happy to help out a young man who obviously took his Hippocratic oath so seriously.

"Of course, there was a NDA attached to the money. Although it was never explicitly said, I had a choice to make. I was given one minute to decide."

I put my empty cup on the ground and reach over and take his hands in mine. "You made the right choice," I whisper hoarsely. "I would have been furious if you'd ruined your life for me."

"You're too good for them," he murmurs, his voice choking with emotion. He gently caresses my hands, withdrawing his own the moment his finger grazes against my wedding band.

"I should go," he says matter-of-factly as he stands, his return to his doctorly demeanor breaking my heart. I grab his wrist, halting him, and stand, looking up at him with tears in my eyes.

"Please," I beg. "Don't go."

"If I stay, I'm going to do something I shouldn't."

"Maybe I want you to."

"You're married," he states simply and without accusation.

"Don't remind me," I chastise as we move towards one another.

I sigh as I look at the pretty blonde in the mirror who looks decades younger than me. Caitlin has asked me a question that I ask her to repeat, and she looks at me quizzically before asking if I have any more wet wipes in the bathroom. I nod, heading towards the cabinet under the sink to fetch another box.

I'm not proud to admit that I cheated on Edward, and never once do I think my infidelity is okay because he cheated on me all the time. After all, two wrongs never make a right. Cash and I fall head over heels for one another, our fondness quickly growing into a love I once thought existed only in fairy tales.

Cash begs me to leave Edward so many times that I lose count, and as much as I want to, I can't. If I leave him, Edward will make certain that I never see Adam again, and there is no way I could live with myself if that happened.

Over the next two years, Edward becomes more and more violent, his rage-filled tirades becoming more frequent as things continue to go badly for him at work. The patron grooming him for higher office runs hot and cold with his support, and during the times Edward's favor is low, he's meaner to those of us he blames for holding him back. Instead of realizing he's working for a lying madman and trying to make something of himself on his own, he takes out his frustrations on Adam and me.

I end up missing a few events I'm supposed to accompany my husband to because I'm genuinely sick with a stomach virus I just can't seem to kick. He's furious each time I cancel, his blows raining ever harder and his words growing increasingly more cruel. But as long as it's me he hurts and not Adam, I'm okay with taking the brunt of his anger. I would endure all of Hell if it means keeping my sweet boy safe.

It's Cash who finally buys the pregnancy test and demands I take it, and when it's positive, all I can do is cry. I have no idea if the child is fathered by the man I love or the man I hate, and at some point, I know there will be terrible choices with even worse consequences for me to make.

I wait until the very last minute to tell Edward I'm expecting because I don't know how he's going to react. At least I don't have to worry about him thinking my baby belongs to someone else, as despite his obvious loathing of me, he still requires I do my "wifely duty" several times a month. Cash and I have been exceedingly careful, and as far as we know, Edward has no idea we've been seeing each other.

Much to my surprise, Edward is delighted with the news of my pregnancy. He brags to his friends and drags me to every media outlet to take pictures and videos of us, the loving couple, thrilled to finally become parents. His campaign manager is over the moon, booking appointment after appointment for me to give speeches to women's groups all over the nation. It sickens me to pretend the child is Edward's, as in my heart, I know Cash is the father.

The last few months of the pregnancy change Edward, who now dotes on me. He comes home from work earlier and earlier to have dinner with me, banishing Adam to his room with threats of violence should he disturb us. When I gently ask Edward to please be kinder to his son, I'm pleasantly surprised when he makes an effort. He even takes time to play baseball with Adam, and on weekends, goes to his Little League games and cheers him on. For the first time ever, he seems genuinely happy with us both.

Apparently all it took to make him happy was for me to get pregnant with another man's child.

I, on the other hand, have never been more miserable. With more demands on my time, and Edward always around, I almost never have time to see Cash. I miss him terribly, and the more I miss him, the more I resent Edward's newfound attachment. Trust me, the irony of him now craving my affection and me not wanting his is not lost on me.

When I go into labor, Edward is out of town. Cash is allowed in the delivery room with me, holding my hand and feeding me ice chips, and I'm thankful I get to share these long, painful hours with him and not Edward. The staff know better than to ask questions, although I do notice more than a few raised eyebrows when he slips a few times and calls me sweetheart.

When the baby is born, it's Cash who cuts the cord, and Cash who tells me the baby is a girl. It's Cash who places her on my chest and cries with joy when I tell him I want to name our baby girl Emma, after him.

I know I'll forever remember every detail of his tear-stained face and enormous smile when, later, safe in my private room, Cash leans over and kisses me tenderly. It's cut short when someone knocks and then barges in without waiting.

I'm sure we both look guilty as sin when my mother, in yet another of her ridiculous hats, enters holding a floral arrangement more suited for a hall centerpiece than in congratulations of a birth. She looks at us with narrowed, suspicious eyes, but says nothing about what she may, or may not, have seen.

Cash leaves a minute later, pretending to have been giving me instructions and telling me he will be back later to check on us. He bids my mother goodbye, her eyes widening in recognition.

When the door shuts behind him, she stares at me furiously and then down at Emma. "She looks just like her father."

I look up at her, ready to pretend, until I see in her eyes there's no use. She knows.

"That child is Edward's, and don't you ever forget it," she hisses. "I went through a lot of trouble for you, and you are not going to embarrass our family now. The media will have a field day if this becomes known. You are going to break off this hateful relationship immediately."

I stare at her coldly. "That's exactly what I plan to do, mother. The second I get out of here."

I try to shake off the memory of what happened next, but it's got me by the throat. I'd been in this very bathroom just a few days later, grabbing the last of the toiletries I was taking with me. Cash and I had just finished a lengthy meeting with our attorney, and I was finally doing exactly what I told my mother—I was taking the children and leaving.

After our attorney said I had more than enough evidence to prove Edward an unfit parent, he filed an emergency injunction awarding me sole custody of Emma and Adam. With no way of knowing how my husband would take the news, we all felt it was safest if the children and I stayed with someone. And the only someone I wanted to be with was Cash.

Last night, I wrote Edward a letter breaking the news. The minute I returned from the lawyer's, I placed it on the front table next to the giant arrangement of flowers where it will be the first thing he sees when he gets home. I feel a strange sense of closure propping the sealed envelope up against the vase, taking one last look at the envelope with his name written on it in my flowing script. By the time he reads it, we will be long gone.

I check my watch, smiling when I realize Cash will be here within the hour to whisk the children and me away. He was supposed to stay and help me pack, but the car seat he bought for Emma is missing a few parts, so he headed back to the store to exchange it.

With my things finally packed, I zip up the large suitcase and try to drag it off the bed, but it's too heavy. I try again, getting it most of the way off when I hear, "Would you like some help with that?"

My blood runs cold, my hand slipping off the handle, the suitcase thumping heavily to the carpeted floor. I reach for it, jerking it upright onto its wheels. I keep my head down, too afraid to look at him.

"I'm glad I decided to come home early to spend time with my family or I would have missed you."

He strides closer, his body next to mine. He reaches forward and brushes my hair away from my face. I flinch.

"What? Don't I get a kiss hello?"

I don't know what to do. Part of me wants to abandon the bag and make a run for it, but there's no way for me to get to Adam, who's happily boxing up his toys in his room. His and Emma's clothes are already waiting at the front door that Edward I'm sure has already seen. . .

Oh my God, has he seen the letter? Fuck!

Searing pain rips up the side of my head as Edward grabs a handful of my hair and forces me to face him. "Look at me when I'm talking to you!"

I haul off and swing as hard as I can, the slap to his face catching him off guard enough to let go of my hair. I run for the door but Edward catches me by the upper arm, his vice-like grip making me call out in pain.

"Let me go!" I scream over and over while trying to fight him off. I scream for help, hoping one of the staff will call the police. Edward slaps me hard enough across the face to stun me, rendering me silent. Blood fills my mouth, my lip gushing from where his wedding ring made contact. I look up at him with a cruel smile.

"You've done it now," I say in a low, menacing tone. "There's not a court in the country that will let you near your children ever again."

His eyes widen as he takes a stumbling step back. "What have you done?" he breathes. "What have you done?"

Something in me snaps. I'm done cowering from him.

I throw my shoulders back and glare up at him. "It's over, Edward. I'm leaving you and taking the children with me."

He stares at me with wide, incredulous eyes as he whispers, "I thought you loved me."

I blink at him in utter amazement, a drop of blood splashing off my chin and landing on his hand. I start to laugh, the noise coming out of my mouth sounding deranged even to me. I wipe away a few hysterical tears as I pull my arm loose from his grip. "Are you fucking kidding me? Is this your idea of a joke?"

He doesn't answer. I step forward, and for the first time ever, he retreats from me. It's a heady feeling, one that gives me a strange form of courage I've never felt before. Never before has the unflappable Edward James Bellamy backed up. From ME. "I fucking hate you, Edward. I have hated you since the day you raped me behind that bar and left me for dead."

I didn't think it was possible, but I've rendered him speechless. He stares at me as if he's just woken from a dream and is so disoriented, he doesn't even know who he is.

I grab the suitcase and head for the door. I'm off balance already from the weight I'm lugging, so when he grabs me again as I approach the stairs, I stumble to my knees. The suitcase falls over on its side.

"I didn't think you remembered," he murmurs, helping me stand. "You never mentioned it."

"I'm sorry if I never found the right moment to bring it up," I snap. "I guess I couldn't decide if that conversation was more suited for during the soup or salad."

He takes a step closer, pulling me to my feet. "Don't fuck with me, Louise."

"You see, that's the beauty of divorce. I'll never be forced to fuck you ever again."

His free hand wraps around my throat and squeezes, his face a mask of fury as he leans in closer, his lips pressed almost against mine. "No. The beauty of divorce is it's not necessary if one of the parties should have a tragic accident before standing before the judge."

Edward drags me to the stairs, and now I have no doubt what he plans. I'd been so stupid coming back here. I should have known I'd never escape, and now the children will be stuck being raised by him.

I refuse to let that happen.

I fight him with every last breath, but he's so much stronger than me. I get enough swipes in to prove there'd been a fight, hoping that at least if I'm dead when the police arrive, that the coroner will be able to pin him as my murderer with his DNA under my nails.

I use the last of my breath to deliver my final parting blow. "Everything you are. . . everything you've done. . . it's over. You came from nothing, and you will die the same way. A nothing with nothing. At least. . .at least Emma's father will take care of the children while you rot in jail."

He lets go, his eyes wild. I lean over and gasp for breath, doing everything I can to not pass out. I'm so dizzy, each inhale making things worse. I fall to my hands and knees, focusing on nothing but my breath.

"She's not mine?"

I'm too busy coughing and sputtering to answer, wiping my bloody mouth on my sleeve and leaving a thick smear of blood. Apparently he didn't see the letter or the copy of the DNA test I had done that proves Cash is Emma's biological father.

Edward repeats the same phrase over and over, each time getting more agitated. I try to crawl away from him, but he grabs me by the hair and drags me to my feet.

"She's not mine?!" he yells in my face, his hand against my throat squeezing harder than ever. I'm about to pass out just as the front door opens.

"Come on baby, let's go!" Cash calls. "We need to be long gone before your soon-to-be ex gets home from work."

If I had an ounce of breath left in me I'd scream for him to run, but I've nothing left. I'm suddenly so afraid, not for myself, but for Emma. For Adam. For Cash.

Edward's going to kill them all.

I feel myself being moved backwards, my feet no longer able to resist, my arms unable to push Edward away. I'm just about to lose conscious-ness when he leans in and whispers, "'Til death do us part, darling. 'Til death do us part."

The memory of being thrown down the stairs is interrupted by the sound of hysterical feminine laughter. I'm slow to regain my bearings, first noticing I'm seated on the little velvet stool in front of the makeup vanity in my room.

Wait—hadn't I just been in the bathroom getting makeup wipes?

I look in the mirror, my hair up in an elaborate, sweeping design, a gold and jewel encrusted crown nestled among the curls. I'm dressed in an elaborate gown, something flowing and feminine with enormous skirts and a tight, corseted waist. I hear the sounds of laughter and the voices of a party in full swing wafting up from downstairs.

My heart thumps heavily in my chest.

"All this time," Caitlin cackles, "All this time, the voice was coming from inside. . . from inside the house. . ."

I turn to face her, surprised to see a time-worn laptop in her hand. She's laughing so hard she's wiping tears from her face. "All this time, it's been you, hasn't it?"

"I don't understand," I tell her honestly. "What's been me?"

My hand reaches under the stool as if of its own accord, my fingertips grazing the folded edge of duct tape securing something to the underside. Although I don't know what's there, I know I need it. I need it desperately. I barely register the pain as my fingertips begin to bleed.

Caitlin rushes for the door, the laptop smashed against her breasts with one arm, her other hand reaching for the handle. I don't know how I know it, but if she gets out, a lot of people are going to die.

I have to stop her.

I rip at the tape, a knife falling from under the cushion and into my hand. I don't know who stashed it under my chair, but I'm glad they did.

In order to stop her, I'm going to need it.

51

Emma

We have the television on, but muted, as we do our chores around the house. It's a mandatory television hour even though it's nothing more than a bunch of reporters standing in front of the home I grew up in as they excitedly discuss the party happening within.

It's hotter than Hell and I feel absolutely miserable, my lower back hurting like nobody's business. It started as a mild twinge shortly after I woke, but now the pain's bad enough to take my breath away.

There's so much to do before the funeral, and all of us are tired and hurting right now, so I don't complain. Sarah suspects I don't feel well, asking me repeatedly if I'm alright, and when I'm finally too tired to move and breathless from the pain, she takes me by the hand and leads me to bed to rest.

I wake up a few hours later with Sarah shaking me. I'm soaked with sweat, the pain suddenly so much worse. "There's a vehicle coming that's not one of ours. You must hide. Hurry!"

I try to rise quickly, but it doesn't happen, poor Sarah having to manhandle me to get me off the mattress just as another vicious pain hits. I cry out and clutch at my back, just as we hear the sound of crunching gravel in the driveway. Pain or not, I must crawl into the hiding space and be silent or we will all die.

"I will come and get you as soon as I can," she whispers as she puts everything back in place and closes me in.

It's so hot I can hardly stand it. The pains come and go, and I do my best to breathe through them, but all that happens is they get worse. I'm so thirsty I'm half tempted to lick the sweat from my arms, but I don't, worrying the salt will only make me thirstier. I try to hear what's being said downstairs, but can't catch much more than a word here and there. I wish that Sarah will somehow hurry along their inspection without seeming suspicious, but when I hear floorboards creak and boots clomp on the stairs, I find myself wishing they remained downstairs.

"It's hotter than fuck in here," one man says. "I'd rather be dead than live like this."

The way I feel right now, I'd be more than happy to help him with that request.

They check the closets and the armoire, looking under the beds and even up in the attic. They bitch and moan about the heat as they head outside to search the barns and outbuildings.

Sarah remains inside, and when the coast is clear, she opens the hatch and hands me a pitcher of water before sealing me back in. "They are here on a search because of the missing officers. They should leave soon. Don't worry, they don't seem as bad as most. I sent the children to Esther's, so they are safe, too."

Every minute in my hidey-hole is misery, and although it feels like I've been stuck in here for days, it's probably only been an hour. What I don't understand is that instead of the heat making them want to finish more quickly, these guys are slower than usual.

When they return to the house, they demand food that Sarah has no choice but to provide. As they eat the dinner she'd been preparing for us, the men alternate between laughing at how the Zooks live like it's the 19th century and complaining about "the vicious one-eared dog that wants to eat them" that's tied up in the barn and still somehow almost managed to get a piece of one of them.

Good boy, Gritty.

When they catch sight of the peach pie cooling in the window, Sarah gives them that, too. By the time they finally leave, I'm so far beyond exhausted there are no words. I'm so stiff and cramped that I don't know how I'll ever untangle myself from the knot I'm in.

It's at least another ten minutes before Sarah comes to get me, I imagine waiting for the alarm to chime that their vehicle turned onto the main road. When she opens the door for me, I promptly fall out onto the floor, my body reveling in its newfound freedom while simultaneously getting even with me with another sharp twinge in my back.

Sarah helps me to my feet carefully, noting how my night dress is soaked through and the floor wet. I'm embarrassed beyond belief to realize I must have peed myself at some point.

"I'm s-sorry I made such a mess," I say while fighting back tears of mortification. "I'll clean it up when I'm—" A breathtaking pain hits me, this one by far the worst yet.

"Emma! Are you having contractions?"

I shake my head. "No, I must have slept wrong last night, and being balled up for so long just made it worse. The pain isn't in my belly. It's in my back."

Sarah speaks slowly to me, like the pain has made me stupid or something. "Emma, sweetheart, your back is fine. Trust me. You are in labor."

I shake my head. "I can't be in labor. It's a full week before my due date and Declan isn't here!"

She laughs. "Emma, I can assure you that many a woman has given birth before their due date as well as when their husbands are out of town."

"I am not having this baby without him," I retort stubbornly.

She laughs again. "Emma, it may be impossible to *conceive* a baby without a father, but I can assure you, it's very possible to *deliver* one without. In fact, men are often terrible in the delivery room."

"Not Declan," I argue. "He's delivered plenty of babies through the years."

"Yes, but none of the women were his *wife*," she explains, choosing her words carefully. "Many of my sisters have allowed their husbands to witness the miracle of birth, thinking the experience will bring them closer, only to find that certain. . . aspects. . . of their married life suffered for it later. It worried me to hear this, and is why Amos has not witnessed any of his children being born. My neighbors think that is why I've ended up pregnant so often."

As it dawns on me what she means, I blush. She chuckles as she helps me undress and get into the tub, the cool water feeling incredible against my overheated skin. When Amos returns from the fields, she sends him off to fetch Rowan while she examines me, happily announcing that everything is progressing as it should, but I still have a long way to go. She leaves me a glass and a pitcher of water and tells me to take frequent, small sips to rehydrate myself while she heads downstairs to restart dinner.

I sit with my cell phone in my hand, wanting to call Declan, but not sure where he is or what he's doing. I know the minute he finds out I'm in labor he will drop everything and race home, and I don't know that I want him to do that, either. Knowing labor can often go on for a very long time, I decide to wait. Whatever he's doing I'm certain is more important than sitting here holding my hand.

"So what if he misses the birth of this child?" I mutter to myself, trying to convince myself that I'm making the right decision as I rub my belly. "He'll just have to make sure he's here for the next one."

52

Declan

When I meet Olesya at the staging area, she's pissed. "I thought you weren't coming?" she snaps as she hands me a garment bag with my clothes in it for the night. My last name is clearly printed on the heavy plastic in block letters.

I cock an eyebrow at her. "This says otherwise."

She shrugs. "I am nothing if not always prepared."

"Sure thing, Girl Scout," I mutter under my breath as I toss the bag over a chair and begin to unbutton my shirt. When I unzip it and see what she expects me to wear, I realize that our plans have changed. Again.

I knew I should have stayed the fuck at home.

I march over to where she's taking a call, grab the phone from her hand and bark, "She'll call you back in a minute," before disconnecting. I round on her, and for the first time in my life, I'm ready to strike a woman and feel absolutely no regrets.

I shove the bag at her so hard she has to back up a step to catch her balance. "I'm not wearing that."

She rolls her eyes at me, then shoves the bag back into my chest. I don't reach for it, so when she lets go, it falls to the floor.

"Stop being such a diva," she spits at me as she wrenches her phone from my hand. "Dressing as a patrolman is the only way I can get you in there armed. As much as you are a massive pain in my ass, I can't afford to have you die tonight. There are things you still must do."

I'm so angry I'm shaking. "So, what? Now you know when I'm gonna die, too? Jesus Christ, Olesya. Do you have any idea just how fucking creepy you are?"

"This is not the time!" she roars, making everyone around us turn to stare. "I'm trying to make this work so you and your family can lead the life you want. The life you deserve. If it fails... No. It *must* not fail. I will not even think it."

Her voice trembles slightly as she steps closer, lowering her voice. "This mission doesn't involve just you. There are many members of the revolution in that house, and we owe it to them and their families to make sure everyone gets out safely. Stop making everything about you. You aren't the only one doing things you don't like tonight."

She looks up at the ceiling, the first hint of fear creeping into her voice. "Sasha and Nina are in there. They've been there since yesterday afternoon. From what I can see, Edward has been pawing at them since the moment he saw them, and he will kill them if they do not get out tonight. Declan, I need you in there to make sure everything goes according to plan."

Oh, fuck...

I gulp down the lump of fear in my throat. Yeah, I should have stayed the fuck home.

What's the worst that can happen? You've already killed one daughter, why not go for the hat trick?

I tilt my head back and close my eyes. My hands fist in my hair as I let out a roar of anger and frustration laced with a heavy dose of fear. My head hurts, my heart aches, and it's got to be becoming clearer to everyone, and not just me, that I'm not in the right headspace for this.

Olesya grabs the bag, takes my arm, and walks me into a small office and closes the door. She points to a small sofa and we both sit. "I am very sorry for your loss," she says quietly. "I know you loved the child. From what I've been told, she was a true daughter of the revolution."

I nod, not trusting myself to speak.

"I know wearing a uniform like that of the man who killed her is no easy thing. I may be a practical woman, but Declan, I am not as cold as you think. If you had more time to process her loss this would be easier-"

"No," I snap. "There's nothing about Keira's death that's ever going to get easier. She never should have been there. She was supposed to stay home and be a kid for a few more years, but that motherfucking Isaac took her with him without my permission. I swear to God, when I get my hands on that little fuck—"

"You will do *nothing*," Olesya hisses. "If you hurt him, you will regret it forever. That I can promise you."

When I wait for her to tell me why, she only stares at me. I roll my eyes. "Oh, for fuck's sake. Can't you tell me anything useful?"

"His is not my story to tell. You need to ask him."

I grab the garment bag and wrap it over my arm and hold it against my abdomen. "Olesya, what happens if we fail tonight?"

She doesn't answer me, instead taking a moment to look at her beeping phone and type out a message. When she looks up, she's back in boss-lady mode.

"It doesn't matter. We simply cannot fail."

* * *

I'm dressed in the hateful uniform of a patrolman and have just popped in the colored contacts I'll wear as part of my disguise. I still think I'm way too recognizable until I put on the ridiculous hat that cuts down not only on my visibility, but manages to somehow make me look completely different with it on. I just hope at no point I have to remove it, or I'm a goner.

The second I step foot inside the mansion, I adopt the persona of the quintessential all-business patrolmen. I have two guys with me, the three of us just one of our many groups of "patrolmen" working to secure the premises. We take our cover seriously, even going so far as to give contemptuous looks at lower-ranked officers kowtowing to the rich and famous guests instead of doing their jobs.

We wander through the crowd, Olesya occasionally asking me to turn my head left or right to get a better look at someone through the camera hidden in my hat. I'm surprised that, after a complete trip around the house, Edward is nowhere to be found until I overhear someone say the festivities won't begin until he and the Lady Consort make their grand entrance.

Of course the motherfucker not only has to have a party for his fuckin' birthday, he needs to make an entrance. Prick.

I snort out a laugh before I can help it, one of the guests looking at me like I've lost the goddamn plot. I narrow my eyes at him and he cowers, turning back to his friends. As I survey the crowds, the same guy makes an incredibly tasteless quip about betting on how drugged Louise will need to be to make it down the stairs.

Just when you think you can't hate these assholes any more. . .

A woman with a tray of drinks walks past, her long skirts tucked up along the sides to keep her from tripping over it. She's dressed as a sexy version of a "serving wench," her stupidly high heels causing her to slip on the polished marble floor. Even without seeing her face I'm almost positive it's Amy. When some brash asshole pinches her ass after taking a drink from her tray, she flat out growls at him while giving him a scathing glare. If we were anywhere but here, I'm certain Amy would kick his ass, but since she doesn't want to end the night face down in the Reflecting Pool, she forces a smile before turning away.

Don't eat anything she hands you tonight, buddy. She's gonna put crushed glass in your food, for sure. . .

We stop to admire the acrobats and jugglers, musicians, and dancers scattered throughout. There's a crowd of people oohing and aahing at something in the conservatory, so we head over there to check it out. I nearly choke to death on my spit when I see who it is.

On a small wood platform surrounded by tropical plants stands Sasha, dressed in what I can only describe as a slutty-looking Genie outfit. Nina sits cross-legged at her feet and is dressed similarly, with some sort of foreign-looking oboe-thingy in her hands. Between them is a good sized wicker basket, and when Nina leans forward to remove the lid, the men ooh at the glimpse of her cleavage while the women shriek in fright at the enormous, and very angry, snake that pops its head up and hisses.

Nina slowly lifts the instrument and begins to play, the snake turning and lunging furiously at her until Sasha moves, prompting it to lunge at her. They play this strange game of monkey in the middle until it gentles, the crowd every bit as mesmerized by their performance as the now sedated-looking snake.

When they are done, and the snake is safely enclosed in the basket, everyone applauds. I pan the crowd as they disband, carefully watching the girls flirt with some of the men who wander over to ogle them more closely. I catch Sasha's eye just as she lifts a watch off some guy's wrist without him remotely noticing. She slips it inside the basket with her reptile friend, a genius idea because no guard is going to want to look in there when they're on their way out. I pretend to cough into my hand to keep from laughing out loud.

I wander among the guests, noting more of my people as they work the crowd handing out drug-laced aperitifs. Aside from the girls robbing a handful of lecherous men blind, nothing of interest is going on in the conservatory, so I head back out towards the main entrance.

There's some sort of excitement at the front door that I decide to investigate, my men following me closely. I stroll towards the noise, making sure to slowly pan the room so the people behind the scenes can see what I'm seeing. Edward's foreign invitees have arrived with Cass by their side, the big soldier keeping the guests bold enough to approach the dignitaries in line with just a simple glower. I catch his eye and he nods in recognition. I quickly turn away, not wanting to risk other members of his group looking at me too closely.

I'm just about to head back into the conservatory when a loud crash from upstairs catches my attention. There are a few loud knocks from inside the room to the left that a number of us turn to face, a lone member of Edward's House Guard heading upstairs and trying the door, only to find it locked. He knocks quietly, trying to not make a scene as he demands entry as everyone below watches. When nothing else happens, everyone grows bored and returns to their conversations, but I'm not so easily convinced there's nothing worrisome going on up there.

"Hold your position. Keep watching," Olesya whispers anxiously in my ear. Now I know something's up. Something out of sorts just happened in that room, and I have a feeling that within the next few minutes, we're all going to find out what.

53

Louise

Dear God, what has happened?

I stare down at my blood-soaked dress, grasping at my chest and torso and trying to figure where it's all coming from. It doesn't take me long to realize I'm unscathed, and at first, I'm relieved.

But if the blood isn't mine, to whom does it belong?

My vanity has been overturned. Tubes and compacts full of makeup have stained the carpet all sorts of pretty colors, and hundreds of tiny, jagged slivers of broken glass shimmer under the lights like diamonds. An acrid stench infiltrates my nostrils as a hot curling iron burns a hole through the plush, once-white carpet.

Although I know that's enough to start a fire, there's considerably more for me to be concerned with. Like what the hell happened in here and who's knocking on the door and demanding entry?

Why can't I remember?

This strange amnesia reminds me of when I woke from the coma I'd been lucky to survive all those years ago. . .

Despite being unable to speak, all sorts of people ask me what happened the day of the "accident." Doctors. Nurses. Therapists. Policemen. A handful of the new political group's personal guard known colloquially as the Purity Police. They all try to communicate with me using everything from white boards to puppets, but although I understand them perfectly, I am unable to communicate.

But just because I can't speak doesn't mean I don't remember.

I remember everything.

In the beginning, Edward visits me daily, always bringing fresh flowers and making a show of fussing over me. He asks the doctors and nurses who are always in the room a million questions, his tone always brimming with concern. He's the poster child for loving husbands everywhere as long as someone is in the room with me, but the looks he shoots me when their backs are turned are enough to set off the alarms on both my blood pressure and heart rate monitors.

It's clear that everyone believes he pushed me down the stairs, they just can't prove it. I overhear the local chief of police warn the hospital staff to keep close watch over me when Edward visits. When no one is around, the nurses beg me to nod, or blink, or just do something, anything, that the authorities can use to put him behind bars.

But I say nothing. I am so weak I can barely move, so if he decides to hurt me, or kill me, there's no way for me to defend myself. If I tell anyone what happened, he could hurt my children. I must not give him any reason to hurt them, and I must stay alive so I can protect them.

As the days turn to weeks, and Edward never once says or does anything remotely threatening, the staff begins to relax. At first they allow him to be alone in the room with me but insist he keep the door open, "just in case my health rapidly deteriorates." After a week or so of that, they allow him a bit more leeway until he's eventually allowed to close the door to "make a quick, private call."

It's then he begins to threaten me. He sees that with each passing day, I'm getting better. He knows it's just a matter of time before I'll recover enough that the police will again wish to speak with me. He threatens to hurt Adam and suffocate Emma in her crib if I tell anyone anything other than I fell down the stairs due to my own clumsiness. He tells me that there are eyes always on me and ears always listening, and if

I mention anything about that day to anyone, he will find out. He places his hand around my throat and squeezes, whispering that the next time I even think of leaving him, he will finish the job he started.

After a few weeks of this, I'm so scared I'd agree to just about anything. Reality becomes fluid; what is real seems like a dream, and my nightmares become material. I begin to wonder if I dreamed trying to leave him, and the beating, and being thrown down the stairs. Maybe I did fall down the stairs.

Through all of this, Cash never comes to visit. I worry about him constantly, but am unable, not to mention, too afraid, to ask anyone about him. As time passes, I wonder if my mind somehow conjured him and he really didn't exist? What if he's nothing more than a figment of a love-starved, lonely imagination? But how can he be mere fiction when I can still feel the way his lips kissed mine?

It takes months of speech therapy before I utter my first coherent word, and a few weeks after that, I take my first steps. It's very hard work, and my conviction to get better wavers. Some days I do everything I can to take one more step, or to clearly speak one more syllable. Other days I'm more than happy to stay in my wheelchair and let myself rot.

When I can finally speak, the questions begin again. Multiple times a day, the doctors ask me if I would feel safe if I were to return to my home. They beg me to tell them if someone's there had been hurting me. They promise they will help me if someone is. I simply say I don't remember.

Because of Edward's prominence in the government, the Purity Police take over the investigation after an anonymous caller to the local police claims they have proof that he pushed me down the stairs. They allow Edward to sit by my bedside as they interrogate me, and I smile and pretend to not be terrified out of my wits. I lie to them, saying my darling husband would never dream of hurting me. I accuse the informant of simply wanting to harm my husband's career, and that there could be no credible "proof" to something that never happened. The investigation is, once again, closed.

The afternoon before I'm set to be discharged from the hospital and sent home, a new doctor, one I've never met before, sits me down and lists every injury I had when I'd been brought in. He explains that over half of them are inconsistent with a fall. He knows that my injuries were caused by a severe beating just prior to "falling" down the stairs. He tells me again what everyone has told me—I'm lucky to be alive, and next time, I might not be nearly as lucky.

The doctor reaches into his briefcase and pulls out a newspaper. He places it before me, tapping his finger next to the headline reading "Renowned Doctor Found Dead at Home."

I snatch the paper from him and begin to read. Deep in my heart I already know what happened and who's to blame even though the police have no suspects. I don't need to know the specifics of how he died, I want to know when. And when I read the time of death is reported to be around the same time as when I was shoved down the stairs, I begin to violently shake. Although the police investigate crimes for a living, I already know without a doubt what happened. Edward murdered Cash shortly after he pushed me down the stairs and then somehow made it look like he was killed at home in a robbery gone wrong. By being with me during the fall, he even has me to use as an alibi for my lover's death.

Suddenly, I can't breathe. I gasp for breath and clutch at my chest where my heart pounds far too fast to be safe. I'm not safe. My children aren't safe. Not anywhere. If I run, Edward will find me. If I tell people what I know, what I've seen, and what he's done, he will kill me. He's too smart, and his reach is too broad. He's become too powerful. I am only safe as long as I remain silent.

The thing about living in fear is it's every bit as deadly as a knife to the throat or a bullet to the brain except it takes much longer to die, and because of that, is much more cruel. Once I come home, Edward forbids me from going anywhere without him. If the children need to be taken anywhere when he's unavailable, they are taken by a member of the household staff. All errands are fulfilled by the small army of workers who watch me carefully, each hoping I'll do something wrong so they can report it to my husband for a reward. The only time I disobey his rules is to visit my father at the hospital, arriving mere minutes before he died of a massive heart attack. Edward beat me so badly for that disobedience that I ended up missing my own father's funeral.

I begin to drink again. I mix it with the pain meds I'm still on from the fall, and would have overdosed multiple times had I not been found or thrown up before passing out. When things get so bad that I can't take another day, I slit my wrists, but I'm found before I can bleed out.

Claiming that I'm a danger to myself and my children, Edward sends me to one of the new State Asylums for the Impure of Spirit where I'm treated horribly. The place is filled with the worst sort of fraudsters who believe every problem can be solved with a healthy dose of religion and inhumane conversion therapies. There are no therapy sessions, no activities, no nothing. Just weeks and weeks of watching the New State Church's religious channels, hours on my knees in prayer, and all the torture one can imagine—as long as the methods do not leave a mark.

Most days I am quiet to the point I'm nearly catatonic. The days I'm not, I am filled with rage. It starts as a seed in my belly and grows within me until its power fills me with the sort of energy only the deepest desire for vengeance can bring. I am hot one day and cold the next, my life becoming one of true disjunction, a dichotomy of dark and light, vicious and sweet. There is no middle ground.

A few months later, I meet Ekaterina. She's the only nurse in this place who doesn't treat me like an animal. She tells me if I ever want to get out of this "shithole" I must learn how to regulate my emotions. I must try to tame this new, swinging energy and bend it enough to my will to appear "cured." Only then will they let me go home where she promises our real work together will begin. She tells me it will take years, but she swears to me it will be worth it when we finally get our revenge.

For the first time in ages, I smile. I tell her I'd be willing to wait a thousand years as long as I can be the one to destroy Edward James Bellamy.

The party is in full swing downstairs, the guests milling about, the servers hard at work. A glimpse at the clock shows I have mere minutes before I must meet Edward on the landing and descend the stairs. There's no time for me to change out of my ruined gown, not that I have anything else appropriate to change into.

A voice at the door demands I open, and when I hurry to do as I'm told, I trip over something and fall to my hands and knees. I manage to get back to kneeling and look back to see what I tripped over. On the ground is a shoe that is far too large to be mine. But it's not just a shoe. It's a shoe, and a foot, and a calf, and a knee. . .and it's all attached to a woman who isn't moving.

What have you done?

I haven't done anything. . .

What have you done?

"I don't know!" I shout.

Blonde hair streams around her face like a golden halo. I crawl over to her and tentatively shake her shoulder, but she doesn't move. Her sightless eyes stare fixedly at the ceiling.

Next to her lies the cracked and broken pieces of a computer, a shield she had valiantly used against her attacker. Not far from her lies the murder weapon that caved in her skull—a heavy marble vase.

I stifle a scream as I cower back, flashes of things I don't remember coming to the forefront of my mind. Caitlin found a computer under my bed. She kept saying the strangest things about "the voice coming from inside the house," and that she was going to tell.

But I've done nothing wrong. The computer isn't mine.

I survey the scene. The turned over velvet stool has duct tape only partially stuck to the underside of the cushion. I vaguely remember there being a knife, and when I look at my hand, I see my fingertips are cut. There are matching slashes on Caitlin's arms and hands that are deeper, but nothing severe.

The flashes grow faster and brighter, the timeline all screwed up, but I'm following them. Caitlin's wild laughter as she hugs the laptop to her chest. Someone knocking on my door. A knife in my hand. A scuffle.

My wrist aches, and when I look again, it's swollen and bruised. It hurts to move. There's glass in it. Glass from the computer screen. The knife knocked from my hand so I reached for the vase on the mantle...

Wait. No. *Trinity* reached for the vase...

No. *I* reached for the vase.

I gasp aloud, tears springing to my eyes. Everything's suddenly so clear I have no idea how it's taken me so long to figure it out.

I am Trinity.

Trinity is *me*.

"My Lady? It's time for you to come out. The Supreme Regent is waiting."

I lean against the wall, my heart pounding. I've been spying on my husband for years, sending classified information to his greatest enemies. I set up cameras and surveillance equipment, recording as much evidence as I could to bring that son of a bitch down and it hasn't been enough.

Now I've killed a woman. They are going to see what I've done, they are going to figure it all out, and then they are going to kill me. All these years of suffering will be for nothing. He's going to get away with it all.

The smell of blood hangs in the air, the sin of murder staining my hands and clothes. The moment I go out there, they will know what I've done. I race to the bathroom and grab a towel, trying to wipe the blood off my hands but it won't come off. I wipe one spot clean only to find another covered in blood. I rub so hard my skin burns.

A key in the door turns and I run to close it, but I'm too late. It's open, but if it opens no further, the body won't be seen. I race past the shocked guard, still rubbing at my hands with the towel, my hands growing raw from the rag and now beginning to bleed.

I hear wild applause but don't look, my focus on my hands as I beg them to come clean. Someone loudly tells everyone to hush, that I'm speaking. The grand foyer immediately goes silent, everyone straining to hear the words that come to me as if I'm channeling the nameless Lady, herself.

""Out, damned spot! Out I say! One, two. Why then 'tis time to do't. Hell is murky. Fie, my lord, fie! A soldier and afeard? What need we fear who knows it, when none can call our pow'r to accompt? Yet who would have thought the vicious crone to have so much blood in her?"

There's mumbling from below, as people stare up at me, wondering what they are seeing.

"The Thane of Fife had a wife. Where is she now? What, will these hands never be clean?"

Edward has come out into the hallway, his hands reaching for me, a poorly-enacted look of sympathy on his face. He's trying to silence me. Trying to herd me back into my bedroom where he'll finally kill me like he's always threatened. . .

I back away quickly, my feet carrying me terrifying close to the top stair. I shake my head and hold out my hands in warning to stay away. I wag my finger at him angrily. "No more o' that, my lord, no more o'that! You mar all with this starting."

There are patrolmen at the bottom of the stairs, the confused men staring up at me. If they think I'm going to hurt Edward they will shoot me. But there are more ways to hurt a man than just physically.

I remember a different part of the Scottish play, a monologue far more fitting for this important moment. "Bleed, bleed, poor country! Great tyranny, lay thy basis sure, for goodness dare not check thee! Wear thou thy wrongs; The title is affeered!"

I laugh loudly as I point at Edward, whose patience is wearing thin. A few people below titter, obviously not having paid attention when Macbeth was taught in high school.

I take a moment to peruse the crowd, my eyes lighting upon Cassiel standing with the foreign dignitaries who look positively shell shocked. I throw my shoulders back and enunciate as if I'm on stage at the old Kennedy Center. But this new speech doesn't belong to Lady MacBeth.

"I think our country sinks beneath the yoke;
It weeps, it bleeds, and each new day a gash
Is added to her wounds. I think withal
There would be hands uplifted in my right;
And here from gracious England have I offer
Of goodly thousands. But, for all this,
When I shall tread upon the tyrant's head
Or wear it on my sword, yet my poor country
Shall have more vices than it had before,
More suffer and more sundry ways than ever,
By He who has succeeded."

Yes, I changed the last line a bit to suit my needs, but it still works the way I want it to. I must admit, the mix of reactions from my audience would be comical if I wasn't expecting to be murdered sometime within the next five minutes. Those who know the script, and know I just performed an execution-worthy piece of Shakespeare, look absolutely terrified but yet unsure how to react. After all, I am *the* Lady Consort. Would I really come out against my husband at his sixtieth birthday party?

Those not familiar with the play look up at me with confusion, but are prepared to applaud raucously, because they think that's what's expected. The foreign leaders speak furiously to one another over by the front door, the tall military officer who escorts them quickly pointing to the exit that another uniformed soldier immediately escorts the dignitaries through.

With a wide smile on his face, the other officer turns towards the stairs and begins to applaud loudly. "Oh, what a fitting start to this fine night by using the Bard's own words," he enunciates carefully, making sure his voice can be heard throughout the room. "We should all applaud the Lady Consort's fine performance, as it has set an exemplary tone for the start of this very memorable evening! Come, let's applaud her fine performance!"

A few people begin to applaud, then more join in, and I know I should feel relieved right now, because the danger of the moment has passed. But it's only been replaced by a more dangerous moment, where mother and son will be side by side for everyone, including his father, to see. I don't know how to stop it, but Edward must never find out...

I feel myself become lighter, a bit woozy, my feet precarious on the edge of the top stair as I start to sway. I try to inhale, to squeeze some air into my tightly-corseted lungs, but I get nothing. The harder I try, the worse I feel, and then everything starts to dim..

Dear God, no...

A few people gasp below, then someone shouts, "Grab her!"

I try to remain standing, but I end up stumbling on the short train of my dress when my heel catches in the thick fabric. It proves to be the final nail in my awaiting coffin.

And before I can utter another syllable, I begin to fall.

54

Declan

I'm the closest "patrolman" to Louise when she starts to sway, and as much as I know it will probably get us both killed, I push the few people in front of me out of the way and sprint up the stairs. I'm not fast enough to stop the first hit to her head, but thankfully I'm able to stop any others. Cassiel's there in less than a second, giving me a hand holding her up while I untangle myself from my wife's unconscious mother. Together we pick her up and carry her back up to her room.

Olesya is losing her shit over coms, telling everyone to abort the mission and get the fuck out. Now. Another patrolman opens the door to Louise's room and mutters a curse, checking out the turned over vanity and bloody handprints that are everywhere. He tries to enter the room but Cassiel tells him to stand down, that he will handle things from here. It's not until I round the edge of the bed that I see Caitlin's body and the shattered computer. Cass curses when he nearly trips over the body, his eyes damn near bugging out of his head.

"We can't leave her here," he hisses to me. "Bellamy's gonna kill her after that. Then finding the dead mistress? Fuck, they're gonna kill her."

"Everything okay in there?" the guy calls from the door.

"Yeah, all good," I yell back. "We're just getting her settled." The last thing we need right now is this asshole coming in here and sounding the alarm.

"Okay. There's a way out of here that she uses to meet with me that she said is practically undetectable. It comes out through a window on the lower west side of the house. I don't know if she has to fuck with the security system to make it work, or if it's just a series of camera blindspots she knows how to use. Either way, she's gotta wake up to talk you through it. Once you get outside the house, I know how to get you the rest of the way."

"Oh, simple as that, is it?" I sneer as I hurry to the bathroom and dampen a cool cloth for Louise's head. It's not until I get back and see Cass shoving the dead woman under the bed, do I realize he said "you" and not "us."

I trip over the computer, once again nearly face planting as I bounce off the edge of the bed. "What the hell is Louise doing with a computer?"

"It's not hers. It's Trinity's."

"How do you know that?" I ask. "And if it's hers, why is it in Louise's room?"

He looks at me like I'm stupid. "They're the same person," he tells me just as Louise starts to wake up.

"What? Is Trinity like an alias?"

"Not quite."

Cass grimaces at me, and suddenly the pieces click together in my mind. In all my years of seeing patients, I've never seen a case of Dissociative Identity Disorder. I guess there's a first for everything.

"How do you know? Did she tell you?"

He shakes his head. "I don't think she knows," he says again. "She always talks about Trinity like she's real. Thinks she's a nurse, or a guardian, or something."

Her eyelashes begin to flutter, a few small moans leaving her lips before finally opening her eyes. She sees Cassiel and smiles. "Hi, sweetheart," she mumbles. "I've missed you so much."

Cass looks at me, a slight blush pinking his cheeks. "Please tell me you aren't fucking her," I demand.

"Ew, Jesus, no. She's my mother, you pervert."

I'm just about to ask if he's been smoking crack when another knock on the door makes us both turn. "Yo, guys, the Supreme Regent wants to thank you. Can you come out here and shake hands real quick so he can get the party started?"

I can't help it. I start to laugh. Can this night get any more fucked up?

"Why is it that the first time you show up here is the night I'm going to get killed?" Cass gripes. "Please, tell me this is a coincidence so I can punch you in the mouth for being a fucking liar."

I laugh harder. We both stand and try to make ourselves looks somewhat presentable and then just say fuck it and head out to the hallway. Cassiel's dark uniform hides most of the blood on him, but my bright white one is grotesquely stained.

"Hey, if we somehow survive this, I fully expect to be filled in on the family drama as soon as humanly possible. By the way, does Emma know?"

He shakes his head. "We thought it best to not tell her. We didn't know how she'd take the news."

"About which part?"

He looks at me knowingly. "All of them."

* * *

When Cass and I exit the room, he stops to tell the nosy asshole at the door to not let anyone in there until he returns. We step out onto the landing, and the minute we come into view, the crowd below bursts into applause. My cheeks heat, the people below probably thinking it's from nerves when really it's from my blood boiling with rage. Less than twenty feet in front of us stands the man of the hour.

I'd give anything to wrap my hands around Bellamy's neck and squeeze until he dies, but I know there's not a chance in hell of that happening. I'd be shot dead before I even lifted a hand. Cass and I stride over and take a knee before him, our heads bent in required submission.

"Men, please. You have done me a great service tonight. Stand up and let me shake your hands."

I've never been more thankful to have on the white leather uniform gloves, as otherwise, this gig would be up right here, right now. Cass goes first, politely, but stiffly, bowing formally, and then standing to accept Edward's thanks and proffered hand. They shake, and Cass then takes a knee to kiss his hand and stand again. As he backs away from Edward, I'm thankfully reminded of the protocol where one is to never turn their back on the Supreme Leader.

The entire protocol took maybe a minute, but when Cass is done, he looks like he's aged five years. He elbows me when I don't move, my cue to get this the fuck over with, but if I were to make a list of all the things in life I don't want to do, bending the knee to Bellamy ranks just under getting a prostate exam from Wolverine.

Any of my former misplaced mirth is gone. My jaw is so tense, my teeth clenched so hard, that I'm abso-fuckin'-lutely doing some serious dental damage. I swallow my pride and bow to the haughty bastard, and when he extends his hand to shake mine, I swear I feel something crack in my jaw.

"I don't think I've met you before," Edward says to me casually, his head cocked slightly to the side as he peers at me more closely. "Yet there's something about you that looks familiar."

Jesus Christ, someone get me the fuck out of here. . .

"I hear that a lot, Sir," I say quietly in a disguised voice. "I imagine I just have one of those faces."

He nods thoughtfully as I back away, giving him room to descend the stairs. It's clear that we are expected to deal with his wife, and it's not lost on either me or Cassiel that Edward never even bothered to ask if she's okay.

We're surprised to find her sitting at the foot of her bed and waiting for us when we re-enter. She's changed out of her bloody dress and is wearing a long, dark gown with a hunter green hooded cape that covers her golden hair.

"We must move quickly," she tells us. "Everyone will be called in to dinner shortly and then we can make a run for it." She gives us thorough instructions, demanding that should things go awry, Cassiel and I are to save ourselves and leave her behind. I look at him and see he feels the same as me—there's no way we're leaving her here. We are all going to get out of here together. Period.

When Louise, or uh, Trinity, asks to use our phone to speak to Olesya, I hand over my earpiece and the two of them speak for about a minute before she hands it back to me.

"If you survive this, I'm going to fucking kill you," she spits before ending the call.

"You're welcome, you pissy bitch," I mutter to myself, eliciting a chuckle from Cass.

"You do know that Hell will freeze over before you get a thank you from her," he laughs.

"Yeah, well I also never thought I'd be shaking hands with my father-in-law at a fancy-ass party in his house, so I guess at this point, anything's possible."

"If you two are done chatting, we need to get moving," Louise says with urgency, even as she sways on her feet. She took a hard blow to the head, so we're going to need to watch her carefully. She stops talking for a moment, pressing her fingers to her bruised temple and closing her eyes with a wince. After a few deep breaths she looks at me, her eyes so much like Emma's, and Cassiel's, I can't imagine how I didn't put the pieces together sooner.

"Listen carefully, boys. This is what we're going to do," she begins, launching into a detailed escape plan. When she's done, Cass and I look at each other and shrug, knowing it's far better than what we came up with, which was pretty much nothing. If all goes as planned, and with a little luck, I just might live to see the sun rise.

"I thought we were here to rescue her?" I mutter to Cass. "But right now, she's saving our asses."

He smiles sadly and shrugs. "She may have her issues, and at times made some really bad decisions, but there's no mother on the planet with more love for her children than her. It's what's kept her alive all these years, and what's going to get you out of here in one piece."

I stare at him for a moment as he hands me his service revolver and points at his head.

"What the fuck are you doing?"

"I have to stay. If I leave with you, you'll lose your last connection to the inside. There's no way for me to explain why I'd go with you. This way, I can just say you attacked me when I had my back turned and you knocked me out."

He kneels down to make the next part of my job easier, making a smart-ass quip about my height. It's not my fault he's a goddamn giant.

"Now make sure you hit me hard enough to actually knock me out with one blow," he winces even as he says the words. "I really don't want you to have to whack me twice."

55

Emma

"How much longer?" I pant while Rowan once again checks my progress. She and Sarah have taken turns being up with me all night, and I have never been more jealous when they fell asleep for a few hours and I didn't.

"You have a while to go yet," she says as she snaps off her gloves. "You're about five centimeters."

"You said I was five centimeters four hours ago!" I wail as another contraction hits.

"I know, I know," she says as she gently pats my knee. "There's no predicting how quickly things will happen at this point, especially with this being your first child. First children always take longer."

"Are there any ways we can speed this up?"

Rowan sighs. "Well, we can go for another walk—"

"I don't want to go for another walk!" I yell through gritted teeth. It's barely 9 a.m., and it's already so hot, and I'm so damn tired, that all I want to do is cry. The kids were all shuttled off to be watched by a neighbor, so at least I don't have to worry about upsetting them with my yelling. I feel badly that I'm not being more stoic, but I never thought labor would be this long or painful. I'm a damn ballerina, for Christ's sake. We pride ourselves not just on our ability to handle pain, but to move beautifully through it. There's *nothing* beautiful about any of this right now.

"Has anyone heard from Declan, yet?"

I broke my promise to myself and called him around two in the morning, leaving him a short message to say he was needed at home as soon as possible. I hoped to hear from him by now, as last night's party was scheduled to end by three am. He *always* contacts me when his missions are over and he's safe, so to have not heard from him by now has me more than a little concerned.

I try not to tear up, but nothing right now is as it should be. Keira's funeral had to be postponed as road closures made it impossible for the New York group to get here until tomorrow at the earliest. I'm in labor, Declan's missing in action, and Rowan and Sarah are exchanging increasingly more worried glances when they think I'm not watching.

"Sorry, sweetie, nothing yet," Sarah says after checking my phone for the millionth time. "Try not to worry so much. I'm sure everything's going to be just fine."

I'm glad she's so sure, because God only knows I'm not sure about *anything* right now. My mind jumps to all the worst case scenarios, and the more time passes, the worse those scenarios get. By noon it's sweltering in here, and Sarah sends Micah to the store to get more ice in an attempt to cool me down. My blood pressure's gone sky high, and now those worried glances have become steady, concerned gazes.

When the local doctor "stops by," I know there's a problem. He's silent and stern as he checks me over, taking my blood pressure multiple times and grunting noncommittally when Rowan tells him I've only dilated another centimeter.

They go into the hall to chat, their voices so quiet I can't hear what they're saying before the doctor says he'll wait downstairs for our decision.

When Rowan comes back into the room, she's ashen faced as she sits next to me on the bed. "Emma, Dr. Stoltzfus thinks you need a cesarean. Your labor's not progressing as it should, and your blood pressure is dangerously high. We are both worried that something could happen if we wait much longer."

I start to cry. "Is my baby alright?" I whisper, terrified of what she's going to say next.

"The baby is showing signs of distress. If we don't do this soon. . ." her voice trails off, the woman too kind to say what I already know.

I lie back against the pillows and place my hands over my face and begin to sob. I can't lose my baby. I just *can't*.

Dear God, if anyone here has to die today, please let it be me. Just please, please, don't let my baby die.

The harder I try to calm myself, the more I fall apart. Rowan does her best to reassure me, but it's not until she tells me I'm making things harder on the baby by becoming hysterical that I can pull myself together. My head is pounding, and my nose is snotty and running all over the place. When another contraction hits, it's the worst one yet. In the middle of it I feel a warm gush of liquid release from somewhere inside me, my eyes refusing to believe it's blood even as it stains everything it touches a deep, dark red.

"Dr. Stoltzfus! Sarah! Come quickly!" The note of panic in Rowan's voice hangs heavily in the air as footsteps race up the stairs. I'm suddenly so dizzy I can hardly raise my head from the pillow, and when the Doctor comes in, he shouts to Sarah in German and she races to the other room to do whatever he demanded. She returns with a tall stack of towels.

"Listen carefully, Emma. We have to deliver the baby now. We're going to do a C-section, just like I explained before. Do you understand what I'm saying? Emma? *Emma?*"

I can feel her hand slapping my face, and hear her panicking words, but my head hurts and my body feels so damn *wrong* that I can barely breathe. She jumps from the bed and helps the doctor set things up, the two of them shouting commands to Sarah, and now to Micah, who stands staring in the doorway. He looks as if he's seen a ghost.

"Mama," he says, his voice shaking, "is she having the baby now?"

Sarah snaps something to him in German, but he just keeps gawking. "Mama, she can't have the baby now."

Sarah huffs out a few harsh sounding words that do little to rouse him, so she walks over to him, grabs him by the good shoulder, and turns him around to march him back down the stairs, but I never hear their heavy boots clomp down them. My vision is barely focusing, and all I can hear is my heart beating too hard and far too fast.

"Save my baby," I whisper, using the last bit of energy left in me. "Tell him I love him."

"Emma, stay with me," Rowan shouts as she dons a sterile surgical gown and gloves and then opens up a kit full of the scariest looking instruments imaginable. She shouts for Sarah, who doesn't respond, and then lets out a string of curses as she attaches a blade to her scalpel as the doctor squirts some sort of brownish liquid on my exposed belly and then places a drape over it. When she holds the instrument up and comes towards me, she's praying to the Goddess Brigid, much to the doctor's disapproval. Just as she's about to cut into me, I hear the unmistakable sound of a gun being cocked as someone large and heavy rushes in the room and demands she stop.

"If I don't get this baby out, Emma's going to die as well as her child. Do you understand me? So shoot me if you want, but then you're going to have to explain to the Supreme Regent why both his daughter and the Heir are dead."

I'm barely conscious, but when I turn my head, there's no mistaking who the officer is before me. For as long as I live, I'll never forget those pale, clear eyes that have haunted my days and terrorized my sleep.

His eyes are filled with glee as he enters the tiny room despite Rowan's command to stay back. He sneers down at me, my eyes barely focusing but still somehow fixated on his terrifyingly cold eyes.

"I could give a shit if she makes it," he drawls, taking a step back to give Rowan more room to work. "I'm just here for the kid."

"You will never take my baby," I grit out just before the scalpel pierces my skin and I scream. Then everything goes black.

56

Declan

I'm shocked how well Emma's mother navigates getting us not only out of the house, but across the grounds and to a gate in the wall without being seen. The property is crawling with patrolmen who, pretty soon, will figure out just how badly they fucked things up when they realize Louise is gone and I'm the one who took her.

I'm feeling exceptionally chuffed after I knock out a chauffeur and steal his jacket, hat and car, tell Louise to sit in the back, keep her dark green hood over her hair and act annoyed should we get stopped. I'm a little anxious as we head for the main entrance, but with security so high inside, I guess they feel no reason to check cars as they leave. We drive off the compound without being given so much as a second glance.

When we are finally out of the Premier City, I ditch the fancy car for one of our old beaters we keep stashed nearby. I change into some jeans and a tee shirt I find in the trunk, leaving behind both uniforms for the patrolmen to find as sort of an extra fuck you. After this, I can guarantee no vehicle will ever leave the Residence without a very thorough search.

Because of the foreign dignitaries, all the main roads are shut down. Louise and I are stuck using only local roads and a route that is seriously out of the way of our destination. We change cars as frequently as we can, not wanting to risk anyone following us back to Lancaster. When dawn comes, I try to call Emma and tell her I'm safe, only to find my cell dead, most likely having broken when I fell saving Louise from bouncing down the stairwell on her skull.

"How's your head?" Louise sits beside me staring silently out the window. She doesn't talk much, and I don't push her to make idle chit-chat. The whole situation is more than a little weird, not just with her being my mother-in-law, but also being the only criminal wanted more than me in this country. Don't get me wrong, I have a lot of questions I'm *dying* to ask, but I don't want to be rude. The last thing I want to do is make a shitty first impression with my mother-in-law.

"I'm fine," she says with a shy smile. Emma looks so much like her mom that I end up wracking my memory to find even the slightest trace of her father in her, but I find nothing. I don't want to stare, but they really look way more like sisters than mother and daughter. When I tell Louise this she laughs, and looks away out the window again, her cheeks pinking just like Emma's do when I compliment her.

Here and there she occasionally pipes up with a question or a story about Emma's youth. Nothing she tells me is Earth-shattering, mainly the sort of chit-chat a guy and his girlfriend's mom get into the first time they meet. I wonder if it's rude to ask if I'm speaking to Louise or Trinity right now, but just to be safe, I table that question for another time.

We eventually stop to get gas, and I tell Louise to stay in the car when I go in to pay. I pull the baseball cap I found in the backseat down over my eyes and the wrist brace I use to cover the brand on the back of my hand, making sure to do nothing noteworthy that might end up biting me in the ass. I grab a cup of nasty gas-station coffee and two bottles of water for the road, and juggle them to the front counter to pay. The guy behind the counter is watching the news on an ancient TV, the static so thick I can hardly hear the commentator.

CHAPTER FIFTY-SIX

"Crazy, ain't it?" the guy says to me. "I can't believe the poor girl's dead."

"What girl?"

I drop the water bottles to the counter and lean over to get a better look at the TV. The footage they show is of the Residence I just left, only it's now decorated with heavy black bunting and matching memorial bows. My grip loosens on the styrofoam coffee cup and it falls to the floor. The guy working there gives me an annoyed glance but turns back to the news, apparently having no interest in cleaning up the mess anytime soon. Like me, he's too busy watching the screen.

"Who's dead?" I choke out.

The guy looks at me like I'm stupid. "Ain't you been watching the reports, buddy? The Regent's daughter died last night giving birth. They say the boy's hanging on for now, but who knows if he's gonna make it."

No. This has to be a mistake. No.

"I don't understand," I say again. "I just saw her a few days ago. She was fine."

He looks at me oddly, then I realize what I said. "On TV," I add quickly. "She looked fine."

He lets out a breath, taking my excuse with a nod. "Yeah, I hear 'ya. We see so much of them on the news it's easy to forget we don't really know them."

I reach into my pocket and pull out a wad of cash, my hands shaking so badly a few bills fall to the floor. I don't bother to pick them up. I leave the water on the counter, the guy calling for me to come back and get them, but I'm already out the door.

I get in the car, and slam the door shut behind me and just sit behind the wheel, dumbstruck. I'm numb to my very core, the world around me nonexistent as I stare straight ahead through the windshield, my brain fumbling the horrific news. I try to remain calm, a part of my brain telling me this can't be real, that if Emma was dead, I'd somehow know it. Feel it. But right now, I feel nothing.

A hand touches my arm and I flinch away as if I've been burned. "Declan?" I turn to face Louise, her face white. "Declan, what's happened?"

Holy fuck, I can't tell her. I can't say the words. I don't *believe* the words. I refuse to believe she's dead until I see her with my own eyes, but that means going back to the city, and heading back there now would be suicide.

Death by patrolman. Would that really be such a bad way to go?

Honestly, no. I have a gun, and if I point it at them, they'll kill me. If it looks like they're going to try to take me into custody, I can use it on myself. My Catholic upbringing says suicide is a mortal sin, but who the fuck am I kidding? No matter how I try to justify the things I've done, I'm going to Hell. So what's the difference if I send myself there a bit earlier than the good Lord intended?

"Declan, you're frightening me."

I shake my head, closing my eyes for a moment, unable to look at the woman who gave birth to my wife. How can I tell her Emma's dead? How will she take the news? She's gonna ask me a million questions, and I have no answers. I should have stayed inside and heard more, and a part of me desperately wants to march back in there and get my answers. But going back in there would be weird, and the last thing I need the clerk to do is call the patrol. No, I have to keep Louise safe. I start the car and drive off.

I decide to not say anything, determined to get back to the farm. But wait—we can't go to the farm. Emma was at the farm. If they know Emma's dead, that means they found us. We'll be walking into an ambush. They'll be waiting for us. Fuck, what do I do now?

I keep the radio off, knowing the news will be everywhere, and as much as I wanted details earlier, I realize now they don't matter. All that matters is my Emma's dead. She's dead because I, once again, put the cause before her. I misjudged my priorities and made the wrong decisions, and had I only been there, maybe she'd still be alive.

I smash my fist into the steering wheel and scream as grief wars with shock to control my mind and actions. It's becoming harder and harder to breathe, so I try to take in more air through huge, gulping gasps. Something tickles my face, and when I swipe at my cheeks, my hand returns wet.

I pull over to the side of the road and get out, marching into an arid, dusty field and screaming at the top of my lungs. My heart has been ripped out and shredded, my mind incapable of thought. Even my body gives up, my legs buckling as I fall to my knees. My guts are so twisted, so painful, I bend over and retch into the sun-baked dirt.

I have no idea how long Louise lets me scream and cry and curse God in wholly unintelligible ways, but eventually I run out of tears and am left destroyed and empty in the dirt. I vaguely feel her presence, her voice soothing and soft and so much like Emma's that at first I think it's her. She approaches me like I'm a wounded, feral animal, taking each step carefully. When she's near enough to touch me, she tells me before she places her hand on my shoulder, before she drops to her knees beside me, before she takes me in her arms and holds me tight. I cry like I've never cried before.

When I've exhausted myself, she helps me up and somehow gets me into the backseat of the car. She tells me to lie down, to sleep, that she will drive for a while. Between my grief and exhaustion, the movement of the car lulls me to sleep.

In my final twilight moment between wake and sleep, I realize I never bothered to ask Louise where we're going, not that it matters. I no longer care about anything or anyone. My wife is dead, and they have my son, and for all I know, he's dead, too.

And if that's the case, there's nothing left for me to live for. Nothing left, at all.

57

Louise

The boy is grieving.

I don't know for whom or what happened, nor do I want to ask. All I know is he's asleep in the backseat, the gun he had fallen asleep with in his hand now safely up here by my side after I'd carefully pulled over and taken it from him. I don't want him to do something rash in the midst of his misery.

I know about rash behavior, and yes, the rumors that I'd tried to take my life multiple times over the years are true. After my "fall" down the stairs, the pain of learning to walk and the difficulty of learning to talk again, had almost done me in. But it hadn't been the physical pain that nearly destroyed me.

After being released from the asylum, I was sent home to languish in the house I'd come to despise. It was a cruel and unusual punishment, even for someone as evil as Edward. The only bright spot in my life was having Ekaterina as a companion. She slowly and carefully brought me back from the brink of madness, reminding me there were reasons to live, even if only for one day at a time. She made me realize that although I lost Cash, I still had our beautiful daughter. I still had Adam. And somewhere out there, I prayed was my beautiful Cassiel. I never told Edward he had another son, the secret one only myself, Ekaterina, and a preacher in Philadelphia and his wife knew. Even now, it gives me great satisfaction knowing something he never will, that there's one weapon left in my arsenal Edward will never see coming until it's too late.

Ekaterina, or Trina, as I called her for short, became my closest friend. She got me off the pain meds and weaned off the alcohol, careful to keep my healing mind and body quiet from Edward. She had the uncanny ability to predict things, some of them so dark and terrible that when they came true, I believed her to be a witch, and even when I mustered the courage to ask, she never confirmed or denied my theory.

Together, we concocted plans and put them into action. We slowly replaced the house staff with people who were loyal to us and not Edward. She procured cameras and computers for inside the house, and once the entire staff was on my side, we spied on my husband and his cronies and fed the tidbits of information to those who could use them best. It still hadn't been enough to stop the war and the madness that happened after, but it gave me great satisfaction to ruin Edward's plans.

Then one day, Trina disappeared. I was never told why or where she went, but I felt her loss desperately. I fell into a terrible depression, my mental state deteriorating to the point I frequently lost great chunks of time. I asked members of my staff what happened during those periods, surprised to find that I'd been acting normally, if a bit bossier.

Now I understand. It was in those forgotten times that I became Trinity, a name I'd chosen in honor of the three children I love so very, very much.

I didn't see Trina again for nearly twenty years, and then one day, I bumped into her in a bathroom at a charity event for the National Ballet. She was dressed to the nines and now had bottle-blonde hair and a thick Russian accent, but I knew it was her. She pretended to not know me, introducing herself to me as Olesya Vasilieva, the mother of the renowned prima ballerina, Anna Vasiliev. She kissed me on both cheeks and made small-talk as she reapplied lipstick while glancing repeatedly at the cameras watching our every move, her way of telling me to be discreet.

It was a strange meeting, as she said she was leaving the country shortly, but was glad we had met. When she kissed me goodbye, she slipped me a paper with three predictions I always knew would one day come in handy.

Today, apparently, was that day.

58

Declan

For a few blessed moments after I wake, I don't remember any-thing. I'm in the backseat of a moving vehicle, the sun low in the sky, the smell of manure and freshly broken soil heavy in the air. My eyes are swollen and itchy, my face stiff from the dried tears on my cheeks.

Just as I push myself to sit up, everything comes rushing back, and the reality knocks the wind from my chest. Louise looks up in the rearview mirror as I gasp for breath and our eyes meet.

"Declan, I have something I need to tell you, and all I ask is that you listen to me before you say anything. Can you do that?"

I look at her wearily, not wanting to come across as a complete prick, but not wanting to listen to a lecture about how life goes on or whatever other happy horseshit she's going to tell me. I nod woodenly.

"I have reason to believe Emma is alive," she says, throwing me for a total loop. "But right now, she's in grave danger."

I try to break in, but she raises her hand to silence me. "Let me finish," she says sternly. "You promised to hear me out."

Part of me is stunned, the other part furious, but it's the unex-pected hope for a happily ever after that seals my lips. Although what she says is the sort of twisted shit you only see in movies, no woman has ever sounded saner. In the end, I have to decide if I want to take a leap of faith and believe the word of someone I've been told is batshit crazy who, right now, doesn't seem insane at all.

So before I can talk myself out of it, I take a chance, and jump.

* * *

When we finally arrive in Lancaster, we expect to see a million patrolmen, but the streets are quiet to the point of silence. We drive past a few farms that look deserted, their barn doors rattling in the wind and unlatched pasture gates opening and slamming shut with the increasingly violent gusts.

"There's a storm coming," Louise says.

"You're goddamn right there is," I growl.

She looks over at me and smiles.

I am so pissed off I can't wait to get out of the car and go fuck some shit up. My hands are clenched into fists, my body vibrating with the need for violence. I give Louise directions to Esther's farm, and I'm glad to see at least her place isn't deserted. Marigold is chowing down in the paddock next to the house, mine and the Zook's kids playing in the yard as if it's just another day in Mr. Rodgers' fucked up neighborhood.

Esther comes out to meet us as we get out of the car, her face haggard and worried. "Declan, I'm so sorry, I heard the news—"

"Did you hear it from anyone around here? Or just on TV?"

"Well, no, I didn't go to the house. I figured you would want your privacy."

Oh, thank fuck. . .

"Listen, I don't think Emma's dead, but I think there's big trouble over there. I need weapons."

"I'll go with you—"

"No," I say quietly. "You stay here with the kids and Louise."

CHAPTER FIFTY-EIGHT

Esther looks over at Louise and finally registers who she is. "Oh, shit..."

But Louise is already over with the children, kneeling in the dirt and speaking quietly to them, even Anya crawling over and examining her with her big, thoughtful eyes. After determining that Louise is okay, she climbs into her lap and reaches for the heavy, jeweled necklace around her neck.

I head inside and take my pick of Esther's weapons. Considering I don't know who I'm going to find at the house, I load up with a few guns and a bunch of ammo, and consider removing my father's knife from my belt and replacing it with another holstered gun, but I change my mind at the last minute. It's always good to have a variety of weapons at hand.

Esther tells Louise she'll be back shortly, and she quickly bridles Marigold and tells me to hop on behind her. The horse is not thrilled to be pulled from her food, but she plods off in the direction of the Zooks at a slightly slower pace than I'd be able to run. I tell Ester to kick the horse into high gear, and she tells me without a doubt that if I fall off and hurt myself, I'm going to be no good to anyone. She's got a point, as of all the things I've learned on this farm, riding hadn't been one of them.

When we get close but are still well covered in the woods, I dismount ungracefully before Esther heads to Adam and Dex's. I'm close enough to the house to see no vehicles out front, but in the distance, I can make out one white and green Ag vehicle.

The property is silent save for the wind whipping the fully dried clothes hanging on the line. I know for sure now that something's wrong, because there's no way Sarah would let clean clothes get rained on. The sky is getting darker with each passing minute, a strange greenish glow appearing in the sky. I don't know what that means, but it can't be good.

I get as close to the house as I dare, listening closely for voices or other sounds telling me where everyone is, but with the wind whipping the trees into a frenzy, I can't hear a goddamn thing.

I know I should wait for Adam and Dex, but when I hear a woman scream from within, I'm in motion before the sound fades. Gritty races out from the depths of the barn barking wildly, nearly strangling himself as he hits the limit of the tether.

A new idea takes root in my mind, and I run to the barn to untie the hulking Shepherd. He takes off so fast the rope burns my palm and I have no choice but to let go. I can't call him back without giving myself away, and when he races to the house, he blows clear through the screen door.

I hear another scream, this time a man's, and it doesn't sound like it comes from either Amos or Micah. Seconds later, Micah is dragging a seething Gritty from the house, the dog snarling and snapping as he tries to drag the boy back inside. They head to the barn and I race around to the back door to meet them inside, nearly scaring the piss out of them both. Then Micah relaxes slightly after realizing it's me.

"Thank God you're here," he tells me as he hands over the leash. "You have to stop him. He wants to take Emma and the baby away."

Micah fills me in on everything that happened, and I'm devastated to hear Emma's in rough shape after an emergency C-section. She has yet to wake from the surgery, but according to the kid, my son appears to be alright.

"There was a great deal of blood lost," he tells me quietly. "Rowan wanted to send me to the clinic to get blood for her, but he won't let us leave. The surgery was over less than an hour ago, but she has yet to wake."

I want to strangle that stupid motherfucker with my bare hands. How dare he not listen to the doctor? This is the sort of shit that could kill her.

"He said the minute she's awake, he will take her back to her father. Rowan said she could die if moved too soon, but he doesn't care. All he talks about is getting in the Supreme Regent's good graces by bringing him the true Heir."

I have no doubt if this guy manages to deliver Emma to Edward, she's dead. Edward won't risk keeping her alive, especially not after telling the nation she died giving birth. He knows she won't stay quiet, and she will never stop trying to escape until she either succeeds or dies in the process.

"How many patrolmen are in there? Has he called for backup?"

"This is the strange thing, Declan. There is only one. He is very proud and sure of himself that he can do this alone and reap the awards for himself. I normally would say you will have no trouble subduing him, but he is very skilled."

"You know him?"

"Yes, I do," he says quietly, now looking down at the ground. "He was the warden at the camp. He did horrible, horrible things to us, the sort of things that aren't... *normal*. He enjoyed torturing us, Declan. It made him... excited."

Holy fuck. It's that same motherfucker who killed Keira. The same son of a bitch who tried to rape my wife. The same cunt pedophile who tortured and fucked countless children who didn't dare fight back.

Usually when I'm this enraged I'm rash and too quick with decisions, but an eerie calmness descends upon me. I help him quickly bridle Gable and boost Micah onto his bare back. It's still far too soon after his own surgery for him to be doing something as active as riding, but desperate times call for desperate measures. Despite the storm quickly rolling in, I send him into town, telling him to ride fast and get the blood Emma needs. He's to return to the barn and wait for my signal. He nods his understanding, then sinks his heels into Gable's side and gallops off.

Knowing there's only one patrolman inside makes things simpler, but Goodman's unpredictable. I have no doubt if I burst in there he'll threaten Emma, maybe even kill her. No, I need to draw the fucker out. Although the smartest way of eliminating me would be to shoot me from afar, Micah's right—he's prideful. He's gonna want to take me alive so he can have the spectacle of marching me, his bloody and broken prisoner, through the streets of the Premier City. Being the man responsible for capturing me will be the highlight of his career.

But for that to happen he needs to take me alive. And being the nice guy I am, I'm going to let him.

I shuck my weapons except for a single Glock and my knife. I rub dirt into my skin and tear at my clothes, using the point of my knife to bloody myself up a bit to make it look like I've been chased through the trees. By the time I'm done, I'm a mess.

The approaching storm has whipped itself into a fury, the first large, fat drops of rain splashing in the dirt as I stagger and limp from the barn towards the house as if wounded. I repeatedly scream Emma's name, the hysteria in my voice and eyes practically palpable despite the rest of my body being ready for action.

Before I even get close to the porch the screen door opens and there he stands. Lightning flashes in a sky nearly dark at night, illuminating the icy, clear blue of his glee-filled eyes. His pistol is pointed at me, his finger aside the trigger. I slide to a halt and stare at him, as if suddenly seeing a ghost. I lift my weapon, staggering a bit before adopting a stance I would never shoot from. I make sure the fake, violent tremor in my arm is erratic enough for him to take notice. "Tell me it's not true! Tell me she's not dead!" I scream.

His face gives away his every thought. The motherfucker's buying my performance lock, stock and barrel. "Put down the gun, Declan," he responds slowly. "Then I'll tell you whatever you want to know."

Like fuck he will. I shake my head wildly, then drop to my knees. "No. If she's dead, I want to go with her." I place the gun under my chin. "I can't live without her. I won't!"

He steps off the porch and into the pelting rain. Unfortunately, the fucker's not dumb enough to lower his weapon.

"Please," I beg. "I want to see her. I *need* to see her. Just let me see her one last time. *Please.*"

It boils my blood to be on my knees to him, but I know my plan's working when he steps closer. The rain is coming down in torrents, making it hard to see clearly despite the short distance between us.

Come on you smarmy fuck, just a little closer. . .

"Drop the gun, Declan. I swear, if you give yourself up, I'll let you see her one last time. Otherwise, you'll never set eyes on her again. Understand?"

"Y-yes," I stammer. "Thank you. Thank you!" I toss the gun away, then let my hands drop to my sides. With me no longer armed, he boldly strides towards me, any pleasantness in his tone gone.

"You stupid motherfucker," he hisses as he raises his gun to hit me in the head. "Do you honestly think I'm going to do anything for you?"

He's now within an arm's reach, but I need him one step closer. I do my best to stare up at him in disbelief, pretending to not understand this strange turn of events while watching the weapon descend towards my head. It's then he takes that last step I need. . .

I fly into motion, blocking the blow with one arm just as my other hand seizes the hilt of my blade and swings it forward and upward, meeting its intended mark in his groin. It sinks in easily, the blade every bit as sharp now as when it was made generations ago.

His jaws fly open and he emits an agonized scream.

Bright red blood blooms like unfurling petals around my blade and stains the fine fabric of his pants. I've hit my mark—the femoral artery—dead on. He drops his weapon and falls to the ground, clutching at the hilt of the knife like he's ready to pull it out.

I *tsk* at him, wagging my finger disapprovingly. "You pull that out, you're only gonna die faster. If I were you, I'd use the five minutes or so you have left to make your peace with God."

"You rotten motherfucker," he spits through his teeth. "I'm going to kill you for this."

I laugh, rising to my feet and picking up his weapon from the ground. "No, you're not." I begin to walk away after he crumples to the ground, the change of position making him scream even louder.

"Is this about the girl?" he yells after me. "Is that it? Are you getting me back for the girl?"

I stop in my tracks, the air suddenly gone as cold as my blood. "What did you say?"

"This *is* about the girl, isn't it? That little redheaded firecracker I stabbed in the woods. She's dead, isn't she?"

The lightning flashes again, and I turn back to face him. The fury in me is unimaginable, my hands fisting and flexing, fisting and flexing, in time with my heart.

"I don't know why you feel you need to avenge the little whore. She spread her legs for every inmate in that place. Had things not gone down when they did, she was next on my list to fuck. I bet she'd have been a real fun ride."

I normally hate to let anyone see they've gotten under my skin, but I cannot stand a piece of shit like him talking about Keira like that. "Take it back," I say quietly, an eerie calmness descending upon me.

"Or what?" he snickers between gasps. "You said I have only minutes left. What are you going to do? Kill me faster? Go ahead. Shoot me and get it over with."

There's no way in Hell I'm going to ease his suffering. I smile as I step closer, unbuckling my belt and pulling it free from my pants. I loop the leather between his groin and the knife and secure it tightly, his scream filling the night until another clap of thunder erases the sound. I drag him to his feet, the rain so heavy I can barely see a foot in front of me, then force him to march in front of me, pushing him to walk faster whenever he slows. It seems to take forever and somehow yet no time at all, to reach our muddy destination.

When I command him to stop, he collapses to the ground. I stand over him like an avenging angel, the flashes of lightning and claps of thunder blinding and deafening as the storm rages.

"You should know I didn't mean to kill her," he pants up at me. "The dog was getting ready to attack me, and I couldn't get my gun out of the holster fast enough. I threw the knife just as she stepped in front of the dog."

For the first time, he looks truly terrified. He's gone terribly pale, his nearly colorless eyes ghostly in the bright flashes of lightning. Even with the makeshift tourniquet still in place, he's losing blood rapidly.

I wonder why he's telling me this now, if he honestly thinks I will show him mercy because it was an accident. But then he smiles, and the look on his face is so smug and oily I know whatever he says next is going to seal his fate.

"What a dumb, fucking cunt," he laughs. "You know, she had me in the crosshairs right before she did that. She could have killed me with one shot, but she saved the dog, instead."

This moment is a clear turning point in my life. It's one of those obvious times I'll later reflect upon and realize had I taken the other road, that everything that followed would have been different. But I'm not looking back, I'm in the moment. I still have time to make the right decision. I'm still capable of keeping myself just this side of doing something unforgivable. There's still one more chance to save my soul.

The only problem is that I don't want to.

It will stay between you and me. No one ever has to know.

I'm not surprised to hear his voice right now, or to feel his presence at this moment.

He's a pedophile. A murderer. A rapist. He starved children and worked them to death.

Yes. . .

He killed Keira. It's because of him that she's dead.

Yes. . .

He laid hands on your wife, the woman you love more than anyone in the world. He was going to rape her and pass her around to his buddies. Are you really going to let him die quickly?

No.

He doesn't deserve a quick or clean death. He deserves a taste on Earth of the Hell that awaits him, and I am going to revel in his screams and delight in his agony.

I'm no avenging angel and I am not God's soldier.

I am a demon made flesh, and I want him to suffer.

With a smile on my lips, I lean down and tighten the tourniquet before removing my knife from his groin. I swear on all things dark and twisted that his screams are the sweetest music I've ever heard. I lose myself in their melodious torment, laughing uproariously at his increasingly panicked pleas for mercy.

What I'm doing is very, very wrong. I've crossed the line from vengeance to devilry, and not only am I fully aware, I don't give a fuck. If there was ever hope for my soul it's now lost as I give in to the darkness.

It is too late, he drags me down; I sink, I sink. . . .

My soul is lost forever.

59

Emma

I am barely conscious when Declan comes to my room, but even in my delirium, I know something is wrong. Even though we lost power from the storm, there are enough candles lit to see he's soaked through from the rain, his clothes torn and muddy, and his hands and torso are coated in blood.

There's a coldness about him that chills me. Something terrible has happened that has changed him forever. The others in the room are equally horrified, only Rowan daring to command him to leave. She instructs him to get cleaned up before he frightens me, whispering something to him I don't catch. She somehow manages to shake him from his trance, and when he looks down at himself, he backs out of the room looking every bit as spooked as the rest of us.

When he returns, he's freshly showered and in clean, dry, clothes, but he's still terribly pale. He speaks to Rowan in hushed tones, the two of them whispering urgently until he hisses, "Enough!" and she silences. A minute later, she speaks again, I think carefully giving him the bad news, and then I know for certain that's what happened when I hear the unmistakable sound of his fist hitting the wall. I'm so tired my eyes close despite desperately wanting to stay awake.

When I wake, Declan and I are alone. He's sitting in the rocking chair with our child cradled in his arms, the only light coming from a single night light plugged into the wall. It's enough to clearly see my beloved, clad only in his pajama bottoms, as he whispers to our son in dulcet Spanish. It's warm and muggy from the rain, and a glance outside at the darkness proves my assumption that it's either very late, or very early.

As if he feels my eyes on him, he raises his gaze to me and smiles softly. "Go back to sleep, mamacita," he whispers. "You need your rest."

"Come here," I whisper back. "I want to see our son."

He pads over to me and sits on the edge of the bed. Declan's a natural with our son, cradling him gently and supporting his head, his love for the only biological child we'll ever have beaming from his eyes. Rowan and Dr. Stoltzfus had no choice but to perform a hysterectomy when they couldn't get the bleeding under control. Our dreams for a huge family are dashed before they've barely begun.

I'm fighting the tears that come with the loss, and manage to blink most of them back. Although it hurts like hell to move, I want to look at my precious baby badly enough that I would crawl through fire for a glimpse. "He's perfect," I whisper as I run my fingers through his thick, inky hair.

"Of course he is," Declan smiles down at his son before giving me a sideways glance. "He's just like his mother."

I chuckle at his sweet words, but wow, does it hurt. My laughter turns to a groan of pain as I clutch at my belly. Declan frowns, asking me a million questions that I wave away, instead telling him I want to hold my son. He places him gently in my arms, carefully arranging pillows around him and me so I will be as comfortable as possible. Declan wraps his arm around my shoulders and snuggles up next to me, resting his head against mine as he stares adoringly at our son.

"He still needs a name," I remind my husband. I don't want to start a fight, not in this tender moment, and it's almost as if Declan knows what I'm going to suggest because he tenses beside me.

He then takes a fortifying breath and lets it out slowly. "While I was getting to know him, a name came to me. I think we should name him Keiran."

"Keiran," I repeat, looking down at the sweet boy nestled in my arms. "Keiran Byrne," I whisper again, already thoroughly in love with the name. "It suits him. I like it." I grin as I look up at my husband, who's smiling from ear to ear, remembering a similar exchange between us from not that long ago.

I look down at our perfect child thoughtfully. "I love it, but I can't help thinking he should have a middle name. How about Keiran Andrews Byrne?"

The bright smile on Declan's face is only marred by the tears in his eyes. "It's perfect," he tells me, dropping a gentle kiss on my cheek before leaning over to whisper, "You're perfect," before planting an even sweeter one on my lips.

I'm so happy my heart could burst, but it's not until Declan gets up and brings our sleeping daughter to our bed that I feel this moment is complete. We snuggle together until sleepiness overtakes me, and then Declan takes both children to the makeshift nursery in Anya's room so I can rest. I fall fast asleep before he returns, the smile on my face still present as I navigate sweet dreams of our little family's future together.

60

One month later

Louise

I kiss my grandson on the top of his little head one last time before handing him over to his mother. I tear up when I look at my daughter cradling the sleeping child in her arms, the love she has for him shining from her eyes.

I don't want to leave them, but I can't stay, either. The search for me is only intensifying; and every day Edward cannot verify that I'm out of the country is another day where my disappearance puts innocent people at risk. I have enough regrets in my life. I certainly don't wish to rack up any more.

I have only minutes left with Emma before Olesya will come to collect me, and I feel the strangest pressure to make certain these last minutes with her are especially meaningful. Since my escape from the Residence, I've reunited with all three of my children. Although I had known Adam was still alive, the chance to see him, to hug him, and most importantly, to beg his forgiveness for my shortcomings, have been some of the most healing hours of my life. Despite having been in contact with Cassiel for years, it is only now I feel we have a real mother/son bond. I leave them feeling relieved beyond measure for their love, their understanding, and their forgiveness.

My time with Emma has been bittersweet. I am so proud of the woman she's become and the loving mother she's proving to be, and yet my heart aches knowing I can take absolutely no credit for any of it.

My regrets tally in the thousands when it comes to my children, and even if I live to be a thousand years-old, I will never feel worthy of the love she, as well as her brothers, so freely bestow upon me. The unfairness of finally being able to start an open, honest relationship with my daughter only to have to leave hurts far worse than anything Edward ever did to me.

After a considerable amount of urging from Emma, I've spent a large amount of time talking to a man everyone calls Brother Love. For the first time in ages, I've had deep, in-depth discussions about psychology, religion, and most importantly, how to learn to be happy after a lifetime of misery.

"Forgive yourself, child," he told me. The fact he called me child made me laugh, as I doubt he's that much older than me. When I said that to him, he chuckled.

"Age is an issue of mind over matter. If you don't mind, it don't matter," he explained before attributing the quotation to Mark Twain. There were many other pearls of wisdom he bestowed during the frequent, lengthy calls that I absolutely plan to continue on a weekly basis so he can keep tabs on mine, and Trinity's, mental health. I've come to the conclusion I'm not a well woman, and probably, never will be. But at least I'll soon have access to medications and therapies that may, hopefully, let my fractured personality finally heal.

"We can still video-chat," Emma encourages, but her wavering smile and glassy eyes prove that she, too, knows it won't be the same.

"And I'm sure at some point we can visit," I say, even though I'm not sure at all.

There's so much I want to say to her, so much I want to make sure she knows, but there's not enough time. So I tell her the only thing I can. "Your father would have been so proud of you."

Emma smiles sadly. "I wish I could have met him. He sounds like he was a wonderful man."

I have to look away when she wipes a tear from her eye because mine also begin to water. I promised myself that I wouldn't cry; I don't want my daughter's last memory of me to be teary. She already has far too many memories of me crying to last her a dozen lifetimes.

"All the best parts of you are from him," I say once I get myself under control.

"No," Emma states emphatically. Then she softens, adding, "Not all."

I take her compliment gracefully, not wanting to argue with her in these, our last minutes together. Anya crawls over to me from where she was playing on the floor and grabs at my pants, using them to pull herself up to standing. Her knuckles are white from fisting the fabric, all of us knowing if she lets go, she'll absolutely fall back onto her bottom and start to scream. I pick her up and set her in my lap as she stares at me thoughtfully.

"I wonder what she's thinking," I muse.

Emma chuckles. "I wonder the same thing all the time."

"She's going to be a handful when she gets older," I warn, but then can't help but smile. "Just like you."

"I hope so," Emma states wistfully. "I really do. This next generation of women is going to need to be the strongest yet. Our fight has only just begun."

We sit together in comfortable silence, Emma lost in her thoughts as I follow mine. We are three generations of women, all from the same family, but our lives are as different as if we'd come from different worlds. Over the past week Emma and I had many uncomfortable chats as I told her every piece of my history no matter how hard it was for me to choke out. Not only did she need to know everything

I'd learned about Edward, I told her every detail I could remember about Cash.

And from the moment I told her she is not Edward's biological child, she stopped referring to him as her father. I can't say that I blame her, as he never once acted towards her as a father should. I've often wondered if I never told him that he wasn't her biological father if he might have been kinder, but in truth, I think not. The only thing Edward cares about is his pride, and I have no doubt that he would have still used Emma any way he could as long as it benefitted him.

I'm so lost in my thoughts that it's not until a car door slams that I realize I've zoned out. Olesya and her daughters smile as they glide towards us, and little Anya breaks out into the widest smile the moment she sees them.

"Louise, have you had a nice visit?" Olesya asks as she swoops down and picks up Anya and promptly kisses her on both cheeks. The little girl laughs uproariously, as if the attention of the three women is the greatest thing to ever happen to her. Nina sweetly drops a kiss to the top of the baby's head while Sasha blows a noisy raspberry against her pudgy cheek that restarts the child's gleeful laugh.

The women then coo over Keiran for a few minutes before Olesya looks at her watch and frowns. "It's time for us to go, Louise. Adam will be unhappy if I get you to the airstrip late."

Emma and I stand, both of us bursting into tears even though we both swore we wouldn't. Nina takes Keiran from Emma so we can hug one last time, and my daughter takes me by surprise when she launches into my arms and hugs me as fiercely as I hug her back.

"I love you, mom," she whispers brokenly, and I can't help but smile through my tears. I've wanted to hear those words from her for far too long.

"Oh Emma," I whisper as I pull her even tighter against me. "Doubt thou that the stars are fire; Doubt that the sun doth move; Doubt truth to be a liar; But never doubt I love you."

Emma pulls away with a laugh as she mops her eyes. "Again with Shakespeare, mom?"

I shrug. She teases me because she now knows that we have yet another thing in common—the Bard is both of ours' favorite author. After Emma told me how she met Declan and about their courtship and secret marriage, I couldn't help but see their impossible love repeating the tale he first told in the late 1500s. I only pray it doesn't end the same way.

Before I fall down that rabbit hole, I tell Emma one last time that I love her, and quickly get in the car before I break down completely. I have complete faith that if there is a way for me to stay that wouldn't risk lives that Olesya would have told me. And if there's nothing else I've learned since we met all those years ago, it's that when Olesya tells you to do something, you do it without asking questions.

She's arranged for me the opportunity of a lifetime to start over, and for the first time in many years, I'm excited about my future. I'm headed to Switzerland, my political asylum already granted in exchange for anything I can tell the Europeans about Edward's regime. I've been advised by several legal experts that my marriage can be annulled, as it was an unlawful agreement due to my youth and nonconsent.

"Did you hear the news?" Olesya asks innocently as she slides into the back seat next to me, allowing the girls to take the front.

I nod. "Yes, I did. Emma tried to keep it from me, but I already knew."

The nation is in deepest mourning this morning after word was released that our *beloved* Mother Barbara died during the night. Along with a handful of others who attended the Gala, she had fallen quickly, and mysteriously, ill shortly after the event. But where the others all passed quickly, she lingered in a coma until her body finally gave out.

"Did they ever find out what caused it?"

Olesya looks surprised before slowly responding, "Last I heard there was some sort of poison in the desserts. Something very difficult to trace. Something plant based."

"How interesting," I murmur. "Do they have any suspects? Could there really be anyone out there who despises our *beloved* Mother Barbara that much?"

Olesya can no longer keep up the ruse. "Louise, come on now! Everyone knows it was Trinity. The Purity Police are fumbling all over themselves trying to figure out how she pulled it off. Edward is furious, and better yet, he's scared. He thought the Residence was impenetrable, and now he's frightened that if she got in there despite increased security, that she can reach him in other places he once believed safe. He knows that had he not broken up the party after your masterful *performance* to deal with the fire and his dead mistress, he'd be dead, too."

"But if everyone left before dinner, how did some of the people get poisoned?"

"This is the interesting part." Olesya leans in conspiratorially and places her hand on my forearm. "They have so far narrowed the poison down to being in some sort of strange, exotic passionfruit dessert. As people waited outside for their cars to be brought around, members of the household staff came around to the guests and offered them something sweet wrapped up in boxes for the trip home. All the boxes with specific names written on them were the ones containing the toxin."

"Mother did always enjoy her sweets," I sigh.

Olesya stares at me for a long moment, her eyebrows rising with surprise. "Are you saying. . .?" her voice trails off.

"Come now, Olesya," I tease in my best fake Russian accent. "I thought that you knew everything?"

EPILOGUE

Emma

"Anya! Stop torturing your brother!" I scold.

She's been stealing Keiran's toys all morning, and although he's not remotely happy about it, he doesn't fuss or cry. Instead, he simply crawls over to another toy, this time a stuffed bone of Gritty's, that he happily squeaks until I think I'll go mad. As if Gritty feels the same way, he lumbers over to our son and nudges him with his nose, flopping down next to him and dropping his twenty-pound head into the child's lap. He gently takes the bone from the boy's hands and flings it across the room and proceeds to rub his damaged ear all over him instead. Always an agreeable child, he takes the ear in his little hands and kneads it roughly. Despite it looking uncomfortable, Gritty loves it, groaning out his pleasure a few times before falling into a deep, drooling sleep.

The two of them are best friends and have been for some time now. We were really worried we were going to lose Gritty after we buried Keira, as the dog grieved her fiercely. Declan had to pick the dog up and manhandle him into our truck when we left the cemetery, as he'd refused to leave her grave. When we got to our new home, we had no choice but to tie him up, because he kept running away, always headed back towards Lancaster and the one he loves the most.

It wasn't until one day that Keiran dropped some food on the floor that Gritty even noticed the little boy, and over the course of a few days, the two became inseparable. Gritty even lets my son ride him like a pony, a sight that used to worry me until I noticed just how careful the big dog always is with him aboard. The two of them sleep together in the same room, Gritty vigilantly guarding our son against monsters under the bed and any and all things that go bump in the night.

We moved from Lancaster as soon as I was well enough, the risks associated with staying being too great for us to stay. Olesya provided us with a beautiful house in the Virginia countryside surrounded by acres and acres of absolutely nothing. The Zooks came with us, packing up all their animals and children and moving into the farm next to ours. Within a month, almost all of Lancaster joined us in an area we renamed New Lancaster. The men have been busy revitalizing the farms they moved into, and everything they grow and raise is now theirs to either keep or sell. They give most of the monetary profits to the war effort, and have resumed feeding those in the communities who are the most in need.

Ezra and Levi moved back from Canada and back in with their family after a few months, with the Canadian government's blessing, of course. They look so normal and healthy now that one would never have believed they'd once spent years in a work camp, but if you look closely at their eyes, it's clear the hell they lived will never be forgotten.

Even Micah has adapted to his new life, finding ingenious ways to do things I never could have thought of. Like Gritty, he too misses Keira terribly, as I firmly believe that the two of them really did love one another despite their short time together. Keira had asked Declan with her final dying breath to tell Micah that she loved him, something she'd been too scared to tell him in person. And when Declan finally worked up the courage to talk to the boy, he came back looking thoughtful, but much more at peace.

"He already knew," my husband responded when I asked how the conversation went. "He told me he already knew."

We are safe here, the land heavily protected by security measures and signal blockers and God only knows what else Olesya, Amy, and my mother came up with. When Declan and I have missions or appearances, we have little worry about their safety, especially when Tetka Olesya or her daughters babysit.

I've come to enjoy her company, but there's still something strange about her and her daughters that I can't quite put my finger on. There are too many times that she's casually mentioned things that later come true, or predicted dates and times of events that inevitably happen. We've learned that all calls from her are emergencies, and we never take her concerns lightly. Even Declan, as cynical as he is, listens to her advice like it's the word of God. Next time I see her, I absolutely plan to ask her how she does it.

I often think back to the day of my presentation, and of the anxious girl who found herself engaged to a monster. She'd been so lost, so broken, never once imagining just weeks later that she would meet the man she would eventually marry, a man who loves her so much he would go to the ends of the Earth to keep safe. I know deep in my heart that he would gladly die for his family, and although at times he takes far too many risks, I can't imagine loving, and being loved, by anyone but him.

As if my thoughts conjure him, a truck pulls into our driveway, the familiar chime of our alarm system telling me he's here without needing to look. I hurry out to greet him, always loving his first blooming, broad smile when our eyes meet. He reaches into the back seat and pulls out a large cardboard box, kicking the door closed behind him. When he turns and sees me, his smile still makes me feel all warm and gooey inside.

"What's inside the box?"

Declan cocks an eyebrow and makes a face of mock disapproval. "Your boy's in trouble," he says, trying to hide his smile.

"Who? Keiran?"

"Nope," Declan responds as he gently lowers the box to the ground so I can see inside. "Gritty."

Inside the box are six orange and black puppies whose parentage is indisputable. They look *exactly* like their father. I start to laugh as I pick one of them up, the squirming bundle of fur licking the tip of my nose when I bring it to my face.

Declan calls for the kids, and Anya comes racing out, screaming, "Da-dee!" at the top of her lungs. She launches into his arms and he catches her, swinging her around as she laughs with delight. The minute he puts her down, she's all about the puppies, squealing and giggling as Declan pulls each of them out of the box and places them in her lap. I've never seen my daughter happier.

I reach over and open the screen door, allowing Keiran to toddle out on his chubby baby legs, his hands making grabby fingers as he beelines for the pups. He plops down on his diapered rear end next to his sister and reaches for one.

"Be gentle, Keiran," she says in her bossiest voice. It always makes me smile when she says his name, the difficult vowel sounds coming out like *Kee-ran* instead of how it should. We sit together and play with the puppies, both Declan and I basking in every glorious second of this happy moment. He slides over to sit next to me, wrapping his arms around me and kissing me soundly. When he pulls away, he looks a little sad.

"What's wrong?" I ask.

"Nothing," he responds quickly. Too quickly. Then one of the puppies toddles off and he's forced to swoop after it before it topples over the edge of the porch. He flips the pup over onto its back and tickles its belly, and when he plops it back onto his lap, it promptly pees on him.

"Oh, dammit!" he gripes as the stain grows and both kids laugh. He shakes his head and then laughs at himself, hopping to his feet and announcing he's going up to shower and change before he sets up a stall in the barn for them. Before he goes inside he stops with his palm on the screen door, that same sad look on his face.

"What are you thinking?" I ask.

He pauses for a second, looking down at me with the most wistful look. "I was just wishing I could live in this moment forever."

*   *   *

Declan

During the course of our marriage, I've only lied to Emma a handful of times, and sadly, this is one of them.

Don't get me wrong, I *do* wish I could live in this moment forever. The times when I can simply be a dad and a husband are precious and far too few. I often spend weeks at a time away from my wife and children, far away from the normalcy of being home that every family deserves. My children deserve to grow up the way I did, well, back in the time before the nation went to Hell. They deserve to be able to see both of their parents every day, go to school, have friends over to play, and go to sleep overs. They should be allowed to leave their home without fear, and explore without worry, but they can't. As Keiran grows, his resemblance to me hasn't diminished. He looks *exactly* like I did at his age, except he has Emma's beautiful sapphire eyes.

It only takes one glance to see he's our child, and it's our child, not the imposter growing up in the Executive Mansion, who is the true Heir. There are grumbles within the nation as Caine grows older and looks nothing like Emma but shockingly like Edward. If you put the boys side by side, it would be clearer than crystal who belongs on the throne, and although they don't know this, I do know they fear the possibility. They will search for my son forever, because as long as he's alive, he's a threat to Caine's reign, and because of this, my son will never be safe.

Anya has a similar problem. Her light caramel skin darkens with even the slightest touch of the sun, and in the summer, it tans to a beautiful shade that sets off her large brown eyes and delicate features. Her hair is thick and very curly, and trying to get a brush through it is a miserable experience for all involved. It's clear she's of mixed race, an "abomination" punishable by death in a nation evermore focused on racial purity.

I wish I was a normal parent, with my worries limited to keeping them healthy and happy instead of hidden and safe. I wish my biggest concerns included saving money for college and not spending sleepless nights worrying about kidnapping. I spend far too many hours anxious about them dying young and in some terrible way because they followed me into war instead of living in peace.

Sometimes, I wonder if I should send them overseas to live with Louise, or to Canada to live with Esther. But then I remember the conversation I had with Isaac not that long ago that put everything in perspective. That he is John and Marta's son was particularly heartbreaking to learn, as he'd missed getting to know them by a matter of months. I told him everything about them I could remember, emphasizing how much they loved him and never stopped praying they would one day meet again.

For being so young he took everything in stride until I teared up telling him how some of his mannerisms remind me so much of both of his parents. I asked him if he was ever upset that they sent him away and he shook his head vehemently.

"They had no choice," he said forcibly. "Had there been any way to keep me, they would have. I cannot fault them for something completely out of their control."

That's what snapped me out of my funk. Although not by much, I'm still in control. Until I am backed against a wall and have no other choice, I will not do what John and Marta and so many others were forced to. I will fight to keep my family together, a family that, because of their selflessness, now includes a new Canadian "brother."

I confided all this to Olesya over drinks after our meeting yesterday. She sympathized with me, which made me feel better, but then she promptly made me feel *worse* by saying that as my children grow older, my worries will only grow with them. By the end of the night I was good and drunk, as I believe was she, although one can never really tell with her.

"I asked you once before, Declan, that if you could have one thing, anything at all, what would you ask for?"

Yeah, I remembered. Even though that was only a year ago, I'm surprised at how much my answer has changed in such a short time. "I want my children to grow up healthy and happy," I tell her. "I want my wife to be healthy and happy."

Olesya nods thoughtfully while refilling our whiskey glasses, not that either of us need more booze at this point. "So, your one wish would be a selfish one? Looking out only for your family? What about the cause? Do you still wish to win this war?"

"Of course, I want that, too," I snap.

"Choose one," she demands, suddenly sounding far too sober for my liking.

"Why? It's not like choosing makes a goddamn bit of difference. More than likely neither are going to happen. If you haven't noticed, we aren't any closer to winning this war than we were right after the fighting ended. It doesn't matter how many people in charge we kill, or if we even get Bellamy out of the Executive Mansion. Fuck, even Louise going public and spilling everything she had on him did absolutely nothing."

"Choose!" she demands.

"Goddammit, Olesya, you know I want it all!"

She sits back in her chair and crosses her legs, as calm as if we're having a leisurely drink at a classy restaurant and not arguing over stupid shit while getting wasted in her living room.

"And what would you be willing to give to have it all?"

"Anything," I answer without thinking.

"That's a very dangerous answer," she responds. "You never want to leave decisions of payment to Fate."

"Like I don't already know that," I mumble into my glass. I drain the last drops of whiskey and tell her I'm going to bed. I don't want to think about this anymore. Thinking is overrated, especially when drunk.

I fall into a fitful sleep that's neither restful nor refreshing. Then I begin to dream.

It's a bright, sunny day. There's a young man with my dark curls and Emma's sapphire eyes laughing and holding hands with a handsome young man who, going by his looks, is of Latino descent. They're clad in jeans and polo shirts and walking in a park, the two of them looking around to make sure no one's watching before ducking behind a tree and kissing each other passionately.

A voice breaks them apart, the sapphire-eyed boy turning pink-cheeked when he faces the disapproving glare of a tall woman with curly dark hair and beautiful brown eyes. She's dressed for business in a pretty navy blue suit and sensible heels, the small American flag pin on her lapel glinting the light. Unable to keep up her charade of disapproval, she laughs, her eyes twinkling as she hugs and kisses both men on the cheek. Then she shields her eyes from the sun and looks around, a small frown on her lips.

Not far off is my Emma, blinking back tears and watching them with a sad smile on her lips. In her hand is a single red rose that she lifts to her nose, smelling deep of the scent before walking to the edge of the Reflecting Pool. There no longer is scummy water or floating bodies, but thousands and thousands of flowers, notes, and mementos. She places a kiss to the petals before tossing the single stem into the pile, where it disappears from sight.

I woke this morning feeling like absolute shit, and I can't stop thinking about that dream. I know it must mean something, maybe even something really good, as aside from Emma looking a bit misty-eyed, everyone appeared happy and healthy, just as I wished.

The house is eerily silent as I head downstairs for coffee. I find it strange that despite the late hour, I'm the only one awake, as Olesya and her daughters are almost always up with the sun. Then, I see the note on the kitchen table.

> *You have seventeen years.*
> *Then, O, woe is me,*
> *To have seen what I have seen.*

I pray that what she's written is some sort of tasteless joke, but Olesya doesn't joke. Panicking, I try to call her, but her phone's been disconnected. So have Sasha's and Nina's. I call around, but nobody's seen them in *weeks.* I ransack their office looking for clues as to where they're headed and come up empty-handed.

She's gone. They're all gone.

I swallow hard, suddenly feeling sick.

Because one of my rare lies had been to Olesya, too.

Last night, I may have told her I'd give anything, but what I'd thought had been different. Worse.

Because I'd sworn I'd give my soul for even the slimmest chance to have it all.

To Be Continued One Last Time. . . .

ACKNOWLEDGEMENTS

I'M NOT GOING TO LIE; there were times during the writing and editing of *The Sentinel's Daughter* that I thought this book wasn't going to happen. Trust me when I say that a metric fuck ton of blood, sweat, and tears (and more than a few panic attacks) went into this one. Now that it's complete, and I can hold a copy of it in my hands, I can honestly say that every ounce of pain to birth this behemoth was worth it. I'm proud of all of my novels, but this one will always be extra special in my heart.

Shortly before *The Prodigal Daughter* was released, I was diagnosed with a degenerative neurological condition that has really tossed a wrench in the daily workings of my life. So, first off, I must thank you, my readers, for patiently waiting for me to get my body and brain well enough to continue Emma and Declan's saga. Writing is hard work, and when your brain decides to not cooperate, it gets a lot harder. I knew going into this novel that this would be my most ambitious storyline yet, so trying to wrestle it into something worth reading with only parts of my brain firing on all cylinders was no joke.

Next on my long list of people to thank are the doctors, nurses, and researchers in the Department of Neurology at Johns Hopkins Hospital, and especially, Dr. Scott Newsome. Without you all, I can guarantee this book never would have been completed.

To my amazing Alpha readers (with everything I've asked of you for this one, you are Betas no longer!), thank you for everything from your friendship to your proof-reading skills. Dr. Alexandra Ranieri-Deniken, thank you for your extensive psychological insights and making sure I'm portraying my characters who suffer from a wide variety of mental illnesses correctly. Of course, this is only secondary in appreciation to the many, many years of friendship we've shared, and all the love and support you've shown me. I love you!

To Marissa Seibel, Queen of the Proofreaders, thank you for your extreme attention to detail, as well as your pithy comments. To Alyssa Moody, thank you for your candor, not to mention your willingness to read and reread as needed. I especially enjoy your real-time, and often hilarious, comments that absolutely brighten my day. Diana Oprea, thank you for your ability to know just when to call with uplifting comments to thwart a whopper of a brewing panic attack.

That leads me to my friend and mentor extraordinaire, David Hazard, who has never stopped believing in both me and this massive project. Thank you for your patience and understanding as I picked this story out of my brain one word at a time. Peter Gloege, you and David knocked *The Sentinel's Daughter's* cover out of the park! As much as I love all the covers, this one is my favorite!

Lastly, to my darling husband, Rich, thank you for being my soulmate, my rock, and the one person I can always count on. Your support through this project, through my illness, and through whatever else that bitch Fate plans to throw our way, means the world to me. I'm proud to be your personal Scheherazade.

Oh, and one more—thank you to all my critters for their snuggles and support during the writing of this book. Although Gritty is a fictitious character, a blend of a number of the beloved dogs I've had the joy of being owned by over the years, Marigold, the enormous Belgian draft horse, is real. Few horses I know of have gone from being rescued at a slaughter auction to being immortalized in print, but girl, you did it, and you very much deserve it. Thank you for all your sloppy kisses, fumble-lipped attempts to take a cookie off my hand, and (no joke) minutes-long, continuous farts. Not a day goes by where you don't make me smile.

"First they came for the Socialists,
and I did not speak out,
Because I was not a Socialist.

Then they came for the trade unionists,
and I did not speak out—
Because I was not a trade unionist.

Then they came for the Jews,
and I did not speak out—
Because I was not a Jew.

Then they came for me—
and there was no one left to speak for me."

— MARTIN NIEMÖLLER

ABOUT THE AUTHOR

NIEMÖLLER'S FAMOUS WORDS are the last thing visitors
to the United States Holocaust Museum in Washington, D.C. see before
they depart the exhibition, and every time I read them, they give me
chills. I found it interesting that when I looked this quotation up, there
were a number of similar quotations attributed to Niemöller, as well.
They all have the same sentiment, but use different demographics. Upon
further research, I learned that he tailored his words to each audience
with the intent of making his sentiments hit that much harder. The fact
that, all these years later, I can find how often he reworked his famous
quotation to fit the crowd says volumes about the self-absorption of
mankind.

　　When I first sat down to write *The Sentinel's Daughter*, I knew I
wanted to dive deeply into the demographic of women in this new
society. By now, you know that the women not considered "pure" are
targeted right alongside the men, but what about those married to the
richest and most powerful men? How are they faring with their new
reality? How did they end up in this miserable new existence? More

importantly, why the hell didn't they fight back? Or if they did, why did their attempts fail?

So, I did a lot of studying. I researched fascist, totalitarian and dictatorial regimes. I read how both men and women were subjugated through fear and violence until they finally gave up and did as they were told out of fear they would be "next." Their losses of freedom occurred more like a death by a thousand cuts than by a fell swoop of a guillotine, and in nearly every regime I studied, the first major cut against any marginalized group was *financial*.

I don't know why that surprised me, as it's already happening here. I don't have to tell you which ethnic and racial groups are being hit the hardest, as I'm sure you already know. But are you aware how much worse off marginalized women are than the men?

As much as many would like us to believe that, in the year 2024, women are equal to men in America, sadly we are not. Statistically, women earn eighty-two cents for every dollar a man makes. Of the 38.1 million people living in poverty, fifty-six percent, or 21.4 million, are women. Native American women have the highest poverty rate at 28.1 percent, African American women (25.7 percent), and Hispanic women (24.0 percent). The poverty level among white women is less than half those previously mentioned, at 11.7 percent. In 2021, children living with only their mothers were more than twice as likely to live in poverty as those living with only their fathers (35.0 percent vs. 17.4 percent, respectively).[1]

You don't need me to tell you that women are far fewer in the ranks of CEOs, CFOs, and board members of Fortune 500 companies, and despite the fact there are currently more women than men in our nation, we are woefully underrepresented in our government. The Equal Rights Amendment, often called "the most popular Amendment

---

1 Data compiled from the Institute for Women's Policy Research, National Women's Law Center, and the U.S. Census Bureau.

to never be ratified," has been doggedly trying to achieve ratification since 1923. (It's currently hung up in Congress over a deadline loophole despite *finally,* in 2020, getting the last state ratification needed to become law. Thank you, Virginia!)

I can go on and on about how underrepresented and unequal women are in our nation, but if you've read this far, I'm preaching to the choir. But just in case I'm not, I'm going to say it one more time.

In our nation, women are not on equal footing with men. We're not even close.

As of the time I'm writing this, it's been nearly two years since *Roe v. Wade* was overturned, and a whopping twenty-one states have already either severely restricted a woman's right to choose or taken the right away completely. Some have even gone so far as to ban abortion in cases of rape, incest, and a few even when a woman's life, or that of the fetus, is in jeopardy. Women are being forced to endure the psychological effects of carrying to term non-viable pregnancies, or suffer the graphic, daily reminder of a sexual assault. Children who have been raped, yet aren't even old enough to drive a car, are being forced to give birth. How are they expected to care for an infant when they are but children, themselves?

On top of all of this, some states are now looking to restrict access to birth control. Restricting access to birth control *and* abortions is only going to increase the poverty rate among women, as I guarantee that the same members of our government wanting to restrict access to birth control and abortions are not planning to increase the social services necessary to help raise these children. For the vast majority of "Pro-Life" politicians, the lives they are so desperate to save are no longer their concern once they are born.

I'm saying it loud and clear right now so every person in the room can hear—A politician's desire to restrict abortions and limit birth control is not a matter of devotion to a collective national morality—it's a way to suppress already-marginalized groups of women by miring them in inescapable debt. Period. They've realized that the key to subjugating women is not moral, it's *financial*, and a great way to keep women poor is to keep 'em pregnant.

Can you tell I'm pissed? You're goddamn right I am.

What surprises me the most about this is how often I find my anger on this topic not reciprocated by other women. In the course of a few of the more civil debates I've had on the topic, the responses I've received have varied. I received more than a few lectures on morality and religion, a handful of stern rebukes about how if I had children of my own I would feel differently, and one particularly memorable flippant statement that if the poor really wanted to rise above their poverty, they should get an education, and/or work harder, and that if they really want an abortion they can just just travel to another state where it's legal. (I must admit that I went rather apeshit on the last person as, damn, that was some *seriously* unconscionable white privilege talking.)

With all this going on in the nation, and all these thoughts about women swirling around in my brain, it's no surprise that *The Sentinel's Daughter* focuses on the women of this new America. Aside from Declan, there are no other male viewpoints in this novel. Except for the scheming Mother Barbara, even the wealthiest women live at the mercy of men. Louise comes from a very wealthy and powerful family, and yet even when she's the Lady Consort, she lives in fear of her husband. Afterall, power corrupts, and absolute power corrupts absolutely.

On the flip side, in the poorer communities that support the Cause, we find that men and women share power far more equally and respectfully. The Mennonites may still divvy up their chores along gender lines, but the husbands and wives work as a team. In addition, Amish and Mennonite men and women have a long tradition of working together on everything from barn raising to quilt making, respectively. Although known today for staying mainly within their communities, war changes people. Once the women realize Rowan and Esther are trustworthy, their circle grows to include them. It's taken until this novel to finally get Emma in a position to fully trust other women, and finding a way to unite these unlikely friends has been some of the most gratifying writing of my career.

I can't help but think that if Niemöller were alive, he would urge us to speak out for our sisters who are unable to rise above their meager circumstances. But before that can happen, we need to listen to one another with empathy just as Emma listens to the women tell about how they lost their children. Just because we have experienced different things, or have different beliefs, does not make one person "right" and the other "wrong." We must begin to understand that what is right for me, or you, is not necessarily right for everyone else. We don't have to step in sync to get along. There's so much we can learn from one another if only we're willing to listen, and so much we can do to help if only we take the time to ask what we can do to help.

The time to speak out for others is now. Don't let the opportunity slip by until it's too late.